Finding Libbie

Deanna Lynn Sletten

Finding Libbie
Copyright 2016 © Deanna Lynn Sletten

This title was previously published by Amazon Publishing.

ISBN–13: 978-1-941212-52-3

Cover Designer: Deborah Bradseth of Tugboat Design

Finding Libbie

Part One

Jack and Libbie

Chapter One

You never know what the day will bring, Emily Prentice thought as she stepped outside her town house into the May sunshine. It was something her grandma Bev always said, and for some reason, those words were echoing in her thoughts this morning.

As she walked to her car in the driveway, she inhaled the cool spring air—a delight after the long months of a northern Minnesota winter. She hopped into her Jeep and drove off through the quiet neighborhood until she turned onto the main road that ran south through town.

Unable to resist the fresh air, Emily opened the window a crack and let it rush across her face. A stray blond hair escaped her ponytail, and she swirled it behind her ear with her fingertip as her blue eyes kept vigil on the traffic around her. It was early morning and cars were rushing about the town of Jamison on their way to school, work, shopping, or any other number of destinations. By now, the local Walmart parking lot would be filling up, as would the Target. School parking lots would be mass confusion as parents dropped off children, and in an hour, the mall would open and shoppers would make their way there.

Emily was happy that she wasn't joining the throngs of people in any of those places. She was headed to the other side of town to her grandmother's farmhouse, where, at least for the time being, it was still peaceful.

Emily followed the road that ran beside beautiful Lake Ogimaa. The area was rich in Ojibwa culture and many of the lakes and landmarks were named using the local Native American language. Ogimaa meant "chief" in Ojibwa. The blue water sparkled in the morning sunshine. The ice had finally melted, and it was refreshing to see the open water. The lake's shore was trimmed with expensive homes on the north bank, resorts on the east bank, and the local park on the west bank where she was driving now. She continued on past Jamison State College, which had sat on the south shore of the lake since the early 1900s, and continued farther south where old farms were slowly being sold off and turned into housing developments to satisfy the needs of a growing community.

Less than thirty-five years ago, housing developments hadn't been necessary for the sleepy town whose only saving graces were the tourists visiting the resorts in the summer and the college students in the winter. The downtown stores supplied all the necessities, and the three gas stations took turns being open on Sundays. Back then, as it had been for over one hundred years, two families owned the majority of the businesses in town—the Wilkenses and the Jamisons—and if one more Wilkens had lived in the town at the time of its incorporation in 1898, the town would have been named Wilkens instead. Of course, that had been a bone of contention between the two families for over a century.

But all that had happened before Emily was born thirty years ago, and she didn't remember how the town looked before the mall opened, the chain department stores bought out the old fairgrounds, or the many franchised restaurants filled the strip between the lake and the mall. She only knew about it from the stories passed down by her grandmother and her father of how the town used to be.

The traffic thinned out as Emily left the southern tip of Jamison and headed out to the new suburbs where nice, modest-priced homes were being built on one-acre lots in a maze of streets. Farther down the road from those, she turned right on old County Road 9, which had been renamed Valley View Drive years ago but which locals still called by its original name. Soon, she was driving past open farmland separated by clumps of pines and scattered oak and birch trees. The fields were just beginning to turn green and sat untended because no one farmed here anymore. Some of the land was still used for grazing horses, but most of it was just sitting there, waiting to be plucked up by the highest bidder to turn it into an oasis of two-story houses with four bedrooms, two and a half baths, and a family/media room. The world had closed in on Jamison, and although growth was welcomed by many, it was resented by those who'd lived there the longest.

Emily gazed around her at the open fields that would soon be dotted with houses. Her heart ached at the thought that this would all be gone soon. No more would there be the sweet smell of fresh-cut hay in the summer or wide-open land where deer grazed and eagles hunted. Century-old farmhouses would be bulldozed, all of the memories inside them brushed away in an instant. Progress was necessary, but Emily wished that some things would never change.

A small rail fence on the left marked the beginning of the Prentice farmland, and Emily smiled when she saw her grandmother's farmhouse in the distance amidst a grove of trees. As she drew nearer, the two front windows on the second floor winked at her like two friendly eyes, and the screened-in porch below them spread across the front of the house like a smile. Many old farmhouses looked creepy, but her grandmother's always looked cheerful and welcoming.

Emily turned her car left and drove up the long gravel driveway past old oak trees that spread out their limbs like welcoming arms and tall spruce trees that stood at attention high up into the sky. An old, faded red barn sat off in the distance, and the small chicken coop beside it sagged a bit to the left. A large building that had once been her grandfather's woodworking shop now sat silent and empty. Since the death of Grandpa Norm in 1998, the outbuildings were no longer being tended to, but the house still looked as clean and fresh as always. Her grandmother might be going on eighty-four, but she was as active as when Emily was a little girl tromping the fields alongside her on her daily walk.

Emily pulled her car up to the back of the house and parked under a maple tree. Stepping out, she looked around slowly, memorizing every bit of the land and the house. Just as her neighbors had done, Emily's grandmother had sold off the farm to developers, and in a year or so, the farmland and house would be a distant memory. Emily felt like all her childhood memories had been sold along with it. She'd never again walk the fields with her grandmother, never explore the inside of the musty old barn, and never be able to bring her own children here—when she had them—to relive the past. The past would be gone forever.

Sighing, Emily walked toward the back mudroom, but before she reached the door, her grandmother opened it and smiled down at her. Emily couldn't help but smile back. Her grandmother's charm was too sweet to ignore.

"There's my Emily," Beverly Prentice said, standing in the doorway and wiping her hands on a kitchen towel. "You're in time for my homemade sweet rolls. They're just out of the oven. And I'll even make you one of your sweet coffees with that fancy machine you all gave me for Christmas."

Emily took the three steps up into the mudroom as her grandmother moved aside to let her in. The two women hugged, and Emily felt comforted by her familiar scent. She smelled of spices from baking and flowery fabric softener that lingered on her soft cotton blouses. To Emily, it was the smell of love.

Emily slipped off her sneakers, and the two women walked into the tiny hallway and took a right into the small country kitchen. Emily inhaled deeply. The sweet aroma of rolls made her mouth water.

"You're going to make me fat," Emily said, taking down two plates and retrieving the forks and napkins. "Did it occur to you that maybe I'd already eaten breakfast?"

Bev shook her head. "I'll bet you haven't. And a couple of sweet rolls aren't going to put an ounce of fat on your lean body." She bustled around the kitchen, turning on the coffee machine and selecting her granddaughter's favorite coffee packet to put in it.

Emily watched her as she took down mugs. She swore her grandmother had more energy than she did. Even though her grandmother complained of slowing down, Emily had yet to see any sign of it. She was two inches shorter than Emily's own five-foot-six frame, and she had just enough padding on her to look healthy. Today, she wore a pale-pink blouse and brown knit slacks with a pair of tan Keds. Her face had been kissed by time, with each wrinkle earned from smiles and worry, but her blue eyes still shone brightly and sparkled with delight at the simplest of things. It was a sweet face that cast its spell instantly over anyone lucky enough to meet her. Her quick smiles and easy ways made people want to sit down and confide in her, and throughout her life, many had.

Once the coffee was poured, Bev and Emily took their treat out into the dining room and sat at the oval oak table. The room held a matching hutch on one side and three large windows that looked out into the fields where her grandfather's cows had once grazed. When Emily was younger, she'd often sit here in early mornings or evenings and watch as white-tailed deer grazed in among the cows. Now the view held only spring grass starting to sprout out of the untended land.

Emily bit into her sweet roll and sighed. It was warm, sweet, and gooey, and it was perfect.

"You're a sweetheart to help your old grandma pack up this house," Bev said, her eyes sparkling at Emily. "It's going to be a big job, going through generations of things in this old farmhouse."

"I'm happy to help, Grandma. We have all summer to do it, so it won't be too bad. We can take one room at a time." Emily glanced around her. "What do you think Grandpa would say about the family farm being sold off to developers? Would he be sad?"

Bev shook her head. "Your grandfather was the one who told me to do it years ago. He said, 'Bevie, don't you worry about this old place when I'm gone. You sell it off to the highest bidder and live it up.'"

Emily laughed. "Is that what you're going to do, Grandma? Live it up?"

Bev chuckled. "Well, first off I'm going to move into that little town house two blocks over from yours, and then we'll see. I might do a little traveling, take a cruise with some of my old lady friends, and maybe even go on some of those casino bus trips. It'll be nice not having to worry about this big house anymore."

Emily smiled. "You do deserve to have some fun."

Bev began stacking the dirty plates to carry into the kitchen. "So, dear, how is that young man of yours? Will he be finished with school this spring?"

Emily hid her grin. She knew her grandmother didn't approve of her boyfriend, but she always asked politely what he was up to. Emily met Jordan Reardon in their first year at Jamison State College, and they had started living together in the town house by the end of their second year. Emily had quit college after finishing her general education requirements because she hadn't yet figured out what to major in and couldn't afford to waste the money. But Jordan had known exactly what course he'd wanted to pursue—a PhD in English literature, eventually obtaining a position as a college professor. So he'd continued his education, while Emily had taken a full-time job at a department store in the mall. That was almost ten years ago, and she was still at the store—albeit now as a manager in the women's clothing department—and Jordan was at the college, working as a teaching assistant and also taking classes for his doctoral degree.

Her grandmother's disapproval of Jordan had nothing to do with his character—he was a good man and a hard worker—it was the fact that Emily had supported him while he pursued his many degrees, making it impossible for her to go back to school. Emily didn't mind helping him, since she still didn't know what she wanted to do with her life. She didn't necessarily like her job at the store, but at least it paid the bills. She figured Jordan would be finished with school at some point and earning a decent income, and then maybe she could go back to college.

"He's still working toward his PhD," Emily replied calmly, as she helped her grandmother wash and dry the few dishes. "But he's been teaching a few undergraduate classes and he should be finished by the end of next year."

"My, but it takes a long time to get through college these days," Bev said, shaking her head. "What about you, dear? Will you be going back to college sometime soon?"

Emily sighed. "I'm not sure, Grandma. I still don't know what I want to do. I'll just work until I figure it out."

"Well, you're a smart girl. You'll figure something out," Bev said with certainty.

Emily wished she felt as certain as her grandmother.

Bev placed her hands on her hips. "Well, dear, where shall we start? The basement, main floor, upstairs, or attic?"

Emily thought a moment. They were going to pack up the items her grandmother wanted to take with her to the town house, then separate out the larger items for either storage or to sell. Her father and brother would come and help with the heavier furniture on the day her grandmother moved. In the meantime, she and her grandmother had to go through all the closets and decide what to do with decades of her grandmother's life.

"Why don't we start up in the bedroom closets and box up the giveaway items and anything you want to take with you that you absolutely don't need right now?" Emily suggested.

"Sounds good," Bev agreed. "All the boxes are upstairs in the guest room."

The two women trudged upstairs where the master bedroom, two small guest rooms, and the one bathroom were. Armed with tape, markers, and scissors, they went into one of the guest bedrooms and began in the closet.

They began sorting items and boxing up the keepers and the giveaways. Even though her grandfather had been gone a long time, Emily's grandmother still had some of his old clothes in the guest closet. They boxed those items up for Goodwill, keeping only his army uniform and the suit he'd worn for their wedding. In the dresser, there were long-forgotten sheet sets, doilies, and other linens that they separated out and boxed. Her grandmother told Emily to take any items she might want—like some of the doilies that had been crocheted by her great-grandmother Prentice—and also gave her the military medals belonging to her grandfather that they'd found in a drawer to give to her brother.

"Maybe Edward would like to have these," Bev said.

Emily nodded. "I'm sure he'd love to."

After two hours in the first guest bedroom, they moved on to the second one. This room was one that Emily knew well. It was the bedroom she'd slept in when she'd stayed overnight as a child, and it was the room that held all the fun toys her grandmother kept for when children visited. The closet in this room was much like the other one, but deeper, and with shelves from floor to ceiling. Games, dolls, Legos, puzzles, and a variety of other toys sat on the shelves, and a few dress-up clothes were stored in an old chest. An antique cake tin held costume jewelry that Emily used to wear when she played dress-up, and she smiled when she pulled it from the closet.

"You have to keep those," Bev said. "You just loved playing with them as a child."

Emily agreed and put the tin aside to take home with her later.

"I wish your mother were here to help," Bev said as they worked. "She'd offered to sort through things with me years ago before she became sick, but we never had a chance. Poor Kate. She was such a sweet soul."

"She would have enjoyed this," Emily agreed. Her mother had died of breast cancer two years earlier, after fighting the disease for four long years. She missed her mother terribly, and she knew her father, Jack, did also. Even at age sixty-four, he still worked five days a week at his garage, fixing cars, tractors, motorcycles, and just about anything else with a motor. In fact, Emily knew he worked even more than he had before her mother died. He rarely left the garage. He was using work to deal with his grief, and Emily found his loneliness heartbreaking.

They separated out which toys to keep and which to give away. As the closet began to empty, Emily stepped inside it and, using a flashlight, searched the top shelf to make sure they'd taken out everything. To her surprise, there was a round box at the very back of the shelf. Using the little stepladder, she climbed up and reached for the box. As she brought it out into the lighted room, she blew on it and a cloud of dust flew in every direction. She took a rag from her pocket and dusted it off, then marveled at how lovely it was. It was a very old hatbox, covered in a creamy-white fabric with soft-pink cabbage roses and green leaves on it. The top of the box was trimmed in eggshell-colored crochet edging. A faded pink ribbon was tied around it to keep the lid secure. The box had also faded over time, but it was still beautiful.

"Grandma? What is this? I've never seen this box before."

Bev turned from where she'd been packing puzzles into a box. She gasped when she saw what was in Emily's hands. "Oh my!"

Emily set the box on the dresser and stared at her grand-mother curiously. "What is it, Grandma?"

Bev walked over to where the box sat and gingerly laid a hand on it. "I'd forgotten all about this," she said softly. "I haven't seen this box in nearly forty years."

Emily watched as a sad expression crossed over her grandmother's face. "Maybe we should just put it away," she suggested.

Bev shook her head slowly. "No, it's been hidden away long enough. Go ahead and open it, dear. The past can't hide forever."

Emily stared down at the box a moment, wondering what memories such a beautiful old box could hold that would cause her grandmother to act so strangely. Carefully, she pulled on the end of the ribbon and the bow came loose, falling away. She put both hands on the lid and lifted it up slowly, so as not to ruin the aging box. Peering inside, she saw the very young face of her father in a black and white photo staring back at her.

"It's old photos!" Emily exclaimed, setting the lid aside and reaching inside the box. She lifted the first photo of her father. He was wearing his high school cap and gown and held a diploma in his hand. Underneath was another one of him in swim trunks by a lake, smiling crookedly at the camera. "He's so young," Emily said, smiling widely. "No wonder I've never seen many photos of him at this age. They were all in this box."

She lifted up a pile of photos and began looking through them. "Look, Grandma. This one must be his high school prom. He's wearing a suit and there's a flower in his lapel."

Bev drew closer and glanced over Emily's shoulder. "Yes, that was his senior prom."

The next picture was in color and was of Jack with a beautiful girl by his side. She was much shorter than Jack and very petite, with light blond hair that fell below her shoulders and large blue eyes. Her skin was creamy white, and she wore a lovely pink satin dress with a lace overlay that was long and skimmed the floor. Emily thought she was the most beautiful girl she'd ever seen. Jack stood behind her, his hands circling her tiny waist as they both smiled brightly.

"Who is she, Grandma?" Emily asked. "She's so beautiful."

"That's Libbie," Bev said softly. "Short for Elizabeth."

Emily glanced over at her grandmother. "Was she Dad's high school sweetheart? Is that why these pictures were put away?"

"Yes, she was," Bev said, looking into Emily's eyes. "She was also your father's first wife."

Emily's mouth dropped open as she stared at her grandmother. "First wife?"

Bev reached out and patted Emily's arm. "I know this is a bit of a shock, dear. It was something none of us talked about. But now there's no reason for you not to know. Let's take the box downstairs, and you can look through it while I make some coffee."

Emily covered the box and followed her grandmother downstairs, dazed. She sat at the table and started pulling photos from the box and examining each one. One was of the couple sitting in a canoe, smiling playfully at each other on what looked to be Lake Ogimaa. The girl was wearing a two-piece swimsuit with a netlike cover-up and Jack was in his swim trunks. Even in black and white, Emily could tell they were deeply tanned. There were more pictures from prom, and a few of her uncle Larry—her mother's brother and Jack's best friend—clowning around with the couple. Another showed Libbie and Jack smiling happily, standing in front of a cottage. Reaching deeper into the box, Emily pulled out ripped up pages that looked to be from a photo album. When she peered closer, she saw that they were wedding photos of her father and Libbie. Some of the pages were torn, as if they'd been ripped angrily from the album. Why?

Emily glanced up at her grandmother as she set a mug of coffee in front of her. "Dad was married before," she said, hardly believing her eyes. She gazed down at one of the photos in her hand. It was her father in a tuxedo with tails, and Libbie wearing a lovely satin wedding gown with lace sleeves and a long train that swirled around her feet. Both she and Jack were smiling happily at the camera. Emily returned her gaze to her grandmother, who'd sat down opposite her. "They look so happy."

Bev sighed as she looked at the photo in Emily's hand. "They were happy, dear. So happy that there was no possible way for anyone to predict it would end as it did."

"What happened?"

Bev lifted the photo of Jack and Libbie in the canoe and gazed at it, looking as if she were trying to remember a long-lost memory. Finally, she set it down and looked into Emily's eyes. "You know that your father loved your mother dearly, don't you, Ems? He wouldn't be grieving so if he hadn't."

Emily nodded. "I know he did."

Bev nodded. "Well, your mother was eight years younger than Jack, and she was Larry's baby sister. The boys really didn't have much to do with her since they were so much older, unless they'd let her tag along every now and again. Libbie, she was the same age as Jack, and they'd known each other since kindergarten. But it was the year he turned seventeen that Jack's eyes were drawn to Libbie Wilkens, and he saw no one else after that."

"Libbie was a Wilkens? One of the rich Wilkenses?"

"Yes. Her parents owned half the businesses in town, what little bit of town we had here in 1968. Of course, they'd been handed down businesses from their parents and grandparents, but her father had built up their legacy even more. They owned the grocery store, hardware store, a furniture store, one of the dime stores, a building supply store, and even owned half of one of the two banks in town then. They lived in a lovely home on the north end of the lake, where Libbie had friends over every sunny day all summer. And it was that summer, between their junior and senior years, that Jack fell head over heels in love with Libbie."

Chapter Two

Jack and Libbie – 1968

Jack stared across the high school gym at Libbie as she danced in Bill Driscoll's arms. She looked like an angel as she glided across the floor in a white dress. The full chiffon skirt that fell just below her knees billowed as she moved. Her long blond hair was pulled up into a loose chignon with tendrils curling down around her face and neck. She was the most beautiful girl at the prom, and every boy wanted to dance with her. Jack wished he could pull her out of Bill's arms and dance with her all night, and he was plotting exactly how to do so at that very moment.

"Hey, at least pretend you're with me and stop drooling over little Miss Sunshine over there," Myrtle Hill said.

Jack turned his attention back to the girl he was dancing with. "Sorry, Myrt. I just wish I could sneak Libbie away from snobby Bill. Even for a few minutes. Just because he brought her doesn't mean he's the only one who can dance with her."

Jack watched as Myrt rolled her eyes. At six feet, Jack towered over Myrtle, who couldn't have been more than five feet, even in heels. She had a little too much padding for her height, and those cat-eye glasses with the fake rhinestones in the corners made her face look wide. But she and Jack had made a deal. Myrtle was madly in love with his best friend, Larry Spencer, and Jack needed a date in order to come to the prom. So she'd agreed to come with him if he'd make sure to get Larry to dance with her, and then Jack could pursue Libbie.

Jack glanced around the gym at the decorations and smiled. He'd spent the entire day yesterday with the other eleventh-grade volunteers, twisting and hanging crepe paper streamers and blue and white balloons from the ceiling. He hadn't done it out of the goodness of his heart or because he'd wanted to make sure the seniors had a beautiful prom—he'd done it to be around Libbie. In their small school, it was traditional for the eleventh graders to host the junior/senior prom. He'd signed up to help with the decorations because he knew Libbie was supervising. From his spot high atop the ladder, he'd been able to watch her move among the other students, giving directions and approving of their work. Twice, she'd stopped under Jack's ladder to look up at him with a grin and say, "Looking good, Jack." He'd smile down at her and nod. He knew she was talking about the streamers, but he could dream she'd meant those words to be about him.

The band stopped playing, and Jack led Myrtle over to the refreshment table for a cup of punch. As they stood sipping their drinks, Larry walked by with his date, Mary Beth Johnson. She was a pretty girl, tall and slender, with long dark hair and warm brown eyes. Larry and she looked well suited, since he also had dark hair and brown eyes and was nearly as tall as Jack. Larry winked at Jack, nodding to Mary Beth as if to say, *Look who I'm with.* Jack couldn't help but smile. Mary Beth came from a devout Catholic family, so there was no way Larry was going to get even so much as a kiss from the pretty girl tonight.

"Larry's never going to notice me since he's with Mary Beth," Myrtle whined. "I shouldn't have come here tonight. It was a waste of time."

Jack knew that was probably true, and he felt bad for Myrtle. He understood how she felt. Poor Myrtle had had a crush on Larry for years, just like he'd had a crush on Libbie since the first grade. But Jack was sure that with a guy like Bill at her side, Libbie would never look twice at him. Steeling himself, he decided it was time to put his plan in motion.

"Don't give up so easily, Myrt," Jack said, taking her hand and leading her back onto the dance floor. The band had started playing a slow song, "This Guy's in Love With You." It was the perfect song for Jack's next move.

He danced with Myrtle slowly across the floor to where Larry and Mary Beth were. "Here's your chance, Myrt," Jack whispered. "Give it your best shot." Jack expertly cut in between Larry and his date. "May I cut in?" he asked, handing Myrtle over to a stunned Larry and pulling Mary Beth into his arms. He moved her away as quickly as the slow tune would allow. He looked back only long enough to see Larry dancing with Myrtle—he'd had no other choice.

"Having a good time?" Jack asked as he danced Mary Beth in the direction where Libbie and Bill were.

Mary Beth was too nice to complain. "Yes, I am," she said.

Soon, they were beside Libbie and Bill. Jack took a breath. *Here I go.*

"May I cut in?" he asked Bill. Just as he'd done moments before, he expertly handed Mary Beth off to Bill and pulled Libbie into his arms, moving her quickly across the floor before Bill could protest.

His heart pounding, Jack tried to slow down so it didn't feel as if he were pushing Libbie around the floor. But she kept up with him perfectly, gliding as if on air. When he finally had the nerve to look down at her, he saw her grinning up at him mischievously.

"Took you long enough to rescue me from boring Bill," she said.

Jack's mouth dropped open and then he clamped it shut when he realized how he must look.

Libbie giggled. "You shouldn't be so surprised. I've seen you staring at me all night. I figured you were waiting for the right time to ask me to dance."

Jack gazed into her blue eyes and smiled. "I thought you'd be mad at me for cutting in."

"Mad? No way. I'm happy someone finally cut in. If I had to hear Bill brag one more time about going off to college in the fall, I was going to barf."

Jack laughed and they continued to dance slowly. Libbie felt so good in his arms. She was a good six inches shorter than he was, but she fit perfectly against him. Her hair gently brushed his neck, and she smelled as sweet as she looked. He'd waited a long time for this moment, and it felt as wonderful as he'd imagined.

As the last notes of the song played, Jack pulled away and looked down at Libbie. "I have a surprise for you. Will you come outside with me a moment?"

Libbie's eyes sparkled. "Okay. But you'd better behave like a gentleman, Jack Prentice."

Jack slipped his hand around hers and led her though the crowd and out the open door into the cool May evening. Outdoor lights lit the way as they hurried down the path that curled around to a spot where there was a bench hiding amongst the trees and bushes.

"What are you up to?" Libbie asked, but she looked unconcerned as she sat primly on the bench and spread her skirt around her.

"You'll see," Jack told her. He walked to a tree behind the bench and bent down, picking something up and then returned to the bench. In his hands were a wine bottle and two glasses.

"Jack! What on earth?"

"I wanted to surprise you with something nice," Jack said, pulling out his pocketknife and snapping out the corkscrew so he could open the bottle. "Everyone always sneaks beer on prom night, but I figured a girl like you would prefer wine." He twisted the screw in the cork a few turns and then pulled it out.

"Well, you did surprise me," Libbie said, accepting a full glass of white wine. "But you'll be in big trouble if we get caught."

Jack lifted his glass and clinked it to hers. "It'll be worth it," he said. "To prom night."

"To prom night," Libbie repeated, and then took a sip.

"How did you manage to get a bottle of wine? You're underage." Libbie asked.

Jack grinned. "Larry helped me out. His uncle has all sorts of booze around the house. He'll never miss one bottle of wine."

"Ah," Libbie said.

They sat there a while, listening to the crickets and frogs singing their nightly songs. The sky was clear, and the stars twinkled high above.

"Another school year has come and gone," Libbie said wistfully. "Can you believe it, Jack? We'll be seniors next year. And then what? Everyone will go in different directions and our lives will change forever."

"Change is a good thing," Jack said. "Life moves on. Kids grow up. That's what we're supposed to do."

"Everything is changing all around us," Libbie said, looking at Jack with wide eyes. "Martin Luther King's assassination and all the rioting last month. The war in Vietnam. College students protesting all over the country. Even though none of that seems to touch our little town, it's still all out there happening. It's scary."

Jack cocked his head and looked at Libbie. "It does affect us, though. We all know someone who's gone off to fight in Vietnam. Look at the Jacksons' son. He died over there. Heck, in less than a year, I'll be registering for the draft, and I could go, too. Even Bill could go."

Libbie closed her eyes and shuddered. "I can't even think about that. It's all too much to deal with."

Jack smiled over at Libbie. "Then let's talk about nice things, like warm summer days and long walks by the lake and the smell of lilacs and lavender growing in the garden."

Libbie giggled. "And who will you be walking with by the lake enjoying the aroma of lilacs, Jack? Myrtle?"

Jack grinned. "Maybe. Would you be jealous if I did?"

"Silly. Why on earth would I be jealous of you and Myrtle? I'll be spending the summer with boring Bill and all my friends."

Jack sat silently and took a sip of wine.

Libbie turned to Jack. "I suppose you'll be working all summer at your uncle's gas station again this year?"

Jack nodded. "Yep. When I'm not helping my dad build and install kitchen cabinets. He's booked for the entire summer. And of course, you'll be having swim parties by the lake and getting a great tan," he said, teasing.

Libbie shrugged. "There's not much else to do."

They sat so close that Jack felt Libbie shiver, so he took off his suit jacket and draped it around her shoulders.

"Well, who knew that you could be such a romantic?" Libbie said, smiling at Jack. "And all along I've always thought of you as the mean little boy who teased me and chased me around the playground when we were in grade school."

"Maybe I was chasing you to steal a kiss," Jack said.

Libbie laughed. "You're crazy, you know that, Jack?"

"Hey, you didn't think I volunteered to decorate the gym just because I like twirling crepe paper, did you?"

Libbie moved even closer to Jack. "Then why did you volunteer?"

Jack ducked his head down toward hers. "So I could be around you."

Libbie giggled and took another sip of wine. "Now you are being silly. You've known me my entire life, Jack, and you've never once shown any interest in me."

Jack looked at her seriously. "We have known each other our whole lives. But you're Libbie Wilkens, whose father owns half of Jamison and who dates the banker's son. I'm just plain old Jack. I never thought you'd be interested in me."

Libbie looked up into his eyes. "If you wanted my attention, why didn't you ask me to the prom instead of asking Myrtle?"

"Everyone knew you'd go to the prom with Bill. Myrtle only came with me because she has a crush on Larry and wanted to dance with him. And I only came so I could whisk you away and be alone with you."

Libbie's eyes softened. "Really?"

"Honest to God."

"That's so sweet," Libbie said softly.

Jack reached for her hand and held it. "I've had a crush on

you since the first grade, Libbie. I'm warning you right now that I'm going to do my best to win you away from Bill this summer and steal your heart."

Libbie gazed at Jack, and then a smile spread across her lips. "Okay, then. I've been duly warned." She leaned over and placed a soft kiss on his cheek. "Good luck," she whispered. Then she stood, dropping his jacket on the bench, and ran back to the gym, giggling.

Jack sat there a long time after she'd left, a big grin on his face.

Chapter Three

Summer came and Jack's days were filled with helping his father, doing chores around the family farm, and working at the gas station. Of all the work he did, he enjoyed working at his uncle Rick's gas station the most. Jack was good with his hands, but woodworking didn't come as naturally to him as it did to his father. Jack was relegated to sanding, staining, and screwing in the door hinges and handles, while his father did the creative work of building his custom cabinets. Then Jack would help install them in the houses of the people who'd ordered them. It took them inside many of the finest houses in town, especially those on the north end of the lake, where the bankers, lawyers, doctors, and rich businessmen lived. Jack would gaze around the beautifully built homes in awe, hoping to one day be able to own such a fine home himself. After all, if he was going to win Libbie's heart, then he'd also have to give her the life to which she was accustomed.

That wasn't going to be easy, though. Jack loved working on engines, and mechanics didn't earn the type of money that bought lake homes. But he loved the process of tearing apart an engine and fixing it. Sometimes, his uncle let him work on small projects in the garage, and that was how he'd decided he wanted to be a mechanic. He'd already signed up for the new program at the high school, where he could spend half of his day throughout his senior year at the local trade school learning auto mechanics. That way he'd get his first year of trade school paid for and have only one year to pay for himself after he graduated high school. He knew his parents would help him as much as they could with their limited budget, but with a younger sister and brother coming up right behind him, money would be tight. His father did well with his cabinet business, and his family grew most of their own food and sold some beef cattle each year, so they weren't at all poor. But they weren't rich, either, so Jack saved as much money from his job as he could to go toward his education. He also had his eye on an old used truck that he wanted to buy by fall.

After the prom, Larry had given him heck about switching out Mary Beth for Myrtle during the dance.

"And after I risked my neck stealing that bottle of wine for you," Larry had complained. "I had to dance with Myrtle for three songs before I could get rid of her and get back to my own date. And Bill was actually flirting with Mary Beth!"

Jack had assured his friend that his being able to spend a few minutes with Libbie had made it all worth it. "I owe you, buddy," he'd told him.

"You bet you do," Larry had said good-naturedly. "When you start dating Libbie, you owe me a double date with one of her cute, rich friends."

Unfortunately, Jack hadn't had as much time to spend pursuing Libbie as he'd hoped. June was already coming to an end, and he'd only seen her when she came into the gas station to fill up her car. She drove the most beautiful candy-apple-red

1966 Mustang convertible with a black soft-top and interior, and Jack practically drooled over it as much as he did Libbie. But it suited her perfectly—it was small, sleek, classy, and beautiful, just like her.

One beautiful sunny morning in late June, Libbie drove up to the gas station and honked her horn. Jack's head was under the hood of a car, and he was pouring new oil in it when his uncle Rick hollered to him. "I think there's someone here to see you," he said with a grin.

Jack walked outside, his coveralls stained in oil, wiping his hands on a rag. There was Libbie in her car. The top was down and she'd sat up on the back of her seat. Her hair was up in a ponytail, and she wore white shorts and a sleeveless white shirt that showed off her tan.

"Well, there you are," she said, smiling as she pulled off her sunglasses. "Will you fill it up for me, Jack?"

"Sure will." He picked up the nozzle and went to the back of the car. As soon as the gas started running, he walked around the side and smiled at Libbie. "And would the lady like her windows washed, too?"

"Isn't this a full service station?" she asked coyly.

Jack chuckled. "Yes, ma'am, it is." He washed her windows, then opened the hood and checked her oil. "Everything looks fine," he told her, as he pulled out the nozzle and placed the cap back on the tank.

"Yes, it does," Libbie said, gazing at Jack.

Jack walked around to her side of the car. "I assume this goes on your father's account?"

"Of course." Libbie looked Jack up and down. "You sure are dirty today. What were you doing, rolling around on the floor of the garage?"

"Yep. That's exactly what I was doing. You should try it sometime. It's fun rolling in grease and oil."

Libbie giggled. "For a guy who's supposed to be winning my heart this summer, you sure have been scarce. When are you going to start?"

Jack stopped short, surprised by her question. Regaining his composure, he said, "I've been working a lot this summer. But don't worry, Libbie. I haven't forgotten you."

Libbie slid down into her seat and turned the car on. "A bunch of us will be at my house on the beach all afternoon. If you can tear yourself away from rolling in grease, then you should stop by." She slipped on her sunglasses.

Jack leaned down closer to Libbie, being careful not to rub his dirty coveralls on her sparkling clean car. "I don't get off until three."

Libbie shrugged. "I'll still be there." She waggled her fingers at him, put the car in gear, and drove away.

"Pretty girl," Rick said from behind Jack.

Jack nearly jumped out of his skin. "Geez, Rick. You scared me to death. How long have you been standing there?"

Rick laughed. He looked a lot like Jack's father, Norman, with his tall, square build, wavy brown hair brushed back away from his forehead, and dark brown eyes. He was a couple of years younger than Norman, and he had an easygoing personality. Rick had served a year in the Korean War in 1952, and Jack always had the feeling that was the reason nothing bothered Rick much. If he could survive the war, then everything else was a piece of cake.

"Sorry, bud," Rick said, slapping Jack on the back. "So, how long have you and the Wilkens girl been an item?"

"We're not—yet," Jack said, grinning. The two walked back

into the garage where Jack headed to the car he was working on.

"It isn't all that busy today," Rick hollered at him across the shop. "Why don't you leave at one instead of three?"

Jack looked up, surprised, but when he saw his uncle wink at him, he smiled. "Thanks, Uncle Rick."

"Anything for young love," Rick said, chuckling.

Jack was out of the shop exactly at one and headed home in his father's old pickup. He had to change into his swim trunks before he could go to Libbie's. His heart pounded excitedly. He couldn't wait to spend time with her.

He ran upstairs to the bedroom he shared with his younger brother, Ray. Digging through his dresser drawers, he finally pulled out a pair of blue swim trunks and slipped them on. He'd had them since last summer and they were faded and worn, but they were all he had. He found a clean T-shirt to wear with them and pulled on his sneakers before heading back downstairs. Before he could run out the door, he heard his mother's voice from the kitchen.

"Jack? Where are you running off to in such a hurry? Aren't you supposed to be at work?"

Jack turned into the kitchen where his mother was busy baking bread. Practically everything Bev served her family was homemade. She had a garden in the summer and canned vegetables and fruit for the long winters. All their meat came fresh from the farm, too, and even their milk was straight from the cow.

"Uncle Rick let me off early today," Jack said, grabbing a cookie from the jar on the counter. "I'm going swimming with some friends."

Bev smiled at him. Her mahogany-brown hair was pulled away from her face and her eyes twinkled. "That sounds nice.

I'm glad you're going to have some fun. Be sure to come home in time for supper, okay?"

"I will, Ma," Jack said, hurrying out the door to his dad's truck.

Jack lived south of town, so it took a good half hour for him to drive to Libbie's house on the north end of the lake. As he parked his dad's old truck among the newer cars that lined the road in front of the house, he felt the first pang of trepidation. Even though Jack knew all the kids his age—they all went to school together and he'd played on the basketball team with several of the rich boys—he'd never really spent time with any of them socially. He was a farm kid, a working kid, and his parents weren't rich. Did he really belong here, among the privileged?

As he walked up the Wilkenses' driveway, music drifted across the yard, and he heard the sound of teenagers yelling playfully by the lake. The Wilkenses' house was twice the size of his parents' farmhouse. It spread out across the lot with an attached double garage and was two stories high. A circular driveway made of cobblestones ran around the front of it. A lush, manicured lawn and well-tended flower gardens spread out around the house. It was all so beautiful and elegant, and with every step down the driveway, Jack's courage faded.

Jack heard his father's voice in his head. *You're just as good as they are.* His dad always told him that when they worked at the rich people's houses installing cabinets, and Jack would sometimes feel overwhelmed. And his dad was right. No one was better than anyone else. Jack stood tall and continued down the driveway and around the side of the house toward the lake.

The yard in front of the lake was even more beautiful, with an expanse of green grass intersected by a brick walkway that led from the house to the lake. Flower gardens lined the lawn on both sides, and roses grew in gardens near the house. A large brick patio ran the length of the house, and the glass on the white French doors glistened in the afternoon sun. Farther down, the lawn turned into a sandy shore by the lake. A long dock stuck out into the water where a speedboat was docked, along with a smaller fishing boat and also a dingy with oars. On the shore sat a hand-carved wooden canoe that gleamed in the sun. Jack marveled at the grown-up toys. He'd love to have a beautiful speedboat like the one sitting there on the water.

"Hey! It's Jack!" a male voice yelled from the sandy shore. Jack turned his attention down toward the lake where a net stood and the other kids were playing volleyball. He smiled when he spotted Libbie, who was walking toward him.

"Finally," the male voice said. "Someone with some athletic skill. He's on our team!"

Jack looked around at the faces and caught sight of who was yelling. He realized it was Ron, a boy he played on the basketball team with. Ron's father owned the most successful high-end resort on the lake, not too far from Libbie's house.

"Sorry, Ron. He's on my team," Libbie called out to him, giggling, as she stepped closer to Jack. "Hey, you made it. I'm glad you came."

Jack smiled widely. "Hi, Libbie." She was wearing a two-piece yellow swimsuit with a net cover-up that didn't really cover much at all. Her body was shapely and slender, and her skin was a soft-golden tan. He'd seen her just that morning, yet right now she looked more radiant and beautiful than he'd ever seen her before.

Libbie laughed softly, reached for his hand, and led him toward the beach. "Say hi, everyone. You know Jack."

"Hi, Jack," they all said in unison and then laughed. Besides

Ron, there was Carol, Libbie's best friend, and Arnie, Matt, Jean, and Barbara. Jack knew all of them and immediately felt at ease.

"Hi, everyone!" he called back, getting another laugh from the crowd.

They started up a game of volleyball with two boys and two girls on each team. After that, they played a game with the boys against the girls, and the girls won. The boys brushed it off, saying it was a girl's sport anyway, and the girls ribbed them about not being able to win a "girl's sport."

Everyone treated Jack as one of the crowd and he felt like he belonged. They laughed, joked, teased, and had a great time. Jack was happy Bill wasn't there; otherwise, he might not have felt as welcomed. Especially since Jack couldn't keep his eyes off Libbie. She was so pretty and fun to be around, and she teased her friends, boys and girls alike, mercilessly. They had all known each other since kindergarten, so there were no secrets among them. And for Jack, the boy from the other side of town, it felt good to be considered a part of this group.

* * *

Libbie watched Jack with admiration as he played volleyball on the boy's team. He'd finally grown comfortable enough to take his shirt off, and he was long and lean, but muscular, too. Surprisingly, he was tanned. She figured he must work shirtless outside on the farm. She liked watching him move. Each movement was precise and fluid. He was a true athlete. And he was absolutely hunky.

The afternoon grew warmer, and everyone soon gave up on volleyball and headed for the water. The girls swam out to the floating dock to suntan, while the boys took the rowboat out to float around the dock and tease the girls. Libbie held back and so did Jack. She wanted to spend some time alone with him, and she could tell he wanted to do the same.

"Do you want a Coke?" Libbie asked. "I'll run in and get us each one."

"Sure," Jack said. "I'll go with you."

"No, you stay here and enjoy the sun. I'll be back in a minute," she told him. She ran up the brick path, which was hot on her bare feet, and slipped through the French doors. Her mother was in the kitchen, getting a glass of water from the tap. She was smoking a cigarette and staring out the windows toward the lake.

"Hi, Mom," Libbie said, heading for the fridge and taking out two Coke bottles. She opened the drawer that held the bottle opener and popped the tops.

"Are you kids having fun?" Abigail asked, turning toward Libbie. Abigail was the same height as her daughter, and Libbie had inherited her petite frame from her mother. At forty years old, Abigail was still slender, almost to the point of thin, even after having two children. But that was where the resemblance to Libbie ended. Abigail had dark brown hair that was swept up in a beehive hairdo, brown eyes, and a thin face that sometimes looked severe. She was always perfectly coiffed, hair and nails done each week at the beauty shop, and her makeup was carefully applied every day. Warmth did not radiate off of Abigail as it did from some of the other mothers who were quick to hug or smile. But she wasn't unkind, either. Her mother was the queen of politeness.

"Yes, we are," Libbie replied, hoping to retreat quickly. She was almost to the door when her mother spoke again.

"Who is that young man out there by the dock? I don't recognize him."

Libbie took a breath. With the crowd of kids here today,

she'd hoped her mother wouldn't notice a new face. "That's Jack. He's in my grade at school."

Abigail turned and stared out the window again, slipping on her glasses that hung around her neck on a gold chain. "Jack? I'm not sure I know him."

"Of course, you do, Mom. Jack Prentice. His father owns the cabinet business. He built cabinets for the neighbor's new kitchen, remember? And his uncle owns the Shell gas station on the corner in town. Jack works there sometimes."

Abigail slowly nodded. "Oh, yes. I recognize him now. He's the young man who's filled up my car at times." She turned and smiled at Libbie. "Well, have fun, dear."

Libbie nodded and ran out the door, relieved her mother hadn't made a big deal over Jack being there. She could tell by her mother's reaction that she hadn't been very pleased by his presence, but she was too polite to say so out loud. Libbie didn't care one whit what her mother thought of Jack. She liked Jack, and that was all that mattered.

Libbie gave Jack his Coke and they both took a sip.

"Thanks," Jack said, giving her one of his sweet smiles.

"Want to take the canoe out on the water?" Libbie asked.

"Sure."

They slipped the canoe into the water and stepped inside, careful not to tip it. Jack took ahold of one paddle, and the canoe began to glide through the water.

"You look like you know what you're doing," Libbie said. "Do you get out on the water much?"

"Sometimes. But not in anything this nice. We have an old rowboat, and I sometimes take my little brother out fishing on a small lake at the back of our property. My uncle has an old wood canoe, too, that we use."

"You have a brother and sister, don't you?" Libbie asked.

"Yep. Janet is two years younger and Ray is five years younger than I am. He's a good kid. He likes it when I let him tag along."

"That must be fun," Libbie said, lying back and gazing up into the sky. "My sister, Gwen, is only three years older than me, but it's always felt like she's decades older. She's married and has a one-year-old daughter. She's always trying to tell me how to run my life. It's annoying. I wish I had a younger sister or brother. That might be fun."

"Maybe," Jack said. "But being older also means you're responsible for them. That can be a drag sometimes."

"I suppose," Libbie said. She still wished she had another sibling. Someone she could be friends with and share secrets with. She adored her best friend, Carol, and they'd known each other for so long, it felt as if they were sisters. But it would be fun to have someone who actually lived with her who she was close to. So often, she felt ganged up on by Gwen and her mother. Those two were exactly alike, and neither understood her. Her father was always sweet to her, but he had no say in what the women in the family did. Her mother was in charge of the children, and that was that.

Libbie watched as Jack paddled the canoe. He was facing her, and every once in a while he'd smile and it made her heart dance. They had gone out a short distance in the water, and then he'd turned the canoe around and headed back to shore.

"Where's Bill today? Doesn't he hang out here all the time?" Jack asked.

Libbie sighed. Bill was another bone of contention between her and her mother and sister. "He's working at his father's bank. And no, he doesn't come here often."

"I thought you two were going steady."

Libbie grinned. "Oh, you did, did you? Then why did you accept my offer to come out here if you thought I was already spoken for?"

Jack smiled back. "Why did you invite me if you were already spoken for?"

Libbie laughed. "Checkmate." She turned and saw they were near the shore, but she didn't want their time together to end. "See that tree over there? The willow tree that's hanging over the water by the shore?"

Jack nodded.

"Slip the canoe under it. It's beautiful."

"Okay." Jack paddled the canoe toward the shore and then turned it so they could glide under the branches that hung over the water. "Wow, you're right. It's neat. It's like being under a tent or something."

Libbie sat up and leaned toward Jack. "You should see it at night under the full moon. It's magical."

Jack moved in even closer. "I'll bet it is."

"Did you have a nice time today?" Libbie asked.

"Yeah. This was fun. It's too bad I have to work so much. I'd like to do this every day."

"Maybe you can come again."

"I'd like that. But what about Bill?"

Libbie waved her hand through the air as if to brush Bill away. "Bill is my mother and sister's idea of the perfect boy for me. I don't even think he's that interested in me. As soon as he goes off to college this fall, he'll find himself a pretty little thing—or maybe several pretty little things. And I don't care a bit."

Jack cocked his head and stared at her. "Well, then Bill's an idiot."

"And why is that?" Libbie asked.

"Because only an idiot would pick another girl over you."

Libbie grinned. "Then we both agree. Bill is an idiot."

They laughed and then Jack said, "Will you come with me to the lakeside movie on Friday night? I'll buy you popcorn."

"That sounds like fun. I've never gone before."

"Really? Well, we can't have that. I'll bring a blanket to keep us warm, and we can watch the movie under the stars," Jack said.

"It's a date," Libbie said softly.

Jack grinned widely as he maneuvered the canoe out from under their hiding place and over to the shore. It was late afternoon, and most of the kids had headed home. Carol and Barbara were still suntanning on the floating dock. Libbie walked with Jack to the front of the house.

"I'll pick you up around eight thirty Friday night, okay?" Jack said.

Libbie hesitated. She knew her mother wouldn't approve of her going out with Jack. "Why don't I meet you downtown by the old pub near the lakefront? That way you don't have to drive so far home after the movie."

Jack looked at her curiously a moment, and Libbie hoped she hadn't insulted him. But then he smiled at her. "Okay. See you then."

Libbie waved at him as he drove off. She didn't care that he drove an old pickup truck or that his parents didn't own half of Jamison. He was sweet and kind, and she loved how his eyes sparkled when he looked at her. She already felt more for him in the short time they'd spent together than she'd ever felt for Bill.

As Libbie walked back to the house, she forgot all about her mother and sister and their constant disapproval. Her mind was already spinning over what she was going to wear on her first date with Jack.

Chapter Four

On Friday night, Jack and Libbie sat under the stars watching the old movie *Roman Holiday* and sharing popcorn. The night was perfect. The sky was clear, the half-moon was bright, and the stars twinkled above as the movie stars glittered on the large outdoor screen. Couples sat on blankets spread out on the park's grassy hill, and as the night air chilled, they wrapped blankets around themselves to stay warm. Jack had brought two blankets, too, and when Libbie shivered next to him, he unfolded the second one and slipped it around them.

"Better?" he asked quietly, enjoying the feel of her body close to his.

"Much better," she said.

Afterward, they stopped at the Dairy Queen and shared a hot fudge sundae and a Coke. They sat close together in Jack's truck while they ate.

"Where did you tell your mother you were going tonight?" Jack asked casually.

Libbie stared at him, surprised, and then looked contrite. "I told her I was going to Carol's and we might go to a movie.

How'd you know?"

"You wouldn't let me pick you up at your house. I figured you thought your parents wouldn't approve of us going out together."

Libbie dropped her eyes to her lap. "I'm sorry, Jack. It's just that my mom and sister are so protective of me. I didn't want them to make it a big deal."

Jack reached over and touched her chin with his fingertip, raising her eyes to his. "It's okay, Libbie. I get it. 'Rich girls don't marry poor boys.' Right?"

Libbie shook her head. "I don't care if you're rich or poor or anywhere in between. Unfortunately, my parents do. But they don't know you yet, Jack. When they get to know you, they'll like you. I'm sure of it."

Jack smiled. "Let's hope so. But it doesn't matter if they like me or not, because I'm crazy about you. I hope you know that, Libbie Wilkens."

Libbie giggled. "You've been making that pretty clear since the prom."

They finished eating the last scoops of the sundae, and then Jack drove Libbie the short distance to where she'd parked her car. Libbie turned to Jack with sparkling eyes. "Want to do something fun?"

"Sure. But shouldn't you be getting home?"

"That's where we'll be. Remember the other day when I told you it was so cool under that tree in the moonlight? The sky is clear tonight, and even with only a half-moon, it would be beautiful there."

Jack hesitated. "What about your parents? What if they see us out on the water this late?"

Libbie brushed his concern aside with the wave of her hand.

"They're probably in bed by now. We'll be quiet. Come on. Let's do it."

"Okay," Jack agreed, reluctantly. He hoped Libbie was right and her parents were asleep. The last thing he wanted to do was anger them before they had a chance to meet him properly.

Jack followed Libbie's Mustang to her house, and he parked his truck out on the road while she drove into the driveway. He caught up with her at the side of the house. "How will we see in the dark?" he whispered.

"With this," she said, holding up a flashlight. "My dad insists I keep one in the car."

Jack took Libbie's hand and they ran to the shoreline to where the canoe sat. Jack motioned for Libbie to get in so she wouldn't get her shoes wet, then he took off his black Converse sneakers and set then in the canoe before shoving it off into the water.

Libbie pointed out the way with the flashlight while Jack paddled. It wasn't long before they had slipped under the hanging tree branches.

The water was calm, so it wasn't any work to keep the canoe in place. Libbie turned off the flashlight. The light of the moon and stars glittered through the branches and leaves of the tree.

"You're right. It's magical," Jack said, gazing up.

Libbie moved forward to the middle bench. "I knew you'd appreciate it."

Jack glanced at Libbie, her blond hair shining in the moonlight. She looked so beautiful that his heart swelled. He could barely believe that he was here with her. He'd had a crush on her for so long that it seemed as if that was all it would ever be. But here he was, only inches away from her, in this enchanted spot.

"You surprise me, Jack," Libbie said softly. "You really are a romantic. Quoting *The Great Gatsby* earlier. You must have been paying attention in English lit this year."

"I liked that book," Jack admitted. "I know the other guys in the class thought it was stupid and sappy, but not me. Do you think that's weird?"

"No. I think it's sweet."

The frogs and crickets sang out around them as Jack gazed into Libbie's eyes. She leaned even closer, and he did also. Unable to resist any longer, Jack reached up one hand and gently touched the side of her face. Their lips met, and they kissed softly. As he pulled away and looked into Libbie's blue eyes, Jack knew for certain that he was in love.

* * *

That summer Jack felt as if he were floating on air. He spent every free minute he had with Libbie. He went to her house on the rare occasions that Rick didn't need him in the afternoons and spent time by the lake with her and the other kids. His best friend, Larry, started tagging along, and the group accepted him as they had Jack. Larry was tall and athletic, like Jack, and he had a wicked sense of humor that everyone loved. And to Jack's surprise, Carol found Larry very interesting, and the two began dating. Sometimes, the four of them would go to the movies, to the local roller rink, or for a burger at the A&W drive-in. Jack was grateful that Libbie liked Larry and they all got along well. It was fun being able to hang out together as a group.

The four went to the Fourth of July carnival in town and watched fireworks over the lake from the grassy hill in the park. They rode carnival rides and ate hot dogs and cotton candy. Jack even won a small stuffed bear for Libbie at the shooting gallery, which she hugged tightly all evening. Their time spent together was everything Jack had dreamed of, and when Libbie kissed him, he felt as if his life was complete.

Jack didn't worry about what Libbie's parents thought of him until one afternoon when reality came crashing down on him. He was working at the gas station when Libbie's mother pulled her Cadillac DeVille sedan up to the pumps. Jack knew who it was immediately and wiped his hands on a rag to try to get the grease off of them. He didn't want to touch her shiny, new, beige-colored car with dirty hands. He walked over and smiled at her as she stared up at him from the driver's side window.

"Hello, Mrs. Wilkens. Fill it up, today?"

Abigail slowly slid her sunglasses down her nose and stared at him over the top of the rims. It was not a friendly stare. "Yes, please," she said.

Jack went about filling up the car, checking the oil, and cleaning the windows. Mrs. Wilkens had stepped out of the car and was standing beside the driver's door, watching him intently. She made him feel even more self-conscious. She wore a two-piece, royal-blue suit with matching heels. A diamond brooch was pinned to her lapel, and she wore several gold and diamond rings on her perfectly manicured fingers. Everything about her screamed money, and the longer she watched him, the more nervous Jack became.

When he'd finished, he walked over to her, being careful not to get too close. His coveralls were so dirty that he thought for sure the grease would jump off onto her nice suit. "Will that be all today, ma'am?" he asked.

Abigail pulled her sunglasses off and stared him in the eye. "You're Jack Prentice, aren't you?"

Jack's hands were shaking, but he forced himself to stand as still as possible and kept a smile on his face. "Yes, ma'am, I am."

Abigail cocked her head. "I've seen you at the house. You and Libbie are friends."

Jack nodded. "Yes, we are, ma'am. And I appreciate you letting me come and spend time with the other kids there. We have a good time."

"Hmm. Well, that's nice. I'm happy that Libbie has so many *friends*."

Jack swallowed hard. The emphasis she'd placed on the word *friends* was palpable.

"Libbie is a sweet girl who is easily swayed sometimes, I'm afraid," Abigail continued. "We have high hopes for her future, as any mother and father would for their daughter." She looked Jack up and down very slowly. "I'd hate to see anything, or anyone, come between her and a *successful* future."

Mrs. Wilkens's words hit Jack like a brick. He knew exactly what she meant. He wasn't ever going to be good enough for Libbie. "I understand," he said stiffly.

Abigail nodded. "Please put the fuel on our account. Oh, and here," she handed him a folded one-dollar bill. "For your services." She slid on her sunglasses, slipped into her car, and drove away.

Jack watched her leave, the dollar bill practically burning a hole in his hand. Never in his life had anyone made him feel so small and insignificant as she had just now.

"Well, she's sure a piece of work," Rick said, coming out of the garage. He walked over to Jack's side. "Ignore her, Jack. All the money in the world doesn't make you a better person. It certainly hasn't helped her become one."

Jack nodded and headed back inside the garage to help Rick. But no matter how hard he tried, he couldn't erase the memory of the look of pure disgust on Mrs. Wilkens's face.

* * *

Later that afternoon, Jack walked into the farmhouse kitchen where his mother was busy cutting up fresh potatoes from the garden to boil for supper. He smelled a roast cooking in the oven, and there were green beans sitting in a strainer, waiting to be washed. They ate well on the farm. And his mother always made sure their clothes were clean and mended. No child of hers went to town with holes in their jeans or buttons missing on their shirts. Jack had always thought his family lived a good life—they certainly weren't poor. But after today, he wondered if he'd been wrong.

"Why the frown, Jack?" Bev asked. "You have a bad day?"

Jack studied his mother. She wore a simple flowered house-dress with an apron over it and an old pair of black flats. Her brown hair was pulled up into a simple bun, and her face was free of makeup. The only jewelry his mother wore was her plain gold wedding band. No expensive suit, no heels, and certainly no diamond jewelry. But his mother had a heart of gold, and that was so much better than anything Mrs. Wilkens owned.

Jack went over to the counter where the green beans sat and began snapping the tips off and breaking them in half. "Ma? Do you think some people are better than other people?"

Bev stopped cutting potatoes and glanced at Jack. "Does this have anything to do with that cute little Libbie Wilkens?"

Jack looked up, surprised. "You know about Libbie?"

Bev chuckled and started cutting potatoes again. "Sweetie, you can't go to the movies or be seen at the Dairy Queen without someone noticing and telling someone else. It's a small town. Of course I've heard about you two."

Jack dropped his eyes. "Then I'll bet that's how Libbie's mother found out. Through other people."

Bev walked over next to Jack. "Why? Did she say something to you?"

Jack looked at his mother. "She made it very clear today that it was okay for me to be Libbie's friend but nothing more. Maybe she's right, Ma. I'm never going to be successful enough for a girl like Libbie."

"That's not true, Jack, and you know it. Anyone can be successful in life; it just depends on what your definition of success is. For some, it's having a lot of money. But for others, it's being happy with the one you care most about. And if you work hard, you can have both."

Jack sighed. "Mrs. Wilkens made me feel like I was nothing."

"And what about Libbie? Does she think you're nothing?" Bev asked.

Jack looked up. "No. She doesn't care if I'm rich or not. She likes me for who I am."

Bev smiled. "Then that's all that matters, isn't it?"

Jack grinned. "Yeah, I guess that is all that matters." He started snapping beans again.

"Good. Besides, Abigail Wilkens has no reason to look down her nose at you or anyone else. She grew up on a farm just like the rest of us. The only difference is she married Randall Wilkens, who inherited his businesses and money. So don't let her intimidate you."

Jack smiled to himself as he finished up the beans and washed them in the sink. His mother was right. As long as Libbie liked him, nothing else mattered.

"You should invite Libbie out to the farm some evening for supper. You two can go horseback riding or something. I'd love to get to know her better," Bev said.

Jack nodded. Maybe it would be fun for her to meet his family. Especially his mother. Everyone who came to the farm liked her. "I'll ask her," he said.

* * *

Libbie sat quietly at the dinner table. Gwen, her husband, Walter, and their one-year-old baby girl, Lynn, were eating with the family tonight. Libbie didn't like Walter all that much. He was always bragging, and he had no reason to. He'd only gone to college for one year, and yet he acted like he had a PhD. He and Gwen had married in a rush a year out of high school, and then Lynn came along. Walter ended up working in the office of his father's construction company, writing up bids for projects. Libbie didn't always like how her sister acted, but she thought Gwen could have married better if she'd been more careful.

They were eating roasted chicken with new potatoes and glazed carrots. Libbie ate but hardly tasted the food. Her mother always took credit for cooking dinner, but truth be told, their housekeeper, Sandra, did most of the work. Sandra prepared the meal, and all her mother had to do was put it in the oven or boil something on the stove. But of course, her father always compli-mented her mother on the delicious meal.

Walter was rambling on about the recent construction bid he was writing up for a new office building going in northwest of town. Randall listened with interest.

"Why would anyone build in that direction instead of closer to downtown?" Randall asked. "There's nothing out there but an old restaurant and hotel. The rest is all open land."

Walter shrugged as his meaty hands reached for another

helping of potatoes. Libbie thought he didn't need to eat any more. He wasn't much taller than her sister's five foot eight, and he was stocky, bordering on fat. At twenty years old, he looked more like forty to Libbie, but then, Libbie thought the same of her sister. Gwen was taller than she was and built wider and sturdier. Her face was more like their mother's, with that straight nose and pinched look. But she still might have been pretty if it hadn't been for her overbearing personality. Gwen was a bossy know-it-all, and Libbie was usually the one she bossed around.

"The owner thinks that the northwest section of town is going to sprout up with businesses over the next few years. I guess he can think what he wants. As far as I'm concerned, the south end is the way to go," Walter said.

"Land is cheap on the northwest side. Might be worth looking into. Maybe this gentleman knows something we don't," Randall said.

Libbie smiled at her father. He was an easygoing man who was usually open to new ideas, especially if there was a profit to be made. That was why he was so successful. He'd inherited businesses from his family, but he'd also expanded those businesses and opened new ones as he saw a need.

Silence filled the air as they continued eating. Gwen was busy trying to entice Lynn to eat her carrots. Libbie thought that she was being too forceful. Gwen ran her household like a prison. Poor Lynn followed a strict schedule of eating and sleeping, even if the little girl wasn't hungry or tired. Libbie decided that when she had a baby, she'd be less rigid about a schedule and enjoy her baby more.

"I saw your *friend* at the filling station today, Libbie," Abigail said from across the table. "Jack, isn't it? The boy who's been coming out here every so often."

"Oh?" Libbie said casually, even though her heart started pounding. If her mother was bringing up Jack, there had to be some motive behind it.

"He seems like a polite young man, despite his working in such a dirty place," Abigail said, wrinkling her nose. "It seems you've been seeing a lot of this boy lately."

"We're just friends, Mother," Libbie said as calmly as possible. "We've gone out occasionally as a group. Carol is dating his friend, Larry, so Jack and I tag along."

"Really?" Gwen interjected with raised eyebrows. "Then why did I see you and this Jack alone at the movie theater the other night?"

Libbie stared at her sister. She hadn't seen Gwen or Walter at the theater. And here she'd thought she was being very careful. "It was just a movie. I'm seventeen years old. Can't I go to a movie with a friend without getting the third degree?"

"Who is this young man you're talking about, dear?" Randall asked curiously.

Libbie let out the breath she'd been holding and relaxed. She knew her father wouldn't judge Jack. "Jack Prentice, Dad. He's one of the boys who comes here swimming sometimes." She turned to her mother. "Just like Ron, Matt, and Arnie do. And no one ever questions why they're here."

"That's because *they* live on the lake and you've known them your entire life," Abigail said.

"I've known Jack practically my entire life, too," Libbie countered. "We go to school together. There aren't separate schools in town for the different social classes, Mother."

"Unfortunately," Abigail said haughtily.

"Jack Prentice?" Randall said, seeming to ignore the tense exchange taking place. "Is his father the cabinetmaker?"

"Yes, he is," Libbie answered.

"Oh, yes. He made beautiful new cabinets for the Andersons just down the road. Remember how you complimented her on her new kitchen, Abigail?"

Abigail glanced up, her lips forming a thin line. "Yes. They were lovely."

Randall smiled at Libbie. "So, is young Jack going into the family business when he graduates?"

"No, Dad. He's more interested in engines. That's why he works at his uncle's gas station. He's going to school to become a mechanic."

"Not much money in that," Gwen sneered.

"And such a dirty job," Abigail said, sipping her tea.

Randall winked at Libbie. "Well, we do need good mechanics to keep our cars running properly, don't we?"

Libbie smiled at her dad. At least someone in her family was on her side.

Later that evening, Libbie had come downstairs for a drink before bed when she overheard her parents talking in the living room.

"I can't stand the thought of our Libbie dating that dirty gas station boy," Abigail said. "What if it becomes serious? What if she ends up married to him?"

"Now, Abbie, don't get yourself worked up. She's only seventeen. I'm sure by this time next year, Libbie will have moved on to some nice young man. You really shouldn't get upset over it."

Libbie stood there in the hall, fuming. How dare her mother talk about Jack that way? She didn't know him. She heard the clinking of ice cubes in a glass, and she knew her mother was on her third or fourth gin and tonic.

"I don't know, Rand. You haven't seen them together like I

have. I think there's more to it than Libbie is letting on."

"Oh, Abbie, you always get yourself into a fret over these things. Believe me, it will all work out in the end."

She heard the sound on the television being turned up, and Libbie knew that was her dad's way of ending the conversation. She slipped into the kitchen for her drink and then quietly headed upstairs again.

They were wrong. She cared more for Jack than for any boy she'd ever dated before. She might be only seventeen, but she knew how she felt. And there was nothing they could do to get between her and Jack.

Chapter Five

"Is that really what she said?" Larry asked Jack a few days later. They'd taken the rowboat out onto the small lake that bordered the farm's back forty acres and were fishing.

Jack nodded. "I guess she's afraid Libbie and I might get serious."

Larry snorted. "Might get serious? Man, you're already there. I've never seen you look at anyone the way you look at Libbie. And I can't blame you. She's not only beautiful, but she's nice, too. Obviously, she didn't get her personality from her mother."

"What about you and Carol? Have you met her parents yet?"

"Yeah, but by accident. We were heading back to my car after walking through the park downtown and there they were. I was holding Carol's hand, and she dropped it like it was a hot potato. Then she introduced me as a *friend* from school."

"Ouch. What happened?"

"Oh, they were very polite and then left. But I could see in their eyes that they weren't happy. I wasn't all that pleased, either, with the way Carol acted like I was nothing."

"Yeah, but you're still seeing her, aren't you?"

Larry grinned. "Yeah. I can't help it. She's cute."

Jack laughed.

"But it's not like you and Libbie, you know? I mean, I'm sure Carol will dump me as soon as school starts, and I don't really care if she does. But you and Libbie, you two really care about each other. It's going to be a rough ride for you with that family of hers."

"I know. But Libbie is worth it," Jack said.

"I sure hope so, Jack. I sure hope so."

* * *

It was late July when Jack invited Libbie out to the farm to go horseback riding and have supper. She was excited to go but nervous, too. What if Jack's parents didn't like her? Or thought she was a snob, like her mother? She wasn't sure what to wear, either. Jeans or a dress? It seemed rude to underdress, but if they went riding, then she couldn't wear a dress. She'd never been more nervous about meeting anyone in her life.

Jack solved the problem for her. "Wear jeans to go riding in and bring something to change into afterward." Libbie was relieved. She had thought of bringing a change of clothes, but then wondered if she'd seem too prissy for them.

"Don't worry," Jack told her. "My parents will love you."

And Jack had been right. The moment Libbie walked into the farmhouse, she was welcomed with a warm hug from Bev. Then Jack took her out to the shop and introduced her to his father. Norman Prentice looked a lot like Jack, but there were smile lines that crinkled around his eyes and strands of grey running through his dark hair.

"It's nice to meet you, Libbie," Norm said as he shook her

hand. "I can see now why Jack took off of work every chance he could get."

Jack's face reddened, and Libbie thought it was cute that he was embarrassed.

She looked around the workshop, amazed at all of the beautifully crafted cabinets. "You made all of these yourself?" she asked Norm.

Norm nodded. "Mostly. Jack helps with the finishing work and staining. I've been letting Ray help a little, too, but he's still young."

Libbie walked over to a table by the wall that held a variety of small, wooden boxes with lids decorated with carved flowers or hearts. They were painted and stained in a variety of colors. "These are lovely," she said, picking one up and opening it. Inside, on the bottom, was a piece of fine velvet.

"They're jewelry boxes," Jack said, coming to stand beside her. "Dad makes them and my mom sells them at the craft fair by the lake every year. She'll be there in a couple of weeks."

"They're beautiful," Libbie said.

Jack and Libbie left the shop and walked out to the barn. In the corral was a white mare with brown spots. The horse chewed on grass and stared at them.

"She's pretty," Libbie said. "Do you have others?"

"Nope. Just her. My mother used to ride, but now we kids ride her most of the time. She's getting old, but she's still a good mount."

"What's her name?" Libbie asked.

"Sprite."

"That's so cute."

Jack walked into the corral and retrieved Sprite. He led her by her halter over to Libbie. "Ready to ride?"

"Aren't you going to saddle her?"

Jack shook his head. "We always ride bareback. It's not the most comfortable way to ride, but it's easy."

Libbie hesitated. "Won't we fall off?"

Jack laughed. "Don't worry, Libbie. I won't let you fall." He pulled himself up onto Sprite's back and then told Libbie to climb on the fence rail so she could get on the horse. With his help, she slipped up behind him. "Hang on to me, okay?"

"Okay." She wrapped her arms around Jack's waist and held on tight. When she saw him take ahold of Sprite's mane, she asked, "Don't you need a bridle and reins?"

"Nah, we never use them. I always ride like this."

They headed off down a trail that led to the back of the property. The day was warm, but there was a nice breeze, which helped to keep the bugs away. Libbie watched as Jack maneuvered Sprite by gently pulling her mane one way or the other. She'd never seen anyone ride bareback before, and it amazed her how he could control the horse so easily.

"I'll take you to the back forty where the lake is that we fish in," he told her.

Libbie held onto Jack tightly, and soon she got used to the rhythm of Sprite's walk. The path turned into a line of trampled-down grass among the foot-tall grass blowing in the breeze. Trees sat here and there, but for the most part, it was all open field. In the distance, Libbie saw a line of trees. She pointed them out to Jack. "Is that where the lake is?"

Jack nodded. "Yep. It isn't far."

"Do your parents own all this land?" Libbie asked. It seemed like so much open space to her.

"Most of what you see we own. It goes back to where the lake is. Everything you see from left to right is ours, too."

"Wow, that's a lot. What do they do with it all?"

Jack chuckled. "Not a whole lot. My great-grandparents owned this land and they used to raise cattle and horses on it, but my dad only uses a portion of the acreage to raise a few head of cattle. He sells some off each year to local people who want fresh beef. Some of the land he uses to cut hay to feed the cattle all winter. Other than that, it all just sits, unused. My dad prefers making cabinets to working a farm."

They reached the trees, and spread out in front of them was a small body of water.

"This is a lake?" Libbie asked. "It's so small."

"Yeah, it's small, but we still catch fish in it," Jack said, pointing to the rowboat sitting on the shore. He slipped off the horse and then helped Libbie down. Sprite took the opportunity to graze in the tall grass.

"Where do the fish come from?" Libbie asked as they walked over to the water.

"There's a small stream that feeds into the lake. Fish come from it. Way out that way"—Jack pointed out into the distance—"there's a river that feeds the stream. When it rains, the lake gets even larger."

Libbie drew closer to the lake and knelt to run her fingers through the water. "It's cold. It feels nice."

Jack smiled. "Want to go out in the boat?"

"Sure."

He motioned for her to get in it and then he pushed it out into the water and jumped in. Slowly, he rowed it a short way into the middle of the lake.

Libbie liked how peaceful it was out here. Birds sang in the trees and frogs croaked loudly. There was no noise from boat engines or kids swimming and hollering, like on Lake Ogimaa.

"I love your lake," she told him. "It's so blissfully quiet here."

"I'm glad you like it. Maybe we'll come out here more often."

Jack had stopped rowing, and Libbie moved to sit on the middle bench beside him. Jack took her hand and held it.

"I really like your mom. She's sweet. And your dad is nice, too," Libbie said.

"That's good, but you only spent a couple of minutes with my mom."

"Yeah, but I felt more warmth from her in that couple of minutes than I have from my own mother my whole life."

"That's sad," Jack said. "I'm sorry."

Libbie shrugged. "I know my mom loves me, she just doesn't know how to show it. And she always thinks she knows better than I do what's good for me. My sister is like that, too. It's frustrating."

"Where did you tell your parents you were going today?" Jack asked.

Libbie looked directly into Jack's eyes. "I told them I was coming here for dinner. I'm not going to lie to them anymore. If they don't like it, I don't care."

Jack's brows rose. "Really? What did they say?"

"My mom got a little huffy about it, but my dad said to have a nice time." Libbie giggled. "My mom didn't like that he said that, though."

Jack's face grew serious. "I don't want you to have problems with your parents because of me, Libbie. Maybe I should come and meet them properly. If they'd get to know me, they might not mind you seeing me."

Libbie sighed. "Maybe." She wished it would be true, but she knew her mother well, and she would never approve of Jack.

They sat in the boat a long while, enjoying the warmth of the sun and the gentle rocking of the water. Libbie lay back against Jack and put her feet up on the edge of the boat. The warm breeze felt good on her face. Libbie had never felt as comfortable with anyone in her life as she did with Jack. At home, she always felt like she was on edge, never knowing when her mother or sister would criticize her. At school, she was supposed to be the perfect, well-behaved girl who made good grades and volunteered for everything. When she'd dated Bill, she never dared get too close to him because he thought it was an invitation to paw at her. But with Jack, it was different. She felt like she could relax and be herself. She loved it when they held hands, and when he kissed her, her heart soared. But he was never inappropriate, and she appreciated that, too.

She gazed up at Jack. "Do you realize that this is the first time we've been alone together?"

Jack smiled down at her. "Yeah, I guess it is. Except for that night under the tree in the canoe."

"That was a fun night," Libbie said dreamily. "I really like being with you, Jack. You're always so sweet to me." She grinned. "And I like kissing you."

"I like kissing you, too," Jack said, gazing down at her. He slowly lowered his head and kissed her lips.

Libbie sat up and raised her arms around his neck, and Jack kissed her again, running his arms around her waist. Chills tingled up her spine. She'd never felt like this when Bill had kissed her. In fact, she'd felt nothing. But with Jack, her whole body came alive every time he touched her.

Jack finally pulled away. He stared down into her eyes as he ran a finger down the side of her cheek, tucking a stay strand of blond hair behind her ear. "We should go back to the house," he said, reluctantly.

Libbie sighed. She supposed they should, but she would have been happy sitting in the boat with Jack until nightfall. "I guess we should."

As he rowed the boat to shore, Jack told her how much his sister, Jan, admired her. "You're like royalty to her," he said, chuckling. "When I said you were coming to dinner, I thought she'd die. She's been in her room all day primping so she'll look just perfect."

"Why?" Libbie asked. She'd never thought she was that special.

"Because you're older and you're going to be a senior this year and you're beautiful. All the younger girls in school want to look and be just like you."

Libbie laughed. "That's silly. I'm nothing special."

Jack helped Libbie out of the boat and stared into her eyes. "You're special to me, Libbie Wilkens. Don't you ever forget that." He placed a light kiss on her lips.

Libbie's heart melted. Hand in hand, they walked back to where Sprite was grazing and rode back to the farmhouse.

* * *

Jack's world was getting better and better. He couldn't believe how lucky he was to have Libbie in his life. After that first time, Libbie had come out to the farm often. Bev had extended an open invitation to her to eat supper there any time she wanted, and Libbie had taken her up on it. Many times, Jack found Libbie's Mustang in the driveway when he came home from work and Libbie in the kitchen helping Bev cook supper. Libbie said she loved helping, something her mother never let her do, and so far, Bev had taught her how to bake bread and cookies and cook different meats and vegetables. As July turned into August, Libbie came to the farm so Bev could teach her how to can vegetables and fruits. Jack found it amusing how Libbie thought this type of work was fun. It even made Jan want to help out so she could be around Libbie.

Jack's family adored Libbie. Not only did his parents like her, but both Jan and Ray loved it when she came to the house, too. Libbie sometimes picked Jan up in the afternoon and took her shopping in town, trying on dresses and shoes just for the fun of it. Jack knew that Jan loved riding around in Libbie's fancy car and being seen with her. It made her feel special, and Jack appreciated that Libbie did that for her. She was also nice to Ray, who had a wide-eyed crush on Libbie. Ray was into superhero comic books and baseball cards, and once in a while, Libbie brought him a new comic book or set of cards from her father's store. Ray thanked her profusely each time, and Bev teasingly told her she'd spoil him rotten. But Libbie told Jack that she had so much fun doing it all. She'd always wanted a family like his, and she loved being a part of it.

They rarely hung out at the Wilkenses' lake home anymore, opting instead to spend their free time either in town or on the farm. Jack and Libbie rode Sprite often, and they sat in the little rowboat on the lake. Sometimes Larry and Carol joined them and they had picnics on the lakeshore. Jack knew Libbie loved Larry's quirky sense of humor. They always had fun when they were all together.

Late in August, Jack bought his very first truck with the money he'd been saving since he was fourteen. He proudly showed off his 1960 Ford F-100 to Libbie the day he bought it from the used car dealer in town. It wasn't new and it wasn't fancy, but it was his, and he beamed with pride when he took it to Libbie's house for her to see.

Libbie had been sitting out by the lake with Carol, Matt, and Arnie when Jack showed up. They all whooped and hollered when they saw his truck, and the girls jumped into the front seat while the boys hopped into the bed to go for a ride. Jack had beamed with pride as they drove around the lake in his truck. Libbie's friends had shiny new cars like she did, but they all acted like Jack had the best vehicle of them all, and he appreciated it. He felt like he was one of them, and it felt good.

Chapter Six

A week before their senior year began, Jack took Libbie out for dinner to a nice restaurant in town. He had a surprise for her, and he wanted to give it to her in the most memorable way possible. They went to the Lakeshore Inn, a steakhouse with a lakeside view. Carol's parents owned it, and it was one of the most expensive places to eat in their little town. Libbie had been pleasantly surprised when Jack had told her where they were dining.

She'd dressed up for him in a yellow sleeveless dress that had a wide white belt. It showed off her slender legs and tanned skin to perfection. Jack, wearing his only suit that was for special occasions, felt like the proudest person in town when he escorted her into the restaurant and to the table.

They felt very grown-up as the waiter asked them for their drink order and brought their sodas. They sat in a half-round padded booth that offered a view of the lake. It was cozy and intimate, exactly how Jack had hoped it would feel.

Libbie smiled up at him as she sat by his side. "This must be a very special occasion for you to bring me here. But it's so expensive," she whispered. "Are you sure you want to eat here?"

Jack reached for her hand. "I wanted to do something special," he said. "Don't worry about the money. Let's just enjoy it, okay?"

Libbie agreed and they both ordered the steak and shrimp dinner. They talked easily as they ate and joked and laughed. Jack loved how easy it felt being around Libbie. She was more than a pretty face. She was smart and sweet and fun to be around. He just hoped she felt as strongly about him as he did her.

They shared a piece of cheesecake for dessert and then left the restaurant, hand in hand. Jack drove them to the other side of the lake to a favorite spot of theirs. It was a small park with huge old oak trees and pines and a narrow trail that ran beside the lake a short distance. It was still light out, so they got out of the truck and walked a short distance down the trail to a tree that grew out over the water. They ditched their nice shoes and carefully climbed out onto the thick trunk, their legs dangling and their toes barely touching the water.

"I love it here," Libbie said, sighing.

"I have something for you," Jack said, growing nervous. He pulled a velvet ring box out of his pocket and handed it to Libbie.

Her eyes grew wide as she stared at the box. "What is it?"

"Open it and see."

Gingerly, she opened the box, and sitting there on the velvet was a brand-new high school ring with a gold chain attached to it. "Jack. This is your school ring. Why are you giving it to me?"

"I was hoping you'd wear it around your neck. Will you go steady with me, Libbie?"

Libbie gasped as she looked up into Jack's eyes.

"I'm in love with you, Libbie. I told you I was going to try and win your heart this summer, and I hope I did. Please say yes, Libs. I want everyone to know that I love you and we're together.

Will you wear my ring?"

Tears filled Libbie's eyes as she nodded. "You did win my heart, Jack. I love you, too," she said softly.

Jack smiled as he lifted the ring and necklace out of the box. Libbie turned slightly and pulled up her hair so he could clasp the chain around her neck. He gently caressed the side of her face before kissing her softly on the lips.

Libbie fingered the ring. "You didn't even get a chance to wear this ring," she said.

Jack grinned. "I didn't buy it for me, silly. I only bought it so I could give it to you."

"Jack, you are the sweetest boy I've ever known. I'm the luckiest girl in the world." She reached up around his neck and kissed him again. They lost their balance for a moment and had to pull apart to steady themselves.

"We'd better get out of this tree before we fall in," Jack said, laughing. He climbed down out of the tree and then helped her down. They stood on the path, holding each other close and kissing until they were both out of breath.

"I want to tell the world that I love you," Jack said.

Libbie laughed. "What's stopping you?"

Jack turned toward the lake and yelled at the top of his lungs, "JACK PRENTICE LOVES LIBBIE WILKINS!" His words echoed across the lake as both teens laughed.

Jack walked her back to his truck with his arm around her. She fit perfectly next to him, as if they were meant to be together. When they got inside the cab, Libbie turned to Jack and reached for his hand.

She looked up at him, a serious expression on her face. "I do love you, Jack. I've never felt like this about any other boy. I just hope you don't mind if we take things slowly. I don't want to end up pregnant and having to get married. It's happened to so many girls I know. I hope you understand."

Jack looked at her tenderly. "I will never ask you to do anything you don't want to do," he said softly. "You'll always be safe with me."

Libbie smiled up at him, and then he started up the truck to take her home.

"Do you think my parents heard you yelling all the way across the lake?" she asked, her eyes sparkling mischievously.

"I don't care if they did. I'll go inside and tell them myself if you want me to." He grinned at her.

Libbie hit him playfully on the arm. "Don't you dare. They'd have a cow. They're still trying to get used to the idea that I spend so much time with you."

Jack glanced over at her. "Okay. Whatever you say. The woman is always right."

Libbie hit him again and then slid over to sit beside him as he drove her home.

* * *

"What is that thing you're wearing around your neck?" Libbie's mother asked her one night at dinner. Gwen and the baby were there, but Walter was at his weekly golf league. All eyes turned to Libbie and the ring around her neck.

It was only a week into the school year. Until now, Libbie had made sure to keep Jack's ring under her clothes whenever she was at home. Tonight, however, she'd rushed home after cheerleading practice and changed quickly for dinner, forgetting about the ring. She looked up at her mother and could tell by the expression on her face that she knew exactly what it was.

"It's Jack's class ring," Libbie said, lifting her chin in defiance. "He gave it to me."

Gwen gasped. "You and Jack are going steady?"

Libbie looked at her father, who sat at one end of the table, and then at her mother. She sat up straight, trying to be brave. "Yes, we are."

Abigail dropped her fork onto her china plate and ran her hand over her forehead. "Oh my God!"

Libbie glanced up at Gwen and saw a smug look cross her sister's face. She was enjoying Libbie's discomfort. To his credit, Randall kept his expression calm and unreadable.

"Do you mean to tell me that you and that *gas station boy* are serious?" Abigail said, her voice rising. "Ridiculous!"

"Now, Abbie. Let's be calm about this," Randall said gently.

"Calm? About our little girl dating *that* boy? Why, he's not good enough to clean her car windows, let alone date her."

"Mother!" Libbie exclaimed, shocked that her mother was being so rude. She knew her mother didn't approve of Jack, but she'd never heard her say such mean things about anyone before. At least not outright.

"Abbie, please," Randall said. "We don't judge people by how they earn a living."

Abigail stared hard at her husband. Libbie recognized that glare. Her mother was about to fly off the handle. Libbie shrunk down into her chair. No one wanted to be in Abigail Wilkens's path when she lost control.

"Don't you dare get on your high horse with me, Randall," Abigail said in a low, menacing tone. "I don't see you inviting your employees from the grocery store, hardware store, or any of our other businesses to come to our home and socialize with you. No, you socialize with people from our own class. I refuse to have our daughter becoming involved with a lowly gas station attendant." Abigail turned her burning eyes on Libbie. "You are *not* to see this boy again, do you hear me? It's over." Abigail stood, threw her napkin on the table, and stormed out of the room.

Baby Lynn, sensing the turmoil in the air, began crying. Gwen lifted her from her high chair and tried comforting her.

Libbie's body shook with fear as tears filled her eyes. She looked at her father for support, but it was useless. He only shook his head and shrugged. Libbie knew he couldn't help her. He ran the businesses and controlled the money, but when it came to the family, her mother's word was law.

"I'm sorry, kitten," he said softly. Then he stood and headed in the direction Abigail had gone.

Libbie knew he was going to try to calm her mother down, but he'd be unable to change her mind.

"It's for the best," Gwen said over baby Lynn's head. "That boy would never be able to give you the life you're used to, if it came to that. Be thankful that Mother sees what a mistake you two are before it's too late."

Libbie narrowed her eyes at her sister. "You mean a mistake like you getting pregnant and having to get married? You're a good one to talk."

Gwen's lips formed a thin line. "You spoiled little girl. You have no idea how difficult life can be when you don't have money. And if you stay with that boy, you'll always be poor. Is that what you want? To live on that farm for the rest of your life? He'll never be anything more than he is now, so don't throw my life back in my face. At least my husband earns enough money to support me properly."

Libbie stood so fast her chair fell back onto the floor with a thud. Lynn began to cry again. "There's more warmth and love at that farm than all the money in the world can buy, so don't you dare say another word against Jack or his family." She turned and ran into the kitchen and up the back staircase to her bedroom, slamming the door behind her.

Libbie dropped onto her bed and sobbed. *They can't make me stay away from Jack! They just can't!* She felt as if her whole world was caving in on her. Just last week, she'd been so blissfully happy, because of Jack. And now she felt trapped.

I could run away and never come back here, she thought. But then what would she do for money? How would she live? She wouldn't be eighteen until next April, so going out on her own would be difficult. And she'd have to give up so much if she did. But there was no way she was giving up Jack.

Wiping her tears away, Libbie sat up and carefully picked up the phone in her room. No one was on the line, so she dialed the number at the farm. After the second ring, Jan answered.

Libbie took a calming breath so she'd sound normal. "Hi, Jan. Can I talk to Jack?"

"Sure. Just a minute," Jan said. Libbie could hear Jan hollering to Jack that the phone was for him. Even in her sadness, it made her smile. She pictured Jack in his room, sitting on his twin bed, doing his homework. She could practically hear him running down the stairs to the only phone in the house, in the dining room, to answer it.

"Hey, Libbie. What's up? I was just thinking about you," Jack said, sounding happy.

His sweet voice made her tears begin to flow again. She didn't want to lose Jack. She just couldn't. "Something's happened. My mom and I had a terrible fight. I need to see you."

"Are you okay?" Jack asked, his voice filled with concern.

"Yes. But I have to see you. Please come, Jack. Park down at Carol's house and I'll meet you there. You can't come to my house. Hurry. Please." She began sobbing again.

"I'll be right there," Jack told her. "I'll hurry."

Libbie hung up the phone and grabbed a handful of tissues to wipe away her tears. Finally, when she felt calmer, she changed into an old pair of jeans and a sweater, then went to her door and quietly locked it. She crossed her room, opened her bedroom window, and climbed out onto the slanted roof. There was a tree that grew close to the house, and she carefully climbed onto the thickest branch and made her way down the tree to the ground. She'd done this many times before, when she'd wanted to sneak out to a party with Bill, and she'd never been caught. Hopefully she wouldn't be caught tonight, or it would make her situation even worse.

Carol lived two houses away, so Libbie headed to the bushes that separated their house from the neighbor's and walked through them, so her parents or sister wouldn't see her. The sun was just setting, so no one noticed her as she made her way to Carol's house. She waited beside a large oak tree until she heard the rumble of Jack's truck come down the road. Just as it came into view, she ran out and he stopped.

Libbie climbed up into the cab and reached for Jack. Tears fell down her cheeks and onto his shirt as he held her tight.

"What happened, Libbie?" Jack pulled away and looked down into her eyes. He wiped the tears away from her cheeks with the side of his thumb.

"My mother saw your ring," Libbie said between sobs. "She went crazy. She . . . she said I couldn't see you anymore." Libbie broke down again, and Jack pulled her close.

"Shh. It's okay, Libbie. Everything will be fine." Jack turned off the truck lights so no one would see them there and held Libbie as she cried. "I'm sorry your mother was upset about us going steady. Maybe if I talk to her it'll be okay. She'll see that I'm not all that bad."

Libbie looked up with wild eyes. "No. You can't do that. It'll only make things worse. You don't know how angry my mother can get. She just goes crazy."

"Okay, okay," Jack said softly. "Does your father feel the same way?"

Libbie sniffled and Jack pulled a few napkins out of his glove compartment and handed them to her. After wiping her tears away, she said, "I don't think so, but it doesn't matter what he thinks. My mom runs the house, and he never interferes. And my sister was siding with my mom, too. They were ganging up on me, like they always do."

"I'm sorry, Libbie," Jack said, pulling her close again and kissing the top of her head. They sat there in the dark cab with the silent night surrounding them.

"I wish we could run away," Libbie said. "I'm so tired of them telling me what to do. I can't live without seeing you, Jack. I just can't." She pulled away and looked up into his eyes. "Let's run away. Tonight. We'd be so happy somewhere far away, together."

"Oh, sweetie, that's a nice dream, but we can't run away. We have to finish school. I'm going to trade school, too, and I need to finish that if I'm ever going to earn a living."

Libbie's heart fell. "I thought you loved me. I thought you'd do anything to take care of me."

Jack took her hands in his, bringing one to his lips and kissing it gently. "Baby, I do love you. I've never loved anyone the way I love you. And I would do anything to take care of you. But running away isn't the answer. You'd miss all your friends, and your family, too. Things will work out, I promise. Your parents will come around."

Libbie shook her head sadly. "My mother will never approve of you, Jack. And she meant it when she said I couldn't see you anymore."

Jack reached over and tilted Libbie's face up to look at him. He smiled at her. "Maybe she did, but she can't stop us from seeing each other at school, can she? And soon, we'll both be eighteen and she won't be able to tell you what to do. I promise you, Libbie. She can't keep me away from you. It'll be impossible."

Libbie wanted to believe that was true, but she knew how stubborn her mother could be.

They sat in the truck, holding each other, until the moon rose high in the sky and the air cooled around them. Finally, Jack said, "You should go home before they notice you're gone. You don't want to make things worse."

Libbie nodded halfheartedly.

"Can you sneak back in without anyone seeing you?" Jack asked.

"I'm sure my parents are in bed by now. If not, I'll climb up the tree and onto the roof."

"I'll walk you back to your house and make sure you get in safely," Jack offered.

Jack wrapped his arm around Libbie's waist and pulled her close as they walked the short distance in the moonlight to her house. Once they were near it, he turned to her and looked down into her eyes. "I love you, Libbie. We'll get through this. Just remember how much I love you, and you'll be fine."

Libbie nodded as Jack kissed her softly on the cheek. "I love you, too," she whispered.

Libbie walked toward the dark house and opened the French

door in the kitchen. Slipping inside, she turned around and saw Jack still standing in the bushes at the edge of their property. She made her way quietly up the back stairs. Everything was silent and dark up there. She took her key from her pocket, opened her bedroom door, and went inside. Then she flicked her bedroom lights twice so Jack would know that she was safely inside the house.

Libbie ran to her window and looked outside, but it was too dark to see if Jack was still there. Exhausted from the emotional turmoil of the night, she went to bed and fell asleep quickly.

* * *

As Jack lay in bed that night, he thought about the wild-eyed look on Libbie's face when she'd told him he'd only make things worse if he spoke to her mother. He'd never seen her look anything but happy. But tonight she'd been shaking and scared as she'd cried in his arms. He'd wanted to protect her from her pain. He would have gladly taken her home to the farm if he'd thought it wouldn't have made things worse for Libbie. But he knew he couldn't, and it had been hard for him to watch her return to her house. He hoped she was okay.

He knew from the incident at the gas station that Libbie's mother didn't like him. But it seemed to him that she'd reacted too severely over them going steady. And to cause Libbie so much pain was cruel. It was difficult for him to understand a mother acting that way, since he was used to his own mother being so kind and loving.

Well, she's going to have to get used to me, because I'm not going away.

Jack's love for Libbie went far beyond puppy love. He knew,

even now, that he wanted to spend the rest of his life with her. He was working hard at school so he could learn his trade well and earn a living to support them. He was never going to be rich; he knew that. But he could still give Libbie a good life, if she'd have him.

As Jack fell asleep, his thoughts were of Libbie and how he'd take care of her and keep her safe for the rest of her life.

Chapter Seven

Abigail didn't leave her bed for three days after her outburst, claiming she was too distraught to get up. Gwen came over every day to care for her and to cook dinner for the family. This wasn't the first time Libbie's mother had taken to her bed after an outburst. It actually happened quite often, and usually after a family quarrel or upsetting news. Libbie always thought her mother did it to get attention or to sway her father to give in to whatever demands she had made. But this time, she knew it was because of her, and she felt guilty for making her mother sick. It also didn't help that Gwen gave her reproachful looks every time their paths crossed.

Everyone tiptoed around the house so as not to disturb Abigail. On the fourth day, Abigail reappeared, looking tired but acting as if nothing had happened. This behavior had always baffled Libbie. How could her mother be so angry that she became sick and yet pretend that all was fine just a few days later? It made no sense, but she was relieved that her mother wasn't angry with her anymore—at least for the time being.

No one questioned Libbie about her comings and goings or

whether she was spending time with Jack. It was as if things had returned to normal, and she didn't dare question it. She kept Jack's ring out of sight, and that seemed to keep her mother pacified.

As the homecoming celebration and dance drew near, Libbie went to her father to ask if it was okay if Jack escorted her. She'd been nominated for Homecoming Queen, and Carol had been nominated as part of the court. But if Libbie couldn't go with Jack, she'd already decided she wouldn't go at all.

"Of course you can go with him, kitten," Randall said, as if the incident at dinner had never occurred. "Why don't you have Jack stop by here before the dance so we can finally meet him properly? I'm sure your mother would like to take pictures, too."

Libbie doubted very much that her mother would want to take pictures, but she didn't tell her dad that. "Thanks, Dad," she told him, kissing him lightly on the cheek before leaving. Maybe he'd talked her mother into accepting Jack as her boyfriend. She hoped so. At least now she felt free to enjoy planning for homecoming and going with Jack.

* * *

Jack stood nervously outside the Wilkenses' front door. He adjusted his tie for the tenth time, and then ran his hand down his suit jacket sleeve, smoothing out imaginary wrinkles. He'd had to buy a new suit for homecoming. He'd grown over the summer, and his arms and legs were too long for the suit he'd worn the previous spring to the prom. He'd even splurged on new dress shoes. Libbie was worth it though, and he felt proud to be escorting the new Homecoming Queen to the dance. He just had to get through meeting her parents without having a heart attack.

Taking a deep breath, Jack rang the doorbell. A moment later, a tall, slender man with dark hair and friendly brown eyes answered.

"Hello. You must be Jack."

Jack relaxed a bit at the man's friendly greeting. He extended his hand. "Yes, sir, I am. It's nice to meet you, Mr. Wilkens."

Randall shook his hand and moved aside to let him inside. "Come in, Jack. Libbie will be down in a moment." He smiled. "You know how girls are, always making us men wait."

Jack smiled back and entered the house. He glanced around as he followed Mr. Wilkens through the large entryway to the back of the house and into the family room. It was just off the large kitchen, and the French doors leading out to the backyard stood between the rooms. They had passed a formal living room on the way there.

"Please, sit down," Mr. Wilkens said, pointing to a sofa. "Can I get you something? A Coke, maybe?"

"No, thank you. I'm fine." Jack sat down gingerly. He placed the box that held Libbie's corsage on the coffee table in front of him. Mr. Wilkens sat down in a recliner opposite him and lit up a cigarette. Jack wondered if Libbie's mother would make an appearance. He wanted her to see that he was a decent person, despite the fact that he was a farm boy from the south end of town.

"I hear you work at Rick's Shell Station. He's your uncle?"

Jack nodded. "Yes, sir. I work there in the summer and on weekends during school. I also help my father with his cabinet business."

"Yes, I've seen your father's work. He does a fine job."

"Thank you, sir."

Mr. Wilkens suddenly stood up and looked across the room.

"Abbie, dear. I'm so happy you were able to come down. I hope your headache is better."

Jack turned and saw Mrs. Wilkens standing there, staring directly at him. He quickly stood, bumping his knees into the coffee table.

"Yes, I'm feeling better," she replied, but her eyes were locked on Jack the entire time.

"You know Jack, don't you, dear?"

Mrs. Wilkens looked Jack up and down very slowly before replying. "Yes. Hello, Jack," she said coolly.

Jack swallowed hard. "Good evening, Mrs. Wilkens. It's nice to see you again."

She only nodded and then walked past him toward her husband. Mr. Wilkens offered her a cigarette and then lit it for her. She stood there, staring at Jack with those cold, sharp eyes, occasionally puffing on her cigarette.

Jack wasn't sure what to say. His palms were sweating, and he was growing hot in his suit. He'd known that Libbie's mother was a formidable figure, but he hadn't realized how absolutely scary she could be. He stood up straighter and tried to remain calm. He was at least a head taller than her, but her glacial stare made him feel two feet tall.

"Ah, there she is," Mr. Wilkens said, smiling toward the doorway.

Jack turned and saw Libbie. All his anxiety drifted away as he gazed at her. She looked beautiful in a long sapphire-blue satin dress. Her hair was pulled up with delicate wisps framing her face, and she wore white gloves that went up to her elbows. She truly looked like royalty.

"You look beautiful," Jack said, forgetting her parents were in the room and walking over to her. He reached for her hands and held them as their eyes met. She smiled, and his heart skipped a beat.

"Yes, kitten, you look lovely," Mr. Wilkens said, coming over to them. He had picked up the box with the corsage in it. "I believe Jack brought this for you."

Jack reluctantly let go of Libbie's hands as the magic of the moment faded away. He took the box from Mr. Wilkens and opened it, showing Libbie the flowers inside—a delicate white orchid with baby's breath tied with a sapphire-blue ribbon.

"Oh, Jack. It's so beautiful. Will you pin it on?"

Jack nodded and took the corsage out of the box. Carefully, he pinned it to her dress, all the while feeling her parents' eyes on him.

"Look, Mother," Libbie said excitedly. "Isn't it beautiful?"

Mrs. Wilkens snuffed out her cigarette in the ashtray on the coffee table and walked over to her daughter, a forced smile on her face. "It's lovely, dear," she said stiffly. "You will make a beautiful Homecoming Queen." She gently hugged her daughter before pulling away and standing off to the side.

Jack noticed that Libbie either chose to ignore her mother's stiffness or she was just used to it. Maybe that was as warm as Mrs. Wilkens ever was. At least her coldness hadn't dampened Libbie's spirit. She was smiling brightly at Jack.

"Are you ready to go?" Jack asked.

"Yes, just let me grab my wrap." Libbie went into the entry-way where the staircase was and lifted a lace shawl off the stair rail.

"We'll be right behind you two," Mr. Wilkens said cheerfully. "We can't miss our baby girl being crowned Homecoming Queen."

Jack turned to Libbie's father and offered his hand. "It was nice meeting you, Mr. Wilkens."

"Nice meeting you, too, Jack. We'll see you in a little while."

Jack looked over at Libbie's mother, who was glaring at him. "Nice seeing you again, Mrs. Wilkens," he said.

She only nodded.

Jack turned, and there was Libbie, her eyes sparkling at him. He smiled and escorted her out to his truck.

Later, as the homecoming program commenced, Jack stood near the back of the high school auditorium with Larry by his side. Libbie and Carol were up on stage wearing their crowns and having their pictures taken with the entire court for the yearbook and newspaper. The whole community had turned out for the coronation, so every seat was filled. Libbie's parents had showed up, as well as Gwen and Walter, and they were sitting at the front near the stage. Jack had met Gwen for the first time that night, and by the cold gaze in her eyes, he knew immediately that she didn't like him any more than Libbie's mother did.

Jack's mother had brought Jan to watch, and they were sitting somewhere in the mass of people. Jan had been starry-eyed about Libbie being named queen, and Jack knew she hoped to one day be just like Libbie.

"You should be standing up there beside Libbie as Homecoming King," Larry said to Jack. "You're just as good-looking as Ron."

Jack looked sideways at Larry. "Uh, I'm not sure if I like you thinking that I'm good-looking, but thanks."

Larry laughed. "You know what I mean."

"Well, you could be up there, too," Jack said.

"Yeah, if I was rich," Larry snorted. "They don't vote for the poor kids."

Jack nodded. Unfortunately, it was true. The popular kids

were usually the rich kids, too.

"You and Carol are still together, though. She must have finally told her parents about you."

"Yeah. They don't seem to have a problem with us dating. I think they actually like me. Can you imagine that? I've been over there a few times for dinner," Larry said.

"They should like you. You're a nice guy," Jack said.

Larry snorted. "I'm not all that nice, and you know it. But I can be polite if I have to be. You, on the other hand, are a nice guy. It's a shame that the Ice Queen doesn't like you."

Jack shook his head. "I doubt she ever will. And Libbie's sister seems to have it out for me, too. But it doesn't matter. We're together whether they like me or not."

"That's the spirit," Larry said. He glanced up at the stage. "You sure are a lucky guy, Jack. I mean, Carol is really pretty, but no one can hold a candle to Libbie. She's in a whole other league. All the guys are jealous of you, you know that?"

Jack turned to Larry. "Are you?"

"Nope. I'm not a sappy romantic like you. I'm never settling down and getting married. Marriage is a trap."

Jack laughed and slapped him on the back. "Right. You just keep on saying that until the right girl comes along."

Later that night, as Jack danced with Libbie in his arms, he knew for sure that he did believe in marriage, because for him the right girl—the only girl for him—had come along.

Chapter Eight

Jack and Libbie's senior year flew by. The holidays came and went quickly, and at the end of January, Jack turned eighteen. Libbie cried the day he went to the courthouse and signed up for Selective Service. He had no choice—it was the law, and their country was in the middle of a war in Vietnam. But Libbie fell to pieces, believing that she'd lose Jack to the war and he'd never come home. It took him hours to calm her down, and for days afterward, she cried at the mere mention of Vietnam. With every boy in their senior class coming of age for the draft, it was hard not to talk about it. Jack did his best not to mention the war so as not to upset her, and in March, when Larry signed up, they only discussed it when Libbie wasn't around.

The world was changing around them. Nixon had become president that year, and although he spoke of the de-escalation of troops in Vietnam, neither boy felt safe from being called up. Students were protesting the war all around the country, and some were even being killed in the process. And the United States was planning to send a man to the moon. It all seemed surreal to the teens in the small Minnesota town, where, for most, the biggest problem was choosing a college or who to take to the prom in April. For Jack, the prom was not a problem at all. He'd have the honor of escorting Libbie, and he had a surprise for her, too.

Not another word had been said by Libbie's mother about the two dating, although Libbie had told him that her mother became upset easily these past few months and often took to her bed for days. Her sister, Gwen, cared for Abigail when this happened, and Libbie also helped, often preparing dinner for the family on the days her mother was incapacitated. Libbie had learned a lot about cooking while visiting the farm and enjoyed it, so it wasn't difficult for her to simply heat up the dinners that Sandra prepared.

At times, Jack noticed that Libbie's behavior was a bit erratic. She'd be excessively cheerful one moment and then depressed the next. Sometimes, they'd be at a movie or hanging out at the burger place with Larry and Carol, and she'd go from happy to crying in an instant. It would take Jack a long time to calm her down after these episodes. If Carol was around, she'd help. Afterward, Libbie would apologize profusely to Jack, saying she didn't know why she was so emotional. Jack attributed her behavior to the stress she was experiencing at home. It didn't happen often, but it worried him that she was under so much stress that she'd break down that way. But his mother told him not to worry too much.

"She's a teenage girl with a stressful home environment," Bev had said. "Hormones are jumping all over the place. She'll be fine when school is out and she can concentrate on her future."

Jack thought his mother was right. Libbie was always happy when she came out to the farm and could relax and not worry about her mother or have her sister berating her. He would do his best to help her through this trying time.

Spring came in April, melting the snow. Libbie turned eighteen, and her birthday was celebrated with as much pomp and circumstance as the prom. Her parents had a big party for her at their house, and even Jack's parents and Jan and Ray were invited to the event, although Jack knew it was at Libbie's insistence they be included. Though the evening was chilly, paper lanterns had been strung around the outdoor patio, and a huge table of food and goodies was set up in the room just inside the patio doors. All of Libbie's friends attended, and when the cake was served, everyone sang "Happy Birthday." Libbie's parents gave her a beautiful gold heart-shaped necklace with a diamond inset. Jack couldn't afford anything as extravagant—he'd been saving his money for something more meaningful and had given her a delicate gold bracelet with a sparkling star charm on it. He knew how much she loved the night sky, and he hoped it would remind her of all their evenings together, gazing up at the stars.

By early May, when it was time for the prom, the trees were budding and the ice had melted from the lake. This year, Jack and Libbie's class would be catered to by the eleventh-grade students, and all they had to do was show up and have a good time.

Jack had been planning this night for weeks. He wanted it to be perfect for Libbie in every way. When he picked her up, her father was friendly and her mother was at least cordial. This year, Jack had rented a tux, with black pants, a white jacket, and black cummerbund and bowtie. When he'd put it on and looked in the mirror, it had struck him how much he'd grown up over the past year. High school was almost over, and then his adult life would begin. He only hoped it would all turn out the way he planned. Tonight would be the deciding factor.

When Libbie came downstairs, his heart flipped. He'd seen

her dressed up many times, but tonight she was more beautiful than ever. She wore a floor-length sleeveless pink satin dress with white-lace overlay and a wide pink sash around her waist. The color made her skin glow, bringing out the natural pink of her cheeks. Her blond hair was pulled up high with loose tendrils framing her face. And when she smiled, her eyes lit up. Jack felt at that moment that he was the luckiest man in the world.

He swallowed hard when she came to the bottom of the stairs and felt as nervous as the first time he had taken her out. Carefully, he pinned on her corsage of pink and white roses with a white satin ribbon. When she looked up at him, her eyes sparkled, and he wanted desperately to kiss her. But he refrained and only smiled. There'd be time for stolen kisses later.

"You look absolutely beautiful, kitten," Mr. Wilkens said, hugging his daughter.

Mrs. Wilkens also hugged her, something Jack rarely saw her do. "You'll be the most beautiful girl at the prom tonight," she whispered to her.

"Thank you, Mother," Libbie said, almost breathless with delight.

Libbie's father took pictures of the couple and then they were on their way. After Jack opened the truck door for her, he kissed her tenderly on the cheek and said, "You are beautiful, Libbie. I love you so much."

"I love you, too, Jack," she said sweetly. "You look so handsome in that tux."

They drove to the prom and went through the picture line before entering the gym. It had been decorated beautifully with their class colors—blue and white—with streamers above creating a colorful awning and glittery stars hanging from the ceiling. The band was already set up on the stage, and refreshments sat on a long table at the side of the room. The lights were dimmed, and glitter sparkled on tables. It was enchanting, and being with Libbie made it seem even more of a fairy tale come true.

Carol and Larry joined them at one of the tables that lined the dance floor. Carol was wearing a lovely blue off-the-shoulder dress that showed off her slender figure and bright blue eyes. Her auburn hair was pulled up, with curls escaping around her face, and she looked very elegant. Larry hadn't been able to afford to rent a tux and wore a navy blue suit, but he looked handsome with his dark hair slightly longer and combed back and his brown eyes sparkling mischievously.

"We're sitting with the two most beautiful girls at the prom," he said, winking at Jack. "How'd we get so lucky?"

The girls giggled and Jack smiled. He felt lucky being with Libbie every day.

They danced close all evening as the band played and stopped only for a drink of punch. Myrtle Hill stopped by their table with her date—one of the very smart boys in their class—and talked for a few minutes. She was excited about going off to college in the fall, and apparently her crush on Larry had subsided because she hardly paid attention to him. Other classmates stopped to talk, too, and everyone seemed to have plans for the future. Carol was already registered to go to college in town, although she wasn't sure if she wanted to pursue an elementary education degree or an accounting degree. Larry had applied for a scholarship at the college and been accepted, and planned on going for a business degree. Despite his carefree attitude, Larry was actually very good at managing and organizing, and he thought it might be a good fit.

Around ten thirty, Jack grinned at Libbie as they danced and said, "Come outside with me a moment, okay?"

Libbie nodded, and they went through the open door and out to the same spot where they had drunk wine the year before. Someone had strung Christmas lights in the trees by the bench, and Libbie marveled at them as she sat down.

"What's going on? Did you do this?" she asked.

Jack smiled at her and reached under the bushes behind the bench, pulling out a bottle of champagne and two glasses. "I wanted to surprise you. Just like last year. Except this year is better, because you're at the prom with me."

"Oh, Jack. You're so sweet. But we can still get in trouble if we're caught. I don't want to get banned from graduation."

"No one will catch us," Jack said. He sat down beside Libbie and did what he'd wanted to do all night—kiss her. Softly, he touched her lips with his as his hand slid up her back. He loved kissing her and feeling her close against him. Libbie responded, wrapping her arms around his neck. Their kiss deepened until, reluctantly, Jack pulled away. He gazed down into her eyes, wanting to remember this moment for the rest of his life. The half-moon shone brightly in the sky above them as the stars twinkled. But what shone the brightest to Jack were Libbie's blue eyes.

"Last year I told you I wanted to steal your heart. I hope I have, Libbie, because you've stolen mine. I love you more than anyone on this earth. I couldn't even think of a future without you in it."

Libbie reached up and tenderly touched the side of Jack's face. "I love you, too. You did win my heart. I don't want to be with anyone else but you."

Jack bent down and kissed her softly. Then he pulled away and went down on one knee while reaching into the pocket of his jacket. Libbie's eyes grew wide as he pulled out a small velvet box, opened it, and showed her the ring nestled inside.

"Libbie. My beautiful Libbie. I want to spend the rest of my life with you. I want to fall asleep with you in my arms each night and wake up each morning beside you. I want to take care of you and love you until the day I die. Please, Libbie, will you marry me?"

Libbie's eyes filled with tears. She looked from the ring in his hand up into his eyes. "Oh, my God, Jack. Yes! Yes, I'll marry you."

Jack stood and pulled Libbie to him, lifting her in the air and twirling her in a circle, making her squeal with delight. They laughed, and then he set her back on the ground and kissed her deeply. They were both breathless when they pulled away. "I love you, Libbie. Forever."

"I love you, Jack. Forever."

Jack slipped the ring on Libbie's slender finger as he gazed into her eyes. "I know the diamond isn't big, but I will make up for it with love," he whispered.

Libbie stared down at the gold band that held a small solitaire diamond. "I love it, Jack. It's perfect. Just like you."

They kissed again, this time even more passionately. Jack had kept his promise to Libbie over the past year and had not pressured her to do anything she wasn't ready for. And tonight he wouldn't either. If she wanted to wait until they were married, he'd patiently wait. He loved her enough to wait.

"Did she say yes?" a voice rang out, and both Libbie and Jack turned to see Larry and Carol standing at the curve of the walkway.

Jack nodded, and Larry let out a whoop. "Hallelujah and praise the Lord!" Larry said, making everyone laugh. "If you'd said no, Libbie, Jack would have offed himself for sure."

Carol hugged her friend and admired the engagement ring, while Larry slapped Jack on the back. "We have to celebrate! Where's that bottle of champagne?"

Larry popped the top and pulled out two more glasses hidden behind the bench. They poured champagne all around. "To Libbie and Jack," Larry said, raising his glass. "May you be happy forever."

The foursome clinked their glasses and drank.

* * *

Libbie was happier than she'd ever been in her life. She constantly looked at her left hand to make sure the ring was there and it was true. She was engaged to Jack. She loved him so much that her heart felt like it would burst. And now she was going to be his wife.

Larry and Carol stayed with them until the bottle of champagne was empty and it was growing late. The prom ended at midnight, and then there was a party being held until two at a student's house on the lake. Everyone was invited, and since parents would be there, the other parents wouldn't worry.

Libbie knew that Carol and Larry weren't going to the party afterward. Carol had confided in her months ago that she and Larry were sleeping together, so they'd sneak away often to their secret spot to be alone. Libbie knew that they were headed there tonight before Larry took Carol home. Over the months, Libbie had wondered how Carol could give herself to a boy she wasn't necessarily committed to. Carol wasn't loose and was a good person, so the fact that she was having sex with Larry had really surprised her. Libbie had also wondered if she would lose Jack if she continued to say no to sex. Not that he had asked her outright to make love to him, but sometimes when they kissed, it seemed as if they would both lose control, and a few times they had come close. Yet each time, Libbie had stopped it, afraid she'd become pregnant and trap Jack. She loved Jack more than anything, but she hadn't wanted to trap him into marriage like her sister had with Walter. She had wanted Jack to want to marry her first.

And now her dream of marrying Jack was coming true.

Jack hid the empty bottle of champagne behind the bench and put the glasses in the bushes to retrieve later. He turned to Libbie with a grin on his face. "Should we go back into the gym?" he asked.

Gazing at him, standing there in his tux, so cute and sweet, Libbie made a decision that she'd been putting off long enough. "No. Let's go somewhere alone."

Jack smiled and reached for her hand. She took it, and they walked around the gym to the parking lot and got into his truck. Jack drove to the spot beside the lake that they loved best, where they could see the moon reflected off the water. It was peaceful there, and no one was around.

"Are you happy, Libbie?" Jack asked, placing his arm around her and drawing her near.

"Yes," she said softly. She looked up into his eyes. "I can't wait until we're married and we can be together all the time."

"Me, too." He dropped his lips to hers and their tongues met and danced. Jack pulled her closer, exploring her body with his hands. She loved his touch, and she responded by running her hands inside his jacket, feeling his back muscles grow taut under her fingertips. She lay back on the seat and Jack moved over her. He kissed her slowly down her neck until he touched the sweet spot at the base of her throat and shivers ran up Libbie's spine.

She wanted more, so much more.

The champagne had made her feel warm and tingly all over, but she wasn't at all drunk. She knew exactly what she was doing, and what she wanted. She pulled away, and Jack instantly thought she meant for him to stop.

"I'm sorry, Libbie," he said, breathing heavily. "I should take you home."

As he sat up and straightened his jacket, Libbie placed a hand on his arm. Jack looked at her, his eyes questioning.

"I don't want to go home yet," she said softly. She reached up behind his neck and pulled him to her, kissing him. But Jack pulled back.

"We really should stop, sweetie. I love kissing you, but it's getting harder and harder to stop at just kissing."

"Then don't stop."

Jack hesitated as he searched her eyes. "Are you sure?"

Libbie nodded. "Yes. I want you to make love to me, Jack."

Jack stared at her, his eyes reflecting his love for her. "I want to. Oh, God, do I want to. But not in the front seat of a truck. We've waited so long. We can wait a little longer. Our first time should be special."

Libbie smiled up at Jack. "I know a place where we can go."

Libbie gave Jack directions, and he drove the truck along the north end of the lake past all the larger homes until they came to a secluded spot with a small, dark cabin.

"Where are we?" he asked, as he parked behind the garage near the road so no one would see his truck.

"This is my uncle's cabin. He's my mother's brother. He lives down in Minneapolis and rarely comes up here to use it."

They stepped out of the truck, and Jack came around to hold Libbie's hand as they walked to the door.

"How will we get in?" Jack asked.

"There should be a key up on the door frame."

Jack reached up and, after getting a handful of dust, found the key. He opened the door and they walked inside. It was pitch-black inside with the shutters covering the windows. "I can't see a thing."

Libbie felt around and found a flashlight by the door. She snapped it on and it glowed dimly. "There's an oil lamp on the table. There must be matches around here somewhere." She went into the tiny kitchen and found a book of matches in a drawer by the stove, then handed them to Jack. He took the glass chimney off the oil lamp and lit it. The lamp gave off a warm, yellow glow.

"Don't they have electricity?" he asked, glancing around.

"No, he never hooked up to it when they ran it around the lake. There's a generator outside, but if we start that someone might hear it."

Jack nodded. He walked over to another oil lamp on an end table in the living room and lit it, too. "These will do," he said.

The cabin was small. The living space, dining area, and kitchen were all in one large room, and there were two small bedrooms and a tiny bathroom. There was a woodstove in the corner for heat. It was clean, except for a layer of dust, and it looked cozy. Libbie went over to the sofa and pushed the small coffee table aside.

"What are you doing?" Jack asked.

"The sofa opens up into a bed," Libbie said. "I don't want to disturb the bedrooms. I doubt this is used much. Come help me." She took off the two cushions, and Jack pulled the sofa bed out. The springs creaked, but it opened up and sat firmly on the floor. Sheets were already covering the mattress.

"Well, it's not the Ritz, but I guess it'll do," Jack teased.

Libbie laughed nervously. He looked at her and their eyes met. Then he walked over and took her hands in his.

"Are you sure, Libbie? We can wait."

"I'm sure. I love you, Jack. I want to make love to you." She turned slowly. "Will you unzip me?"

Jack came up behind her and gently unzipped her dress down to the middle of her back. Without turning, Libbie slipped the dress off her shoulders and let it drop to the floor. Underneath, she wore a white satin slip. Jack placed his hands on her waist, kissing her bare shoulder. Shivers of excitement danced through Libbie.

Jack removed his jacket, tie, and cummerbund and laid them carefully over a chair. Libbie turned to face him, and he came to her and pulled her into his arms. Once they kissed, the nervousness subsided, and Libbie no longer felt self-conscious. This was Jack, the man she loved, the man she was going to marry. She trusted him completely.

He pulled away and lifted Libbie's slip over her head. Underneath, all she wore was a bra and panties. His sharp intake of breath made her look up into his eyes, which were dark with desire. He drew her to him, slowly exploring her body with his hands.

"You're so beautiful," he whispered in her ear.

Her own desire growing, Libbie unbuttoned his shirt and pushed it away. He wore a T-shirt underneath, and she pulled it up so he'd take it off, too. They'd seen each other like this before many times, in their bathing suits. But this was different. Tonight, they held each other close, feeling the sensation of their bodies melding together. Libbie had never felt this beautiful before, or this desired. She loved the feel of being in Jack's arms, against his warm skin.

Backing away, Libbie lifted her arms and pulled out the pins that held up her hair. Jack sat on the bed watching her, his breathing deepening. Once the pins were out, she brushed her fingers through her hair and shook it loose. Jack reached out and drew her to him, kissing her flat stomach while caressing her with his hands. Pulling her down beside him, they lay on the bed, holding each other close.

"Libbie," Jack whispered, as she lay naked in his arms. He rose above her and she reached up and caressed his cheek.

"I love you, Jack," she said. And when they finally came together, Libbie knew that she'd love Jack for the rest of her life.

Chapter Nine

Jack lay curled up beside Libbie, still mesmerized by how deep his feelings ran for her. After they'd made love, he'd grabbed the afghan that was folded up over a chair and covered them against the chill in the cabin. The oil lamps flickered and gave the room a warm glow, but it was nothing like the warmth he felt inside.

He'd known that he loved Libbie for a very long time, and tonight had only made their connection stronger.

He lifted himself up on one elbow and bent to kiss her gently on the cheek. "Are you okay?" he asked, worried that she didn't feel the same way he did.

Libbie rolled over and snuggled up beside him. "Yeah. I was just thinking."

"About what?"

She grinned. "About why we waited so long to do this. If I had known how amazing it would be, I would have seduced you a long time ago."

Jack laughed heartily. "Well, I hear it gets better as time goes on," he said. "With lots of practice."

Libbie giggled. "You're just saying that so I'll always say yes."

He ran his fingers through her silky hair, pushing it behind her small ear, and then dropped a kiss on her forehead. "I hope you'll always say yes," he said softly. "I love you so much, Libbie. I've loved you for so long that tonight is a dream come true. I'm afraid I'll wake up and it will be just that—a dream."

Libbie cupped his face in her hand. "My sweet, romantic Jack. It's real. All of it. And I can't wait to spend the rest of my life with you."

He kissed her tenderly and then sighed.

"What's wrong? Are you tired of me already?" she teased.

"Never. But it's really late. I should take you home."

Libbie sighed then, too, and nodded. After one last kiss, they got up and dressed. Jack zipped up her dress and she smoothed it out as best she could.

"What about your hair?" Jack asked, growing nervous. "What if your parents are waiting up and see that it's down?"

"Don't worry, they won't be up. They go to early church service on Sunday. Besides, if they are up, I'll just say I took it down at the party. They'll never question it."

Jack nodded. Once they were ready, they pulled the sheets off the bed and closed it up. "What about these?"

Libbie thought a moment. "I'll hide them in here and come back during the day and wash them. If anyone asks why I'm here, I'll just say I'm cleaning up the cabin for my uncle. No one will think twice about that."

"Hmm. You're pretty good at this sneaking around thing. Should I be worried?" Jack asked, grinning.

Libbie shook her head. "With my parents, I had to learn to sneak around a little. They're always so worried about what everyone thinks. But I'll never lie to you, Jack. I want our marriage to be honest from the start. I hate having secrets."

"Me, too," Jack said.

They closed up the cabin and left. On the drive to Libbie's house, Jack said, "I think you should hide the engagement ring until we can talk to your parents together. I want to be there when you tell them. I have a feeling it won't be easy."

"Okay. Maybe you can come over tomorrow night after dinner and we can tell them then. I don't want to wait too long."

"The sooner the better," Jack said. He pulled up in front of her house and walked her to the door. It was dark inside except for a light on in the entryway.

"See? They're in bed," Libbie said.

Jack reached for Libbie and held her close. "Tonight was amazing. Every minute of it. I love you so much, Libbie." He kissed her, then reluctantly stepped away to leave.

Libbie grabbed his hand and pulled him close one last time. "I love you, too. Don't ever forget that. No matter what happens. Okay?"

Jack nodded. "Goodnight, Libbie."

"Goodnight, Jack."

He walked back to his truck and watched as she entered the house and closed the door. Then he turned his truck around and headed home, still unable to believe that he was soon going to have Libbie beside him forever.

* * *

"You're what!" Abigail screeched from across the dining room table. Jack and Libbie sat at the other end, holding hands. Gwen and Walter were there, too, with little Lynn in her high chair, happily eating her apple pie as if nothing was happening around her.

"Now, Abbie, stay calm," Randall said soothingly.

"We're engaged, Mother," Libbie said softly. As planned, Jack had come over after dinner for dessert to announce their engagement. He'd dressed in a button-up shirt, slacks, and dress shoes, as if here were going to church. Libbie had found it endearing that he'd made the effort to look nice, but she knew it wouldn't make a difference to her mother.

"No! Absolutely not," Abigail said, her face turning red. "I do not approve of you marrying this boy. It was one thing for you to date him, it's quite another for you two to get married. I forbid it!"

Randall reached over and placed his hand over Abigail's. "Abbie, please. Let's all discuss this calmly."

Abigail turned burning eyes on her husband. "*You* said this was just a childish crush. You assured me that it wouldn't last. But look at what's happened now. We should have stopped this a year ago. Can you honestly tell me you want our daughter to marry *him?*"

"Mother! Don't talk about Jack like that. I love him. I want to spend the rest of my life with him."

Gwen had been sitting there quietly, watching the scene play out. But at Libbie's words, she snorted. "Love? Really, Libbie? You're not old enough to understand what a big commitment marriage is. How can you possibly know that you love this boy?"

Libbie glared at her sister. "Who are you to talk? You weren't much older than I am when you got married. At least I'm not pregnant and don't *have* to get married."

"Libbie!" Abigail said, looking aghast. "Don't you dare talk to your sister that way. At least she married a man of means."

Libbie was so angry, hot tears formed in her eyes. She fought to hold them back, not wanting her mother and sister to know how badly they were hurting her. She felt Jack squeeze her hand, and it gave her strength.

"Ladies, please," Randall said more forcefully. "Enough. We will discuss this in a dignified manner." Everyone around the table quieted. Randall composed himself and turned to Jack. "Tell me, son. What are your plans for the future? How do you propose to support our Libbie?"

Jack sat up straighter. "I've already completed a year at the local trade school for mechanical training. I have one more year of school, and then I will be able to get a good job as a mechanic. I've already spoken to the head mechanic at the Ford dealership here in town, and he said he'd be interested in hiring me when I'm finished with school. Until then, I'll work at my uncle's garage and with my dad."

"Mechanic," Abigail said with disdain. "A dirty, low-paying job. You'll never support Libbie in the way she is accustomed."

"Maybe not at first, ma'am," Jack said, turning to Abigail. "But I'll be trained in both regular engines and diesel. I'll earn more than a regular garage mechanic when I'm done with school. Eventually, Libbie and I should have a good life."

"Eventually," Gwen interjected. "But what about now? What about a year from now, and the year after that? I suppose you'll expect our parents to give you money in order to put a roof over your heads and food on your table?"

Libbie was about to lash out at her sister when she felt Jack squeeze her hand. She turned and saw the determined look on his face and the hard set of his jaw.

"I don't expect handouts from anyone," he told her decisively. "I will take care of Libbie without help from any of you."

Libbie beamed up at Jack, so proud of his being able to stand up to her family.

"Well, you are a determined young man," Randall said, a small smile on his face.

Jack turned to Libbie's father. "I love your daughter, sir. And I respect her and only want the best for her. I will do whatever I have to to take care of her. She will always be safe with me, I promise you."

Randall nodded. "Well said."

Abigail stood, throwing down her napkin. She glared at Jack. "I don't care what you say. You are not good enough to marry my daughter, and I will not let you." With that, she stormed out of the room.

Gwen set her lips in a fine line, glaring at Libbie. "See what you've done? You've upset Mother—again." She also left the table and followed the path her mother had taken.

Randall sighed and Walter kept silent, wiping the pie crumbs from his daughter's face.

"Don't worry about your mother," Randall said, giving Libbie a weak smile. "She will come around. She always does." He stood up and extended his hand to Jack.

Jack stood quickly and shook his hand.

"I'll hold you to your promise, son," Randall said, but his expression was kind. Then he walked over to Libbie and gave her a kiss on the cheek. "Congratulations on your engagement, dear. I'm sorry the news wasn't as well accepted as it should have been."

"Thank you, Daddy."

Randall left the room, also heading upstairs to Abigail.

Jack and Libbie turned and looked at each other. They sighed in unison.

"Never a dull moment in this family, eh?" Walter said with a grin.

Both Jack and Libbie turned and stared at him in surprise. Then Libbie couldn't help it—she broke out laughing, and so, finally, did Jack.

* * *

After the disastrous announcement at Libbie's house, Jack drove her out to the farm to announce their engagement to his family. Unlike the Wilkenses, however, Jack's family was delighted to hear that Libbie would soon join their family.

"Congratulations, sweetie," Bev said to Libbie, giving her a warm hug. "I'm so happy for you both. She gave Jack a hug, too. "I'm thrilled to have Libbie as a daughter."

Norm also hugged both Libbie and his son. "Such a wonderful surprise," he said.

"And you'll be my sister!" Jan squealed, hugging Libbie tightly. "I've always wanted a sister."

"Will you live with us?" Ray asked. "Are you going to be sharing our room with us?"

Everyone laughed as Jack explained that after they were married they'd have a place of their own. Ray seemed to like that idea better. "Then I get a room to myself," he said cheerfully. "That's even better."

"Let's celebrate," Bev said. "I have a chocolate cake in the kitchen. Jan, come help me serve it, okay?"

"That sounds delicious," Libbie said. She squeezed Jack's hand. "I love your family," she whispered to him before heading into the kitchen to help. After what she'd just gone through with her family, Libbie appreciated Jack's loving family that much more.

Bev asked for all the details of how Jack had proposed and

Libbie told them, leaving out the part about the champagne, as they all ate their cake.

"That's so sweet," Bev said. "I didn't know my Jack was such a romantic."

Jack reddened and everyone laughed.

"Have you picked a date?" Jan wanted to know. "Will it be a big wedding? Can I be a bridesmaid?"

"Jan, dear. Give them some time. They just got engaged," Bev said, laughing.

Jack and Libbie looked at each other. Libbie knew he was thinking the same thing as she was. They had a lot of planning to do. And after her mother's reaction, there might not be a big wedding.

"We'll have to wait and see," Libbie told Jan. "We haven't talked about the wedding yet."

They left shortly after that, with Bev telling Libbie to come out to the farm as often as she wanted that summer. There was only a week left of school and then graduation. After that, except for marrying Jack, Libbie really had no other plans.

On the drive back to Libbie's house, they started discussing their future.

"I guess we should think about a wedding date," Jack said.

Libbie was sitting close to Jack and turned to him. "I want to get married as soon as possible. After last night, I can't stand the thought of us being separated for long."

Jack smiled down at her. "Me either. Last night was incredible. I can't wait until we can be together every night."

"Then let's get married this summer, Jack. Please? I don't care if I have a big wedding or even if my mother approves of us. I just want to be with you."

Jack pulled the truck over at their favorite spot by the lake and parked. He turned to Libbie and took her hands in his. "I want to be with you, too, Libbie, but we have to think about our future. I should finish my second year of school before we get married. There's really no way I can pay for school and support us if we get married this summer. But if we wait, then I can get a better job and we can start our lives right."

Libbie's face fell. She had so hoped they'd get married right away.

"Hey?" Jack caressed the side of her face, and she lifted her eyes to his. "It's only a year. It'll go fast. Besides, I know you wouldn't be happy just running off and getting married. I'm sure your mother will come around, like your dad said, and you can have the wedding of your dreams. Don't you want that?"

"I just want you, Jack. So much could happen in a year. What if you don't love me a year from now?"

"That could never happen," Jack said. He drew her close and kissed her softly. "I will always love you, Libbie. Always."

Libbie nodded and Jack drove her home. She knew he was right and that they should wait, but she was eager to start her life with Jack. If her mother continued to protest their marriage, the next year would be hell.

Chapter Ten

Abigail stayed in her room for five days, the longest Libbie could ever remember her hiding away. Libbie was worried about her, even though her father said she'd be fine. She felt guilty, since it was her fault her mother had taken to her bed. Also, graduation was on Saturday, and Libbie didn't want her mother to miss it. On Friday evening, Libbie knocked softly on Abigail's bedroom door, and when she didn't hear a response, she tentatively opened it. Gwen had just left for the evening, and her father was down in his study, reading.

"Mom? May I come in?" Libbie looked inside the room. The lamp on the bedside table glowed softly, and her mother was propped up in bed on a pile of pillows, but she looked to be sleeping. Libbie rarely visited her mother in her bedroom. Her parents had separate rooms, which hadn't seemed odd to Libbie until she grew older. She'd asked her mother once why they didn't sleep in the same room, and her mother had looked embarrassed by the question. She'd explained it away as her father not wanting to disturb her sleep when he rose early in the morning. Libbie had thought it made sense at the time, but she knew now that she never wanted to have separate bedrooms once she and Jack were married. What would be the point of being married if they couldn't sleep in each other's arms every night?

Just as Libbie was about to turn and leave, her mother's eyes opened.

"Libbie? Is that you?"

Libbie walked over to her mother's bed. "I just wanted to check on you, Mom. Are you feeling any better?"

Abigail slowly pushed herself up higher in the bed. To Libbie, she looked like a frail old woman twice her age. It was as if she'd aged decades in the last five days. Libbie's heart broke. Her mother could be difficult, but she still loved her. She hated seeing her mother so sick.

"I'm doing better, dear," Abigail said. She reached out her hand and touched Libbie's arm. "I'm happy you came in to see me."

Libbie was unnerved by her mother's touch. Abigail rarely showed signs of affection. Libbie had never taken it personally—her mother rarely touched anyone—but when she did, it always took Libbie by surprise. Libbie moved closer and bit her lip. "I'm sorry you're sick, Mom. I feel like this is my fault."

Abigail nodded. "Don't worry, dear. I'll be fine. Come, sit awhile."

Libbie sat carefully on the edge of the bed. She noticed that there were empty glasses on her mother's nightstand and bottles of prescription medicine there, too. Libbie wondered why her mother would need medication when she was just upset about her marrying Jack. When she turned and looked into her mother's eyes, she thought they look odd. Her pupils were dilated, and they looked glassy.

Abigail ran her hand up and down Libbie's arm. She

attempted a smile. "You know that I only want what's best for you, don't you, Libbie?" Abigail asked. "That's why I was upset. I want you to have everything I've had and more."

Abigail was slurring her words. It frightened Libbie to hear her talk this way. She wondered if it was because of the medicine. "I know you do, Mom. I'll have everything I need. I love Jack and he loves me. We'll be happy together."

Abigail dropped her hand to her side and sighed heavily. "Oh, baby girl. If only love were enough."

Chills rippled through Libbie's body. What did her mother mean? Love was everything.

"Dear, I was young once, too. I know that first love can be exciting and you think that you can live on love only. But there is so much more to life, and it can be much harder than you think. Security is the most important thing a woman can have. Otherwise, all the love in the world won't do you any good."

Libbie stared at her mother, trying to understand what she was saying. Hadn't her mother married her father for love? Or had it just been because he came from a family with money?

"Jack will take care of me, Mom. I can count on him. He comes from a good family, and they are all hard workers. They have all they need, and love, too."

Abigail sighed. "Oh, Libbie. I hope you're right."

"Will you be able to come to my graduation tomorrow afternoon?" Libbie asked hopefully. "I'd miss you if you weren't there."

Abigail nodded. "I'll be there. I wouldn't miss it. And we'll take you out to dinner for a celebration. How does that sound?"

Libbie smiled. "I'd like that, Mom."

"Let me sleep now. Tomorrow I'll be better."

Libbie nodded and left the room. As she went to her own

bedroom, she worried about what she had seen on her mother's nightstand. Libbie knew that Gwen would know, but she didn't think her sister would tell her. Those types of things just weren't discussed in their house, so she decided not to say anything. She was just relieved her mother was going to make an effort to come to graduation. And maybe, after a time, her mother would get used to the idea of her marrying Jack. Then everything would be fine.

* * *

Libbie's mother kept her promise and showed up for graduation along with the entire family. Jack's family was in the stands, too, and Libbie felt so proud to walk across the stage and accept her diploma. They were all adults now, and soon everyone would be going their separate ways. She felt excited and scared, all at once.

And, just as Libbie's father had promised, her mother finally came around and accepted that Libbie was marrying Jack.

"Well, it looks like we have a wedding to plan," Abigail said one morning at breakfast, as she sipped her coffee.

Libbie stared at her in disbelief. "Really, Mom?"

"Of course. We can't have our daughter marrying without a big celebration, can we? We'll get started on the plans today, dear."

Randall smiled and winked at Libbie, and she squealed, jumped up, and hugged her mother.

"Oh, thank you, Mom. I'm so excited!"

"You're welcome, dear," Abigail said.

"Well, try not to put me in the poorhouse with this wedding, okay, ladies?" Randall said as he stood to leave for work. He laughed, and Libbie smiled brightly at her father. She was so happy that her parents had accepted her engagement to Jack and wanted to give her a nice wedding. She couldn't wait to tell Jack.

* * *

"That's wonderful," Jack said when Libbie drove into the gas station later that morning to tell him. "I told you they'd come around. Let's set the date."

Even though Libbie was anxious to get married, she settled on waiting one year. They picked the first weekend in June of the next year, June 6, 1970. Libbie was thrilled—she finally had a wedding date. What she didn't realize was how many problems would arise when planning her wedding.

Her mother insisted the wedding be held at their own church, the First Lutheran Church of Jamison. All the prominent people in town attended that church and many would be invited. She also wanted the reception to be at their country club on the lake. Libbie was worried at first about the choice of the church until Bev set her mind at ease.

"We're Lutheran, too, dear. The only difference is we go to the smaller church on this side of town. I'm sure your church will be lovely," Bev reassured her.

Libbie spent the summer making wedding plans, choosing her bridesmaids, and trying to narrow down the wedding guest list. Her mother thought two hundred people would be fine, but that number made Jack gasp.

"Two hundred people? Is she inviting the entire town? Only about twenty of those will be my relatives."

Libbie promised she'd try to talk her mother into a smaller guest list, but as the summer wore on, it continued to grow larger. Her mother wanted to invite out-of-town relatives, business associates, and, it seemed, everyone they'd ever met. As always, changing her mother's mind was proving to be very difficult.

Libbie had chosen Carol as her maid of honor, and Jan would be a bridesmaid along with Barbara and Jean. Jack picked Larry as his best man and Ray as a groomsman, but still had to come up with two more friends to balance out the wedding party. The larger the wedding became, the more nervous Libbie grew. She felt like things were slowly spinning out of control, and it made her anxious.

As Jack worked his jobs and saved money for school and their future together, Libbie picked out napkin colors, flowers, and bridesmaid dresses. Even to Libbie, it seemed out of balance. She felt like she should be contributing more to their future but wasn't sure how. She'd never before considered finding a job or going to college, even though she'd earned good grades in high school. No one had ever encouraged her to plan a future other than getting married and having children. And even if she'd wanted to find a job, she had no idea what she'd want to do. Her parents had always provided for her, and now Jack had promised to take care of her. It was all she'd ever known—after all, her mother and sister had never worked; in fact, most of the women Libbie knew didn't work. Yet she still felt strange about not helping Jack by earning money, too.

This summer wasn't like the summer before. Libbie didn't spend much time by the lake with her friends, choosing instead to go out to the farm when she and her mother weren't working on wedding plans. Libbie loved spending time with Bev and had learned to cook and bake even more since the previous year. Libbie also hung out with Jan, but not as much as before. Jan was sixteen, and she'd found a part-time job at the Dairy Queen so she could save money for a car. Libbie was kept busy between planning the wedding, cooking with Bev, and being around Jack as much as possible.

Libbie loved the nights that she spent alone with Jack. They'd sneak away often to her uncle's cabin and spend hours exploring each other's bodies and making love. After that first night together, Jack had driven to another town fifty miles away where no one knew him and bought condoms at the drugstore. Libbie had found that funny, but she knew why he'd done it. Their town was small and people would talk. He didn't want anyone to say a bad word about Libbie. She loved that he protected her that way, and she loved their evenings together.

"I can't wait until we don't have to sneak around anymore," she told him one evening as they lay on the sofa bed in the cabin. "This wedding is getting so complicated that I sometimes wish we could run away and get married."

"I know," Jack said, running his fingers through her silky hair. "But it will be worth the wait, I promise you."

In August, Gwen announced that she was expecting another baby, and Libbie thought she didn't look very happy about it. Gwen already had a busy toddler, and Lynn would only be three years old when the new baby arrived the following summer. In addition to that, Abigail had been taking to her bed more often than before, and Gwen always took it upon herself to care for her. Libbie was never asked to take care of her mother. If Gwen couldn't come and help her, Randall would do it. Libbie thought it was strange that she was never asked, yet she was relieved, too. She didn't understand why her mother fell ill for a day or two and then was better. She'd never questioned her mother's illnesses as a child—it was just a fact of life—but now she wondered about it. Yet she was still afraid to ask Gwen or her father about it. It just wasn't discussed. So Libbie tried putting it out of her mind to focus on her own future instead.

Fall came, and Jack went back to school and worked some evenings with his father and weekends at the gas station. Larry and Carol were in college and busy with their own lives. Many of Libbie's other friends had either gone away to college or were working at their parents' businesses. Even Jan was busy in her junior year of high school and with her other friends. Libbie felt restless. She spent less time with Jack than she would have liked, and she had very little to do. Even when she did spend an evening with Jack, going to a movie or just sitting in his truck under the stars, he was usually distracted and would even sometimes fall asleep.

"Is this how it's going to be when we're married?" Libbie said one evening as they sat on the sofa at the farm watching TV. Jack had fallen asleep, and Libbie had angrily poked at him to wake him up. "Are you already bored with me? I might as well go home and be alone than be with you."

Jack apologized profusely, but it didn't seem to make a difference to Libbie. Thank goodness the rest of Jack's family was busy in other parts of the house and hadn't heard her complain.

"I'm sorry, Libbie. I'm just so tired going to school and working so much. I promise it will get better when I'm finished with school. And when we're living together, we'll be together every night."

Tears filled Libbie's eyes. "I'm sorry. I don't know why I'm so agitated. I know you're working hard, and you're doing it for me. I'm just so stressed about the wedding and not being able to spend time with you." Tears fell down her cheeks, and Jack held her close.

"It's okay, sweetie," he said soothingly. "It'll get better, I promise."

Libbie nodded and wiped away her tears. There was so much more that was causing stress in her life than the wedding and not seeing him, but she didn't want to bother him with it. Her mother was constantly taking to her bed, causing Gwen to be angry for having to help. She blamed Libbie for upsetting their mother so much. Libbie had no idea why her mother was having such a hard time. They'd be having a nice day, but out of nowhere her mother would become angry and storm off to her room. Libbie tried being as nice as possible and helped out around the house to take the strain off her mother, but it didn't seem to help. Libbie would go to bed each night feeling the tension in the house and wishing she could leave now to be with Jack. She couldn't wait for June to come so she could finally get out from under the stress of her mother's dark moods.

* * *

Jack and Larry sat in the rowboat on the lake at the farm. It was mid-October and the day was unusually warm. Libbie and her mother had gone to Minneapolis for the weekend to shop for a wedding dress, and Carol had gone along as well. Since the summer and fall tourist season was winding down, Jack had a rare day off from the gas station. So for the first time in weeks, the guys were able to hang out together.

Larry leaned back against the front of the boat and propped his feet up on the middle seat. He pulled something out of his shirt pocket, put it in his mouth, and lit it with a lighter. Taking a long drag, he blew the smoke out and said, "Ahh."

Jack frowned at him. "Are you smoking grass?"

"Yep. Want a drag?"

"No," Jack said angrily. "Since when do you smoke pot?"

Larry laughed. "Since around the same time the whole world started smoking pot. Geez, Jack. Everyone at the college smokes it. You should go into the dorm rooms sometime—the haze is suffocating."

"Where'd you even get that stuff? You don't have any money to buy it."

Larry grinned. "Carol gave it to me."

"Carol smokes pot, too?"

"Of course she does. Jack, you're the only kid I know who doesn't do drugs."

"So she buys it for you?"

"Heck no, she steals it from her parents' stash."

Jack stared at Larry in shock. "Are you messing with me? Carol's parents smoke pot?"

Larry nodded. "Yep. And so do all their highfalutin' friends. They have parties and drink and smoke and God knows what else." Larry laughed. "They probably even wife-swap."

"That's terrible, Larry. Who told you all this? Carol?"

"Yeah. And Barbara and Ron and Matt. All the rich kids around here know their parents do this shit. They just don't tell anyone."

"Well, don't tell Libbie about it. She'd freak out. She has enough to worry about with the wedding and her mother being sick all the time."

Larry took another puff and stared at Jack. "You know, Libbie's mother isn't really sick. Word around town is she drinks like a fish and takes prescription meds that knock her out. Valium. Carol's mother takes them like candy. Carol says they make her mother as cool as a cucumber. But Libbie's mother takes them with alcohol and they really do a number on her."

Jack pointed a finger at Larry and said sternly, "Don't you

ever say a word about that to Libbie. Do you hear me? She doesn't need to hear all this shit. Besides, no one knows for sure, so don't spread it around, you hear?"

"Fine, fine. Take it easy, Jack. Hey, you want a puff?" Larry reached the joint toward Jack.

"No. And keep that stuff away from my house. I'm not going to ruin my life getting caught with that crap."

"Okay, okay." Larry put it out and pocketed what was left.

Jack sat there for a long time, thinking about what Larry had said. He wondered if Libbie knew that her mother had a drinking problem. As far as he knew, Libbie thought her mother just got upset easily and needed rest. Why would a woman who has everything need to hide from life by getting drunk and high? He decided the sooner he and Libbie were married, the better it would be for her.

Chapter Eleven

The minute Libbie tried it on, she knew it was the dress. She, her mother, and Carol had gone to the chicest bridal salon in Minneapolis, and for over two hours Libbie had tried on dress after dress. Her mother had picked out several long-sleeved dresses with full skirts, but Libbie wanted something a bit more modern. Carol brought her dresses that were too modern. But when the sales lady brought her this dress, Libbie fell in love. And once she had it on, she knew it was *the one.*

Libbie stepped out of the dressing room and stood, holding her breath as her mother studied her. The dress was a cross between elegant and modern. It had white applique flowers on the form-fitting bodice, a sweetheart neckline, and cap sleeves. A long, narrow satin underskirt fell to the floor with a full lace overlay that billowed out into a train in back. Libbie had on a matching, full-length lace veil that hung down over the train.

Carol gasped and clapped her hands in delight with she saw it. Her reaction made Libbie smile, but she knew the most important opinion would be her mother's. When her mother finally gave her a small smile, she knew she approved.

"You look lovely, dear. I think you've found your dress," Abigail said. She stood and walked over to Libbie, placing her cheek against her daughter's. "Absolutely breathtaking."

Libbie squealed and stared at herself in the mirror as Carol buzzed around her, arranging the train and veil. She couldn't believe how grown-up she looked in this dress. And she couldn't wait until Jack saw her on their wedding day.

* * *

Winter blew into their northern Minnesota town by early November and was there to stay. Jack jokingly told Libbie he sometimes questioned his decision to work on automobiles when temperatures outside were freezing, and inside the school garages it wasn't much warmer. He swore that if he ever had a business of his own, he'd have a heated garage.

On December 1, the first draft lottery drawing was held. The rules of the draft had changed—instead of drafting nearly every man who came of age, they would hold a lottery and those with the lowest numbers would be drafted first. In 1969, they drew numbers for men born in 1950. Jack and Larry were safe for one more year. Their birth year—1951—would be drawn for lottery in July 1970.

While they let out a sigh of relief that their lives wouldn't be affected by war for at least another year, Libbie was at her wit's end. The draft lottery drawing brought up all her fears again that Jack would be sent to Vietnam, and it was all Jack could do to calm her down almost every time they were together. The nightly news about the war gave her nightmares, and she told him that she'd often dream of him lying dead in the jungles of Vietnam. She'd wake up screaming with no one there to comfort her.

"I can't bear for you to leave me," she said, crying uncontrollably. "They can't take you! We'll barely be married and you'll be sent away to war."

Jack tried without success to console her. "I may not even get drafted," he told her. "I might get a high number and never be called. Please don't worry, Libbie. We'll live our lives and see what happens."

But Libbie couldn't go on as if everything was normal when the idea of losing Jack was constantly at the forefront of her mind. Even the Christmas holiday didn't cheer her up. Her appetite dwindled and she lost weight. Sleep eluded her. She didn't want to close her eyes for fear that she'd have another nightmare.

The heavy hand of stress was weighing Libbie down. The wedding planning was wearing on her nerves as well as her mother's episodes, which were occurring more frequently. And nothing Jack or anyone else said would get her mind off of Vietnam and losing Jack. By the middle of January, she looked pale and drawn with dark circles under her eyes.

Gwen, now seven months pregnant, finally took Libbie aside one day and gave her a little yellow pill. "Take this. It'll calm your nerves and help you sleep."

Libbie looked at the pill in her hand and then up at Gwen. "What is this? Where did you get it?"

"Don't worry about that. It's safe. Just don't take anything else with it and you'll be fine. If it helps to calm you down, we can get you a prescription."

Libbie wasn't sure she wanted to take pills, but she was desperate for sleep. She finally took it, and soon she felt calmer and more relaxed. It worked like magic.

Two days later, Gwen took her to their family doctor, and Libbie got a prescription for Valium. The doctor told Libbie to only take one every evening before bed, if needed, and no more. But Libbie found that taking one in the morning helped her start the day feeling calm and then one at night lulled her into sleep. She kept the bottle hidden away in her bedroom. She didn't want Jack to know about the pills. Libbie told herself that this was only temporary and that as soon as they were married, she'd be able to stop taking the pills. It was her little secret.

But Jack noticed right away how much calmer Libbie seemed. "You look like you're feeling better," he'd said one night after they'd eaten burgers at the Dairy Queen. They hadn't been to the cabin in weeks because it was much too cold there, and they didn't dare start a fire and attract attention. They both missed spending time alone, but they knew that it wouldn't be long before they were married and spending every night together.

"I am," Libbie told him, feeling more at ease. "I've been able to sleep again, and that makes a big difference. Like you said, I shouldn't worry about something that hasn't happened yet."

Jack lifted his hand and caressed the side of her face. "I'm glad. I was so worried about you. It won't be long now. Just a few more months. As soon as spring comes, we should look for a place to rent until we can afford to buy our own house."

Libbie's eyes let up. "Really? Oh, that will be fun! A place of our own. With all the wedding plans and my not feeling well, I'd forgotten that we'd need a house! I can't wait."

"Me, either," Jack said smiling. He kissed her softly. "Together every day and night. It will be wonderful."

In March, Gwen gave birth to a healthy baby girl and they named her Leslie. Libbie stayed a week at Gwen's house to help her with Lynn while she recovered. It had been a difficult week for Libbie. No matter how hard she tried to help, Gwen criticized everything she did, from changing the baby's diapers to dressing

Lynn. Libbie cooked dinner each night for the family—dishes she'd learned to cook from Bev at the farm—and Walter complimented her on the nice meals, which only angered Gwen more. After a week, Libbie couldn't take Gwen's constant criticism anymore and went home, only to find her mother had become ill again. It was more than Libbie could handle, and she began sneaking in a pill or two during the day to cope.

Winter finally melted away into spring, and a week after Libbie turned nineteen in April, she and Jack started searching for a place to rent. Their choices were limited, as they quickly learned that they couldn't afford to rent a house—even a small one—and pay the utilities. They looked at the few apartments available, but they were small or older run-down places. The apartments for rent over downtown businesses weren't any better and smelled musty. Libbie wanted a place they could call their own, but she felt discouraged. She didn't want to live in a shabby place. Jack was disappointed, too, but he told Libbie they'd find the perfect home eventually.

"We just have to keep looking," he said.

The wedding was drawing near, and Libbie was feeling the strain of her mother constantly taking ill and her father working long hours at his office, staying away from the house more and more. Gwen's resentment grew each time she had to come help care for their mother. Libbie offered to help, but Gwen flatly told her no. "You wouldn't know what to do," Gwen would say. She would bring both kids over to the house and rush between their needs and her mother's. Libbie hated having Gwen around and being treated like she was useless. She wanted so much to get away from them all, but at least she had her pills to take the edge off of her nervousness.

* * *

At the end of May, Jack received his diploma for his two-year mechanical degree. They celebrated with friends and family at the farm with a big supper and Jack's favorite dessert, chocolate cake. Carol and Larry were there, as were Jack's uncle Rick and his wife, Sarah. Jan had turned seventeen that year, and she invited her new boyfriend, Justin. Jack felt so proud to finally be finished with school. He'd already talked to the garage manager at the Ford dealership and been hired, starting the middle of June, a week after the wedding. It was a better wage than at his uncle's garage, and he was excited to start their life with a new job.

During the evening, Jack noticed that Libbie was unsteady on her feet several times and yawned constantly. He asked her if she was feeling okay.

"I'm fine, worrywart," she said. "I'm just tired. Dealing with Gwen and my mother, not to mention the wedding, has worn me out."

Jack nodded, but he thought her eyes look more glassy than tired. He hoped she was fine and not coming down with something. It was only a week before the wedding, and he wanted her to enjoy her special day.

After the celebration, Jack, Libbie, Carol, and Larry went to Carol's house to sit in the screened-in gazebo by the lake. Carol's parents were away for the weekend, and since she was the last of their children who lived at home, they had the place to themselves. They lit a candle in a big hurricane lamp on the table in the center and sat in the dim light, listening to the lake water gently splash against the shore. It was chilly out, and Carol had brought along two large blankets they could wrap around them.

"I brought something to keep us warm, too," Larry said, pulling out a bottle of vodka from his jacket pocket.

"Ooh! I'll get some 7 Up and glasses from the house," Carol said, dragging Libbie along to help. They were back in a flash and soon everyone had a drink in their hand. Carol had also brought out maraschino cherries to put in their drinks.

"Now we're having a party," Larry said, laughing.

"Who'd you swipe the booze from this time?" Jack asked. He only took a few sips from his drink. He didn't want to have too much and then drive back to the farm. The last thing he needed was to be picked up for underage drinking before he started his new job.

"Carol's parents, of course," Larry said. "They have a ton of booze in their bar. I think they buy it in bulk." Larry and Carol laughed. They both drank down their first one quickly and made a fresh drink.

"This tastes good together," Libbie said, finishing hers off. "I'll have another one."

"Don't drink too fast," Jack said. "I don't want to take you home drunk. Your parents will kill me."

Libbie turned glassy eyes on Jack. "Hey, I'm nineteen and I'm going to be married in a week. My parents can't tell me what to do anymore. I can do whatever I want." She emptied half the glass in one long drink.

Jack held his tongue, but when Libbie asked Larry to make her a third, Jack interceded. "We should head out," he said.

"Don't be such a drag," Larry said. "I love you, man, but you need to relax and have some fun."

Jack glared at Larry. He and Carol were on their way to getting drunk. They were just students. They had no responsibilities. He had a lot more to lose.

"Yeah, stop telling me what to do," Libbie slurred. "You're marrying me, but you don't own me. Fill it up, Larry." She raised her glass toward Larry.

"No. You've had enough, Libs," Jack said. He took the glass away from her and placed it on the table.

Libbie stared at him with wild eyes. She stood, swaying, and shot out her hand, connecting with the side of Jack's face. She hit him so hard that he reeled back and almost fell off the bench. He regained his balance and looked at her, stunned.

"Don't tell me what to do! I don't have to listen to you." Libbie turned and ran out of the gazebo, but she stumbled on the steps and fell to the ground.

Jack was up in an instant and by her side, but as he tried to help her up, she started swinging at him again and yelling, "Let me go! Let me go!"

The situation sobered up Larry and Carol pretty quickly and they came to Jack's aid. Jack let go of Libbie, and even as drunk as she was, she got away from him and headed into the dark, toward the lake.

"Get one of the blankets," Jack told Carol. She did and they all ran to Libbie. She already had her feet in the freezing water. Her shoes were soaked. Jack put the blanket around her quickly and bundled her up tightly so she couldn't fight him. Then, amidst her screaming, he lifted her up and carried her out of the water.

"Let me go! Let me go!" Libbie screamed. She wriggled and kicked, but Jack held on tight.

"Take her inside the house," Carol said, rushing ahead of him to open the door. Larry followed behind.

Jack carried her inside and set her on the sofa. Libbie was struggling so hard that he had to straddle her to keep her from falling off.

"I'll make coffee," Carol said, running to the kitchen.

"Libbie! Stop! You're going to hurt yourself." Jack leaned down close to her face, trying to get her to focus on him. "Libbie!" he yelled. "Look at me. Look at me!"

Libbie thrashed around as much as she could, still bound in the blanket and with Jack on top of her. Finally, exhaustion fell over her, and she stopped moving. Her eyes met Jack's.

"Libbie. Sweetheart." Jack's eyes pooled with tears as he stared down into her flushed face. She'd looked like a wild animal only seconds before, and now she only stared at him with dead eyes. "Libbie. Say something. Are you okay?"

Libbie gazed at him until, finally, recognition appeared in her eyes. Her face softened and tears filled her eyes. "Jack? Oh, Jack. I'm so sorry," Libbie said, sobbing uncontrollably.

Jack sat up and pulled her to him, holding her close. "Shh, sweetie, shh. It's okay. You're okay," he said quietly as he rocked her gently.

"I'm so sorry, I'm so sorry," Libbie kept saying pitifully as her tears fell.

Carol came over with a cup of coffee, but Jack waved her away. Libbie was fading fast. As Jack rocked her in his arms, she fell into a deep sleep.

"She's going to have to stay here tonight," Jack said softly to Carol.

Larry and Carol were both sitting on the opposite sofa, looking dazed. Carol nodded. "I'll call Mr. Wilkens and tell him she's staying here tonight so he doesn't worry."

"Is there somewhere I can lay her down?" Jack asked.

He lifted Libbie in his arms, and Carol led him upstairs to her bedroom. Carol pulled down the blankets on one of the twin beds, and Jack carefully laid Libbie down. Her face and hands were dirty from falling in the mud, and her shoes were soaking wet. Jack gently took off her shoes and socks and then pulled the blankets up over her.

"Can you get me a wet washcloth?" he asked Carol.

She did, and he gently wiped the dirt from her face and lovingly brushed her hair back with his fingers. He wiped her hands and arms clean, also. Her breathing was shallow but steady. He wished he could stay with her and make sure she was okay, but he knew he shouldn't. He bent down and kissed her on the cheek. "Goodnight, Libbie. You'll feel better tomorrow."

Larry and Carol had gone into the hall to give him privacy. He walked out there and turned to Carol. "Will you sleep in there with her tonight and make sure she's okay?"

Carol nodded. "Of course I will. You go home and get some rest. Libbie will be fine."

Jack turned and walked down the hall and downstairs with Larry at his heels.

"Hey, man, I'm so sorry," Larry told him once they were both in the kitchen. Carol had stayed up in the bedroom with Libbie. "I've never seen anyone react that way to alcohol before. I'm sorry."

Jack sighed. "It's not your fault. But let's keep the booze away from Libbie from now on, okay?"

Larry nodded. "That's a nasty bump on the side of your face. We should get you some ice."

Jack raised his hand to where Libbie had hit him. He felt it swelling between his cheek and temple. "I'll be okay. I'm heading home. You want a ride?"

"No, I'm staying here tonight. But don't worry, Carol will stay with Libbie. I'll sleep down here on the couch. We'll make sure she's okay."

Jack's brows furrowed. He hated leaving Libbie when he wasn't sure if she was okay. But she was sleeping soundly, and Carol had promised to watch her.

"Hey, Jack," Larry said, placing a hand on his arm. "I promise she'll be okay. If there is even the slightest sign of a problem, we'll call you and get her to the hospital as fast as possible."

Jack looked into his best friend's eyes. Larry was serious, he could tell. Finally, he nodded and left the house.

No one was awake when Jack got home, and he walked quietly through the house and up to his room. Ray was sound asleep, and Jack undressed in the dark and slipped into bed. But sleep eluded him. Every time he closed his eyes, he saw the wild look in Libbie's eyes as she flailed her arms and yelled at him. He wondered how his sweet Libbie could be so furious after a couple of drinks. She'd been so calm and content the past few months, despite being so agitated by the draft lottery in December. In all the years they'd known each other, he couldn't remember her ever having any kind of mood swings.

It must be the stress of the wedding that's getting to her, he thought. And her mother being sick more often. Plus, they still hadn't found a place to live. *Of course, that's what's wrong. She had to blow off steam somehow.*

Jack finally fell into a restless sleep. First thing in the morning, he was going to check on Libbie and make sure she was all right.

Chapter Twelve

Libbie awoke the next morning with a splitting headache and feeling disorientated. She gazed around the room, wondering for a moment where she was until she finally recognized Carol's bedroom. *Why am I here?*

She sat up slowly and glanced around. The other bed had been slept in, but Carol was gone. Looking down, she realized she was still wearing her clothes from the night before. Libbie grimaced. Her head hurt so badly she had to lie back against the pillows again.

She tried to remember the previous night. She knew she'd gone out to the farm to celebrate Jack's graduation. Then they'd come to Carol's house to sit in the gazebo. As she wondered what could have made her feel so terrible, she slowly recalled the vodka that Larry brought and then it hit her. She'd drunk a few vodka & 7 Ups. How many? She couldn't remember. She must have been completely drunk if she had to stay here.

"Great! You're up. How are you feeling?" Carol came into the room with a tray. She walked over to Libbie's bed and set the tray down beside her. It had toast, orange juice, and coffee on it.

"I've got a headache, but otherwise I'm fine," Libbie said groggily. She pointed to the toast. "Is that for me?"

"It sure is. I'll go get you an aspirin for your headache. Eat some of the toast. It might help you feel better."

Libbie sat up in the bed as Carol left the room. She picked up a piece of toast. Her stomach rolled and she set it down again. Libbie looked around the room. She'd been in Carol's room dozens of times and had even spent many nights here when they were younger. The room hadn't changed much, except for the posters on the walls. Over the years, kitten and puppy posters had been changed to rock bands. The bedspreads were pink and fluffy, the furniture was white-and-gold French provincial, and the carpet was a cream shag. Pink flowered curtains crisscrossed over blinds on the one big window in the room. Sunlight peeked through the closed blinds, making Libbie wonder what time it was. She saw the round alarm clock on the nightstand between the two beds and turned it around. It was a little after noon.

Did I sleep that late?

"Here you go," Carol said, bringing in the bottle of aspirin.

Libbie swung her legs over the side of the bed and immediately felt woozy. "It's already past noon. My mother will kill me! I need to get home and help her set up for the bridal shower tonight." She slipped her foot into one of her shoes, grimaced, and looked up at Carol. "Why are my shoes wet?"

Carol sat down beside Libbie, a worried frown on her face. "Don't you remember what happened last night?"

Libbie looked at her friend. "I remember being in the gazebo and having a couple of drinks, but after that I don't remember anything."

As Carol told her what had happened the night before, tears filled Libbie's eyes. Why had she acted so crazy? And how could she have been so cruel to Jack—the person she loved the most?

"Don't cry, Libbie," Carol said, getting her a box of tissues. "It wasn't your fault. Larry probably made your drinks too strong, and you're not used to drinking."

Libbie grabbed a handful of tissues and wiped her eyes. "But I reacted terribly. Poor Jack. He must hate me!"

Carol smiled and shook her head. "Not at all. He loves you more than anyone could love another human being. He held you until you fell asleep, and he washed away the dirt on your face and hands so lovingly, it melted my heart. You're so lucky to have him, Libbie. If I thought Larry loved me even half as much as Jack loves you, I'd marry him in an instant."

Libbie sat there, letting Carol's words wash over her. She wondered if it was the alcohol that had affected her so strongly, or if it had been a combination of the alcohol and the pills she had been taking. She silently vowed to never again drink so much that it made her behave that way.

"I'd better leave," Libbie said. "My mother will be worrying about the bridal shower."

"Don't worry about the shower," Carol told her. "I've already talked to your mom and told her I'd be there soon to help. Plus, she said Gwen had taken charge of everything so we don't have to worry. She told me to tell you to get some rest so you feel fine for tonight."

"What did you tell her?"

"I told her you were exhausted from the excitement of the wedding and you needed some sleep. She believed me, or at least I think she did."

Libbie sighed with relief. "You're a good friend, Carol. Thanks."

Carol smiled. "Hey, I'm the maid of honor. I'm supposed to

do that kind of stuff." She handed Libbie two aspirin and made her take them, then went to her closet and took out some clean clothes. "Change your clothes and shoes so you won't go home looking dirty. Your shoes are pretty much ruined. We'll probably have to toss them."

Libbie nodded. Carol was right. The leather was ruined.

"Oh, and Jack stopped by first thing this morning to check on you. He's so sweet. He said to let you sleep and he'd stop by your house later to see you. He was really excited about something. He said he had a surprise for you."

A surprise? After how she'd acted last night, Jack had a surprise for her. She felt like the luckiest girl in the world.

* * *

Jack was all smiles when he drove to Libbie's house Saturday afternoon. Earlier that morning, he'd driven over to the northeast side of the lake to help his father unload cabinets for a new house that was being built. Ray had come along to help Norm install the cabinets, and Jack had gone on to Carol's house to check on Libbie.

He'd awoken with an ugly bruise on the side of his head that morning, and there had been no hiding it from his mom. He'd explained it away by telling her he'd swerved to miss a deer on the road and had hit his head on the door frame. She seemed to believe him, which was a relief.

But Jack wasn't thinking about his bruise when he arrived at Libbie's house. He had a surprise for Libbie—one he hoped she'd like.

Libbie's mother answered the door and there was a bevy of activity going on inside. The formal living room was being decorated with crepe paper and paper umbrellas by Carol and Barbara, and Gwen and Sandra were in the kitchen making appetizers for the shower that night.

Before going upstairs to tell Libbie that Jack was there, Abigail had given Jack the once-over. "What happened to the side of your head?" she asked, one eyebrow up.

"I almost hit a deer last night and hit my head on the door when I swerved," Jack said.

Abigail pursed her lips but didn't reply. She went upstairs to get Libbie.

Libbie came down looking tired but otherwise fine after the previous night's ordeal. Jack grinned at her and took her hands in his. "Are you feeling better today?" he asked quietly so her mother wouldn't overhear.

Libbie nodded, and Jack could tell she was trying to hold back tears.

"Can I steal you away for a little bit? I have a surprise for you."

Libbie nodded again, and Jack held her hand as they walked together toward the door. On the way past the living room, he told Carol they'd be back in a little while.

No sooner were they in Jack's truck than tears started streaming down Libbie's face. "I'm so sorry, Jack. I don't know what happened last night. I don't remember any of it."

Jack drew her close. "It's okay. Don't worry about it."

"But I hit you," Libbie said, pulling away. She reached up and gently touched the side of his face. "Look what I did. How could I hit you like that? I'm so sorry."

"I'm fine, Libbie. Really. Let's just forget about last night and think about our future instead." He smiled at her. "I have a surprise for you that will make you feel so much better."

Libbie brushed her tears away and nodded. They drove off down the road past Carol's house.

"Where are we going?" Libbie asked.

"You'll see. It's just down the road." Jack drove along the lake road and then turned into a driveway that had a sign that read Blue Water Resort. The view from the road was blocked by trees and bushes, but when they drove into the resort area, it opened up to a large expanse of water and beach. There were cottages sprinkled about the property and a larger building that was the main lodge. A long dock jutted out into the water, and small fishing boats were tied to it. Two wooden canoes sat up on the beach, glistening in the sunshine.

"This is lovely," Libbie said, gazing around her. "But why are we here?"

"You'll see," Jack said with a grin. A middle-aged man in overalls and a flannel shirt came over as Jack and Libbie climbed out of the truck. He handed Jack a key.

"Is this your future bride?" he asked, nodding to Libbie.

"Yep," Jack said. "Libbie, this is Clem. He owns this resort."

"Nice to meet you," Libbie said.

"Well, ain't you a pretty thing. It's nice to meet you, too, young lady," Clem said. "You two go ahead and look. Let me know what the missus says."

Clem walked away toward the other side of the lodge, and Libbie looked up at Jack, confused.

"What's going on?" she asked.

Jack took her hand and led her across the yard. "This morning after I helped my dad unload cabinets down the road from here, I drove this way to Carol's to check on you. On the way, I saw a sign, so I stopped in to check it out. Here we are." Jack stopped in front of a cottage with the number 3 on it. The cottage was larger than the other two they'd passed and it had white wood siding and sky-blue trim.

"I still don't understand," Libbie said.

"Let's go inside and I'll explain."

They stepped up on the covered wooden porch, and Jack unlocked the door. He opened it and let Libbie walk in first. They stepped into a large, rectangular room that held a nice-sized kitchen on the right and a large living room on the left. In the corner of the living room was a barrel-style woodstove. The furniture in the living room was worn but clean, and the kitchen had a wooden table painted white with four chairs. Light blue, navy, and white were the colors of the furniture and curtains, and the walls were whitewashed.

"There's two bedrooms down the hall and a bathroom," Jack said. "What do you think?"

Libbie turned to Jack. "It's adorable. But you still haven't told me what this is about."

"I was thinking, if you want to, that we could live here."

Libbie stared at Jack, surprise clearly written on her face. "At a resort?"

"Yeah. Clem doesn't want to run this as a resort anymore, so he's renting the cottages long-term. We'd still have access to the lake and can use the boats and canoes. And the cottage is furnished, so we wouldn't have to worry about buying furniture. What do you think?" Jack held his breath. He could afford the cottage on his income, and they could save for a place of their own. It seemed like the perfect place for them.

Libbie walked down the hall and looked at the two bedrooms and the small bathroom. "Well, everything looks clean and nice," she said tentatively.

Jack let out his breath. "You don't like it," he said, disappointed.

"No, I didn't say that. You just caught me off guard." She looked around again. "It is cute and cozy. And we have more room here than any of the apartments we looked at. And living on the lake would be nice . . ." She turned to Jack, and a smile slowly appeared on her face. "I love it! Oh, Jack, it's such a great idea."

Jack was so happy he grabbed her around the waist, lifted her off her feet, and swung her around in a circle. Libbie laughed, and when he set her down, he kissed her. "We finally have a place of our own," he said, wrapping her in his arms. "It's affordable, too. And we can save money to buy a house someday." Jack looked down at Libbie. "Seven more days. Only seven days and we can finally be together. I can't wait Libbie. I love you so much. We're going to be so happy."

"We are," Libbie said, her eyes shining brightly. They kissed again, and Jack reluctantly pulled away.

"Let's go tell Clem we're taking the cottage," Jack said. Libbie nodded and they walked hand in hand over to the lodge.

* * *

Libbie's bridal shower was lovely, and she received many wonderful gifts from her friends and relatives. To her surprise, Libbie's parents had given her a complete set of the china she'd picked out. It was beautiful, and extremely expensive, and Libbie smiled to herself when she thought of her and Jack using that fancy china in the little cottage by the lake.

When Libbie's mother found out that they were going to live in a cottage at a resort, she had a fit, but once again Randall calmed her down. "Jack is a hardworking boy. I'm sure he will buy our Libbie a house in no time. Until then, think of how much fun they'll have living by the lake. And she'll only be a short distance from home."

Abigail had to admit having Libbie living so close would be nice, so she didn't say anything more about it. She also never asked to go see it, either. Gwen dropped by for just a minute to inspect the cottage and only wrinkled her nose at it. But Libbie didn't mind. She stopped by the cottage every day to bring her things there and put them away. She replaced the resort's worn dishes and silverware with her new ones and also made the bed with new sheets she'd been given at the shower.

Bev stopped by and told them how much she loved the little cottage. "It's enchanting," she said, glancing around. "It's the perfect little honeymoon cottage." She'd made them a beautiful wedding ring quilt and Libbie loved it. Their little home was becoming their own, and Libbie couldn't wait to move in permanently.

Libbie was happy. After the terrible episode the previous week, she decided to take her pills only if she absolutely couldn't sleep. It had scared her how she'd blacked out that night, not remembering a thing about it, and she feared she could become dependent on the pills. Besides, once she and Jack were together, she knew she would be happy. Jack was all she needed.

* * *

On their wedding day, Jack gasped when he saw Libbie in her beautiful gown walking down the aisle to him on her father's arm. Jack, too, looked handsome in his black tux, and the entire wedding party looked lovely. There wasn't a dry eye in the church when the two vowed to love, honor, and cherish each other for the rest of their lives. And when Jack lifted Libbie's veil and gazed down into her eyes, she knew he'd meant every promise. *I'll always be safe with Jack.*

For the town of Jamison, Libbie and Jack's wedding was the celebration of the decade. There had never been a more beautiful wedding, nor a more beautiful bride than Libbie. And the reception at the country club was talked about for years to come. The decorations, the flowers, the incredible meal, and even the wedding cake were all extravagant and memorable. But it was the bride and groom that stood out more than any of the trimmings. The love in their eyes for each other was real, and everyone saw it. And when Libbie and Jack danced their first dance as husband and wife, women could be seen brushing away tears from their eyes, and men cleared their throats in an attempt not to show their emotions. It was evident to everyone who attended—no couple had ever been more in love than Libbie and Jack.

That night, long after the last bit of champagne had been drunk and guests had gone home, Jack held Libbie in his arms, tucked away in their bed in the little lake cottage. They'd made love slowly and sweetly, and afterward they held each other tightly and cuddled under the sheets.

"We're married," Jack whispered in Libbie's ear as his body curled around hers. "Even after everything today, I still can't believe it."

"We're married," Libbie said softly. Then she giggled. "You're stuck with me now, Jack Prentice."

"It's a pleasure to be stuck with you, Libbie Prentice," Jack said, kissing her cheek. And they made sweet, passionate love once again before falling asleep in each other's arms.

Chapter Thirteen

Libbie and Jack lived in a state of pure bliss. They couldn't afford to go on a honeymoon, and Jack had to work, but they spent every spare minute together taking walks in the woods, canoeing on the lake, or curled up together in their cottage, making love. They both felt relaxed, content, and carefree.

The first few weeks Libbie stayed busy putting away their many gifts from the wedding, writing thank-you notes, and organizing the little cottage to make it feel like home. She cooked dinner for Jack every night and baked cookies and cakes like his mother did. There was a laundry room at the main lodge, and she washed clothes twice a week. In that time, she'd met Clem's wife, Edith, and the two women got along well despite their age difference.

Larry and Carol came over one Sunday evening in late June, and they all sat at the small kitchen table and played card games and ate snacks that Libbie had made.

"You're becoming a regular little Suzy Homemaker," Larry said, winking at Libbie. "And your brownies taste as good as Jack's mother's."

"Thanks, I think," Libbie said, laughing and grabbing another Coke from the small fridge for herself. Larry had brought along a bottle of gin, but Libbie didn't drink any of it. She noticed Jack only had one drink, while Larry and Carol had a few and were getting silly.

"You sure you don't want another drink?" Larry asked Jack, pouring himself one.

"No, you go ahead," Jack told him, looking up at Libbie. They smiled at each other. She was happy that he didn't get drunk like Larry did. She adored Larry—he was always sweet to her and he loved to tease and have fun—but he wasn't as responsible as Jack.

"Well, you'd better have your fun now, Jack, 'cause after the draft lottery in July, you might have a one-way ticket to Nam," Larry said, laughing.

Libbie's eyes darted up quickly, and she caught Carol hitting Larry's arm and shushing him. "What are you talking about?" she demanded.

Larry opened his mouth to speak, but Carol punched him again and he quickly closed it.

Libbie turned to Jack. "What's he talking about? What draft lottery? I thought that was months from now."

"Oh, wow, Jack. I'm so sorry," Larry said. "I thought Libbie knew. It's been on the news and in the paper."

Libbie stood up, angry now. "What is he talking about?" she yelled.

Jack placed his hand on her arm. "Please don't get upset, sweetie. Sit down and I'll tell you."

Libbie sat, watching him intently.

"The draft lottery for men born in 1951 is being held on July first," Jack said, holding her hand.

Chills ran down Libbie's spine and tears filled her eyes. "You mean I could lose you as soon as July?"

"No, no, no," Jack said, jumping up and wrapping his arms around Libbie from behind, touching his cheek to hers. "Even if my birth date draws a low number, even if I get drafted, it won't be for at least another six months. We have plenty of time together. And I may not be drafted at all."

Libbie felt the shaking start from deep within until her entire body began to quiver. Jack must have felt her shaking, too, because he held her tighter, as if to stop it. She jumped out of her chair with such force, it pushed Jack back, and she turned and faced him. "Why didn't you warn me about this? Why were you hiding it from me?" she yelled, angry tears streaming down her face.

"I'm sorry, Libbie," Jack said, coming to her with open arms. But Libbie stepped back and wrapped her arms around herself. "Libbie, please don't be angry. Please. I didn't want to upset you. That's why I didn't say anything. You were so troubled after the last draft that I didn't want you to worry like that again. I may not even be chosen. We just have to wait and see."

Carol came over to Libbie and wrapped her arm around her. "Let's not worry about it tonight, okay, Libbie? We can go back to playing cards and having fun. And you made so many wonderful treats. Come on, let's sit down."

Libbie stood there, holding herself tightly as she looked into the faces around her. How could they all be so calm? The thought of losing Jack terrified her. She loved him so much; it would kill her if he had to go off to war. How could they all not know that?

Breaking away from Carol, she ran down the hall and into their bedroom, slamming the door. She heard their muffled voices but didn't care what they were saying. Her heart was pounding fiercely and her mind was racing. A cold sweat covered her body. Bile rose up in her throat and threatened to choke her. She hugged herself tightly and rocked back and forth, trying to soothe herself, but it didn't help. She had to calm down, and she knew she couldn't do it on her own.

Walking slowly to the dresser on shaky legs, she opened her lingerie drawer and dug around until she found the pill bottle hiding in the very back. She grasped it tightly and stared at it, thinking how she hadn't needed to take these since their wedding day. Libbie opened the bottle and took out one pill. Then, quickly, before she could think about it, she popped it into her mouth and swallowed. It would calm her down. It would make the pain go away. She only needed it this one time, she told herself, to get through tonight. Then she hid the bottle back in her drawer and lay down on the bed.

* * *

"Dammit, Larry! Why did you have to bring up the lottery?" Jack glared at his friend. Larry just looked back at him with glassy eyes, and Jack realized he'd had more than just alcohol. He'd probably smoked pot before coming over.

"Yeah. Way to go, idiot," Carol said, crossing her arms.

"I'm sorry, man," Larry said, ignoring Carol. "I really am. I figured she already knew. Besides, she'd have found out in a few days."

Jack sighed heavily. These past three weeks with Libbie had been incredible. They'd lived in a bubble of happiness, oblivious to the world around them. Now reality was crashing in much sooner than he would have liked. "I have to go check on Libbie."

"We'll get out of your way," Carol said, smacking Larry on

the shoulder as she walked past him. "Come on, big mouth. I'll drive you home."

She gave Jack a hug, and Larry apologized once more before they both went out the door. Jack packed the food in containers and put them away. He set the dishes in the sink and ran water over them. Then he headed into the bedroom to check on Libbie.

When he opened the door, he was surprised to see her lying peacefully on the bed, half-asleep. He'd never seen her calm down so quickly before. He had thought she'd be upset about this for days. He walked over and lay down beside her, brushing her hair away from her face.

"Libbie? Are you okay?"

She turned her head and opened her eyes. Jack frowned. Her eyes looked glassy, just as they had on the night of the gazebo incident. "Libbie?"

"I'm fine," she said sleepily, then shut her eyes again.

"I'm sorry I didn't tell you. I didn't want you to worry."

Libbie sighed. "I know." She stood and walked to the closet to undress and slip on her nightgown. Jack watched her and noticed that her movements were unsteady.

Maybe she's just really tired, he rationalized. He pulled the blankets down and slid into bed, and soon after Libbie did, too, and turned out the light.

Jack curled up next to Libbie, holding her close. Just as he thought she'd fallen asleep, she startled him by speaking.

"July first is only three days away."

"I know," he said quietly.

"I can't live without you, Jack. I just can't."

Jack pulled her closer and kissed her bare shoulder. "I'm not going anywhere, Libbie. And even if I do, I will come back to you. You have to believe that."

"You can't promise me that. You know you can't," she whispered.

"Oh, Libbie." Jack sighed, dropping his head on his pillow. "I'm just as scared as you are. Don't you know that?"

She turned and looked at him. "I'm sorry. I was so afraid that I never thought about how you felt."

Jack ran his hand tenderly across her cheek and through her hair. "We'll get through this, hon. You'll see. You're stronger than you think."

Libbie laid her head on his chest and curled up next to him. "I'm so tired, Jack. So, so tired."

He kissed the top of her head. "Go to sleep, sweetie. Tomorrow things will look better."

* * *

Libbie spent the next four days in a blur. When Jack was at work, she cleaned the cottage until it was spotless, then she cleaned some more. She washed all the curtains and linens in the house and even cleaned the windows inside and out. She scrubbed and polished until she was so exhausted that she fell into bed each night, hoping for sleep. But even then, sleep eluded her. She'd gone back to taking Valium in the morning and before bed. She needed their calming effect all day and again at night to fall asleep. But even with the pills, she still felt strung out at times, so she kept herself busy.

Carol had come over to check on Libbie that Monday and told her how happy she was that she was feeling better. They'd sat on the front porch in new wooden rockers that Libbie had bought for cost from her father's furniture store. Carol told Libbie she'd broken it off with Larry.

"You did? Why? I hope it wasn't because he told me about the lottery," Libbie said, shocked.

Carol shook her head. "No, not because of that. There were a lot of other things. He's a nice guy and can be really sweet, but he has so much growing up to do. He drinks way too much and is hardly ever serious. We don't love each other as much as we should. In fact, I don't think we've ever loved each other."

"I'm sorry, Carol," Libbie said. "You two have been together as long as Jack and I have. I guess I thought you did love each other."

Carol shrugged. "I told myself I loved him, but then I realized that it wasn't true. He and I aren't anything like you and Jack. You remember that night you freaked out and stayed over at my house? Well, I saw how much Jack truly loved you. He took care of you, and his only concern was that you were okay. I think that was the night I realized I wanted someone to love me as much as Jack loves you. I'm not sure I'll ever find a guy like that, but I know Larry isn't that guy. So, I'll keep looking."

Libbie had been amazed by what Carol had said. She'd thought about it often. She already knew she was lucky to have Jack, but the fact that Carol saw how strong the love was between them surprised her. That was why she couldn't lose Jack. She would never find anyone she'd love as much as Jack or who'd love her as much as he did.

July 1 came and went, and the draft lottery numbers were printed in the July 2 newspapers. Jack was getting ready to leave for work that morning when the paper arrived at the main building of the resort. Libbie saw it, too, and without a word, they walked over to the other building, picked up the paper, and Jack unrolled it. He looked at Libbie, and she bit her lip and nodded. Taking a breath, he opened it to the page that had the number chart and looked for his birthday.

Libbie stood there, hugging herself tightly. It was a warm morning, but she felt a chill run through her. She watched as Jack slid his finger down the dates. Finally, he stopped at his birthday—January 28.

"What is it?" Libbie whispered.

Jack turned and gave Libbie a small smile. "It's a good number, Libbie. A good number. It's 346. That's high. There's a really good chance I won't be drafted."

Relief flooded through her. She reached out and hugged Jack as tears spilled from her eyes. "Are you sure? Are you sure you won't be drafted?"

Jack pulled away and gazed down at her. "They'd have to go through a lot of men before they hit my number, Libbie. I can't promise, but I should be safe."

Libbie sighed. Then her eyes grew wide. "What about Larry?"

Jack turned back to the paper and looked up Larry's birthday, March 2. Libbie saw him frown.

"What it is? What's his number?" Libbie asked.

"It's seventy-seven," Jack said.

Libbie gasped and covered her mouth with her hands.

"I'm afraid he'll be drafted for sure," Jack said, his shoulders slumping. Slowly, he folded the paper and rolled it up neatly, replacing the rubber band. They left it on the porch where they'd found it. Jack placed his arm around Libbie's waist and walked her back to the cottage.

* * *

Jack and Larry sat on the cottage porch that evening while Libbie finished cooking dinner inside. He'd asked her to let him talk to Larry alone for a few minutes, and she'd nodded her understanding.

Larry took a swig of his beer. "It doesn't seem real yet. I mean, I knew there was always a chance I'd go, but now that it's going to happen, it's strange."

"I'm sorry, Lar," Jack said.

"It's not your fault, man. It was fate."

Jack sipped on the beer Larry had brought. They were still underage at nineteen, but Larry never seemed to have a problem getting beer and booze.

"Some of the guys in the shop were talking today," Jack said. "They said it was best to enlist before you're drafted so you might have a better chance of not going to Nam."

Larry nodded. "Yeah, I've heard that from guys, too. I have to check into it. I was thinking of trying to enlist in the Air Force, or maybe even the Coast Guard."

Jack laughed. "The Coast Guard? You've never been to the ocean in your life. You haven't even been to the Great Lakes. What if you get seasick?"

Larry chuckled. "It would be better than the Navy. I can't see myself stuck on a ship for months at a time. I could try the Marines, too. I don't know. Some college students get a deferment until they graduate. I could try for that. That would give me three more years."

"Yeah. That would be good."

Larry glanced over at Jack. "You're so lucky, man. You married the prettiest girl in town and you drew a high number. I'm glad you did, though. Libbie needs you here. It wouldn't be good for her if you left."

Jack looked at Larry curiously. "Why do you say that?"

"Ah, no reason. It's just that Libbie has a soft heart. She

needs someone beside her to keep her strong. Nothing wrong with that. You're her sturdy arm to lean on, man. Without you, I'm afraid she might crumble, and that would be a shame."

"Dinner's ready, guys," Libbie called out the window.

"Yeah! Chow. I'm starved. Let's go eat," Larry said, heading for the door.

Jack thought about what Larry had said all that night and the next day. Did Larry believe that Libbie was weak? Jack had never thought of Libbie that way. She was smart, confident, and hardworking. Sure, she could be emotional at times, but weren't some women like that? His sister was like that, although his mother wasn't. Did Larry see something in Libbie that Jack hadn't?

Jack finally chalked up Larry's words to too much beer. Larry always spoke nonsense when he drank. Libbie was a strong girl. She could stand on her own if she needed to. Jack was just happy that she wanted him beside her.

Chapter Fourteen

Libbie lay curled up beside Jack in bed with her head on his bare chest. They'd just made love, and she adored snuggling beside him until they fell asleep. Except sleeping was the last thing she felt like doing just then. She'd been thinking for days about something and wanted to talk to Jack about it when she found the right moment. She took a breath—this had to be the right moment.

"Jack?" she asked softly, hoping he hadn't already fallen asleep.

"Hmm?"

"Let's have a baby."

Jack's eyes popped open. "What?"

Libbie sat up and looked at him. She talked quickly. "I want to have a baby. A little Jack or Libbie. Wouldn't that be wonderful? And, if we have a baby, they won't be able to draft you. I read that somewhere. At least, they'd be less likely to since you're the sole supporter of the family."

Jack sat up and stared at Libbie. "That's not a good reason to have a child," he said. "I thought we weren't going to worry about the draft anymore. We'll just take each day as it comes."

Libbie looked down as she wrung her hands. They hadn't talked about the possibility of his being drafted for a few weeks. It was mid-August, and summer was going by fast. They'd celebrated the Fourth of July at her parents' house with all their friends, and they'd enjoyed many lovely evenings walking the nearby wooded trails or floating on the lake in the canoe. But the fear of Jack being drafted continued to plague Libbie's thoughts.

"Don't you want to have children?" she asked.

Jack reached out and took her hand. "Of course I do," he said gently. "But I figured we'd wait a while and enjoy our time together before we start a family. And it would be nice to save and buy our own house before we have children."

Libbie dropped her eyes. "But I want a baby," she said. "Not only because of the draft, but also to have someone to love and take care of. You go to work every day and I don't have much to do except clean and cook. If I had a baby, I'd be busy taking care of her or him."

"Libs, I don't think having a baby is the answer to you being bored," Jack said.

Libbie pulled away from him, her eyes flashing. "You just don't understand."

Jack looked at her tenderly. "Sweetie, I do understand. And I do want children. But I think we should wait a little longer. We're young. We should enjoy this time alone before we start a family."

Libbie sighed. "But everyone has something they're doing. You work. Carol will be in school. Most of my friends go to college, work, or have left town. What am I supposed to do with myself?"

Jack sat there looking thoughtful. "What about school? You're really smart. And your parents offered to pay if you wanted to go to college."

Libbie shrugged. "I never really thought about going to college. I don't even know what I'd major in. All I ever thought I'd do was get married and have a family."

Jack smiled. "I'm happy I was the lucky guy you married."

Libbie grinned.

"Maybe you could work for your dad, like in his office or something."

"Oh, no, I don't think he'd give me a job. My mom would kill him. She says Wilkens women don't work."

"But lots of women work nowadays. I don't see why you shouldn't, if you want to."

Libbie thought about what Jack said. True, women were working more than before. And it might be fun to work somewhere. And she could even earn a little money to help save for their house. She looked up at Jack. "Where would I work?"

"I'm not sure, but there must be ads in the newspaper. You should look at them tomorrow and see if anything interests you."

The more Libbie thought of it, the more she liked the idea. "Yeah, I'll do that." She grinned up at Jack. "But you haven't talked me out of having a baby. I still want to have children. But I guess I can wait awhile longer."

Jack pulled her into his arms and she fell on top of him. "In that case, we should practice and practice before we really try making a baby."

Libbie giggled, and then lost herself in Jack's love.

* * *

The next morning, Libbie borrowed the newspaper from Clem

and studied the help wanted ads. There were a few, and some of them were for her father's businesses, so she didn't even consider those. A few others were for businesses owned by the Jamisons. Her father would disown her if she worked for his rival, so those were out, too.

She continued reading down the column of ads. There were ads for a waitress, a fry cook, and a job selling tickets at the local movie theater. She didn't think she'd make a good waitress, didn't want to be a fry cook, and figured the movie theater job would be at night, so that was out. Evenings were the only time she had to spend with Jack. Then she saw a job listing for their local library. It was two days a week, six hours a day, and only involved checking out books, re-shelving them, and helping library patrons. Libbie liked books and thought it would be fun to work around them. It said to come in and pick up an application between nine and three o'clock.

"I'll do it today," Libbie said to herself excitedly. She went to her bedroom and rummaged through the closet. She hadn't brought all of her clothes to the cottage, leaving many of her dressier clothes at her parents' house. She knew she couldn't go there and pick up a dress or her mother would ask her why. And if Gwen were there, she'd bug her until she told her. So she picked out the best dress she had on hand and slipped it on. It was a sleeveless dress of soft yellow with white piping trim and a wide white belt. It fell just above her knees, which Libbie thought would be good for a library. Even though short dresses were the style, Libbie's mother had never let her wear them, so Libbie didn't own any miniskirts. But this would be perfect for job hunting. She slipped on a pair of white flats and pulled a white purse out of the closet to match. As she applied a little makeup and pushed her hair back with a headband, she grew more excited. Working somewhere might be fun. She could dress up and keep her mind busy so she wouldn't have time to dwell on things that upset her. She hoped she'd get this job.

Libbie hopped into her Mustang and followed the lake road, then turned to go downtown. The Jamison Public Library was a small three-story brick building on a corner just across from the lake. It had been built in 1901, originally as a Carnegie library, and had wide steps in front with two tall white pillars on each side. Libbie remembered going there ever since she was a little girl, picking out colorful storybooks to read.

The only parking was on the street. She found a spot around the corner and walked the short distance. It was a beautiful day with the sun sparkling off the lake. Traffic was heavy on the main street through town due to it being tourist season. It wouldn't be long before college students replaced tourists and the small town went back to its normal, quieter routine.

Libbie walked into the building and was greeted by cool air. She glanced around with a smile. She loved the feel of the old building and the unique smell of books lining the shelves. The floors were polished oak and there were two small staircases— one leading upstairs and one leading downstairs to the lower floor. Carved walnut handrails that swirled at the ends lined the staircase walls, and all three stories had a fireplace in each room from the days when there was no central heating.

The librarian desk was on the third floor, so Libbie went up the steps and walked across the room to the long desk where books were checked out and returned. A woman about her mother's age stood there, stamping the inside of books that she took from a tall pile. She looked up when Libbie approached.

"Libbie, dear, how nice to see you," she said.

Libbie smiled. "Hi, Mrs. Thompson. How are you?" Miriam

Thompson had been working at the library ever since Libbie was a small child. Everyone in town knew her.

"Oh, I can't complain. I saw in the paper that you got married this summer. Congratulations, dear. Are you enjoying married life?"

"Oh, yes. We're very happy."

"That's good to hear. What can I do for you today, Libbie?"

"I came to apply for the part-time job."

The woman's soft blue eyes lit up. "Wonderful. Let me get you an application." She reached under the desk, pulled out a sheet of paper, and handed it to Libbie along with a pen. "You can sit right over there and fill it out." She pointed to an empty table that sat by the bookshelves.

"Thank you," Libbie said. She sat down, then perused the sheet of paper. She'd never filled out a job application before. She went through each question, and except for personal information, she had nothing to write. She'd never worked before, and she hadn't done much volunteer work, either. She hoped that they would give her a chance anyway, based on what a good student she'd been in school.

Libbie brought the application back to Mrs. Thompson. "I'm afraid I couldn't fill out too much," she told her. "I've never had a job before, but I'm a quick learner and I used to be in charge of many of the dances and activities when I was in school."

"That's fine, Libbie. We all have to start somewhere, right?"

"Yes, ma'am."

"We haven't had many applications come in, and I think it would be a breath of fresh air having a young girl like you working here with us old ladies," Mrs. Thompson said, smiling. "We'll be going over the applications at our next board meeting on Wednesday, and then we'll choose someone."

"Okay. Thank you, Mrs. Thompson."

Libbie waved goodbye and left, her heart beating with excitement. She hoped the board would hire her. She liked Mrs. Thompson, and thought she'd do a good job there. Crossing her fingers, she hopped into her car and buzzed home.

When Libbie pulled up to her cottage, she saw a bustling of activity going on in the cottage closest to theirs. Two old cars sat in the driveway as well as a truck, and an older man was carrying boxes into the cottage. A woman was running back and forth, bringing in the smaller items, and two college-aged girls were helping them. One of the girls smiled and waved at her, and Libbie waved back before going inside. Libbie hoped it was the two girls moving in. Of the six cottages available for rent, only three had been filled so far. Libbie hadn't gotten to know the other renters well because they were all men who worked construction and wouldn't be there once winter came. But these girls looked to be Libbie's age, and she thought it might be nice to have someone around she could talk to.

Later that afternoon, Libbie went outside on the porch to shake out a rug and noticed that the truck was gone but the two cars were still there. She decided she would be a good neighbor, so she put several freshly baked chocolate-chip cookies into a container and walked over to the cottage. She hadn't even knocked yet when the door flew open and one of the girls smiled broadly at her.

"Hi! I saw you coming over. I'm Candace, but you can call me Candy. What did you bring?" the girl said excitedly.

Libbie smiled. Candy had long, straight, black hair, bright blue eyes, and a friendly smile. She was tall and slender and very pretty. "I'm Libbie. I thought I'd welcome you by bringing over some homemade cookies."

"Isn't that sweet?" Candy said. "Come on in. We're unpacking our stuff. Jackie! Come meet our neighbor. She brought cookies."

The other girl was the exact opposite of Candy. She had pale blond hair that was cut in a pixie style, and she was shorter and much curvier. She had a pretty face and a welcoming smile.

"Cookies?" Jackie said, coming out of one of the bedrooms. "I can never say no to cookies."

Libbie introduced herself, and soon they were all sitting at the kitchen table eating cookies and drinking Cokes.

"We're in our second year of college," Candy told Libbie. "We're both elementary education majors. We lived in the dorms last year but wanted our own place this time around. Too many rules and not enough fun. Do you go to college, too?"

Libbie shook her head. "No, I just got married this summer. My husband works at the Ford dealership in town, in the garage. But I did apply for a job today that I hope I'll get."

Jackie's eyes grew wide. "Is your husband that cute guy with the wavy brown hair and delicious brown eyes? He drives the old blue truck. We saw him the other day when we came to look at the cottages to rent."

Libbie smiled. "Yeah, that's him. He is pretty adorable."

"Oh, my goodness, he's a hunk!" Candy said. "You're so lucky, and I'm so jealous. It's hard finding a nice guy and one who's cute on top of it."

Libbie laughed. "I do feel lucky. He's a wonderful guy."

"So, where did you apply for a job?" Jackie asked.

Libbie told them all about the library job. They told her they were from Minneapolis but wanted to go to college far from home. It had been Candy's parents who'd helped them bring their stuff up that day. They talked nonstop, and finally Libbie had to leave so she could start dinner.

"Thanks for the cookies. I'm glad we have a nice neighbor. Drop by anytime we're here," Candy said.

Libbie said she would, and that they could come over anytime, too. She went home with a smile on her face. She really liked the two girls and hoped she'd see a lot of them.

When Jack came home, she excitedly told him about the library job and meeting the two girls next door.

"The job sounds perfect," Jack said as they ate their dinner. "It shouldn't be so much that you'll feel overwhelmed with it and home, and it will give you something interesting to do."

Libbie nodded. She didn't want to get her hopes up, but she really wanted that job.

The next three days, Libbie kept busy around the house and running to town for groceries. She stopped by her parents' house to pick up more of her nice dresses and shoes in case she did get the job. Gwen and the two children were there when she arrived, and her mother was up in her bedroom.

"Is Mom not feeling well again?" Libbie asked. She picked up her littlest niece and held her. She was only five months old, but she was quite heavy. Libbie felt bad that she hadn't seen much of little Leslie or Lynn over the past couple of months, but she'd wanted to spend every free moment with Jack.

Gwen sighed. She looked tired and had dark circles under her eyes. "She's been sick more than usual. She hasn't been the same since you moved out. You really should visit her more often so she doesn't feel so depressed."

Libbie frowned. "Why is it my fault? She was sick even when I lived at home."

Gwen shook her head. "Never mind. You wouldn't understand anyway."

Libbie didn't want to fight with her sister. She'd been feeling really happy about the prospect of the library job, and she wasn't going to let her sister ruin her good mood. "I'll try to stop by more and see Mom," she conceded.

Libbie ran upstairs to her room and rummaged through her closet. She had an extra suitcase in there, so she pulled it out and packed up several pairs of shoes and a few purses. She sifted through her dresses and pulled down a few, laying them on the bed.

She went down the hall and peeked into her mother's room. The shades were drawn and the only light was from the lamp on the nightstand. She knocked softly. "Mom? It's Libbie. I just wanted to say hello."

There was no answer, so Libbie slowly crept inside. "Mom?" She wrinkled her nose. The air was stale and there was a strong scent. It smelled like the liquor her father usually drank before dinner. "Mom?"

Libbie came to her mother's bedside. Abigail was sleeping. Her face was slack and her hair was mussed. Libbie had seen her mother sick many times before, but she'd never looked this bad. As a child, she remembered her mother having episodes, as they called them then, only once or twice a year. But as Libbie had grown older, her mother's episodes had increased.

Abigail stirred and opened her eyes. She stared at Libbie but didn't seem to recognize her. "Gwen?"

"No, Mom. It's me, Libbie. I just wanted to check on you and make sure you were okay."

Abigail pushed herself up a little. "Will you hand me my glass please, dear?"

Libbie noticed her mother's words were slurred. She reached over and picked up the stout glass on the nightstand. Looking into it, she wondered, was her mother drinking alcohol in the middle of the day?

"Libbie. Please."

Libbie handed her mother the glass, making sure Abigail had it firmly in her hand before letting it go. Her mother took a long drink and then lay back against her pillows, sighing.

"Thank you, dear," Abigail said. She closed her eyes.

Libbie took the glass and set it back on the nightstand. That was when she saw the bottle. It had been hidden from view by the lamp. Slowly, Libbie turned the bottle so she could read the label. Bourbon Whiskey.

Libbie pulled her hand away quickly as if the bottle had stung her. She stared at her mother incredulously. Her mother wasn't sick—she was drunk.

Libbie ran from the room quickly, retrieved her clothes from her bedroom, and went down the stairs. She left the house without saying goodbye to Gwen. She couldn't bear to face her. Gwen had to know that her mother was drunk, not ill. But there was no way she could discuss this with Gwen right now. Maybe not ever.

Chapter Fifteen

Libbie didn't mention her mother's drinking to Jack when he came home that night. She couldn't bring herself to tell him. She was afraid he'd think less of her and her family if he knew. As she thought it over, she wondered if she'd been too quick to judge. Maybe her mother really was sick and in pain. She could be drinking the bourbon to lessen her pain. Her mother took several different types of pills, so she must be under a doctor's care.

Libbie tried to remember if her mother had ever drunk excessively when she was a child. Abigail had always been the picture of decorum. Libbie never once saw her mother act strange or slur her words. If she were an alcoholic, wouldn't she be drunk all the time? Libbie didn't know any alcoholics, but she thought they couldn't get through a day without being drunk. That wasn't how her mother was. So maybe she needed a few days of relief every now and then.

Libbie forced herself to push aside thoughts of her mother's condition. Maybe she'd ask Gwen about it at some point. But until then, she wanted to feel good about the possibility of working at the library.

Thursday afternoon Mrs. Thompson called her.

"I'm happy to tell you that the board decided to offer you the job, Libbie," Mrs. Thompson said. "I hope you still want to work for us."

Libbie wanted to squeal with delight but she didn't think that would be very professional. "Oh, yes. I definitely still want the job."

"Wonderful. You'll be working every Monday and Wednesday, nine to three. Come in on Monday, and I'll show you around and get you started."

When Libbie hung up, she danced around the room and finally let out a happy squeal. Moments later, there was a knock on the door. Candy was standing there, looking worried.

"I was getting out of my car and I heard you yelling," Candy said. "Are you okay?"

Libbie laughed. "I'm fine. I just got a call from the library saying I got the job! I was too excited to hold it in."

"That is exciting. We have to celebrate. Come over to our place. Jackie's home, too."

Libbie followed Candy to her cottage and told Jackie the good news. Jackie clapped her hands in delight. "I'm so happy for you, Libbie."

"Let's celebrate!" Candy said, heading over to her fridge. She pulled out a cheap bottle of red wine and a bottle of 7 Up.

Libbie watched as she filled three glasses half full of wine and then filled them the rest of the way with the 7 Up. "I've never seen anyone do that before," Libbie said as Candy handed her a glass.

"It's really good," Jackie said. "And it makes cheap wine taste a lot better." She giggled.

Candy raised her glass. "To Libbie's first job," she toasted.

The three girls clinked glasses and then took a sip.

"This is good," Libbie said. She took another sip. It was sweet yet smooth, and since it was only half wine, she figured it wouldn't be too strong. "What's it called?"

Jackie giggled. "It's a cheap version of a spritzer."

Libbie didn't know what a spritzer was, but she knew she liked this drink.

That night at dinner, Libbie made spritzers for her and Jack. She'd told him about getting the job, and he'd offered to take her out for dinner to celebrate, but she'd decided to eat in instead.

"What's this?" Jack said, staring at the wine glass.

"The girls call it a wine spritzer. Try it. It tastes really good."

Jack took a sip. "It is good. Sweet, but I like it." He smiled over at Libbie. "Where'd you get the wine?"

"The girls let me buy a bottle from them. It's really cheap wine, but with the 7 Up added, it tastes good. I thought we'd celebrate."

Jack lifted his glass. "Well, then. Here's to you and your new job."

Libbie lifted her glass and clinked his, then took another sip. She'd drunk only one of these in the afternoon with the girls, and it had made her feel warm inside, but otherwise she'd felt fine. And now, as they ate dinner and drank their wine, that warm, cozy feeling washed over her again.

"Your cheeks are flushed," Jack said. "You look adorable."

Libbie giggled.

"I could get used to this," Jack said, reaching over and kissing her lightly on the cheek.

"Used to what?" Libbie asked.

"Wine at dinner. I feel like we're being fancy." He winked.

"Maybe after dinner we can celebrate a different way," Libbie said, winking at him.

Jack stood and picked Libbie up into his arms. "I'm done eating right now," he said, laughing.

Libbie laughed along with him as he carried her to the bedroom to celebrate.

* * *

Libbie loved her new job. She'd been working there for a month, and she enjoyed every minute of it. On her first day, Mrs. Thompson explained the work she'd be doing and that she'd be paid $1.45 an hour. Her duties included checking books in and out, reshelving books, and helping to tag new books when they came in. She was introduced to the other full-time employee, Ardith Haag, a sweet lady in her mid-fifties. Libbie liked Ardith immediately and felt comfortable around both ladies. There were several volunteers who worked there on a regular basis, too, and they all welcomed Libbie warmly when they met her.

Libbie almost wished she worked at the library more than twice a week. She felt important and useful, and she loved helping people find books. Mothers with little children came in regularly, and Libbie had fun helping the little kids find picture books and storybooks. She took pride in her work and was often asked for recommendations, and people said they liked her choices.

When she wasn't at work, she had plenty to do at home, but she grew bored easily. The first couple of months, running her own household had been exciting, and she did enjoy cooking and baking. But now the housework and laundry were growing old fast. She still didn't mind cooking, but everything else bored her. She'd been used to having Sandra clean her room and do her laundry at home, and she hadn't realized how nice that had been until she started doing all the work herself. But she didn't complain to Jack because she knew she should be grateful that he worked so hard to support them and that she should want to help by doing the work at home.

This is what you decided you wanted when you married Jack. So stop complaining.

Still, she didn't get the same feeling of accomplishment in cleaning and cooking as she did at the library.

To take the edge off of her long, boring days, Libbie had a wine spritzer with lunch every afternoon. She'd stopped taking Valium in the mornings because it made her feel slow and fuzzy all day. But the wine made her feel warm and happy, so she didn't think it would hurt to have just one glass a day. Occasionally, she had a glass with dinner, too, but she tried not to drink too often in front of Jack. He never said anything to her about it, but she was sure he was thinking about that night when she'd freaked out with the vodka. The wine didn't affect her that way, so she figured it was safe. She enjoyed how calm and content it made her feel.

The first week in October, as Libbie worked behind the desk at the library, she heard a familiar voice say her name. She looked up. Her mother was standing there, staring at her incredulously.

"What are you doing behind that desk?" Abigail asked. "Are you working here?"

Libbie stood there, stunned, her mind spinning. She could lie and say she was a volunteer, but she knew her mother would find out the truth eventually. She took a deep breath and said, "Yes, Mother. I work here."

Abigail's eyes narrowed. She walked closer to the desk and spoke quietly so no one else would hear. "Did that boy make you get a job? Why on earth didn't you tell me you needed money? Your father would have helped you out."

Libbie feigned a smile. "Mom, I like working here. Jack didn't make me get a job. I was bored, and I wanted to do something that made me feel useful. And it's nice earning a little extra money of my own."

Abigail straightened her back. "Wilkens women do not work. We volunteer, we don't work. We didn't raise you to support a deadbeat husband. We raised you to be a lady and be treated like one."

"Mom! Jack's not a deadbeat. He works really hard, and he treats me like a princess. Besides, I'm not a Wilkens anymore. My last name is Prentice." Libbie immediately regretted that last sentence the moment she saw the shock in her mother's eyes.

"Well, then. Fine. I guess I failed with you. Thank goodness I still have Gwen." Abigail set down the books she was returning, turned on her heel, and walked away with her head held high.

Tears filled Libbie's eyes. Her heart pounded and she felt like she was going to faint. She ran into the ladies' room and hid in a stall as her tears fell. *I failed with you.* She couldn't believe her mother had said that to her. Her mother had never been the affectionate type, but Libbie always thought her mother loved her and was proud of her. Telling Libbie she was a failure felt devastating.

She drove home and the first thing she did was pour herself a glass of wine. She didn't even bother putting 7 Up in it. She drank half the glass, then sat on the sofa and waited for the warm, comforting feel of it to flow through her. She drank down the rest of the glass and poured another. She just wanted to wipe away her mother's words, no matter how many glasses it took.

* * *

Jack walked into the cottage at five thirty and was surprised the kitchen light was off and Libbie wasn't cooking dinner. He hung his jacket by the door and turned toward the living room. There, lying on the sofa, was Libbie, sound asleep. An empty bottle of wine sat on its side on the coffee table with an empty glass beside it.

"Libbie?" Jack walked quickly to her side and tried to wake her up. "Libbie. Wake up."

She stirred, then rolled over and went back to sleep.

Jack sighed with relief. She was breathing normally and seemed to be fine. He picked up the wine bottle and stared at it. *Where is she getting all this wine?* he wondered. *She couldn't go to the store and buy it legally. The college girls next door must be buying it for her.*

He took the bottle and glass into the kitchen and then went into the bathroom to shower. He always took a shower before dinner since he got so dirty at work. He put on a clean shirt and jeans, and went back out to the living room. Libbie was still sound asleep, curled up on the sofa.

Lifting her up carefully, he carried her to the bedroom and laid her on the bed, covered up with an afghan. Once he made sure she was breathing steadily, he went back out to the kitchen to make himself a sandwich.

As he ate, he worried about why she'd drunk so much that she'd passed out. Was she tired from working and doing so much around the house? He decided not to make a big fuss about it. It wasn't like she did this every night.

The next day, as Jack ate a bowl of cereal for breakfast, Libbie staggered out of the bedroom and into the kitchen. She was still wearing her dress from the day before.

"How are you feeling this morning?" he asked, smiling up at her from the table.

Libbie grimaced, pulled out a chair, and plopped down. "What happened last night?"

Jack's brows rose. "Don't you remember?"

She shook her head.

"I came home last night and you were passed out on the sofa."

"Passed out?"

"Well, there was an empty bottle of wine and a glass on the table. I'm not sure how much of the bottle you drank," Jack said.

Libbie sat silent a moment and then a tear fell from her eye. "I remember now. My mom came into the library yesterday and said some really nasty things to me."

Jack went over to Libbie and kneeled down in front of her. "Why would she do that?"

"She was angry because I was working. She said something mean about you and told me 'Wilkens women don't work.' I got mad and told her I liked working there, and besides, I was a Prentice now. That really angered her. She told me I was a failure." Tears slid down her cheeks. "I felt so terrible when I came home that I had a glass of wine to relax and it must have knocked me out."

"Oh, Libbie." Jack wrapped his arms around her. "I'm sorry your mother feels that way. Don't let it get to you. I'm so proud of you, and you love working at the library. Your mother will get used to the idea of you working."

Libbie sniffed and nodded. "I know. It just hurt."

Jack kissed her lips gently. "I hate that I have to leave, but I'll be late if I don't go now. Will you be okay by yourself today?"

Libbie nodded. "I'll be fine. I'll probably just sleep a while."

"Okay. You get some rest and I'll see you tonight." He kissed her again and headed out to his truck.

The morning breeze off the lake was chilly, reminding Jack that winter was around the corner. As he drove to work, he wondered how much wine Libbie had really drunk. He knew she'd had more than one glass—she'd been out cold last night. But why would she lie? He decided that it wasn't a big deal. He couldn't blame Libbie for wanting to relax after the nasty way Abigail talked to her. By the time he was elbow deep into a car engine, he'd forgotten all about it.

Chapter Sixteen

For the next two weeks, Libbie tried to forget her mother's harsh words, but it was difficult. Libbie had always been the good child, the perfect student, the shining star of the family. Being told she was a failure in her mother's eyes had devastated her.

Making matters worse, winter seemed to be in a rush to hit the north woods. Nights were extremely cold, and the wind off the lake was bitter. Jack started a fire in the woodstove every night to ward off the chill, but Libbie felt cold in bed anyway. She began to dread winter for the first time in her life. Thinking of being stuck there at the cottage almost every day alone depressed her. Carol was busy with school, and so were the girls next door. She could always go visit Bev at the farm, but as soon as the temperatures dipped below freezing, she'd have to stay and keep the fire going at the cottage. She had loved the cottage in the summer, but now she wished they lived in a regular house with a heating system.

The last week in October, Libbie was standing at the stove, stirring rice in a pan for supper. It was five fifteen, and she had a chicken cooking in the oven. She'd make gravy for the rice as soon as Jack came home. The phone rang, startling her, and she ran to pick it up.

"Hello?"

"Hey, hon. I'm sorry, but I need to stay late at work."

Libbie frowned. Jack had never stayed late at work before. "Why?"

"A man's car broke down late this afternoon, and he needs it fixed before tomorrow morning. The boss asked if I would stay late and finish up the job. It will probably be two more hours. The good news is I'll get overtime pay."

"What about dinner?" Libbie asked. "I have it cooking right now."

"I'm so sorry, Libs. Why don't you ask the girls next door to come over for dinner? I'd hate to see it wasted."

Libbie thought about that a moment, then smiled. That might be fun. "Okay. I'll save you a plate of food, too."

"Thanks for understanding, hon. See you in a while."

Libbie hung up and quickly stirred the rice again, then turned down the burner's flame. She went out on the porch. It was icy cold outside, but luckily, no snow had fallen yet. She figured that by the first week in November they'd have snow for sure.

She glanced over to the girls' cottage and saw both cars. Running over there, she knocked on their door. Jackie answered.

"Hey, Libbie. Great to see you. What's up?" Jackie asked.

"Hi, Jackie. I have a whole chicken in the oven and rice cooking, and I'm making gravy, too. Jack just called and said he'd be late and miss dinner. Would you both like to come over and eat with me?"

"Would we?" Candy said, coming to the door. "Are you kidding? Lead the way."

The girls followed Libbie back to her cottage, a bottle of wine and one of 7 Up in hand, and they all had wine spritzers while Libbie finished making supper. Libbie had already drunk half a glass of wine earlier, so the second glass made her feel silly and light-headed.

She took out the chicken and made the gravy, then placed it all on the small table.

"Wow!" Jackie said, watching as Libbie served the food. "How do you know how to cook so well?"

"Jack's mom taught me. When I was growing up, our house-keeper made all our dinners, so I never learned to cook until I started hanging out at the farm with Jack."

"Housekeeper, huh?" Jackie said. "I figured you must have been a rich girl from the car you drive, but you must have been really rich if your family had a housekeeper."

Libbie shrugged as she passed out the plates. "I never thought about it. It's just the way we lived."

They all sat down and served themselves. Candy had already refilled their wine glasses, using the last of the wine and Seven-Up.

"Oh, Libbie. This is delicious," Candy said. "You can cook for us anytime you want."

Jackie agreed. "This is amazing. Thanks so much for inviting us. We haven't eaten this good in weeks."

The girls talked about school, their part-time jobs, and the boys they'd dated since school started. "You're so lucky to have Jack," Candy said between mouthfuls of food. "He's so nice, and a hard worker. All I meet are guys that think they'll get sex if they buy me a burger and fries. Can you imagine? It may be the swinging seventies, but that doesn't mean I'll give it up for a burger."

Jackie giggled and Libbie followed suit.

"How did you and Jack meet?" Jackie asked.

Libbie told them her story as they finished eating and emptied their glasses. She felt warm all over, and everything that was said made her giggle uncontrollably. If one of the other girls giggled, she'd start, too.

On slightly wobbly legs, Libbie cleared the table and the girls helped her. She rinsed the plates and stacked them. Her heart was racing wildly and she felt like she had enough energy to run a mile. She liked how happy and energized she felt and she didn't want it to end.

"We're all out of wine," Candy said, tossing the empty bottle in the garbage. "And there's no more at home, either."

"Let's go get some more," Libbie suggested quickly. "I'll buy it since I drank yours. The liquor store doesn't close until eight."

The girls were more than willing to go. "Can we take your car?" Jackie asked hopefully. "I've been dying to ride in it."

"Sure." Libbie grabbed a coat, her wallet, and keys. They all piled into the car, with Jackie in the front seat and Candy in the back.

The three talked and giggled on the ride into town and no one noticed Libbie swerving slightly as she drove. She parked at the liquor store and gave Candy some money.

"Can you get two bottles?"

"Sure can," Candy said. She and Jackie went in and bought the two bottles of wine using their fake IDs. They picked up a six-pack of 7 Up, too. They were out in a flash and Libbie drove the dark streets home.

"I'll bet this car can go really fast," Jackie said. "Like a race car."

"Sure it can," Libbie said. They were on the dark lake road now. They'd passed her parents' house already but weren't at the resort yet. "Want to see how fast it can go?" she asked, and then stepped down on the accelerator.

The girls whooped and hollered in delight as Libbie took first one curve and then another. Libbie squealed along with them. She'd never done anything like this in her life, and her heart raced with excitement.

Just as she hit the third curve, a deer ran out onto the road in front her. Libbie swerved to the right, and her car careened off the road. The last thing Libbie heard was Jackie screaming before everything went black.

* * *

Jack drove along the lake road a little past eight thirty. Fixing the car had taken much longer than he'd anticipated, but it had given him three hours of overtime pay, so it was worth it. He was putting a little money away each check to buy Libbie an extra-special Christmas present. She deserved it. He knew that her life had changed drastically since marrying him and that things weren't always easy, yet she never complained. And she'd also been giving him the majority of her checks from the library so he could add it to their savings for a house. He knew he was lucky to have Libbie in his life, and he wanted to show her on their first Christmas how much he appreciated all she did.

As Jack rounded the last curve before the resort, he saw the glint of a car's taillight on the side of the road in someone's yard. Suddenly, two girls came running out onto the road in front of him, and he had to swerve and stomp on his breaks to miss hitting them.

"Jack! Jack! It's Libbie. Hurry!" The girl with dark hair yelled as he rolled down his window. He suddenly realized that these were the neighbor girls. He looked ahead to where the car was and could see in the beams of his headlights that it was a Mustang, slammed into a thick tree trunk.

"Libbie," he gasped, as he realized what he was seeing.

He grabbed a flashlight from the glove compartment and jumped out of his truck, running to the Mustang's driver's side. The girls were next to him, crying. "She's stuck behind the wheel and she won't wake up," the dark-haired girl said. Jack didn't know if she was Jackie or Candy. He'd never spent enough time around them to remember who was who.

Jack ran around the back of the car and crawled into the passenger seat, and that was when he realized how badly crushed the Mustang was. The hood was smashed up like an accordion, almost all the way to the front seat. The driver's side had taken the brunt of the hit, and Libbie was pinned behind the steering wheel, her head against the back of the seat. There was only enough room for him to squeeze in beside her with the passenger seat pushed all the way back. The window had shattered and glass was everywhere.

Jack turned his flashlight on Libbie. There were cuts on her face, and a huge bump was already swelling up on her forehead. "Libbie?" he said softly. "Libbie? Wake up, sweetie. Please wake up." Tears filled his eyes. He held his breath and strained to hear her breathe. He was relieved when he finally heard her softly inhaling.

"What's going on out here?" An older man wearing a robe over pajamas came out of his house with a flashlight in hand. He walked up near the car, his face suddenly appearing shocked at the scene before him.

Jack pulled himself out of the car. "Call an ambulance!" he said. "My wife is hurt. She's stuck in the car."

The old man didn't even question Jack. He turned and ran

back to his house.

The girls were still standing out by the car, crying softly. Jack turned to them. "Are you two okay?"

The blond girl nodded. "We're fine. We just want Libbie to wake up."

The cold night air seeped through Jack, making him shiver. "Can one of you get the blanket from under my truck seat?" he asked quickly. "And then you two should go inside the truck and sit. It's warm in there."

The dark-haired girl nodded, and they both ran to the truck. She brought back the blanket and handed it to Jack. "I'm so sorry, Jack. I really am. We never meant for this to happen."

Jack just stared at her, unable to process anything other than the fact that Libbie was hurt. "Go back to the truck. It's freezing out here."

She ran off, and Jack squeezed his way back into the car. He tried placing the blanket around Libbie as best as he could. She was pinned in so tight he couldn't get it around her very well.

"Libbie, please wake up," Jack said, his voice cracking. He carefully picked away the glass from her hair and clothes. "I love you so much, Libbie. Please, please wake up," Jack whispered.

Libbie's eyelids fluttered, and she rolled her head in Jack's direction. "Jack?" she asked softly.

"Libbie. Oh, Libbie. Are you okay?" Jack asked.

"My arm hurts," Libbie said, before closing her eyes again.

Jack ran the flashlight over her but couldn't see much of her arm. It was tucked tightly to her body, pinned under the steering wheel. "An ambulance is coming," Jack told her. "It'll be here soon."

The elderly man came back out and checked on Jack, saying the ambulance was on its way. He'd brought out blankets for the girls and took them over to the truck. All Jack could do was sit there beside Libbie and wait.

Finally, the ambulance came along with a police car and a fire and rescue vehicle. After examining the situation, the responders were able to push Libbie's seat back far enough to lift her out of the car and onto a stretcher.

Jack stood by nervously. "Please be careful. She said her arm hurt."

The girls came out of the truck and an EMT checked them over, too. Other than a few cuts and bruises, they were fine, and neither wanted to go to the hospital. A police officer offered to drive the girls home in Jack's truck so Jack could ride in the ambulance with Libbie.

Jack answered the EMT's questions as the ambulance buzzed into town to the hospital. Yes, she'd woken up for a few seconds. She'd said her arm hurt but didn't say which one. No, he hadn't been in the car during the accident.

Once at the hospital, Jack was held back to fill out forms while they wheeled Libbie into Emergency. When he was finished, they still wouldn't let him go back with Libbie. The receptionist told him to wait until a nurse or doctor came out to talk to him.

He paced the hard linoleum floor of the waiting room for over an hour. The lights were harsh and glaring, and it smelled of antiseptic. He couldn't understand why he wasn't allowed to be with Libbie. He was her husband, for God's sake. He should be back there. Finally, a woman in a white uniform and cap came out and walked over to him.

"Are you Mr. Prentice?" she asked.

Jack nodded. "Yes. How is my wife?"

"She's fine. She has a broken wrist and a large bump on her

head, but there is no sign of concussion. The orthopedic special-
ist will be in tomorrow to set and cast her wrist," the nurse said.
"For now, we're moving her to a room for the night."

"I want to see her," Jack said.

The nurse shook her head. "She's sound asleep. The doctor
gave her a sedative to calm her down. She was pretty shaken up.
You should go home and get some sleep and come back in the
morning."

Jack could only imagine how terrified Libbie had been,
waking up in a hospital without anyone she knew with her. It
broke his heart just thinking about it. "I need to see her," he
insisted. "I need to see for myself that she's all right."

"You can see her in the morning," the nurse repeated. "Believe
me, she'll sleep through the night." With that, the nurse walked
away, back through the emergency room doors.

Jack walked through the halls of the hospital until he found
the waiting room and the night receptionist desk. He told her
who he was and to let him know if anything changed with
Libbie. Then he walked over to a corner of the room where it was
darker and sat in one of the hard chairs. He'd wait all night until
he could see Libbie.

Chapter Seventeen

Jack awoke early the next morning when the sunlight streamed in over him through the big plate-glass window. He was scrunched down in the chair, and someone had draped a light blanket over him during the night.

He sat up, feeling the strain in his back muscles from lying in the chair all night. Running his fingers through his hair, he hurried up the stairs to the second floor and found Libbie's room. She was sitting up in bed with a tray of food in front of her on a table. There was a cast on her arm and small cuts on her face that were already scabbed over. She looked up at him sorrowfully.

Jack ran over to Libbie and carefully wrapped his arms around her. He kissed her cheeks and gently wiped her tears. "Oh, Libbie. I was so scared. I'm glad you're okay."

"Where were you?" Libbie said groggily through her tears. "I kept asking for you last night but they wouldn't bring you to me."

Jack pulled back and looked into her eyes. He could tell she was still drugged. "I was here all night. I slept in the waiting room."

"Oh, Jack. I'm so sorry. I don't even know what happened. I was driving with the girls in the car, and then I woke up with the doctor and nurses around me. No one will tell me what happened. Are Jackie and Candy okay?"

"Yes, they're fine. An officer drove them home in my truck. I'm sure they'll be by today to check on you. They were very upset last night. But right now, all I'm worried about is you. How do you feel?"

"I have a terrible headache, and my wrist hurts. They're giving me medicine for it, but I'm still in pain. They woke me up early this morning and the doctor set my wrist and put the cast on. He said it has to be on for at least six weeks." Tears welled in Libbie's eyes. "I feel so terrible, and stupid. We were just having fun last night, and then this happened."

"Shh, shh," Jack said soothingly, wrapping her in his arms. "All that matters is you're alive. You don't know how scared I was last night when I saw your car. I love you so much, Libbie.

Jack sat on the bed beside her and held her until her tears finally stopped. A nurse came in and took the food tray away and smiled reassuringly at him. Libbie fell asleep in his arms, and he gently laid her back against her pillows and carefully moved off her bed. He decided this would be a good time to call her parents, so he walked across the room and was almost to the door when it flew open and Randall and Abigail came storming in.

"Where's my daughter?" Abigail screeched, glaring at Jack. "Why didn't you call us? I had to learn from a neighbor that my daughter was in the hospital."

"I was just going to call you," Jack said, but a soft cry from Libbie made them all turn toward her.

Libbie sat up in bed, staring at her parents, a hazy look in her eyes.

"Libbie. My baby. What happened to you?" Abigail wailed, rushing to her side. "Look at you. My poor, poor girl."

Randall followed her to Libbie's bedside while Jack stood across the room, dazed. He watched as Abigail fussed and Libbie began to cry again. Anger welled up inside him. Abigail wasn't comforting Libbie, she was agitating her.

"How are you, dear?" Randall said, his voice soothing.

"I feel terrible," Libbie said, tears falling down her cheeks. "My head hurts so bad and my wrist hurts. And I wrecked my beautiful car, Daddy. I'm so sorry."

"Now, now, sweetie. You don't have to worry about that. We can replace your car. Let's just worry about getting you well again."

"We need to get you in a private room," Abigail said sharply. "And I want to talk to the doctor immediately. You shouldn't be in any pain." She pushed the buzzer for the nurse. Jack stood there, dumbfounded, as he watched Abigail order the nurse around and insist Libbie be moved and that the doctor be called in right away.

"Mom, please don't make a fuss," Libbie said in a small voice.

"My daughter deserves the best of everything," Abigail insisted, turning to stare at Jack. "How could you have let this happen? Where were you last night that you couldn't drive our little girl to town? Out sitting in a bar somewhere, no doubt."

Jack's mouth dropped open. What was wrong with this woman? How could she be so nasty at a time like this? "I was working late. I was on my way home when I found her."

"Work? I'll bet you were. You should have been home with our daughter. What kind of a husband leaves his wife all alone to fend for herself?"

"Mom, it wasn't Jack's fault," Libbie said, but her words

sounded weak. Jack could see that all the tension in the room was wearing on her.

"We should leave her alone and let her rest," Jack said.

"Not until I speak with the doctor," Abigail shrieked. "You leave. I can take care of my daughter."

Jack had never talked back to a parent in his life, but he was just about to tell her to leave when the doctor came into the room and Abigail's wrath was turned on him instead. Jack took a deep breath and walked over to hold Libbie's hand. By now she was crying uncontrollably, and he couldn't get her to settle down.

A nurse came in and, on the doctor's orders, gave Libbie a sedative. Everyone was told to leave the room, but not without first promising that Libbie would be moved to a private room. Once in the hall, Abigail turned on Jack again.

"The next time something happens to my daughter, you'd better call me immediately. Do you understand?" She turned on her heel and walked down the hallway.

Randall placed a hand on Jack's shoulder. "She's just upset, son. Don't let it get to you. And don't worry about the hospital bills. We'll take care of it." He gave a small smile and then headed in the direction his wife had gone.

Jack dropped into a chair in the hallway, completely drained by all that had just happened.

* * *

That evening Jack reluctantly left the hospital when visiting hours were over. He'd called Larry to come and drive him home, and then promised Libbie he'd be there first thing in the morning. She'd been given some strong pain medication by then and was drowsy. When Larry popped in to say hi, Jack wasn't even sure Libbie knew he was there.

Jack sighed as he climbed into Larry's car. It had been a long, emotional day. After Libbie had been settled into a private room, her mother finally left with the promise she'd be back again the next day. Jack had been relieved to see her go. She'd done nothing but upset Libbie the entire time she was there. Then Jackie and Candy dropped by and brought Libbie flowers and a stuffed kitty. As they left, they took Jack aside and apologized profusely for the accident.

"I should never have asked Libbie to drive last night," Jackie told him. "I just wanted to ride in her pretty car, and now look what happened." Tears filled her eyes. "She shouldn't have been driving."

Jack assured her it hadn't been her fault, but he wondered what she'd meant by "she shouldn't have been driving."

Carol dropped in and brought flowers. Gwen came by and wasn't any nicer than Abigail had been. Jack was happy to see her go. Mrs. Thompson popped in after the library closed and also brought flowers. She assured Libbie her job would be waiting for her as soon as she was feeling better. Even the older couple whose tree Libbie had hit stopped by for a few minutes to check on her. Jack thanked them profusely for their help the night before and apologized for any harm to their property. The older man had waved his apology aside.

"That's a bad corner," he said. "I'm surprised there aren't more accidents."

When Bev, Jan, and Ray stopped by after school, it was a welcome relief to Jack. Bev's warm presence was the opposite of Abigail's harsh one, and she had Libbie smiling in no time. Jan had brought her some sweet-smelling bubble bath for when she went home, and Ray gave her a little plastic pumpkin full of candy.

"I didn't want you to miss Halloween," he said with a crooked grin.

Libbie had seemed calmer after their visit.

Now, as Jack sat in Larry's car, he felt the weight of the past twenty-four hours hit him.

"I went to the junkyard and saw the Mustang," Larry said. He whistled softly. "Man, Libbie is lucky to be alive. I'm surprised they could get her out of there, it was so smashed up."

Jack nodded. "I know. It was pretty scary."

"They gave me her personal items from the car. The guy at the yard knows we're friends. It's not much, just her wallet and a few other things."

"Thanks, Lar. I hadn't even thought about that."

"No problem. I stopped by the accident scene, too, just to make sure nothing was left behind. Did Libbie tell you why they had driven to town that night?" Larry asked.

Jack turned and looked at him curiously. "No. But Jackie said something strange today. She said she shouldn't have let Libbie drive. Why? Do you know something?"

Larry glanced at Jack. "I found a couple of broken bottles of wine and a few of 7 Up. I'm assuming they'd been drinking and then went to town to get more."

Jack sat quiet. He'd wondered about that earlier, but hadn't wanted to believe it. "So you think Libbie was drunk?"

Larry shrugged. "That's my guess, but you should get the story from her. I'm surprised the cops didn't pick up on it. In fact, I'm surprised they didn't search the area and find the bottles first."

"It's amazing what the police around here will overlook when you're a Wilkens," Jack said, hating to say it but knowing it was true.

They pulled up in front of the cottage and Larry let the car idle. "Winter is almost here. It's already too cold for me."

Jack looked over at his friend. "Have you decided what you're going to do about the draft?"

Larry nodded. "I'm just going to enlist and take my chances. There's a waiting list for all the good spots, and I can't get a deferment and stay in college. I guess I'm exactly what Uncle Sam wants and he's going to make sure he gets me."

"I'm sorry, Larry. When are you going?"

"I'm not going to wait for my letter. As soon as winter quarter is over, I'm going to enlist. That will give me until after Christmas before I'll have to leave."

"That soon?" Jack said, stunned.

"I just want to get it over with."

Jack felt guilty that he wasn't being drafted like so many other men his age. But then, he had Libbie to take care of, and he didn't want to leave her, either.

"Let's not say anything about it to Libbie yet, okay?" Jack said. "You know how much it upsets her."

Larry nodded. "Yep, no bad news for Libbie. We all know how fragile she is."

Jack frowned at Larry. "What's that supposed to mean?"

Larry shook his head. "Nothing, man. Sorry. I didn't mean it that way. Libbie's sensitive. She just upsets easily."

"She's had a lot to deal with lately, you know that. Libbie's a strong, confident girl. She's always been strong. You remember how she was in high school," Jack said, irritated.

"Yeah, Jack. I do remember how she was in high school. But she's changed a lot over the past two years. She's just not the same as she was back then. But you're right—she's had a lot to deal with."

"I thought you liked Libbie," Jack said.

"I do. I love Libbie. She's amazing. Hey, man, don't even listen to me rattle on. I have a lot on my mind. Of course, I won't mention Nam or the draft to Libbie. I don't want to upset her. She needs all her strength to heal after that terrible accident."

Jack opened the car door and stepped outside into the brisk night air. "I didn't mean to jump on you, Lar. Come by and see me again soon, okay?"

Larry handed Jack the plastic bag with Libbie's belongings in it. "Will do," he said, grinning. Then he drove off into the night.

As Jack started a fire in the woodstove, he thought about his conversation with Larry. He had to admit that Larry was right—Libbie had become fragile. He thought about her drinking and her neediness. She cried easily and continued to worry about the draft, even though he'd assured her there was little chance he'd be called to serve. He'd marked her behavior down to the changes in her life over the past few months, but he could no longer ignore it—Libbie was not the same girl he'd proposed to. The Libbie he'd known in high school had been independent, strong, and confident. She'd lost that strength and confidence somewhere along the line, and Jack didn't understand why. Wasn't she happy being married to him? Was she sorry she hadn't married someone with money who could give her more than he could?

Jack glanced around the cottage. It wasn't much, and it wasn't theirs. It had been the perfect place for a newly married couple—cozy and romantic—but with winter coming, it was just small and cold.

"I'll try to make things easier for Libbie," he said to the

empty room. He'd buy an electric heater for the bedroom so it wasn't so cold at night and fill the fridge with groceries so she wouldn't have to worry about that for a while. He'd try harder to make Libbie happy. She deserved better, and he'd try his best to give her everything she needed.

Chapter Eighteen

The first snow of the season fell on the day Libbie came home. The hospital had kept her an additional day because she'd complained her head still ached and they wanted to be sure it wasn't serious. The doctor sent her home with pain pills for her wrist and headaches. He didn't know she was already taking Valium, and she hadn't told him, either. The pain pills made her feel tired yet so agitated that she couldn't sleep. She hoped the Valium would help her sleep better.

After making sure Libbie was comfortable on the sofa, Jack carried in all the beautiful flowers and gifts people had brought her. The cottage was clean and warm with the fire crackling cheerfully in the woodstove. But Libbie didn't feel cheerful, despite the lovely flower bouquets set around the living room.

Jack came over beside her and kissed her softly on the cheek. "Are you feeling okay? Do you want to go lie in bed for a while?" he asked, wrapping his arm around her.

Libbie gave him a weak smile. Jack had been so attentive to her needs, and she was so thankful to have him in her life. She couldn't imagine anyone else loving her as much as Jack did. "I would go in the bedroom, but it's warmer out here," she told him. Truth be told, she really just wanted to slip on warm pajamas and crawl into bed. She felt like she could sleep for a week.

Jack smiled widely. "I bought an electric heater for the bedroom so you'd be warm. And an electric blanket, too."

"Really? That was so sweet of you. Then I'll go to bed. I'm really tired."

Jack helped her into the bedroom and got her flannel pj's from the dresser. "Do you need help changing?"

Libbie laughed. "I'm not an invalid."

"I know. But you look worn out."

"I'll be fine, silly."

"Okay. Do you want something to eat? My mom brought food that I can heat up."

Libbie shook her head. "I think I'll just sleep right now. Can I have some water, though?"

"Sure. I'll get you a glass." Jack left and returned with a glass full of water and ice cubes. "Let me know if you need anything else," he said before leaving.

Libbie changed into her pajamas. She pulled the bottle of pain pills out of the suitcase Jack had brought to the hospital. Then she went to her lingerie drawer and pulled out her Valium. She took one and hid the bottle away again. Then she swallowed a pain pill, too. Slipping under the warm electric blanket, she hugged the striped stuffed kitty that the girls had given her and waited for the sweet release of sleep.

* * *

The next two weeks dragged by for Libbie as the snow continued to pile up outside and the cold wind blew through the cracks in the old cottage. Jack had stayed home that first Monday to help Libbie, but after missing two days of work, he reluctantly went back on Tuesday. Libbie tried going back to her normal routine around the cottage, but it was much harder to clean and cook—or even heat up food—with the cast on her arm. She still had a headache, and the lump on her forehead throbbed when she stood for too long. She'd take a pain pill for her headache but they made her heart race, so she'd take a Valium, too. Then she'd have to lie down because she became drowsy. She tried watching television, but she'd soon doze off, and before she knew it Jack was home. Most nights, he'd heat up food for dinner because Libbie was too tired to do it. Jack told her often that he didn't mind, he just wanted her to rest and get better, but she still felt guilty. She should be taking care of him after a long day of work, not the other way around.

At Libbie's mother's insistence, Sandra came to the cottage twice a week to clean since it was difficult for Libbie to do much with the cast. Sandra also took their dirty clothes to the Wilkenses' house to wash and then dropped them back off at the cottage. Because Sandra was doing the majority of the work, it meant Libbie had even more time to dwell on her boredom and growing restlessness. Other than Sandra and sometimes Bev, who continued to bring meals that could be heated up, no one came to the cottage. Carol was busy with school, as were Candy and Jackie. Libbie wondered if the girls were avoiding her because of the accident. Nothing had ever been said to her about the fact that there had been wine in the car when they crashed. Maybe the girls were afraid they'd get into trouble for underage drinking and having fake IDs. Libbie didn't mention anything to Jack about that night, either. He'd be so disappointed in her if he knew the truth, and it would make her feel even worse than she already did.

Three weeks after the accident, Libbie's father surprised her by driving up in a brand new 1970 Mustang. Libbie had been napping when she heard the knock on the door. She'd woken up slowly and opened it, and her eyes grew wide when she saw the blue convertible sports car sitting there, sparkling in the winter sun.

"Surprise, kitten!" her father said, a big smile on his face. Gwen had followed him in his car to drive him back to the office. She walked over to stand on the front porch, without even a trace of a smile on her face.

"Daddy! Thank you," Libbie squealed, wide-awake now. She reached up, hugged him, and he kissed her tenderly on the cheek.

"I hope you like the color. It was this or a black one, and I thought the blue would match your eyes," Randall told her, obviously pleased by her joyful response.

"I love it," Libbie told him.

"You should," Gwen grumbled. "Not everyone gets a brand new car handed to them—twice."

Libbie glanced at Gwen but ignored her comment. It wasn't Libbie's fault Gwen had two children and drove a station wagon. She went inside, grabbed her coat and slipped on her boots, then ran out and slid into the driver's seat. The interior was black and it had a stick shift like her other one, which she liked, and there was even a cassette tape player, too.

"How does it feel?" Randall asked, coming to stand beside the car.

"It's perfect, Daddy," Libbie said, grinning up at him. "I can't wait to get out of this cast so I can drive it."

"Oh, I'm sure you'll be able to drive it sooner," he told her. "Just be careful this one doesn't wrap itself around a tree." He winked at her.

"I'll be careful, I promise. Wait until Jack sees it. He'll be surprised."

Jack was surprised that evening when he got home and saw the brand new Mustang parked beside the cottage.

"I see your father bought you a new car," he said as he stepped inside. Libbie had been so excited about the new car that her spirits were high and she hadn't taken her afternoon pain pill. She was carefully placing a casserole dish in the oven, and there were cut carrots waiting to boil on the stove.

"Isn't it beautiful?" she asked cheerfully. "I can't wait to drive it."

Jack smiled. He walked into the kitchen and pulled her into his arms, kissing her softly. "You must be feeling better. You look happy."

Libbie giggled. "I am. I've been moping around in this cottage for three weeks now. I think it's time I get busy again. I want to go back to work next week. Do you think I could drive the car even with this cast on?"

"I suppose, as long as your arm feels fine. You know next week is Thanksgiving, right?"

Libbie stopped and thought a moment. "I forgot all about that. But the library will still be open Monday and Wednesday. I really want to go back to work. It's depressing sitting around here all day with nothing to do except watch it snow and put wood on the fire."

"Then you should go back to work," Jack told her. "Whatever makes you happy makes me happy."

Libbie hugged Jack tight. "You've been so good to me these past few weeks. I'm lucky to have you, Jack. I love you so much."

"I love you, too, Libbie." He grinned mischievously. "You know, there is a way you can thank me for being so nice."

Libbie saw the teasing look in his eyes and laughed. "Let's at least eat dinner first," she told him. "Then we'll see about that."

* * *

Libbie called Mrs. Thompson the next day to ask if she could return to work on Monday.

"Of course you can, dear," she told her. "We can't wait for you to come back."

On Monday morning, Libbie dressed in a warm sweater dress with a matching coat and knee-length boots and got behind the wheel of her new car. She drove carefully, and much slower than she would normally drive. The roads were plowed and clear and the sun was out, but she felt nervous driving the curvy lake road for the first time in weeks. It was awkward, shifting with her cast on, too, but she managed.

Everyone at the library was happy to see her, and Libbie felt good being back at work again. But as the day wore on, she found herself growing tired and agitated. She hadn't taken a pain pill that morning, or her Valium, and now she wished she had. Her hands shook as she tried to stamp books or put them away on the shelves. Many people who came in asked her about the accident and that made her nervous, too. She didn't want to talk about it, but it was difficult avoiding their questions without appearing rude.

By the end of the day, she was worn out both physically and mentally. Mrs. Thompson noticed how tired she looked.

"If you only want to work half days for a while, that would be fine," she offered. "I know it's difficult for you to work with that cast on. But you'll be getting it off soon, won't you?"

Libbie nodded. She only had to wear it two more weeks. "I'll try to work all day on Wednesday and see how it goes," she told Mrs. Thompson.

When she got home, the fire had gone out and it was cold in the cottage. She turned on the oven, hoping it would heat up the room a little while she fumbled around, trying to start a fire. She was so tired; all she wanted to do was lie down. After she finally got a fire started, she took a pain pill and dozed off.

* * *

They spent Thanksgiving afternoon at her parents' house. Jack had both Thursday and Friday off, so they were going to spend the next day at the farm. Working both days that week had left Libbie feeling tired. With Gwen's two little girls running around and Walter talking on and on, Libbie's nerves were frayed. She asked her dad to pour her half a glass of wine.

Jack glanced at her, one eyebrow cocked. "Should you have that with the pain pills you've been taking?"

"It's just a little wine," she snapped, and then immediately regretted it. "I didn't take a pill today," she said more gently, although it was a lie. She'd taken both the pain pill and a Valium, but it hadn't been enough to get through today.

"Here you go, kitten," Randall said, handing her a glass. "Not too much, though. It can hit pretty quickly."

After the glass of wine, Libbie felt calmer.

* * *

At work the next week, things hadn't become any easier. Libbie had taken her pills before going, and soon she felt drowsy and lightheaded. She did her best to focus on what she was doing, but it was hard. Libbie didn't understand why she wasn't feeling better after all this time. Without the pills, she was jittery and her head ached. With them, she couldn't focus and all she wanted to do was sleep. She was so frustrated by the middle of the day that she finally had to tell Mrs. Thompson she needed to go home and rest.

"Go ahead, dear. We have enough volunteers to help."

When Libbie got home, the fire had already gone out and the cottage was cold. Starting the fire all over again took time, and she was exhausted. She shoved paper under the wood, but no matter how much paper she used, the wood wouldn't burn on its own. It was cold, she was tired, and her pills were wearing off. Frustrated, she picked up a piece of starter wood and threw it across the room. It hit the windowsill where she'd lined up the pretty vases from all the flowers she'd received at the hospital. One vase fell to the floor and crashed into pieces.

Tears filled Libbie's eyes. "I hate this place!" she yelled into the empty room. She grabbed the pain pills off the kitchen counter and took two pills out of the bottle, swallowing both with a glass of water. She turned on the electric heater in the bedroom and also the electric blanket and without even changing out of her dress, she crawled into bed and squeezed her eyes shut, waiting for the pills to take effect and lull her to sleep.

* * *

Jack came home and immediately noticed how icy cold the room was. He flipped on the lights and looked around. A small piece of wood was lying on the kitchen floor next to a pile of broken glass. He frowned. Where was Libbie?

Jack walked to the bedroom and peered inside. The room

was dark, but he saw that Libbie was tucked into the bed and the heater was running. Still, it was cold in here.

"Libbie?" he said softly. "Libbie? Are you okay?" When there was no answer, he grew worried. He walked closer to the bed and bent down to look at her. She was sound asleep, so he walked back out into the living room to start a fire.

Two hours later, Libbie still hadn't woken up. Jack was worried. Her breathing seemed normal, but why was she still sleeping? The living room was toasty warm, and he'd heated up some food for himself. While he'd waited for the food to heat, he'd noticed the bottle of pain pills on the counter and picked them up. Peering into the bottle, he saw that there were only two left. He looked at the date on the bottle. It read November 20. That meant she'd had them refilled since the hospital had given her a bottle of pills on the first. Why? Was she still in that much pain?

He went into the bedroom again and leaned over her, brushing her hair back with his fingertips. "Libbie? Are you awake? Libs?"

She stirred and then gazed up at him. "Jack?"

"Yeah, sweetie. I heated up some food. Do you want to eat?"

Libbie sighed. "No, just let me sleep." Then she closed her eyes again.

Jack gave up. He washed the dishes, put more wood on the fire, and then crawled into bed next to Libbie's sleeping form. "Goodnight, hon," he said, kissing her on the forehead. "Feel better soon."

He really hoped she would.

Chapter Nineteen

December came, but Libbie continued to feel strange. Their first Christmas together wasn't the joyful time it should have been. Even though her cast had been taken off, Libbie's wrist still ached, and she constantly had headaches. The doctor gave her one more refill for pain pills and then suggested taking aspirin after that. But for Libbie, the aspirin wasn't enough. Once again, she began taking Valium twice a day, and most afternoons and evenings she drank wine to ease her pain. She felt calm and mellow from the wine and Valium, but then she'd also feel tired and her head was fuzzy.

She found that despite being underage, she could go into the liquor store and buy wine if she asked the owner to put it on her parents' account. The owner never questioned it, she was a Wilkens, after all, and her parents paid the bills and never asked her about it either. She hid the wine from Jack. She didn't want him questioning her about it or worrying that she might get into an accident again. She felt guilty about hiding it, but decided it was for the best.

They decorated the little cottage with a blue spruce tree and garland all around, and although they'd had fun trimming the tree together, Libbie just couldn't get into the holiday spirit. They spent Christmas Eve with Libbie's family, and then Christmas Day they went out to the farm for a big, old-fashioned holiday meal. Libbie had enjoyed the warmth of the family Christmas at the farm much more than the stuffy atmosphere at her own parents' house. Jack's parents gave down-to-earth gifts from the heart. His father made a jewelry box just for her like the ones she'd seen in his shop, except hers was bigger, with a removable compartment inside. It had a carved rose on top and was stained a light oak color. Libbie loved the gift more than if it had been bought in a store.

"And here's something to put in it," Jack said, smiling warmly at her.

Libbie opened the small gift box. Inside a velvet box was a lovely blue topaz ring set in yellow gold. "Oh, Jack. It's so beautiful!" Libbie squealed, quickly slipping it on her right hand.

"It reminded me of your eyes," he told her.

Libbie's heart swelled with love for Jack. His gift was so sweet, and he was so good to her. She wished she felt better, but it seemed out of her control. She tried her hardest to act happy for Jack's sake, but her heart wasn't in it.

* * *

On New Year's Eve, Carol and Larry came over for a quiet celebration. Even though the two weren't dating anymore, they still got along well, and the four always had a good time. Larry brought vodka and a bottle of champagne, and Carol brought wine. All evening, Libbie felt Jack's eyes on her every time she took a drink of wine, and it annoyed her. She knew he was just worried about her, but she didn't want him counting every sip. By midnight, she'd drunk too much despite Jack's warning glances, and she fell asleep soon afterward. Their first New Year's Eve as a married couple should have been sweet and romantic, but she ruined it by drinking too much and, again, she felt guilty.

Libbie felt as if a dark cloud was casting shadows over her and she couldn't shake it off. The cold weather bothered her more than it ever had before, mostly because she felt lonely during the day and grew weary of keeping the fire going. Cooking dinner and doing laundry grew tedious and tiresome. And even her job at the library was getting on her nerves. She didn't know why, and she didn't know how to dig her way out of the unhappy state she was in. Worst of all, Jack was always so sweet and understanding, even after working hard all day, yet she'd find herself snapping at him unprovoked. Then she'd break down into tears for having been so cruel.

One night in mid-January, Libbie yelled at Jack when he came home and found her asleep on the sofa—again. He'd only suggested they go out for a bite to eat since she was so tired, and she started complaining about all she had to do around the cottage.

"I know you think I don't do anything around here all day but sleep, but I do! Keeping that damned fire going, cleaning, and laundry doesn't do itself, you know," she yelled, her heart pounding furiously. "All I do is work! I never have any fun anymore."

"I know you do a lot around here, Libbie," Jack said soothingly, although his expression had been one of confusion at her sudden outburst. "I only suggested we go grab a burger so you wouldn't have to cook dinner. I don't mind going out."

Libbie dissolved into tears then, hating the way she constantly felt and the way she spoke to Jack. "I sound like a bitch," she said, weeping. "How can you stand to live with me? I'm always unhappy and complaining, and I don't even know why."

Jack sat beside her on the sofa and wrapped her into his arms. "Don't cry, Libbie. I understand. I know you have so much to do around here, plus your work at the library. And winter has been hard for you. And then there was the accident. I'm sure you're still healing from that. Please don't cry, sweetie."

Libbie looked up at him with swollen eyes. "I feel so sad all the time. And then I get so angry, I feel like I'm going to blow. I've never felt this way before. I thought we'd be so happy once we were married, and I was, but now I just keep ruining everything with my moods."

Jack tenderly brushed his fingers through her hair, sweeping it away from her face and behind her ear. "Is it me, Libs? Do I make you angry and unhappy? Tell me what I'm doing wrong or what I can do to make things better. I'll do anything to make you happy."

Libbie's heart swelled at the troubled look on Jack's handsome face. "No, it's not you," she said softly. "You do everything right. I love you so much. It's just me, and I don't know why I'm feeling this way. I want to be happy. I don't understand why I can't control my emotions anymore."

"Maybe you should talk to the doctor," Jack suggested. "There has to be some reason you're feeling this way."

Libbie nodded. She hated going to the doctor, but maybe Jack was right. She couldn't continue feeling so out of control.

* * *

When she did see the doctor, she was surprised by his suggestion. "It could be that the birth control pills are causing your hormones to fluctuate," he suggested. "Maybe you should try going off of them for a while to see if you feel better."

Libbie hadn't even given the pills that much thought. She'd started taking them right before they were married and never even considered that they might be playing havoc with her emotions.

The doctor also reminded her that she'd recently had an accident and a bad bump to the head. "You may just need some extra time to let your body heal from the accident. Just because you look fine doesn't mean your body isn't stressed."

When Libbie told Jack what the doctor had said, he looked thoughtful.

"Maybe you should stop the pill for a while. We'll just be careful," Jack told her.

Libbie stopped taking the pills, but her emotions were still all over the place. The doctor had said it might take a few weeks to feel normal. The problem was, Libbie couldn't remember what normal felt like anymore. Her emotions fluctuated from angry and agitated to excited and energetic all in the span of a few hours. After a spurt of energy, she'd again feel drained and depressed. It was a vicious cycle that left her exhausted. Desperate for relief, Libbie started taking Valium three times a day. The effects of the pill didn't last as long as they had a year ago when she'd first started them. Taking more each day, plus a glass of wine before Jack came home, allowed her to feel calmer, even though her mind felt fuzzy. At least she wasn't snapping at Jack like before. And she let Jack believe she'd calmed down from stopping the birth control pills instead of telling him the truth about the Valium and alcohol.

"The doctor was right. The birth control pills must have been the problem," he said one night as they sat eating dinner. "You seem calmer. Are you feeling better?"

Libbie nodded. "Yeah, I feel a little better." She hated not telling him the truth, but she was afraid Jack would be upset if he knew about the Valium. He might think less of her, or that she was somehow damaged because she needed pills to keep calm, and that would break her heart. As long as the pills worked, Libbie didn't feel the need to tell him.

* * *

Jack's twentieth birthday came and went. They spent the evening having supper at the farm. Jan already had a new boyfriend, and Ray was growing up fast. Libbie felt that time was running away from her. Every day was more and more of a struggle to get through, and everyone else seemed to just glide along in their lives. She wished she could feel that carefree again.

But as the cold days of February dragged on, Libbie found that even three pills a day weren't enough. She felt like she'd fallen into a dark pit and couldn't pull herself out. The combination of Valium and wine continued. Some days she could barely get out of bed, other days she felt better, almost exuberant, and couldn't wait to face the day. She'd miss making dinner some nights because she'd drink herself to sleep by late afternoon. Some mornings she just couldn't get up and go to work and would have to call in sick. She managed, but Libbie felt like she was lost half of the time. And she wasn't sure what to do, because she didn't want to admit to anyone, least of all herself, that she was losing control.

* * *

Jack saw that Libbie was struggling, but he had no idea why—or how to help her. Some days she'd be so happy and upbeat. They'd have snowball fights in the yard or glide around the icy lake on skates, and then go home to their cozy cottage and make love. Those days were precious to Jack. Other days, however, he'd come home from work and she'd be asleep on the sofa. She slept so soundly, she never heard him come in and start cooking something for them to eat. It would take him several minutes to wake her up, and if she did stay awake to eat dinner, her eyes were glassy and her movements slow and unsteady. Jack didn't understand what was happening to her. It was as if he was married to two women—cheerful Libbie and depressed Libbie. But when he'd try to bring up the subject of her health, Libbie wouldn't discuss it.

"I'm fine," she'd say bluntly. "Winter is just dragging me down. I'll be better in the spring."

Jack hoped that was true.

The last Sunday in February, Larry dropped by. Jack stepped outside a moment to speak to him before he came inside.

"How is she today?" Larry asked softly.

"It's been a good day," Jack told him. He'd confided in Larry about Libbie's moods. "I've already told her you enlisted a few weeks ago, and she took that pretty well. Saying goodbye might be a lot harder, though."

"For me, too," Larry said with a grin, but there was no mirth in his smile. A soft crying sound came from Larry's coat pocket.

Jack's brow wrinkled. "What was that?"

"You'll see," Larry said. "Let's go inside. I'm sure Libbie already knows why I'm here."

Jack opened the door and led the way. "Larry came to say hi," he said cheerfully.

Libbie was curled up on the sofa with an afghan wrapped around her. She and Jack had been watching *Bonanza* on television. She smiled up at Larry when he came in. "Hey, Larry. How's it going?"

"Pretty good." He smiled and walked across the room to her. "I brought you something that I hope you'll take care of for me." Larry reached into his pocket and pulled out a tiny, orange-striped kitten. The little ball of fur mewed softly.

Libbie squealed with delight and reached out her hands to hold it. "Oh, Larry. It's adorable. It's so tiny."

"Yeah, he is. One of our barn cats had an early litter, and this little guy was the runt. The bigger ones kept pushing him away from the mother, so I took him in and fed him milk with an eyedropper. I was thinking that maybe you might like to have him. He could use some extra loving care."

Libbie held the little kitten close to her. "I love him, Lar. Jack, we can keep him, can't we?"

Jack smiled. "Of course we can. I'm sure you'll give him all the love he needs."

"I'm going to get him a litter box and keep him inside so he doesn't drown in the lake or get hurt by a wild animal," Libbie said. She beamed up at Larry. "I'll take good care of him."

Larry sat down beside her. "I know you will," he said softly. "Since I'm leaving tomorrow, he'll need you to take care of him."

Libbie's eyes went wide. "You're leaving? Tomorrow? For the Army?"

Larry nodded. "Yep. I'm taking the bus tomorrow morning, and in two days I'll be at the Army camp, ready for them to make a man out of me." He grinned crookedly.

"Oh, Larry." Libbie's eyes filled with tears. She reached out and hugged him with one arm, holding the little kitten between them. "I'm going to worry about you every moment you're gone."

Larry pulled away and looked down at her tenderly. "Now don't you worry about me. I'll be just fine. You love that little kitten and take care of this big oaf here, and the time will go by quickly. Before you know it, I'll be home again." He kissed her softly on the cheek.

Libbie nodded, but she was too choked up to speak. She sat back and hugged the kitten close to her, tears streaming down her cheeks.

"Maybe you can name that silly kitten after me," Larry said, a glint of mischief in his eyes. "Larry's a good name for a cat."

Libbie laughed and Jack snorted.

"Larry is a terrible name for a cat," Jack said. "I wouldn't do that to the poor kitten."

Libbie looked thoughtful a moment. "I know. I'll name him Spence. That would be cute, and it still has part of your last name in it."

"Spence is a great name," Larry said softly. He bent over to pet the kitten, then kissed Libbie on the cheek one last time. "Take care of Spence. When I come back, I'll expect to see a big, fat cat, all lazy and spoiled."

Libbie smiled at him. "Goodbye, Larry. Please be careful and come home to us."

Larry nodded. He stood and then walked over to the door. "Goodbye, Libbie. Take good care of yourself, too." He waved and walked out the door with Jack behind him.

After Jack closed the door, he stood next to Larry, not knowing quite what to say.

"Hey, no frowning, Jack. We've known each other a long time, and you know that I'm tough and crazy. If anyone can come home from Nam, it's me."

"I expect you to keep that promise," Jack said. For the first time in their friendship, a handshake wasn't enough. They hugged each other, and then Larry left with a grin and a wave.

Jack watched him drive away, then took a deep breath to clear his head and went back inside. Libbie was still hugging the kitten tight.

"He'll be okay," Jack said, sitting down beside her and petting the tiny kitten.

"I hope so," Libbie said. She dropped her head on Jack's shoulder.

Jack hoped so, too. He sent up a little prayer to the heavens that his best friend would be safe and come home soon.

Chapter Twenty

Libbie thought of Larry every day, and she was thankful to have the playful kitten around the cottage. He brightened the long cold days that still continued through March. Unfortunately, little Spence didn't help to calm her nerves, and she still relied heavily on her Valium and wine.

One morning, as Libbie was folding laundry and laughing at Spence trying to climb into her basket of towels, the phone rang. It was Gwen.

"Hi, Gwen. What's up?"

"I need you to go sit with Mother for a couple of hours. Dad has a meeting at his office, and I'm still trying to bathe and feed the kids."

Libbie grimaced. Memories of the last time she had seen her mother lying in bed still haunted her. She'd avoided going to the house while her mother was having an episode. It gnawed at her nerves.

"Libbie!" Gwen shouted.

"Fine. Okay. I'll go over and sit with her."

"Good. I'll get there as soon as I can. Just don't let her take any meds, and see if you can get her to eat something. Bye." She hung up before Libbie could respond.

Libbie scooped up Spence and held him close. He had grown a lot in the past three weeks. She no longer put him in a box to sleep—he just crawled out of it anyway. She stroked his soft fur and kissed his head before setting him down again. She stacked wood in the fire so the cottage would stay warm in her absence, then slipped on her coat and boots. Every movement was exaggerated. She really didn't want to go to her parents' house, and she was trying to pull whatever courage she had left from deep down inside her.

As she put a shaking hand on the doorknob, Libbie thought of the bottle of Valium in her lingerie drawer. She'd already taken one that morning, but her nerves were so frayed she thought she might need another one. She hesitated. Could she get through the next few hours without taking one? Biting her lip, she realized that she couldn't. She hurried and got the bottle, took a pill, then headed out.

When she arrived, the pill was already calming her tense nerves. Her dad met her at the door.

"Hey, kitten," he said, kissing her softly on the cheek. "I'm glad you could come. I have a meeting at noon that I just can't miss. And Sandra had to run errands all day for us. I'm sure you'll only have to stay a couple of hours—Gwen said she's hurrying."

Libbie nodded and waved goodbye to her father. The house seemed oddly quiet and empty. This was the home she'd grown up in, yet there was nothing about it that felt warm and inviting. She wondered, as she walked into the kitchen, if it had ever felt like a real home. The Prentice farmhouse was warm and welcoming, as a family home should be. She always felt at ease there. Sadly, Libbie didn't feel that way here.

She made two slices of toast with apricot jam—her mother's favorite—and poured a glass of orange juice. Arranging it on a serving tray, she took a deep breath and walked upstairs. Her mother's bedroom door was slightly ajar, and the drapes were drawn, making the room dark and foreboding. The light by the bed was on, as usual, but it did little to cut through the gloominess of the room.

Libbie tentatively walked inside. "Mom? It's Libbie." Libbie wrinkled her nose. There it was again—that odor of alcohol and stale air. It made her stomach turn over.

"Mom? I brought you something to eat."

Abigail stirred. She was sitting up against a pile of pillows, but her eyes were closed. Her pill bottles and a glass of bourbon sat on the nightstand beside her. "Libbie? Where's Gwen? Where's your father?" she said haltingly.

"Father had to go to work, and Gwen is busy with the children," Libbie said, walking up to the side of her mother's bed with the tray. "I made you toast with apricot jam. Why don't you have a bite or two?"

Abigail slowly pushed herself up higher and finally opened her eyes. Her usually sharp eyes were a dull brown. Her hair, that she had styled weekly at the beauty shop, was crushed against her head, and her face looked pale and thin.

Libbie swallowed hard, trying not to flee the room. She set the tray on her mother's lap and made sure it was steady before letting go. "Should I open the drapes a little? The sun is shining today. Maybe it will help you feel better."

"I prefer the dark," Abigail said.

Libbie watched as her mother slowly lifted a piece of toast to her lips, took a small bite, then set it down. Her hand was shaking, just as Libbie's hand had shaken before she'd taken another

Valium that morning. A chill ran up Libbie's spine as she pushed that thought away.

"Where is Gwen?" Abigail asked again, her brow creasing as if she couldn't remember what Libbie had just told her.

"She had to tend to the children. She'll be here shortly."

Abigail waved the tray away. "I'm not hungry," she said.

"You might feel better if you eat," Libbie coaxed. "Can you try to eat just a little more? There's orange juice on the tray, too, if you're thirsty."

Abigail shook her head. "No. Please take it away."

Libbie picked up the tray and walked over to her mother's desk, setting it down. She couldn't bear the silence in the room, so she started chattering. "Mom, you should see the cute orange kitten that Larry gave me before he left. It's just a tiny thing, but I'm taking very good care of him and he's growing quickly. His name is Spence. This morning he was so cute. He kept trying to jump into the warm towels that I was folding."

Abigail sighed. "Dear. Would you please hand me that pill bottle?" She pointed to the one closest to her.

Libbie stared at the pills and then at her mom. "Gwen said you should wait until she gets here to take any pills."

Abigail glared at her. "Hand me the damned pills!"

Libbie was so taken aback that she stood rooted to the floor.

Her mother took a deep breath. "Dear. Please. Hand me the pills."

Libbie walked over to the nightstand and picked up the bottle. She peered at it under the light. Valium. Just like she took. She stared at it, stunned, squelching the urge to drop the bottle and run out of the room.

"Libbie!"

"Mom, you really should wait until Gwen gets here," Libbie

said, her voice shaking.

Abigail put out her hand. "Give them to me."

Reluctantly, Libbie handed her the bottle. Abigail struggled to open it, but finally did, and took out one pill. She put it in her mouth and swallowed. Libbie watched with trepidation, hoping it had been at least a couple of hours since she had taken her last one.

Abigail sat back against her pillows, sighing. Libbie took the pill bottle from her hand and set it next to the others. Her mother's breathing became slow and steady, so Libbie knew she was asleep. She picked up the tray and silently left the room.

An hour later, Gwen came in looked harried with the two girls. Libbie had stayed downstairs in the kitchen. She'd been too stressed out from her encounter with her mother to sit still, so she'd kept busy by baking a batch of chocolate chips cookies.

"See. It didn't kill you to help out, did it?" Gwen said as she unwrapped the kids from their coats, scarves, and boots. Lynn was almost four years old now and the baby, Leslie, was one. When Lynn was finally free of her winter outerwear, she ran off to the living room where toys were kept in a basket by the sofa. Little Leslie toddled after her on unsteady legs.

"I baked cookies if the girls want any," Libbie offered. Her nerves were stretched to the breaking point. Even as she baked, her mind kept returning to her mother's clawlike hands struggling to open the Valium bottle and then the look of pure satisfaction on her face when she'd swallowed one. Twice, Libbie had almost poured herself a glass of wine to calm her nerves, but then she saw her hand reaching for the bottle and pulled back sharply. It reminded her of her mother, drinking down the bourbon and taking the same pills she did. It had scared Libbie so much that she'd quickly walked away from the bar.

"That's the last thing the girls need right now," Gwen said, heading into the kitchen to start a pot of coffee. "But it does smell nice in here."

Libbie took that as a compliment since compliments came so rarely from Gwen.

Gwen poured herself a cup of coffee when it was ready and then made an all too familiar expression of satisfaction, as if she was as addicted to the caffeine as her mother was to pills and booze. The look made Libbie shiver.

"Tell me why Mom is sick so often," Libbie asked, using all her courage to do so. "And why does she drink bourbon and take all those pills?"

Gwen sat at the breakfast table by the French doors. The afternoon sun shining through the windows did little for her hard features. Libbie's sister was only three years older than she was, yet she might as well have been twenty years older by the harsh look on her face. "Why don't you answer that question? You take Valium. And you drink, too. Why?"

Libbie's mouth dropped open.

"Oh, please. Did you really think no one noticed that you bought wine on our parents' account? Mother told me you've been buying quite a lot. Where is all that going? I imagine Jack is more of a beer guy."

"Jack rarely drinks at all," Libbie said defensively. "And neither do I," she lied. "I occasionally have a glass of wine. So what?"

Gwen snorted. "Okay. Whatever you say. All I know is Mom gets anxious and nervous, and then she heads off to bed for a few days. She's told me she feels like she's in a dark hole that she can't climb out of. Personally, I think she's just being selfish and dramatic, just wanting attention. We all have bad days, but we don't all crawl off and hide."

She feels like she's in a dark hole that she can't climb out of. Those words hit Libbie hard. How often had she felt that very same way? But why? She wasn't bitter and angry like her mother, yet they both felt the same way. Her father was so kind and caring, much like Jack was to her, yet it seemed as if her mother didn't appreciate him. Libbie's skin prickled. Was she acting the same way toward Jack?

"You're thinking about it, aren't you?" Gwen said with a smirk.

Libbie looked up at her. "About what?"

"That maybe you and Mother aren't so different after all."

Libbie inhaled sharply. She heard Gwen laugh, as if it were the funniest joke in the world. The problem was, the joke was on her.

Libbie ran to the door, quickly slipping on her boots and grabbing her coat. She had to get out of there. She couldn't stand to hear one more nasty word from Gwen. It was all too much to bear.

That evening, Libbie didn't drink any wine, determined to prove Gwen wrong. She wasn't like her mother. She didn't hide away in her bed for days at a time, drinking and taking pills. But the sad fact that haunted her was how many times she had fallen asleep from drinking and not made dinner for her and Jack. Was that how it had started for her mother? A day lost, then two, then a whole week? Would that happen to her?

Not if I don't let it happen.

Libbie made a nice dinner for them that night, and Jack was all smiles when he came in to the warm kitchen that smelled heavenly. She did take a Valium that night before bed and hated herself for sighing with relief at its calming effect on her.

Determined not to become her mother, she told herself she would stop taking the Valium, too.

The next morning, she ignored her body's craving for Valium and headed off to work at the library. By mid-morning, though, her hands were shaking and she was jittery. Her headache was back, and she felt so tightly wound up that she could snap at any moment. When she left for the day, she drove past the liquor store even though she would have loved to stop and get a bottle of wine. But she was determined to stop drinking no matter how she felt.

She forced herself to make dinner that night despite her shaking hands. Then she sat on the sofa watching television with Jack while holding the kitten close. Her nerves were raw but she forced herself to sit still, and holding Spence as he slept helped.

As she got ready for bed that night, she stared at her reflection in the bathroom mirror and saw how tense her face muscles were. She took a deep breath, but the tightness remained. No matter how hard she tried, she couldn't relax. She knew she'd never sleep without the help of a Valium, so she took one, and finally a soothing calm washed over her. As she fell asleep curled up next to Jack, she was proud of herself for not taking pills or drinking wine for almost two days, except for the Valium at bedtime. *I'm not like my mother.* She fell asleep, comforted by that thought.

The next day, however, was even harder than the previous two. From the moment she woke up she craved a Valium like most people craved coffee. Twice she picked up the bottle and opened the lid, but both times she saw her mother's slack face and claw-like hands opening the pill bottle, and she threw the Valium back into the drawer. She fed the kitten and cleaned out his litter box, then worked on the fire to keep the cottage warm. But the bottle of Valium beckoned to her like an old friend. Libbie had to put distance between her and the Valium. She slipped on her coat, grabbed her purse and grocery list, and headed out into the crisp March day.

Driving to town, she felt a little better. She went to the grocery store, then to the meat market, where she bought a small beef roast to cook that night. She thought she'd make mashed potatoes and roasted carrots, too. Jack would like that.

Passing the liquor store, her heart began to beat faster. She pulled into the parking lot and argued with herself for a few minutes. Would it really hurt to have a glass of wine with dinner, especially since she wasn't taking Valium anymore? She'd been doing so well; didn't she deserve a treat?

Then she remembered Gwen's sneering face. *You and Mother aren't so different after all.*

Libbie shuddered. She was nothing like her mother. Hadn't she proved that the past couple of days?

She looked down at her hands and saw the slight shake. Her mouth went dry, and she licked her lips. "Just one bottle, and I'll only have one glass at dinner." She ran into the store before she could change her mind.

Libbie carried in her groceries and set them on the counter, then put more wood on the fire. The kitten came running and crawled between her legs, and Libbie lifted Spence up and hugged him, giving him soft kisses on the head.

As Libbie put the groceries away, she couldn't stop her hands from trembling. *Maybe just one Valium. Just one is all I need.* She fought with her thoughts, all the while seeing the image of her mother, lying in her bed, drinking and taking pills.

You and Mother aren't so different after all.

Libbie struggled to push that thought out of her head. Her

mind raced and her heart pounded in her chest. *You and Mother aren't so different after all.*

"Shut up! Shut up!" she screamed into the quiet cottage.

The kitten ran off into the bedroom, frightened by Libbie's screams. Tears filled Libbie's eyes as she ran after him, remorseful for yelling. But little Spence had crawled under the bed and wouldn't come out.

You and Mother aren't so different after all.

Libbie couldn't stand to listen to the voices in her head any longer. She went to her lingerie drawer and pulled out the bottle of Valium. She swallowed one pill, and then went into the kitchen and pulled the wine out of the bottom drawer of the fridge. Fumbling with the bottle, she finally opened it and poured a glass. After a long drink, she closed her eyes and relished the feel of the cool liquid running down her throat. Carrying the bottle, she walked into the living room and set it down on the coffee table. Libbie lay back against the sofa and waited for the Valium and the wine to push those awful thoughts out of her head.

You and Mother aren't so different after all.

Hand me the damned pills!

You and Mother aren't so different after all.

She pictured Gwen's face and then her mother's. They wouldn't leave her alone.

Her heart racing, Libbie took another Valium and drank down her glass of wine. Her hand shook as she poured more wine into her glass and drank it down, too. She had to make them go away. She couldn't bear to see their sneering faces.

You and Mother aren't so different after all.

Libbie took another pill, lay back against the sofa, and waited to fall into the sweet release of sleep.

Chapter Twenty-One

Jack walked through the cottage door at five thirty that evening, tired from a long day at work. His back ached from leaning over car engines all day, and his feet and legs were sore from standing on the garage's cold cement floor. He was looking forward to a warm meal and snuggling in front of the television with Libbie.

When he entered, though, there was no aroma of food cooking, and the air was chilly. The little kitten came scurrying up to him, crying his small, pitiful cry.

"Hey, Spence. Haven't you been fed yet?" Jack asked, picking up the kitten and cuddling it against his cheek. "Where's your mommy?"

The little kitten cried again. Jack turned and looked over into the living room. Libbie was lying crookedly on the sofa. A wine bottle sat on the coffee table, and a glass lay on the floor, red liquid seeping onto the carpet.

Jack's heart skipped a beat. He set the kitten down and ran over to the sofa. "Libbie? Libbie! Wake up!"

Libbie didn't stir. Panic ran through Jack. He'd seen Libbie passed out on the sofa many times before, but never like this. It looked as if she'd just fallen down from a sitting position. He glanced over at the bottle of wine on the coffee table and picked it up. It was empty. Then he spotted the little orange pill bottle lying on its side. He frowned as he picked it up and read the label. Valium. Elizabeth Prentice.

Why is Libbie taking Valium?

Suddenly, a chill ran up his spine. The pill bottle was empty.

He stuffed the pill bottle into his coat pocket and turned back to Libbie, shaking her again. "Libbie! Libbie!" He dropped his ear to her chest and could barely hear her breathing.

She needs help. Now!

Jack grabbed the afghan off the back of the sofa and wrapped it around Libbie, then lifted her up into his arms. He had to get her to the hospital. He couldn't wait for an ambulance. He could drive her there quicker.

He ran out the door, slamming it shut, and carefully laid Libbie on the seat of the truck. Then he ran over to the other side, hopped in, and drove off.

The hospital staff in emergency went straight to work when he carried Libbie in and said she was nonresponsive. They hurried him into a curtained cubicle, and he laid her on the bed. He saw that her lips were turning blue, and panic enveloped him. *I can't lose her.*

A nurse pulled him from the room as a doctor and other nurses worked on her.

"What happened? A fall? Did she take something?" the nurse asked him hurriedly.

Jack felt dazed. His mind was on Libbie, behind the curtain.

"Young man. What happened?" The nurse insisted.

That was when Jack remembered the pill bottle. He pulled it

out of his pocket. "I found this," he said. "And she drank a bottle of wine."

The nurse read the label and handed it back to him. Then she rushed inside the curtained room. No sooner had she left than another woman in uniform gently took Jack by the arm and ushered him to a small waiting room down the hall. "You can wait in here," she said kindly.

Jack walked in and dropped heavily onto a plastic chair.

What has Libbie done?

His eyes focused on a telephone on the wall across the room. A phone book lay on the table beneath it. In a daze, he walked over and picked up the book, looking up Gwen's phone number. He didn't want to call the Wilkenses. He couldn't bear hearing Mrs. Wilkens's shrill voice yelling at him right now. He decided it was best to let Gwen tell them where Libbie was.

Her phone rang three times before she picked it up. "Hello."

"Gwen? It's Jack. Something's happened to Libbie." He didn't mince words. He wasn't close to Gwen, but he knew she had a straightforward personality, so that was how he was going to talk to her.

"Where are you?" she asked, not missing a beat.

"The hospital. I couldn't get her to wake up when I came home tonight. The doctor is with her now."

"I'll be right there," she said, her tone flat.

"Will you please call your parents for me?" Jack asked.

"I'll come there first." She hung up.

Jack stood there, feeling lost. Then he remembered the little kitten, all alone in the cold cottage. He didn't know the last names of the girls next door, so he called Clem at the resort and asked him to go to the girls' cottage and ask them if they'd care for the kitten overnight. Clem said he'd be happy to do that and told Jack he hoped Libbie would be okay.

Then Jack called his mother. Bev answered cheerfully.

"Mom, something's happened to Libbie. I have her at the hospital right now, and I'm waiting to hear how she is."

"Oh, my goodness," Bev said. "I'll be there as soon as I can."

"No, Mom," Jack said. "I know you're cooking supper right now. I just wanted to let you know. I'll call you as soon as I know how she is."

"But I can't bear to think of you there, waiting all alone. I should be with you."

"I'll be fine, Mom. I'll call you as soon as I know something."

Bev agreed to wait and said to tell Libbie she loved her and hoped she'd be fine. After Jack hung up, he walked wearily over to the plastic chair and sat down. All he could do now was wait.

A few minutes later, Gwen strutted through the waiting room door like she owned the place. "What happened? Where is she? How is she doing?" She shot the questions off at Jack in rapid succession.

Jack stood. "I don't know anything yet. She was lying on the sofa, barely breathing, and I couldn't wake her up. I brought her here as fast as I could."

Gwen's lips formed a hard line and she put her hands on her hips. "Why would she be passed out? Did you hit her?"

Jack's mouth dropped open. How could she ask him such a question? "No," he said sharply. "She drank a bottle of wine. And I found these." He pulled the prescription bottle out of his pocket and showed it to her.

Gwen snatched the bottle from his hand and stared at it. Then she looked up at Jack. "Do you know how many of these she took?"

"No. I was at work. I didn't even know she had these. Do

you know anything about them? How long has she been taking them?"

Gwen stared at him for a long time, and then she shook her head slowly. "You clueless boy. You honestly didn't know that Libbie was taking Valium? My God. She's been taking it since right before you two were married. I can't believe she's hidden these from you for almost a year."

Jack was stunned. "Why? Why does she take them?"

"Oh, please. Why do you think? Libbie gets nervous, or haven't you noticed? She was stressed over the wedding and the fact that you might get drafted. If it isn't one thing, it's another. She's *sensitive*," Gwen said snidely. "Just like our mother. She can't face reality without booze and pills."

Jack stared at her, trying to grasp what she was saying. He knew Libbie drank wine, but he hadn't thought too much about it. Sure, she was worried often, but she'd had good reason to be worried. First there was the wedding, then the draft, and then her accident. She'd just had a lot on her mind. He'd never really thought of it as a problem before. But now . . .

Gwen snorted and caught his attention. "You're thinking it all over, aren't you? How many times did you come home to her passed out on the sofa? Huh? Did you really believe it was just the wine that did that? She's been taking Valium all along, but this time she must have taken one too many along with the alcohol." She stared him straight in the eye. "Is there any reason you can think of why she'd want to overdose?"

Overdose? Oh my God. Is that what Libbie has done? Why?

The room suddenly felt small and airless. Jack turned away from Gwen and walked over to the window. This was more than he could handle. He had to think it through. Behind him, he heard Gwen calling her father to tell him about Libbie. Her voice was hushed, and he paid no attention to what she was saying.

She's sensitive. Just like our mother, Gwen had said. Jack tried to understand what she'd meant by that. Libbie did worry. She upset easily. But was that a bad thing? Was she so upset all the time that she needed to take Valium and drink herself into a stupor? Why?

He remembered the conversation he'd had with Larry about the rumor that Libbie's mother drank and took pills. He hadn't taken it too seriously then. Small town gossip wasn't always reliable. But now he couldn't ignore it, because it was affecting Libbie.

A tap on the shoulder brought him around to stare into Gwen's cold eyes. "My father is coming over but I have to leave. Mother's having one of her *episodes,* so she can't be left alone." With that, she turned and left.

Jack's eyes followed her out the door. He couldn't believe that Libbie and Gwen were sisters. Libbie was so sweet and kind-hearted, while Gwen had ice water running through her veins.

Drawing a deep breath, Jack sat down again and waited. He pushed aside his thoughts about Libbie having a problem with drugs and alcohol. He didn't want to assume the worst. He'd wait until he could talk to her about it.

Randall walked into the room half an hour later looking worried and tired. There were dark circles under his eyes and he was pale. He tried to smile, but it was a feeble attempt.

"Have you heard anything yet?" he asked.

Jack shook his head, and Randall sighed heavily as he sat down beside him. He looked like a man who held the weight of the world on his shoulders.

"She'll be fine," Randall said softly.

Jack nodded, but after so much time, he was worried. He hoped Mr. Wilkens was right.

A doctor finally came into the room with news about Libbie. He was an older man, short and stout, wearing the requisite white lab coat. Both Jack and Randall stood, anxious to hear how Libbie was.

"She's resting quietly now," the doctor said. "We pumped her stomach to make sure no more of the pills or alcohol went through her bloodstream. Since we were unsure of how many Valium she'd taken, we wanted to be safe. Her breathing and blood pressure are both back to normal now." He turned his attention to Jack. "It's a good thing you brought her in, son. I'm afraid any longer and she might have died."

A chill ran down Jack's spine. What if he hadn't brought her in? Thank God he had.

"We'd like to keep her here a couple of days. I'll be contacting her regular physician, so he is aware of the situation. While I'm sure it was an accidental overdose, I'd still like to speak with her about what happened."

"What do you mean?" Jack asked.

The doctor cleared his throat. "I'd liked to make sure her mental state is stable. If she is having other problems, or if this wasn't accidental, then she may need other treatment."

"You think she tried to kill herself?" Jack asked, stunned.

Randall placed a hand on Jack's shoulder. "Of course she didn't," he said confidently.

The doctor glanced from Randall to Jack before speaking again. "As I said, I'm sure it's an accident. It happens. Sometimes patients forget that they've taken a pill and may take another one. I just want to make sure she's fine before she goes home."

Jack stood silent. He was processing the idea that Libbie

might have tried to hurt herself. Randall placed a reassuring hand on his shoulder while he talked to the doctor. Randall was so calm about it all that it was as if he handled this type of situation all the time.

Jack finally found his voice. "Can I see Libbie?"

The doctor shook his head. "She's sleeping now, son. I think you should go home and get some rest. You can certainly see her tomorrow." With that, he turned and left the room.

Jack turned to Randall. "Do you think Libbie overdosed on purpose?"

"No, I don't," Randall insisted gently. "Our Libbie is a strong girl. She has everything to live for. I'm certain it was an accident."

"I don't understand," Jack said, running his hand through his hair and walking across the room. "I didn't even know Libbie took these pills. Why does she need them? Isn't she happy married to me?"

Randall followed Jack and sat in one of the hard chairs. "Sit down a moment, Jack," he said.

Jack did and looked over at Randall.

"Libbie's a bright, sweet girl," Randall said. "But you have to understand. The Wilkens women are sensitive, delicate women. Libbie has always been tenderhearted, so it doesn't surprise me that she may be a little upset or anxious at times. You have to be patient and extra gentle with her. If she needs to take a pill every now and again to calm her nerves or get a good night's sleep, then there's nothing wrong with that."

Jack tried to understand, but it was hard. It didn't make sense. The Libbie he'd known in high school was strong and self-assured. Why had she changed so much over the past two years?

"Women are delicate creatures, Jack. I know today there's all that talk about women being equal to men, but the truth is, they need us to watch over them. Believe me; you'll learn to deal with it." Randall stood, but he looked weary, as if he could barely hold up his own weight. His shoulders slumped. "I have to go home so I can let Gwen get back to her family. Think about what I said, son. And please tell Libbie I was here and that I'll come see her as soon as possible."

Jack nodded and watched as Randall left the room. Once again, he was left all alone in the hospital, waiting for Libbie.

There was a tattered sofa at the other end of the room and an old television hanging in the corner. No one else was in the waiting room, so he went and lay down on the sofa. He was completely drained yet so worried about Libbie. He couldn't leave the hospital knowing that Libbie had once again almost lost her life. He'd stay here all night, like he had when she'd had her accident, and wait to see her first thing in the morning.

* * *

Jack awoke right before eight a.m. feeling like he'd been hit by a bus. His neck ached from lying awkwardly on the old sofa, and he had a splitting headache. He went down the hall to the bathroom and splashed cold water on his face, then ran his hands through his hair to push it back. There were dark circles under his eyes, and his skin looked deathly pale.

I look as old as I feel today.

He called his boss to let him know he wouldn't be at work today. He didn't elaborate on what had happened, saying only that Libbie was sick. Jack knew how quickly rumors flew around this small town, and he didn't want Libbie to be the subject of gossip.

Afterward, he went to the receptionist desk to get Libbie's room number. When he quietly entered her room, she was sleeping. She was in a private room—he supposed the hospital staff knew to put her in one by now—so at least he didn't have to worry about bothering anyone else. He sat down in the chair beside her bed and gently took her hand in his.

Looking down into her face, he saw dark circles under her eyes, and her skin was ashen. He lightly brushed her hair away from her face with his fingertips. He loved her so much. No matter what, she was his beautiful Libbie, and he'd do everything he could to care for her.

Libbie stirred and her eyelids fluttered. She looked up at Jack with a dazed expression.

"Jack?" she said hoarsely.

"I'm here, Libs," he said softly. "I stayed all night. How do you feel?"

Libbie blinked several times and tried to swallow but coughed instead. "Can I have some water?"

Jack saw a jug of water on the nightstand, so he poured a little into a glass. He found the button to raise the bed up and helped Libbie into a sitting position before handing her the glass.

After taking a few sips, Libbie handed it back to him. "My throat feels so raw," she said. Then she looked around her and back at Jack. "What happened? Why am I here? Did I have an accident?"

Her voice was so small, it broke Jack's heart. "No, sweetie. You didn't have an accident. I brought you here last night. You were passed out on the sofa, barely breathing. Do you remember anything from last night?"

Libbie gazed up at the ceiling. After a time, tears trickled down her cheeks. "I had gone shopping, and then went home.

But their nasty words kept ringing in my ears. I tried not to drink anything, but I just wanted to make their words go away."

Jack pulled the bottle of pills from his pocket. "What about these, Libbie?" he asked gently. "I found this bottle on the table, too. How many did you take?"

Libbie stared at the bottle in his hand and her tears came faster. "I'm sorry, Jack. I'm so sorry."

Jack sat on the bed beside her and pulled her into his arms, letting her tears fall on his jacket. "You don't have to be sorry, Libs. Please don't get upset. I'm worried about you. You can tell me anything. You know I'll love you no matter what."

Libbie pulled away and stared at him, her eyes small pools of tears. "I should have told you about the pills a long time ago. I didn't want you to think badly of me. I didn't want you to think I was like . . ." she faltered and raised her hands to cover her face.

"I'd never think badly of you, Libs. I love you. God, I love you so much. I was scared to death last night when I thought I might lose you."

"I'm sorry, Jack. I'm so sorry." Libbie's voice was tiny, like a small child's. Jack pulled her to him again. He wanted to reassure her that he meant what he said. He loved her deeply.

"I want to go home," Libbie whispered into his ear. "I promise I'll try harder to be perfect. I won't take pills and I won't drink anymore. Please, just take me home."

Jack's heart broke for her. She sounded so scared and sad. "As soon as the doctor will let you, I'll take you home," he said. He continued holding her, thinking about her pitiful words. *I promise I'll try harder to be perfect.* He'd never wanted her to be anything other than who she was—his sweet Libbie. Had she thought he was unhappy with her?

After Libbie settled down a little, Jack pulled away and she sat back against her pillows. He found a box of tissues, and she wiped her eyes and nose.

"Libbie, I need to ask you something. Do you remember why you took the pills and drank so much last night? Were you upset with me? Did I do something wrong?"

Libbie closed her eyes and shook her head slowly. "It wasn't you. It was me. I just had to wipe their words out of my head."

"Whose words?" Jack asked.

Libbie shook her head. "I don't want to talk about this anymore."

Jack took her hand in his. "Please don't get upset, Libs, but I need to know. Did you take all those pills on purpose?" His voice cracked. "Did you try to kill yourself?"

Libbie's eyes grew wide. "No. Oh no, I wouldn't do that. I couldn't. It was an accident. It had to be. I just took a pill, and when I didn't feel better, I took another. I didn't mean to, Jack. I swear."

Relief flooded over him. "I'm so glad." He sat with her until she dozed again. None of what happened made sense to him, but he was relieved he hadn't lost his Libbie.

Chapter Twenty-Two

Two days later, Libbie was sent home from the hospital with two prescriptions and orders to rest. Her own physician had come to visit her in the hospital and, after a long talk about how she felt, he'd prescribed an antidepressant and told her to continue with the Valium. "But no drinking alcohol," he'd insisted. He'd diagnosed her with anxiety and depression and told her she should stop working at the library for now so she wouldn't feel overwhelmed. Libbie was upset about having to quit her job, but she was determined to do what the doctor said. She truly wanted to feel well again.

Overdosed. That word caused cold chills to run up her spine. Libbie knew she hadn't meant to overdose—she hadn't tried to kill herself—but the anxiety she'd felt over Gwen's words and seeing her mother's condition had stretched her nerves to their limits. She'd wanted so badly to wipe away their words that she hadn't been careful about the Valium. It had been an accident. But it scared Libbie that if she'd done it once, she might do it again.

Being diagnosed with depression had shocked Libbie. Yes,

she knew she'd felt down at times, and she did experience anxiety often, but she hadn't thought it was so bad as to be diagnosed as a condition. Didn't everyone experience ups and downs with their emotions? It worried her that Jack would think less of her now that she'd been labeled as depressed. She was determined to prove that she was fine. She'd take the antidepressant and Valium as directed and prove she could control her emotions.

The first thing she did when she got back to the cottage was hug Spence. She'd missed the kitten and carried him all over the little home with her nearly all day. Bev had left food in the freezer and fridge so they could heat it up for dinner over the next week. She'd left a delicious pan of frosted brownies on the table, with a note saying that she hoped Libbie would feel better soon. Libbie's heart warmed at the thought of Bev and Jack's entire family. They were so kind to her. She felt lucky to have them as her family, too.

For the next two weeks, Libbie felt useless in her own home. Her father had sent Sandra over to help with the cleaning and laundry so Libbie could rest. Carol came to visit often—more than she had all winter—and Bev and Jan came to visit in rotation, too. Candy and Jackie also stopped by on a regular basis—something they hadn't done since the accident. Libbie suspected that the visitor schedule had been orchestrated by Jack so she wouldn't feel alone while he was at work. It made her feel that he didn't trust her to be alone during the day. But she didn't mention it to him. Even with her new medication, she felt fragile, like she could fall to pieces at any moment. The visits actually took her mind off of how she felt.

April brought warmer weather, and soon the snow melted and the lake opened up to blue water again. Jack and Libbie began taking evening walks along the lakeshore and drives to the Dairy Queen for a treat or to the A&W for a burger. Jack promised Libbie they'd have a wonderful, peaceful summer at the cottage again this year, and then if they had enough money, they'd look for a house of their own in the fall. Libbie hoped they could. She no longer loved the cottage as she had that first summer. She was looking forward to a place of their own.

The first part of May, the girls next door said goodbye. They were moving back home to Minneapolis for the summer and weren't sure where they'd be the next winter.

"We're thinking of finishing our next two years at a school closer to home," Candy said. "It'll save money for us and our parents."

Libbie waved goodbye as they drove off. Even though they hadn't spent much time together since last October, she was going to miss them. Since she'd graduated high school, she'd done nothing but say goodbye to friends, and it made her sad.

By now, Larry had been gone for ten weeks. He was in a training camp in South Carolina, which seemed so far away to Libbie. Occasionally, they'd receive a one-page letter from him saying he was fine and surviving boot camp, but with no details. She'd sent him a photo of her and Spence in her last letter, and he remarked on how big the kitten had grown. Libbie was surprised at how much she missed Larry. She thought about him often and hoped he was doing well.

Summer was difficult for Libbie despite the nice weather and longer days. She tried, for Jack's sake, to enjoy rides in the canoe, walks along the lake, or going to the outdoor movies in the park, but nothing helped to lift her mood. In fact, she felt nothing at all. *Dull*, that was the only word she could come up with to describe it. The days Jack worked were long and boring for her, and some days she didn't have the energy to go outside and enjoy the weather. She'd sit inside, holding Spence, watching television and taking naps. But she always made sure to have something cooking for dinner by the time Jack came home. She didn't want him to know how terrible she felt. She watched every word she said around him and pretended to be happy, even when she just wanted to crawl off to bed and sleep. She put on a good show, but it drained her. She was afraid of how he'd react if he knew how unhappy she was. What if Jack decided he'd had enough of her and left? Her whole reason for living would be gone.

And then maybe the thought of overdosing wouldn't be so scary after all.

* * *

Jack knew Libbie was struggling despite the medication she was taking. Her eyes no longer sparkled, and it seemed as if she cared about nothing. When he'd suggest a fun outing to cheer her up, he could tell she was just pretending to be excited. That made him sadder than if she'd just told him no.

On their first anniversary, he surprised her with flowers and dinner out at the Lakeshore Inn, the restaurant they'd eaten in the night he had given her his class ring. Afterward, he took her to the same park they used to love going to, where the old tree hung over the water. Laughing, they took off their shoes and climbed out onto the branch, where they sat and watched the sunset, their feet skimming the cool water. It had been such an intimate moment, and Jack kissed her as the sun touched the lake, turning everything around them a soft orange. For a few hours, he felt like he had the old Libbie back, the carefree girl from high school. But the moment they returned to the cottage, her demeanor changed, making Jack feel as if there were a wall rising between them.

They rarely made love anymore. At night when they'd go to bed, Libbie rolled over and fell asleep quickly. Jack missed holding her in his arms. But he didn't complain. The doctor had said it might take weeks before she felt like her old self again after starting the antidepressant. It had been three months, and still she seemed unhappy. He just wanted Libbie to feel good again, like the girl she used to be, for her sake more than for his.

On a Saturday in mid-June, there was a rapping on their cottage door. Jack and Libbie had been getting ready to run errands in town and neither expected visitors. When Jack opened the door, there stood Randall, smiling, with Abigail.

"Hello, Jack," Randall said in a booming voice. "We have a surprise for you and Libbie. Can you come with us for a little while?"

Libbie had walked up beside Jack, slipping her hand around his arm and holding on tightly. She looked nervous to see her parents. Randall came in and hugged her close, and Jack saw her relax. He realized it was Abigail who intimidated her, and he didn't have to wonder why. Abigail intimidated everyone. She stood stiffly on the front porch, her hands clasped tightly in front of her. Jack noticed that Abigail looked even thinner and paler than when he'd seen her at Easter. She seemed different, too. Not as self-assured. It made him wonder all over again about what Gwen had said in the hospital after Libbie's overdose. *She's sensitive, just like our mother. She can't face reality without booze and pills.* Those words had stuck with him all these months, and he wondered how true they were. Was Abigail an alcoholic? Is that why she looked so sickly? He'd broached the subject with Libbie a couple of times, but she'd turned away each time and said she didn't want to talk about it. So he'd let it be.

Now, looking at the older woman, he put on a smile and said, "Hello, Mrs. Wilkens. Please, come in."

Abigail seemed to tighten up even more, her mouth a thin line and her hands clutched together. "I'm fine right here," she said. "Randall, shall we go?"

"Ah, yes, let's. I can't wait for the kids to see our surprise."

They all got into Randall's Cadillac, and he drove to the north road that led away from the lake. About a mile up the road, he turned right, and then right again, into a new housing development that had sprouted up about two years ago. Each house stood on an acre of land, and most of the lots had been sold and houses built on them. They were modest houses, but nice, and the yards were kept up well, too. Children were playing in yards and riding their bikes on the sidewalks. Randall drove down to the end of the street where it formed a cul-de-sac and stopped in front of a tan ranch house with brown trim and shutters. It had a large bay window in the front, a door with gold glass inserts, and an attached double garage.

Randall parked and stepped out of the car, going around to open Abigail's door and help her out. Jack turned to Libbie, but she shrugged, looking as confused as he felt.

Soon they were all standing on the sidewalk in front of the house, staring at it.

"Well, what do you kids think?" Randall asked, smiling widely.

Jack wasn't quite sure what to think, so he politely said, "It's very nice."

"Come on, let's go inside," Randall said. He wrapped one arm around Libbie's shoulders and the other around Abigail's, then walked up the sidewalk to the house. Jack followed.

Randall pulled a key out of his pants pocket and unlocked

the door. He stood aside so the ladies could enter first, then waved Jack through. They all walked into the entryway.

Jack looked all around. There was a small glass chandelier hanging in the entryway and light hardwood flooring. A coat closet was on his left, and the living room ran the full length to the right. Gold shag carpeting and gold drapes decorated the large room. Randall led them through the living room, turning left into the connecting dining room, and then another left through an arched doorway into the kitchen. A bar-style pass-through between the kitchen and dining room stood to the right, with tall barstools on the dining room side. The kitchen had a light-gold tile floor, harvest-gold appliances, and dark wood cabinets. Everything was sparkling new.

Jack watched as Libbie gazed around her. Her eyes were shining with excitement. "Look, Jack. A dishwasher! Wouldn't it be nice to have one? And everything is brand new."

Jack nodded. It did look nice. And expensive.

Randall took them on a tour of the rest of the house, which included a laundry room, a master bedroom with attached bathroom, another smaller bedroom, and a guest bathroom. After circling back to the living room, Randall clapped his hands and asked, "What do you think?"

"It's so cute," Libbie said. "But why are you showing us this house? Is someone we know going to buy it?"

Randall grinned. "It's already been purchased. I hope you love it, because this is your new home."

Jack stared at Randall in disbelief, while Libbie squealed and ran over to hug her father.

"Really, Dad? Ours? But how? Did you buy it?"

Randall hugged her, obviously pleased to see his daughter so happy. "Yes, Libbie, really. It is yours. But don't give me all the credit. It was your mother's idea."

Libbie turned to her mother who'd been standing quietly beside Randall, her arms stiff at her side. "It was your idea, Mom?"

Abigail nodded and gave a small smile that looked more like a grimace. "Yes, dear. I knew how unhappy you were living in that old cottage. Now you can live in a real house, where you'll be warm all winter and have all the luxuries you deserve."

Libbie hugged her mother. "Thank you, Mom. I love it."

Abigail hugged her back stiffly.

Jack stood, speechless. He'd watched as Libbie's eyes lit up with happiness, and he didn't want to be the one to snuff it out. It had been so long since he'd seen her this excited. But he couldn't let her parents buy them a house. And he knew there was no way he could afford a nice new house like this one, either.

Libbie ran over to Jack, her face beaming. "Don't you love it, Jack?"

Jack took a deep breath to steel himself. "Yes, it's very nice. But sweetie, I'm not sure we can afford this house." He watched as her face fell and it tore at his heart.

"But you said we could look for a house this fall. Can't we live here?"

Her voice was so sad, so pitiful, that Jack was at a loss as to how to answer. Randall came over and wrapped his arm around Libbie and smiled at Jack. "You don't have to worry, Jack. We made the down payment for you, and the monthly payments are low. I knew you'd be too proud to let us buy you the house, but I'm sure you can easily afford the payments."

"I'm not sure about that, sir," Jack said. "This must be an expensive house."

Randall brushed aside Jack's concern with a wave of his

hand. "Don't be silly, son. It's not bad at all. Let us do this for our Libbie and for you."

Libbie grabbed Jack's hands and stared up into his eyes. "Please, Jack? It's so nice, and we'll have our own home. Please say yes."

Jack wavered a moment. Libbie's happiness was all he wanted, but he was worried about more than just the monthly payments. Now there'd be an electric bill, heating bill, and the cost of furniture for a place this big. He wasn't sure he earned enough to cover it all. Jack glanced around him again, and his eyes settled on Abigail's.

"You do want our Libbie to be happy, don't you?" Abigail said, glaring at him.

Jack stared at Abigail. She'd been the one to upset Libbie at every turn, yet she had the nerve to put him on the spot. But denying Libbie the chance to live in this lovely home wasn't an option, either. He didn't feel as if he had a choice.

"Sure, sweetie. Of course we can live here," Jack said.

Libbie squealed and hugged Jack, kissing his cheek. "We're going to be so happy here. I can't wait to move in." She ran around hugging her father and mother again, bringing smiles to their faces, then grabbed her mother's hand and pulled her toward the kitchen. "Let's see everything again," she said cheerfully.

Abigail smiled indulgently and followed her daughter.

Randall walked over to Jack and slapped him on the back. "I knew you wouldn't let our Libbie down," he said.

That was exactly what Jack was afraid he'd do if he couldn't afford to keep this house.

* * *

They moved into their new house immediately, and Libbie asked Jack if she could use the money they'd been saving to buy furniture. He didn't really have a choice—they had to have furniture—but he asked her to be careful because he worried he would need some extra money for bills. He had to admit, though, she was careful spending the money and did get every-thing for cost from her parents' furniture store. But their savings dwindled regardless and Jack began to panic. He had an oil tank to fill up for their furnace before winter and other bills to pay. He knew his income wasn't going to cover everything, and he'd have to find a way to earn extra money on the side. But he didn't complain to Libbie. She was happier than she'd been since she'd overdosed, and he didn't want to burst her bubble. He'd find a way to make things work out.

Chapter Twenty-Three

Libbie adored her new home. She also loved every piece of her new furniture, from the oval, smoked glass dining room table to the brown suede sofa and tan swivel recliner. She'd paid Sandra, who was an excellent seamstress, to make a gold tufted pillow for the bay window seat, and Spence lay there daily, soaking up the sun. Libbie hung spider plants, Boston ferns, and ivy in the sunniest windows, and had colorful throw pillows set all around. Every room looked warm and cozy, and she felt so safe and secure in their new home.

They had a large backyard with a cement patio, where she'd placed a table and chairs, and a barbeque grill, too. It wasn't long before the neighbors came over to introduce themselves, and Libbie was thrilled to make new friends. Many of the women were a few years older than she, and they already had two or three children, but they eagerly welcomed Libbie into the neighborhood. Most were full-time mothers, although a couple did have part-time jobs, so there was always someone home to visit with during the week. And on weekends there was always a neighborhood gathering where everyone was invited over for burgers on the grill. For the first time since graduating high school, Libbie had friends she could spend time with and she loved it.

For the rest of the summer, Libbie put all her energy into turning the house into a home, and she cleaned constantly, making sure everything was always perfect. She wanted Jack to know she appreciated his letting her buy so many nice things for the house, so she treated everything like she would a newborn infant—with tender loving care. She was so happy living in their new house and neighborhood that she stopped taking the Valium because she didn't need it to fall asleep at night. She no longer worried or stressed over everything. She felt like her old self again.

And when August slipped into September, Libbie's biggest fear evaporated. Jack's time for the draft was up. There was no chance of him leaving her to go to Vietnam. It was such a heavy weight off of her. She felt like she could finally relax and enjoy their future together, now that she knew they had one.

As time went on and Libbie no longer felt stressed or depressed, she decided she didn't need to take the antidepressant anymore. She hated how dull it made her feel, so when she ran out, she didn't refill it. She was content with her life with Jack in this wonderful home and neighborhood—she didn't need pills anymore.

* * *

Jack noticed the change in Libbie immediately. She was excited and energetic again, and that made him very happy. She kept the house spotless, cooked and baked, and spent time with the other women in the neighborhood. He knew how good it was for her to have friends, and he was glad he'd made the decision to live here after all—at least for Libbie's sake.

For Jack, though, it took a little getting used to. He'd never lived in a brand new home with all new furnishings, and he was afraid every time he walked through the door that he might ruin the carpet or a piece of furniture. The glass dining room table scared him to death. What if he dropped a plate on it and cracked the table? Libbie laughed at him for being so fearful and told him to relax and enjoy the place. "There's nothing here that can't be fixed or cleaned," she'd told him with a warm smile. He knew it was true, but it made him uncomfortable just the same.

As summer changed into fall and their savings dwindled, Jack worried how he'd pay the bills. Everything except for heat was electric in the house, so their bill was quite high, especially with the hot water heater and the new clothes dryer running so often. He filled the oil tank so they would be ready to heat the house when winter arrived, and that cost a large chunk of money. Worse yet, the oil deliveryman told Jack that he would probably have to fill it monthly. Jack wasn't sure if he could save enough money every month to do that.

Jack worried a lot now.

But the fact that Libbie was feeling better made it all worth it to Jack.

That fall, changes were taking place in Jack's family as well. Jack's sister, Jan, had graduated high school in the spring and headed off to college at the University of Minnesota in Minneapolis. She hadn't wanted to stay in Jamison for college; she'd wanted to move to the city and have new experiences. She'd received a grant to cover her college expenses and Jack's parents said they'd help her with living expenses, but she'd also have to find a part-time job. Jan said she didn't mind. She was ready to fly the coop. So, in late August, they'd all had a party at the farm and said goodbye to her. It had been a month since she'd left, and Bev told Jack that Jan was loving it down there. She'd found a waitress job close to campus and had already made new friends. Jack found it hard to believe that his little sister was living on her own—he still thought of her as being ten years old—but he was proud of her.

Larry had written staying he'd survived boot camp and would be transferring to another unit to await his orders for shipping out. It was all becoming very real—Larry was going to Vietnam. A small part of Jack felt guilty that he was not with his friend, but he also knew his place was here with Libbie. He hoped that Larry would be okay.

Over the summer, Jack and Libbie had become close with two other couples in the neighborhood, June and Adam, and Steve and Natalie. Both were young couples, but they already had small children, and sometimes the six of them would get together and play cards on a Tuesday night or have dinner together on a Saturday night. Jack knew how much Libbie enjoyed get-togethers with their neighborhood friends, so even when he was bone-tired he never complained. As winter drew closer and the cooler temps made outdoor barbeques impossible, the dinners moved indoors. Sometimes, Jack worried about Libbie when they all got together. It wasn't unusual for beer and wine to be passed around, and often one neighbor or another would drink too much. He hoped Libbie wouldn't feel pressured to drink. He knew she wasn't supposed to drink while she was on her medication. She always seemed fine, though, and he'd see her politely decline when offered a glass of wine or a beer. They'd been so happy since moving to the new house that he didn't want anything to change that.

In late October, Jack told Libbie he'd be working at his uncle's gas station on Saturdays to help supplement their income.

"But that's the night we get together with our friends," Libbie said, looking disappointed.

"I'll only work until five," Jack told her. "He needs the help, and we need the extra income. I'm hoping I can take on a few repair jobs as well on Saturdays while I'm there. I may even do some on weeknights. I've had a lot of people ask me if I'd work on their cars on the side. It would help us with the bills."

Libbie was sitting on the bed watching as Jack undressed. "Are we really doing so poorly that you'll have to work more?" she asked.

Jack sat down beside her. "Things are just a little tight right now," he said, not wanting her to worry. "Our bills are higher in the winter because of running the heat, so we could use the extra money."

"But none of the other husbands around here work after hours."

"They're probably more established in their jobs and are making more money than I am, Libs. Plus, most of the guys who live here are older than me, so they've been working longer." When he saw the unhappiness in her eyes, Jack took her hands in his. "It's going to be fine, Libs. I want you to be happy. I don't mind working a little more so we can live in this nice home."

"But I won't be happy if you're gone all the time. I like it when you're home."

Jack grinned. "Well, I'm glad you like having me home." He ran a finger down her back, making her jump and giggle from the chill it gave her. "I'm home now. Do you want to show me how much you like having me here?"

Libbie laughed and Jack captured her lips with his. They fell back onto the bed as Jack showed Libbie just how much he loved being with her, too.

* * *

With the onset of the holiday season, Libbie went into a decorating frenzy. She started right before Thanksgiving, and the decorating continued into December. Their house twinkled and glistened in every corner, and she also baked dozens of holiday cookies and shared them around the neighborhood. She wanted this Christmas to be extra special in their new home. She borrowed decorations from her parents and asked Jack to string lights around the outside of the house and around the tall pine that grew in the front yard. Jack did, and everyone else in the neighborhood jumped in and decorated their houses as well. It soon became obvious that Libbie's decorating spree had started a competition for the best-lit house.

They had spent Thanksgiving at the farm because Abigail wasn't feeling well enough to host a dinner. Libbie thought it was just as well. She was sorry her mom didn't feel well, but she enjoyed the farm much more than her parents' home. Jan came home for the long weekend and everyone had a good time.

The Saturday before Christmas, Libbie had invited their two favorite couples over for dinner, and then the rest of the neighborhood was invited over for dessert and drinks. It was a bring-your-own-booze type of affair, so it wouldn't be too expensive. She'd also invited Carol and her new boyfriend over for dinner, too, and couldn't wait to show off her house and hostess skills to her old friend.

As Jack readied for work that Saturday morning, he pulled Libbie into his arms. "I know you're excited about tonight," he said. "I am, too. I'm a little worried, though. You've been working so hard, I'm afraid you might get sick."

Libbie frowned. *Sick?* "I feel fine," she said defensively.

He kissed her on the tip of her nose. "I know. I just worry about you. You've been pushing yourself so hard over the past few weeks to make everything perfect—and it is. I want you to enjoy the holidays, too."

"I am. I love doing all of this," she said. "Just make sure you're not late coming home. I want tonight to be perfect."

Jack promised he'd leave work early so he could shower and dress before their guests arrived. Once he left, Libbie went straight to work.

With boundless energy, she cooked and cleaned, and when everything didn't look perfect to her, she cleaned some more. Twice she mopped the kitchen floor, and when she saw a crumb in the refrigerator, she cleaned it top to bottom. She wanted everyone to think she was the perfect wife and hostess. Nothing could be out of place.

She was serving roasted duck with orange-ginger glaze, wild rice, and asparagus tips. She'd also baked several pies the day before—apple, pumpkin, pecan, and lemon meringue—to serve when all the neighbors came over later.

By the time she put the duck into the oven to roast, she was tired, but she thought it was a happy tired. Still, Jack's words came back to her. *You've been working so hard, I'm afraid you might get sick.* She'd resented the implication of his words. He wasn't worried she'd get sick; he was worried the added stress would make her start drinking again.

"Well, I'm just fine," she said aloud. "I've been fine for months."

She went to her room to shower and dress for the evening.

Once her makeup and hair were done, she put on her new dress. It was tea length, made of sapphire-blue satin, and had a form-fitting bodice that fell into a full skirt from the waist. Libbie had also bought new matching satin pumps to wear with it. Her mother had an open account for her at the local dress shop, and although she rarely used it, she had for tonight. She wanted to look beautiful for Jack, and for him to be proud of her. As she twirled in front of the full-length mirror, she felt like a princess.

Half an hour before the guests were to arrive, Libbie went back into the kitchen and slipped a full-length lacy apron on over her dress. The duck smelled heavenly. She had the asparagus ready to roast. She pulled the duck out of the oven and slipped in the asparagus, then lifted the lid to check the duck. To her dismay, it looked a bit overcooked. Biting her lip, she rationalized that once the oranges and glaze were on it, the duck would be fine. She carefully transferred the duck onto a serving platter, covered it, and began making the glaze.

* * *

Fifteen minutes later, when Jack came through the kitchen door, he found Libbie on the floor, sobbing.

"Libs, what happened? Are you okay?" He ran to her and dropped down beside her.

"I've ruined everything," she said between sobs. "The duck is overcooked, the glaze didn't turn out, and the wild rice is clumpy. I can't do this. I'm a failure."

Jack pulled her into his arms and held her tight. "I'm sure it's all fine," he said, trying to soothe her, but she pulled away and glared at him.

"No, it's not!" she yelled as she stood up. "I've worked so hard all day and now it's all ruined. I can't serve this to our friends." Tears streamed down her cheeks, leaving black trails of mascara behind. Jack stood and tried to calm her down, but she backed away. Libbie picked up a serving spoon and threw it across the room. It clattered against a wall before dropping to the floor.

"Libbie. Don't. Tell me what needs to be done and I'll try to help you fix it."

Libbie turned on him with wild eyes. "No! Nothing can fix this mess. You were right, I tried doing too much and now I've ruined everything. I'm a failure!" She ran to the bedroom and slammed the door.

Jack stood there, stunned. The manic look in Libbie's eyes had taken him by surprise. It was almost time for their friends to arrive and he still had to shower and change. What was he going to tell them? He glanced around the kitchen and assessed the situation. Going to the stove, he saw that the glaze in the saucepan was lumpy and too thick to pour. He took it to the sink and ran water into it. He smelled something still cooking in the oven and checked. The asparagus looked cooked, so he pulled it out and covered it. Then he found the duck recipe that Libbie was using and looked it over. He sighed. *I don't know what I'm doing.*

He picked up the phone and called his mom. "I need your help," he told her.

Just as he finished doing as his mother instructed, the doorbell rang and he went to answer it. Carol and her new boyfriend were standing there. She wore a silky red dress and heels, and he was wearing a suit.

"Aren't you a little underdressed?" Carol asked, giving Jack a teasing smile.

"We're running late," he told her. "Can you greet the other

guests for me? I'll get Libbie and we'll be out as soon as possible."

Carol nodded. "Of course. This is Jim, by the way. Jim Simmons."

"Hi," Jim said, extending his hand.

"It's nice to meet you Jim," Jack said. "I'm afraid I'm too dirty to shake your hand, though. Can I catch you later?"

Jim laughed. "You bet."

Jack walked to their bedroom and stepped in quietly. Libbie was lying on the bed, tears still falling. He went over and sat on the bed beside her. "Libs? Sweetie? Please stop crying. Carol is here. And her new boyfriend seems nice. Why don't you freshen up while I shower and then go out and say hi?"

Libbie sat up and looked at him, her eyes red and swollen. "I'm sorry I yelled at you," she said with a shaky voice. "You were right—I was trying to do too much and I failed. I just wanted everything to be perfect. I wanted you to be proud of me."

"Oh, Libs. You don't have to prove to me that you're perfect. I already know you are." He slipped his arm around her and pulled her to him, kissing her softly on the lips. "I married the most beautiful girl in town, and the smartest and sweetest, too," he whispered. "I knew I was lucky the day you said you'd marry me."

Libbie sniffled. "I'm not perfect. I ruined dinner. I try too hard and then ruin everything. I'm not good at anything. I'm a failure."

"You're not a failure," Jack insisted. "Everything you do is amazing. Look at all the beautiful pies you made, and the delicious cookies you shared around the neighborhood. And what about all the decorations? They're beautiful. Just because one thing went wrong doesn't mean you're a failure."

"But what about dinner? It's ruined. What am I going to do?"

Jack grinned. "It's not ruined. The duck looks delicious. With my mom's help, I fixed it and it'll be fine. She also gave me a tip on how to save the rice. And I took the asparagus out of the oven in time. It's all fine, Libbie. But if we don't get out there and eat it soon, it will be ruined."

"You fixed it? After I yelled at you?" Libbie asked, surprised.

"Sure. I'm hungry." He laughed.

A small smile tugged at Libbie's lips.

"I have to shower and change. You'd better fix your makeup before you go out there. You have raccoon eyes."

"Thanks, Jack. You're always saving me."

Jack kissed her again. "I'm happy to do it."

Libbie hurried and fixed her makeup and hair then went out to greet her guests. The dinner did taste fine after all, and everyone complimented Libbie on it. And when the neighbors came over for dessert, everyone told her how wonderful her pies were. Jack watched as she graciously accepted their praise. She looked so beautiful, and he was very proud of her.

Later, after everyone had left, they sat together on the sofa in the darkened living room with only the Christmas tree lights on, enjoying the quiet.

"You were incredible tonight," Jack told her, slipping his arm around her.

"I'm sorry I yelled at you," Libbie said softly. "I don't know what got into me. Everything was going fine, and then it all fell apart. And then I fell to pieces, too."

"It's okay, Libs. I know you didn't mean to. You try so hard to make everything perfect and it stresses you out. I was worried that you were working too hard."

Libbie looked up at him. "I don't know what comes over me. One minute everything is fine and the next I'm an emotional mess. It's like I don't have any control over my emotions. And the harder I try, the worse it gets. I should have listened to you and not pushed myself so hard."

"It's okay, Libs. I'm just happy that tonight turned out so well. The neighbors loved your dinner, and your pies were a success."

Libbie dropped her head on his shoulder. "I couldn't have done it without you."

"And my mother." Jack chuckled.

Libbie smiled. "And your mother."

"I love you, Libs. Just you. You don't have to be anything or anyone else for me. You're perfect just as you are. Don't forget that, okay?"

Libbie nodded her head. Jack stood and lifted her into his arms, carrying her off to bed as she laughed warmly.

Chapter Twenty-Four

Jack and Libbie celebrated the New Year at June and Adam's house, along with a dozen other neighborhood friends. New Year's Eve was on a Friday night, so everyone let loose and had a good time. When midnight rolled around, June, with Libbie and Natalie's help, passed out glasses of champagne to everyone. Jack and Libbie clinked glasses as the clock struck twelve, then kissed after sipping their champagne.

"Happy New Year, honey," Libbie said into his ear.

"Happy 1972," Jack said, kissing her once more. They laughed and joined in with their friends, giving hugs all around.

Libbie hadn't had a drink since her overdose, and the smooth, sweet taste of the champagne felt good as it slid down her throat. She'd meant to put the glass down right away, but it was hard to resist. She drank it all, and then set it down, but when June poured her another one, she accepted. What would it hurt for her to drink just a little more?

By the time they left the party, Libbie was more than a little tipsy. Jack helped her on with her coat and wrapped his arm around her as they walked back to their house.

Both of them were in a blissful mood, and they made slow, sweet love that night. Afterward, Libbie lay curled up beside Jack with her head on his bare chest. She could hear the steady beat of his heart, and she loved feeling his warm body next to hers.

"Where do you think Larry is tonight?" Libbie asked quietly.

"I was wondering the same thing at midnight when everyone was celebrating," Jack said. "I know he's in Vietnam, but he hasn't written since he shipped out in December."

"I hope he's safe somewhere, having a drink and thinking of home," Libbie said.

Jack pulled her closer. "Me, too."

They lay there a while longer before Libbie broke the silence again. "Jack?"

"Hmm?"

"Let's have a baby."

Jack lay silent, not answering for a while. Finally, he looked at Libbie. "I don't know if this is the right time, Libs. Maybe we should wait another year or so."

Libbie rose on one elbow and looked down at the outline of Jack's face in the dark room. "But you said when we had a home of our own we could start a family. Now we have this nice place, and this is a wonderful neighborhood. I really want to start a family. I don't want to wait anymore."

Jack reached up and tenderly brushed his fingertips along the side of Libbie's face. "I want a family, too, but don't you think we should wait? Babies are a lot of work and can wear you down. I'm worried it may be too much stress for you. Maybe you should talk to the doctor first to see if it's safe to get pregnant while you're on medication."

Libbie stiffened. "You mean you're afraid I'll freak out and overdose again."

"Libs . . ."

"Jack, I haven't had a drink, except for tonight, since last March. And I'm no longer taking my antidepressant or the Valium. I stopped taking them after we moved in here."

Jack sat up. "Why didn't you tell me you'd stopped taking your medicine? Is that wise?"

"I don't need them anymore. I've been so happy here that I was no longer sad or depressed. Besides, those pills made me feel awful—like I had no feelings at all. I'm happier now. And I don't need alcohol or Valium to feel happy."

"What about what happened over Christmas?" Jack asked. "You said you didn't feel like you could control your emotions. Maybe that's because you stopped taking the antidepressant."

Libbie frowned. "I was just stressed about making everything perfect for our friends. It was just one instance. Other than that, I've been fine."

"I'm glad you feel better," Jack said. "But shouldn't you have talked to the doctor first before stopping the medication?"

Libbie sighed. "He would have told me to stay on them. I don't need them, Jack. My life has changed. I'm not worried about losing you to the war anymore, and we have a wonderful home to live in and a good life. I'm happy." She reached over and ran her fingers through his brown hair. "And I want to have a baby with you," she added gently. "I love you."

Jack slid down in the bed and pulled Libbie on top of him as she giggled.

"I love you, too, Libs. I want to start a family, too. If you're sure it will make you happy, then I'm happy."

Libbie kissed him as he slid his hands down her waist to the curve of her hips. "We could start trying now," she said.

Jack laughed. He was only too happy to comply.

* * *

Jack turned twenty-one at the end of January, and Libbie threw him a surprise birthday party, inviting the entire neighborhood along with his family and their other friends. It was that night that Carol told Libbie she and Jim were engaged and wanted a July wedding.

"But you hardly know him," Libbie said, surprised.

"Actually, I've known him since I started college, but we started dating last August," Carol said. "He's a good person and I really love him. Be happy for me, Libbie."

Libbie was happy for her and told her so; she just hadn't realized Carol had been dating Jim since the previous August. They hadn't seen much of each other over the past few months and it made Libbie sad. She'd made a lot of new friends, but Carol had been her best friend her whole life, and she felt bad that they weren't as connected anymore.

"Don't worry," Carol told her with a wink. "You're not going to get out of having to wear some god-awful maid of honor dress at my wedding."

"Really? You want me to be the maid of honor?" Libbie hugged Carol, then pulled away and frowned. "Ugh. That means I'll be the matron of honor."

Carol laughed.

By February they'd heard from Larry, but he hadn't written any details about where he was stationed in Vietnam.

I don't want my friends and family watching the nightly news and worrying something has happened to me, so I'm not telling you where I am, he wrote. *Besides, I'm doing fine and I plan on being out of this place by Christmas.*

Libbie was relieved he was fine, and she sent up a little prayer for him.

Libbie was so excited at the prospect of getting pregnant that she began making plans for the baby-to-be. Their guest room was small but would be perfect for a nursery. She threw herself into painting the room a soft sage green—"It's perfect for a boy or a girl," she told Jack—and had Jack take out the existing bed and other furniture and store it at her parents' house so she could make room for baby furniture.

"Aren't you getting a little ahead of yourself?" Jack said when she'd asked him to remove the furniture.

"I know I'll be pregnant any day now," she said confidently.

Jack just smiled and moved the furniture.

As February turned into March, Libbie began to worry because she wasn't pregnant yet. When April came and she was still not pregnant, she went to see the doctor, but he told her she was perfectly healthy and to be patient. He also reminded her that if she did become pregnant, they'd need to reevaluate her antidepressant medication. She only nodded and didn't tell him she'd already stopped taking it. She didn't need a lecture about staying on her medication. In her mind, she was fine.

Summer came to the north woods and the days grew warm. It should have been a happy time for Libbie, but each month that she found she wasn't pregnant, Libbie grew more discouraged. In June, she broke down crying one night when Jack came home from work.

"I'm not pregnant—again!" she wailed.

Jack tried his best to calm her down, but she was inconsolable. "Libs, you can't keep doing this to yourself," he said, pulling her into his arms. "Maybe if you just relax and enjoy the summer, it'll happen."

Libbie pushed Jack away. "How am I supposed to relax or enjoy the summer? All you do is work. I'm alone every day and most nights and weekends. We never have fun because you're never here."

Jack sighed, running his hand through his hair. "I'm sorry, Libs, but if I didn't work the extra jobs, then we wouldn't be living here. And if we have a baby, there'll be even more expenses. I'm just trying to pay the bills."

"*If* we have a baby? What do you mean by that? I knew you didn't want to have a baby. You're already complaining about what it will cost."

"Libs, I didn't mean it that way. You have to calm down. Getting upset isn't going to help."

Libbie ran to their bedroom and slammed the door. She knew she was acting crazy, but she couldn't control it. She wanted a baby so badly, and she didn't want to listen to reason.

Jack slept on the sofa that night, and in the morning, Libbie came out and crawled under his blanket with him. "I'm sorry, Jack. I want a baby so much. I know you're working hard to pay the bills and I do appreciate it. I don't know why I get so crazy sometimes. I'm so sorry."

Jack pulled her close. "I know, Libs. We're both tired and stressed. I hate being away from you so much, too, but it's the way it has to be for now. Let's try to enjoy the summer and see what happens, okay?"

Libbie nodded. She knew she should calm down and relax, but it was hard. Her emotions were running rampant, and all she could think about was having a baby. It nearly drove her crazy.

"Besides," Jack said, "we can't make a baby if I'm sleeping on the sofa." He chuckled.

"Oh, hon. I'll try harder not to act crazy about it."

And she did try, but it wasn't easy. Her nerves were on edge by the time Carol's wedding came in July. As the matron of honor, it was her job to host a bridal shower and a bachelorette party for Carol, and although she usually loved doing those things, her heart wasn't in it. She was actually relieved when the wedding was over. She was tired and felt drained, both physically and emotionally.

As summer wore on, Libbie began to withdraw from her usual activities. She started spending more time alone while Jack was at work and begged off from card night on Tuesdays and neighborhood barbeques on Saturdays. She rarely visited the neighbor women during the day anymore, either. June and Natalie stopped by often to ask how she was, and she always put on a smiling face for them and said she was fine. In truth, Libbie no longer enjoyed being around the women who had children. It reminded her that she wasn't pregnant, and that upset her more.

Jack was so tired at night when he came home from work that he didn't complain when she canceled get-togethers with the neighbors. He told her he was happy spending time alone with her. More and more, he was working at his uncle's gas station on weeknights, fixing cars for extra money. He'd come home late, eat leftovers from the night before, and drop into bed. Libbie no longer complained that he worked too much. She was too wrapped up in feeling miserable about not being able to get pregnant.

After another one of Libbie's breakdowns, Jack gently suggested she should try taking her antidepressant again to see if she'd feel better. Libbie refused to even talk about it. "I won't take it," she said defiantly. "I hate how it makes me feel. I'm fine." Jack didn't say anything more about it after that.

In October, Libbie ran into Carol at the grocery store. She

immediately felt guilty for not having seen her since the wedding. But Carol was beaming and had exciting news to share.

"I'm pregnant!" Carol announced. "Only two months, but I'm so happy, I could burst. I knew you'd be happy for me, too."

Libbie's heart sank when she heard the news. She feigned excitement for her friend and promised to keep in touch. But when she got back to her car with her groceries, Libbie burst into tears. She'd been trying for months to get pregnant, yet Carol was pregnant only a couple months after getting married. It wasn't fair.

Libbie passed the liquor store on her drive home, and for the first time in a year and a half, it beckoned to her. She pulled into the parking lot and sat there a long time, debating what to do. She really wanted a drink. No, she needed a drink. Her mouth watered at the thought of the sweet liquid sliding down her throat, and the warm feeling it gave her. But could she drink only one glass? Was she strong enough to control how much she drank? Just one couldn't hurt. She was stronger now. She'd proven she could stop drinking for over a year. She'd have one. Only one. Before she could change her mind, she went inside and bought two bottles of wine and 7 Up, charging them to her parents' account.

Once at home, Libbie put away her groceries, but her thoughts were on the wine in the fridge. She'd placed the bottles in the vegetable drawer, knowing that Jack never looked in there. Finally, with shaking hands, she opened a bottle and poured half a glass, meaning to put 7 Up in with it. But after one sip, she decided against making a spritzer. She took another long sip and closed her eyes, enjoying the sweet taste. Soon, that warm sensation from the alcohol ran through her, and she sighed with relief. *Just one glass,* she told herself. *That's all I need.*

By three o'clock, she was passed out on the living room sofa.

* * *

Libbie told herself she had her drinking under control. On the nights Jack came home on time, she always had dinner waiting and was in a cheerful mood. She'd control how much wine she drank in the afternoon—just enough to feel good but not enough to fall asleep in the middle of the day. But on the nights she knew he'd be late, she'd unintentionally drink too much and pass out. But Jack never knew. She'd always go to bed before he came home and would be sound asleep.

By early November, as the first snow fell outside, Libbie once again discovered she wasn't pregnant. She had thought for sure she was, but her body betrayed her once more. It was only ten in the morning when she took her first sip of wine. *Just one small glass,* she told herself, *to calm my nerves.* She walked around the house, trying to find ways to take her mind off of her problems. Nothing needed dusting, the carpet was vacuumed, and even the kitchen was spotless. She didn't have to think about cooking dinner that night because Jack was working on a neighbor's car at the garage. There was nothing for her to do.

That's when it hit her hard. If she never became pregnant, if she never had a family of her own, what would she do with the rest of her life? How would she fill all the empty hours of the day while Jack was gone? What would be her purpose in life? Those thoughts weighed heavily on her. All she'd wanted was to have a family with Jack. Maybe it would never happen. Then what good was she?

Several times she passed the bedroom that was supposed to be a nursery, and finally she closed the door so she wouldn't have to be reminded of her failure to become pregnant.

Libbie went to the kitchen and opened another bottle of wine. She drank a glass and then poured another. She felt so drained emotionally. Her whole body felt weighed down with sorrow, yet she couldn't even cry anymore. The tears just wouldn't come. She'd cried them all out. Her pain was that deep.

That's when she remembered the Valium pills still sitting in the medicine cabinet.

Unsteadily, she walked to the bathroom and opened the cabinet door. Pulling out the bottle of pills, she stared at them. She hadn't had one of these since July of last year. But today, her sadness was too heavy. She saw the dark hole again, waiting for her to fall into it. She needed help desperately.

Opening the bottle, she took out one pill and held it in the palm of her hand. It was such a tiny thing, yet it could relieve such heavy pain. She walked out to the living room and picked up her glass of wine, put the pill into her mouth, and swallowed it down with a sip of the red liquid. Closing her eyes, she sighed with relief. That sigh triggered a memory, but she just couldn't remember what it was. She walked into the bedroom and crawled onto the bed, setting her wine glass on the nightstand. Lying back on the pillows, she closed her eyes and waited for the pill to take effect. Her thoughts drifted to another room, another bed, another nightstand with a glass on it. That's when it hit her—she'd become her mother.

Chapter Twenty-Five

Jack was worried about Libbie. As winter settled in, her behavior was becoming erratic. There were nights he'd come home from work and she'd be full of energy, having cleaned until the entire house was spotless and cooked a big dinner. Other nights, she'd be dragging, to the point where she just sat on the sofa covered with a blanket, staring blankly at the television. Her highs and lows were so pronounced he began asking her if she should see the doctor about taking her antidepressant again. But she'd snap back at him that she was fine, and sometimes it led to her screaming at him, followed by her crying and apologizing.

"I'm just tired," she'd tell him. "I use up all my energy working around the house and wear myself out. I have to try not to overdo it so I don't get so tired."

Jack accepted her excuses. On the nights he came home on time from work, she always had dinner ready, and the house was always spotless. He could understand how she might be overdoing it on those days. Besides, he was too tired from working so much to fight.

By December, he realized that she no longer talked about

getting pregnant. The guest bedroom door was always closed, and if he opened it, she'd get upset and shut it again. He hated seeing her so sad over not yet being pregnant.

"We can keep trying," he told her gently. "It just takes time. And we're so young; we have years ahead of us to have babies. It'll happen, Libs. Don't give up."

She'd give him a half smile and nod, but Jack could tell she'd already lost hope. And since he worked so many nights, they rarely made love, making the chances of her getting pregnant even slimmer. There wasn't much he could do, though. Prices continued to rise, heating with oil was getting more expensive, and there were all the extra expenses like house and car insurance and keeping his old truck running. He didn't even want to think about when he'd have to replace it. Still, he felt guilty leaving Libbie home alone so much when she was feeling sad.

A week before Christmas, they received a letter from Larry saying he'd survived his year in Vietnam and was now in California finishing up his days in the service. He said he'd be discharged in February and then he'd head home, but California already looked pretty good to him. *Palm trees, sunshine, and warm days in the winter,* he wrote. *And girls in bikinis everywhere! It's a bachelor's dream.*

Jack was relieved that Larry had made it through his tour in Vietnam. He couldn't wait to see his old friend again. Libbie was happy he was okay, too. It was the first time in ages Jack had seen a spark in her eyes. She'd picked up Spence and held him close and said, "Wait until Larry sees Spence. He won't believe how big he is."

That year at Christmas, Libbie didn't put as much energy into celebrating and didn't invite the neighbors over for a party. She told Jack she was too tired to put in the effort. They did go to Steve and Natalie's for dinner a few days before, but Libbie seemed distant. Christmas Eve was spent at her parents' house, which only upset Libbie more. Her parents drank too much, and Gwen and Walter argued. The little girls were the only ones having any fun with the presents they'd received.

Christmas Day at the farm was a much happier event, and Jack was relieved that Libbie seemed more relaxed. Norman had built her a beautiful jewelry armoire that stood about four feet tall and had velvet-lined drawers and doors with hooks where she could hang necklaces. Inside, Jack had placed her present. She unwrapped it and smiled brightly. He'd given her a lovely necklace and earring set with blue topaz stones. "I love it!" Libbie told him as she hugged and kissed him. Jack was pleased he'd been able to make Libbie smile.

Jan came home for Christmas break and everyone was excited to see her. She was in her second year of college and loved living in Minneapolis. Ray was now sixteen years old and had earned enough money helping his father to buy an old beater truck to drive. He was growing into a handsome man, but he still blushed when Libbie said he must be breaking all the girls' hearts in high school.

On New Year's Eve, Jack and Libbie went to a neighbor's party but it wasn't the joyous occasion it had been the previous year. Jack watched as Libbie went through the motions of being polite to everyone, but he could tell her heart wasn't in it. In fact, they'd had a fight before coming—she'd wanted to stay home, and he had told her it would be good for her to be out with their friends. She'd conceded, reluctantly, and they'd gone, but he could tell she wasn't enjoying it. She'd worn a lovely blue dress and the new necklace and earrings he'd given her. Her blond hair was down, but she'd curled it, and it hung softly around her face. He thought she was the most beautiful girl in the room. Despite the hard times they'd had, he still loved her as passionately now as when he'd proposed. He wished he could find a way to help her go back to being the carefree, happy girl she'd once been. However, he had no idea how to do that.

As midnight struck and everyone raised their glasses to toast 1973, Jack pulled Libbie close. "I love you, Libs," he whispered into her ear. "I hope all your dreams come true this year." They clinked their champagne glasses and sipped, but Libbie just gazed around blankly, as if she hadn't even heard what he'd said.

At home afterward, Libbie was already curled up under the blankets and sound asleep by the time Jack got into bed. Jack sighed, disappointed, but kissed her softly on the cheek and snuggled up next to her.

* * *

On a crisp night in February, Larry showed up at their door with a wide grin. "I'm back," he said, laughing.

Jack hugged his friend, excited to see him. "I can't believe you've been gone for two years," he said as he led Larry inside. "It went so fast."

"Not fast enough for me," Larry said.

"Larry!" Libbie ran out from the kitchen and into his arms, hugging him tightly. When she finally pulled away, she beamed at him. "I'm so happy you're safe and at home."

"Me, too," he said, kissing the top of her head. He looked around. "Hey, is that Spence? He's a monster now!"

Libbie laughed and picked Spence up to show Larry. "Isn't he adorable? And he loves it here. He has a sunny window seat to sleep in every afternoon."

Larry scratched the cat behind the ears. "I don't blame him for loving it here. These are quite some digs. What happened? Did you win a lottery or something?"

Jack explained how they ended up with the house, as they all sat in the living room. Libbie sprang up to get the pan of brownies she'd made earlier, and Larry praised her profusely for the treats.

"You don't get these in the army," he said as he stuffed a second one into his mouth.

He told them he was staying at his parents' house for the time being, until he could find a job and get his own place. He wasn't sure if he wanted to finish school or just work. Then he sang praises about how beautiful southern California was and how he would have preferred to stay there.

"But you'd miss all of us," Jack said, grinning.

Larry laughed. "I'd miss these brownies, that's for sure."

As they talked, Jack noticed the change in Larry. He still teased and joked, but his eyes didn't shine the way they used to and he seemed tense. Jack hoped someday Larry would share his experiences in Vietnam with him so he'd understand it better, but not today. Today was for celebrating and catching up with his old friend.

March and April flew by. Change was constantly in the air. Their next-door neighbors sold their house and moved to Minneapolis. Good jobs had always been difficult to find in their little town, and with the downturn in the economy, it was getting harder. In addition, inflation was causing the price of everything to go up and making it difficult to raise a family on small-town pay. Jack felt lucky that there was always a need for mechanics, so his job was secure. But with the rise in prices, it continued to be necessary for him to work many nights a week repairing cars on the side. Libbie no longer complained about his long hours. He figured she was used to it by now, although he worried about her constantly. Her moods changed so quickly, he never knew from one minute to the next if she was happy or if she'd start yelling at him or crying. He had trouble understanding her behavior. When she was happy, she was almost exuberant. Her eyes shone brightly, and she'd do the work of two people around the house. But when she was down, she could barely function. He did his best to lighten her mood as much as possible, but with his own limited energy, it was difficult.

Often, when Jack worked late at night on a car at his uncle's garage, Larry would show up with a six-pack and keep him company. Jack never drank while he worked on engines, but he enjoyed listening to Larry ramble on. Larry was working construction with a local contractor building houses. It was only part-time, since building was down right now, but it was something.

Jack confided to Larry his concerns about Libbie. There was no one else on earth he'd trust telling their personal problems to except his best friend. Larry listened and commiserated, but he never gave advice. He seemed to know that Jack just needed an ear to vent his frustrations to. Jack was relieved he finally had someone to talk to again. Between Libbie's moody behavior and his constant working, Jack was exhausted. But he had to keep going, for Libbie's sake.

* * *

Libbie knew she was losing her battle with pills and alcohol, but she simply didn't have the energy to fight it anymore. Since the day she'd started the Valium again, she'd been unable to stop.

Now she was taking up to five a day and drinking wine, and it was a wonder she could function at all.

She'd been successful at hiding her drinking from Jack all these months. On days she knew he'd be home, she forced herself to drink less so she could function enough to cook a meal. It wasn't easy, because her body craved the alcohol as much as it craved Valium. Her nerves were raw and her hands shook if she waited too long to take a pill or have a glass of wine. But keeping it from Jack was paramount. Libbie couldn't bear for him to find out. He'd want her to see the doctor again, and she'd have to take those dreaded antidepressants. And he'd be disappointed in her, something she couldn't even bear to think about.

Sometimes she'd wake up with renewed energy and buzz around the house with such intensity, it surprised her. Her heart raced, blood pounding in her ears until she couldn't take the nervousness any longer and needed to take another pill or have another drink to relax. Other days, she could barely drag herself out of bed. These highs and lows drained her physically and emotionally. She lost weight, and her already petite frame became even smaller. When she looked in the mirror, she barely recognized herself. Shadows framed her eyes, and her skin and hair no longer shined. There was a tightness around her mouth that reminded her of her mother. But even that realization couldn't stop her from finding solace in one more glass of wine or one more pill.

Libbie hated that she often snapped at Jack but couldn't control herself. One moment, they'd be sharing a joke and laughing, the next moment she'd be yelling at him for not putting his clothes in the hamper or for leaving his shoes out. Her nerves walked the tautest tightrope, and the smallest infraction made her snap. Afterward, she'd fall to pieces, cry, and apologize profusely to Jack for yelling.

Libbie was losing control of her life and had no idea how to stop it.

In June, Libbie heard that Carol had given birth to a healthy baby girl. Carol called her several times to invite her over to see the baby, but Libbie made excuses each time. The last thing she needed to see was how happy Carol was with her new baby when Libbie couldn't have one of her own. Finally, the calls stopped. A small part of Libbie was sad about ignoring her friend, but she knew that, for her own sanity, it was for the best.

The empty house next door was purchased in June by a single woman, and it wasn't long before the neighborhood women began spreading gossip about her. Libbie rarely saw her friends anymore, but one day Natalie and June dropped by, and they warned her to watch out for the new neighbor.

"She's divorced," Natalie said in a hushed tone. "And you know what that means. She'll be after all our husbands."

"I heard she cheated on her husband, and that was why he left her," June said.

Libbie listened to her friends with little interest. She didn't care who the woman was or what she'd done. When Libbie finally met her one sunny day, she was struck by how stunning the woman was. She was tall and slender, with long, straight dark hair and big dark eyes fringed in thick lashes. Her skin was tanned a golden brown, and the sundress she wore showed off her shapely figure. Libbie was sitting outside at their patio table, trying to concentrate on a magazine article and failing misera-bly. The woman walked over, smiling brightly, and introduced herself.

"Hi. I'm your new neighbor," she said, raising her hand to shake Libbie's.

Libbie shook it. "Hello. I'm Libbie."

"I'm Alicia. Alicia Alexander. It's nice to meet you, Libbie."

They talked about the weather and what Alicia did for a living. She told Libbie she worked as a secretary at a local law firm. She seemed nice, so Libbie didn't give her a second thought. That is, until she saw Alicia talking to Jack one evening. He had just come home, and Libbie heard his truck drive up. She'd walked into the living room to glance out the window and see why it was taking him so long to come inside. He was standing on their lawn, talking to Alicia. He was smiling and nodding, and at one point Alicia squeezed his arm with her hand and Jack laughed.

Libbie's heart pounded. She suddenly understood why the neighborhood women didn't like Alicia.

When Jack came in, she jumped him immediately.

"What were you and Alicia talking about?"

Jack looked at her, surprised. "She came over and introduced herself. Then she commented on my uniform and asked if I was a mechanic."

"You both were laughing like old friends. What was so damn funny about that?"

Jack grinned. "I said, 'No, I just like to roll in grease all day.'"

Libbie felt angry heat rising up to her face. That was exactly what Jack had said to her, years ago, when she was flirting with him at the gas station. That had been their joke, and he'd used it on Alicia. She turned on her heel and stormed off to the kitchen. She wanted a drink so badly, but she didn't dare have one in front of Jack.

Jack followed her. "What? We were just talking."

"Yeah, right. I see how pretty she is. And she's divorced. She's probably looking for husband number two." Libbie stood over the stove and stirred the gravy for the pot roast. Her motions were so violent, the saucepan spun on the burner.

"Hey, careful there," Jack said soothingly, coming up behind her and gently placing his hand on her arm. "We don't want you to get burned."

Libbie dropped the spoon and spun to face him. "What do you care? You can go running to Alicia if I drop dead."

Jack frowned. "Don't talk like that. Why is this such a big deal? She came over and talked to me. I didn't start the conversation. Besides, she's at least ten years older than we are."

Libbie pulled her arm away from him and ran out of the kitchen and into the bathroom, slamming and locking the door. Her heart pounded and her hands shook. She leaned against the counter, hugging herself and rocking back and forth. *Stop acting crazy. He'll leave you for sure.*

Jack knocked on the door. "Libbie? Come on. I didn't do anything wrong."

Libbie grabbed the bottle of Valium out of the medicine cabinet, opened it, and took one. She leaned against the wall, waiting for the pill to take effect so her heart would stop pounding and her thoughts would stop racing.

"Libbie! Please. Open the door!"

Libbie slid down the wall and sat on the floor as tears filled her eyes. She couldn't have a baby, she'd lost control of her life, and next, she'd lose Jack.

* * *

Jack avoided his new neighbor at all costs after the scene Libbie had made over his talking to her. He only waved when he saw Alicia and continued on his way as fast as he could. He hadn't understood Libbie's jealousy that night, and he didn't understand it now. But he didn't want a repeat of Libbie's jealous behavior.

After Libbie had locked herself in the bathroom, it had taken him an hour of coaxing through the door to get her to unlock it. He'd been ready to knock it down, but thankfully, he hadn't needed to. Libbie had finally come out, meek as a kitten, and hugged Jack close, crying on his shoulder. He'd held her a long time as she cried and apologized, then cried some more.

He didn't understand her moods, and it was wearing on him as much as it was her.

He knew something was terribly wrong with Libbie. She'd lost so much weight that her clothes hung on her, and her eyes looked dull and lifeless. He asked her over and over again if she felt okay, and each time she brushed his concerns away: *I'm tired; I just overdid it today; I'm getting a cold.* Those were her excuses, but he knew there was more going on than tiredness or a cold. But when he asked if she should see a doctor, she flew into a rage and stormed into their bedroom, refusing to come out. So he gave up asking.

Time was wearing Jack down. Two years of working full-time and taking on additional work had taken its toll. He worried constantly about paying the bills and about Libbie's health. Instead of feeling like a kid of twenty-two, he felt like an old man. He barely had the energy to keep himself going, let alone take care of Libbie when she fell to pieces. He tried, but he knew he was failing, and that made him feel even worse.

On a hot August evening, Jack came home directly from work instead of heading over to his uncle's garage to work on a car. He was so tired; he just didn't want to look at another engine that day. He hadn't called to tell Libbie he'd be home early. He figured he'd shower, change, and then take her out for dinner. He hoped it would cheer her up.

When he walked into the house, he immediately noticed how quiet it was. Spence came over to greet him, and Jack scooped the cat up. Suddenly, an eerie feeling crept over him. It felt like he'd done this before. He shivered, despite the heat of the day. Turning toward the living room, he saw Libbie. She was lying on the sofa, one arm hanging limply to the floor. On the table beside her was an overturned bottle of red wine. It had left two tiny droplets of red liquid on the glass coffee table. They looked like blood.

Jack's heart pounded. He dropped the cat and covered his face with his hands. "Oh God, no. Please, not again."

Chapter Twenty-Six

For the next two months, Jack came home most nights to Libbie passed out on the sofa or lying in bed. There was always a bottle of wine with her, and he knew now that she was also taking the Valium again. That first night, he thought for sure she'd overdosed again but was relieved to find that her breathing was normal. She'd passed out from drinking too much. He'd carried her off to bed and then lain down beside her for a long time, making sure she was okay. Tears stung his eyes to see her this way. She'd been such a vivacious, spirited girl when they'd first dated and married. What had happened? Her entire personality had changed, and Jack had no idea what he could do to make things better.

Libbie had broken down in tears the next morning when he'd asked her why she was drinking again. She'd apologized and promised she wouldn't do it again. He wanted to believe her, but when each night came and he found her either passed out or staggering around trying to make dinner, he knew she couldn't keep her promise.

He tried taking on less work and coming home early more

often, but soon the bills piled up and he had to start working nights again to pay them. Besides, it didn't matter if he came home on time or not now; Libbie would almost always be drunk or on her way to being so by the time he came home. It had become routine for him to come home, feed Spencer, and then carry Libbie off to bed. The refrigerator soon emptied of anything edible, and Libbie no longer shopped to fill it up. Yet she always had a bottle of wine and Jack had no idea how she got it or where she was hiding it. He searched the house several times, but never found where she kept it. Was someone bringing it over? And how was she paying for it? He'd stopped giving her money and had opened accounts at stores around town so she wouldn't have cash on hand to buy wine. But that still didn't stop her from getting it.

Fighting had also become the norm in their household. If Libbie was awake when he came home, she'd pick a fight with him: *All you do is work. You don't care about me anymore. You don't appreciate all I do.* It went on and on. Excuses for why she hadn't made supper or gone shopping or done laundry. He never pointed a finger at her or complained. He didn't want to stress her out more. Jack would stop by the grocery store after work and pick up food or bring home burgers for dinner. He did his own laundry, and hers, too, if she hadn't done it. He never said a word to her about it, even when he was too tired to do it all. But she'd find a reason to fight, and it always ended with her running off and locking herself in the bathroom or bedroom. Jack gave up trying to coax her out. He was too drained.

Jack began blaming all their troubles on the house. He hadn't wanted to accept the house from Libbie's parents in the first place—he had known they couldn't afford it. He'd agreed to it to make Libbie happy. But the house didn't make her happy. He obviously didn't make her happy, either. He soon began to resent and hate the house, as if it was at the core of all their problems. If they didn't have the house, he wouldn't have to work long hours, and Libbie wouldn't have gone back to drinking again. At least that was what he thought, because he couldn't bring himself to believe the alternative—that he was the reason she drank.

One chilly evening in early October, Jack came home around eight, after another shift at his uncle's shop. It was dark out, and winter was already in the air. When he pulled into the driveway, he was startled to see the front door open. Hurrying inside, he saw Libbie lying on the sofa, a bottle of wine on the table. He wondered why the door was open. Had someone been here?

Then he remembered Spence.

He ran all over the house, searching under tables and beds for the orange tabby. He opened every closet and cupboard, checked the laundry room, and even pushed aside the shower curtain to check the tub. Spence was nowhere. Jack bent over Libbie, gently shaking her, trying to wake her up.

"Libs! Libs! Wake up! Spence is missing."

She only raised an arm to push him away and curled deeper into the sofa.

Jack hurried outside and began looking through every bush and up in every tree for Spence. The cat had never lived outside, and Jack worried that he might get into a fight with a stray and get hurt. He knocked on doors telling everyone who answered that Spence had gotten out and was missing. Soon, the entire neighborhood was searching with flashlights for the cat.

"Where's Libbie?" June asked. "She must be frantic."

Jack lied and said she was too distraught to come out and look. He couldn't bear to say she was passed out on the living room sofa.

An hour passed, and Jack was in a panic. He feared for the cat, but his worst fear was how Libbie would react if anything happened to Spence. She loved that cat dearly, and if he never came home, it would tear her apart. Especially if she found out she'd been the one to let him out.

Finally, a neighbor at the end of the block called out that he saw a cat in the bushes, and Jack ran there to check. He got down on his knees and flashed his light under the thick bushes, and there was Spence, huddled and shaking.

Jack heaved a sigh of relief. "Come on, Spence. It's okay. I'll take you home," he said softly to the cat. Jack reached out and pulled the cat to him, picking him up and holding him tight. Everyone who'd been searching was circled around him, cheering that he'd found Spence.

Jack thanked his neighbors and hurried home. When he got there, he placed the scared cat in the kitchen and fed him. Then he walked on tired legs to the living room and looked down at Libbie. She was sound asleep, completely oblivious to the drama that had taken place.

He knew that he could no longer ignore Libbie's condition. By leaving the door open, she'd put herself in danger. What if a stranger had come inside? Or she'd stumbled out into the night and become lost. As painful as it was to do, it was time he admitted she had a problem. He had to do something to help her.

* * *

Jack entered Mr. Wilkens's office tentatively. He'd taken an hour off of work to come see Libbie's dad and ask for help. He hated asking, but he'd decided that if anyone knew what to do in this situation, it would be him.

"Hello, Jack," Mr. Wilkens said, standing up from behind his heavy mahogany desk to greet him. "Isn't this a surprise."

Jack walked over to the desk and sat in the chair that Mr. Wilkens had motioned to.

"What can I do for you, son? You look tired. You must be working too hard."

Jack stared at Mr. Wilkens as he tried to find his voice. Jack hadn't seen him in a while, and he noticed that he looked older and thinner. He, too, looked tired.

"Libbie isn't doing very well," Jack began, and he saw a worried crease form between Mr. Wilkens's brows. "She's been drinking again and taking pills. I don't know what to do about it anymore. I thought you could help me."

Mr. Wilkens ran a hand across the back of his neck and his face dropped, as if the smile he'd been wearing when he'd greeted Jack was all that was holding it up. He sighed. "I told you before, son. Libbie is sensitive. She's like a delicate flower and needs extra care. You have to take care of her. She's your responsibility."

Jack stood and circled the chair, coming to face him again. "I have been taking care of her," he insisted. "But I can't be there twenty-four hours a day. I have to work. I've done everything I can to keep her from buying alcohol, but she still manages to get it."

"Then you have to try harder. You have to spend more time with her."

Jack slammed his hand down on the back of the chair. "How? How can I do that when we have that damned house to pay for and all the other bills? I'm working day and night just to keep us afloat. I can't be with Libbie all the time."

Mr. Wilkens stood and walked around the desk to face Jack. "What do you expect me to do? I already have my hands full between running my businesses and Abbie being sick so often. Even with Gwen's help, I'm burning the candle at both ends. I can't take on your problems, too."

The two men stared at each other, each with frustration creasing his face. Jack had never heard Mr. Wilkens yell like that before—he was usually so calm and even-tempered.

Jack dropped into the chair, defeated. "I don't know what to do. I love Libbie so much. But she needs help. I'm afraid for her."

Mr. Wilkens pulled a chair up next to Jack's and sat, placing his hand on younger man's shoulder. "I'm sorry, son. I'm just so frustrated myself. I had no idea Libbie was doing so badly. I've been consumed with her mother's problems."

Jack stood. "I'm sorry I bothered you. I just thought that you might know what could be done to help Libbie. I'm at my wits' end." He turned and walked to the door.

"Jack."

Jack turned and looked at Mr. Wilkens, watching as the older man took a deep breath.

"There is a place where Libbie could go. It's a nice place, where doctors would treat her problem and help her to get better."

Jack stepped closer. "What kind of place?"

"A hospital of sorts, with a peaceful country setting on a lake. It's more like a retreat, where she can relax and get healthy again. Doctors will set up a treatment plan for her, and she'll no longer have access to alcohol."

"How long would she have to be there?"

"Probably two weeks. Maybe longer. It will be up to the doctor to decide."

Jack stood quietly a moment, thinking about his options. He couldn't help Libbie get better on his own. But sending her somewhere for a long period of time scared him, too.

"I can see you're hesitant, son," Mr. Wilkens said. "I understand. But it is a good place for her to get well. I promise you. I'd never send Libbie anywhere I didn't trust. You know that."

Jack looked up at him. He knew it was true—Mr. Wilkens loved his daughter dearly and wouldn't suggest anything if he thought it wasn't a good idea. "Has Mrs. Wilkens ever gone there?" he asked.

Mr. Wilkens nodded. "Yes, she has. But she was much older than Libbie when she went and more set in her ways. Libbie is young. Maybe if we catch her problem now, she can beat it and won't have to fight this the rest of her life."

Jack nodded. "Okay. How do I set this up?"

"I'll take care of the arrangements," Mr. Wilkens said. "And of course, I'll pay for it. I'll let you know as soon as everything is set up."

"Thank you, Mr. Wilkens."

"No thanks necessary, son. We're family. Family helps each other. We're going to get our Libbie well again, okay?" He looked optimistic.

"Yes, sir," Jack said, before leaving the room and walking out into the crisp October day. *We're going to get our Libbie well again.* He prayed that Mr. Wilkens was right.

* * *

On Friday, Jack took half a day off work and headed home. He hadn't told Libbie that he and her father were going to take her for help with her drinking. He figured if he told her only minutes before they had to leave, there would be less of a struggle. When he arrived home, Libbie, not surprisingly, was already halfway through a bottle of wine.

Libbie looked up at Jack in surprise when he walked through the front door. "What are you doing home so early?" she asked, slurring her words.

Jack walked over to where she sat on the sofa. She had the television on and Spence was snuggled up on the blanket in her lap. Jack kneeled down in front of Libbie and took her hands in his. "Libs, I came home early so your father and I could take you to a retreat to get well. You can't keep going on like this, sweetie. I'm afraid I'll lose you if we don't do something to help you feel better."

Libbie's eyes grew wide. "Go away? No. I'm not going anywhere. You can't make me go."

"You're not well, Libbie. You've lost so much weight, you're not eating enough, and your drinking is out of control. You need help. And your father has assured me that you'll be going to a wonderful place that will help you get well again. Please, Libs. Please do this. For me. For us."

Libbie pulled away from him so violently, Spence flew out of her lap and ran out of the room. Libbie stood and backed up several steps from Jack. "I'm not sick. I don't need help. You're just trying to get rid of me. You think I'm crazy and you want to lock me away. I won't go. I won't!" She ran into the bedroom and slammed the door behind her.

Jack's heart broke. She'd looked like a wild animal caught in a trap. He went to the bedroom door and walked inside. Libbie was lying on the bed, her face in her pillow, sobbing. Jack sat on the edge of the bed and gently rubbed her back. "Please, Libbie. I'm not trying to get rid of you. I want you to feel well so we can be happy again. I miss you. When you drink and take pills, you're no longer yourself. I love you, Libs. I only want to help you."

Libbie turned, tears streaking her cheeks. "I'll quit drinking, Jack. I promise. I'll do it right here. I can stop anytime I want. I don't need to leave you to do it. Please, please don't send me away." Her voice was small and pitiful, and Jack thought he was going to break down and give in at any moment. But he had to be strong. He wanted his Libbie back, and it wasn't going to happen if she didn't get help.

Jack pulled Libbie into his arms and held her tightly. "I don't want you to go, either, sweetie, but you have to. I promise, you'll feel so much better if you do. Please do this. If you keep drinking and taking pills, I'm afraid I'll lose you. I can't live without you, Libs. Please. Let me take you to get help."

Jack held her in his arms for a while before Libbie finally agreed to go. After packing a small bag, she calmly walked outside with Jack to where her father's car was waiting. Jack sat beside her on the ride there, holding her hand and reassuring her that everything would be okay.

But when he had to tear himself away from her as she clung to him at the door, he felt like he had betrayed her. They wouldn't let him stay with her while she was checked in or settled into a room. And he was told he couldn't visit her while she was there. His heart broke as he forced himself to walk away with Mr. Wilkens, the sound of Libbie's sobs following him down the sidewalk.

Once Jack was home, he got into his pick-up and headed straight for the little bar on the edge of town where he knew Larry spent a lot of his free time. He walked in, sat down on a stool beside Larry, and ordered a beer.

Larry, who was drinking whiskey, waited until Jack had drunk down half his beer before speaking. "You did the right thing. She's going to be fine."

Jack nodded, but he still felt his heart being ripped apart at the thought of Libbie crying and calling for him to come back.

"I want everything to be like it was before," Jack said, feeling like he'd lived a hundred years already.

Larry shook his head. "Sorry, pal. Nothing is ever going to be the same again. You just have to hope for better days to come."

As pessimistic as that sounded, Jack understood it was true. Their life together would never be the way it was the first time they'd kissed or the day they were married. He still loved her as fiercely now as he did then, but those days were gone. He just had to make the best of the times to come.

Chapter Twenty-Seven

Libbie got out on a Sunday afternoon two weeks after Jack had dropped her off at the center. When she saw him walking up the sidewalk, she couldn't stop herself from running to him and throwing herself into his arms. Tears ran down her cheeks as she held him tightly, not wanting to let him go for fear of his leaving again.

Before leaving the center, Jack and Libbie met with the doctor to discuss her treatment plan. Dr. Lingby explained to Jack what medications Libbie was taking and the doses, and that she wasn't to take more than prescribed or touch alcohol. He gave them a sheet with the medications and doses written out. Libbie watched as a frown creased Jack's face, but he only nodded. She feared he was upset at the thought of having a wife who was dependent on so much medication just to act "normal," but he didn't let on that it bothered him. When they left, he carried her bag with one hand and slipped his other around her waist as he walked her out to the truck.

They made small talk all the way home, as if they were strangers sharing a ride. Libbie chose her words carefully. She was fearful that one wrong word would send her back into the care center. Not that it had been a bad place—the doctors and nurses had treated her kindly—but she never wanted to be locked away like that again. The first week had been hell as she "dried out" from alcohol and Valium. She'd trembled, had hot and cold sweats, and vomited her way through that week. But as the poison left her system, she'd felt better through the second week. She had long sessions with the psychiatrist about the triggers that caused her to drink and take pills, and group sessions with other patients discussing their experiences. Libbie hadn't liked any of it, had only participated so she would be able to go home. Now, armed with a strong antidepressant, sleeping pills, and Valium for anxiety, and the knowledge of her triggers for alcohol and pill abuse, she was told she could resume normal life.

The problem was, Libbie no longer knew what normal was.

One thing she knew for certain—the pills dulled her senses and made her feel sleepy most of the time, and she hated feeling that way.

* * *

Winter settled in and Libbie watched as the trees shed their leaves and snow covered the lawns. She rarely saw the neighbors anymore, just a wave here or a hello there. Her father stopped by occasionally to visit with her, but he was all she saw of her family. He said her mother was having a rough time that winter and Gwen was too busy with her girls and helping with Abigail to do much else. Larry stopped by some evenings when Jack was working, and Libbie knew that he was checking up on her for Jack. She believed it was the same when Bev would stop by unannounced in the afternoon to drop off chocolate chip cookies or a loaf of banana bread. They all acted like it was normal to stop by, but Libbie knew otherwise. Jack was afraid she'd relapse, so he sent people to check on her.

Jack no longer trusted her to be alone.

Libbie didn't trust herself, either.

She spent her days cleaning the house, cooking, baking, and doing laundry. She went to the grocery store, tried not to glance longingly at the liquor store when she passed it, and filled her prescriptions regularly at the drugstore. Every other night Jack was home for dinner, and the other nights and Saturdays he worked on cars at his uncle's garage. Sundays they spent together, either going to the farm for dinner, taking in a movie, or going out for a burger. Their life was in perfect order so that nothing would upset the balance that Libbie needed to stay well.

Libbie felt that her life had become an endless stream of nothingness.

Christmas was a quiet event that year. They had dinner with her parents on Christmas Eve. Her mother looked pale and drawn, despite having spent the day before at the beauty parlor. Her father also looked tired. Gwen had gained more weight that year, which made her even crabbier, and Walter was his usual bragging self. The girls were growing, now ages six and three, but Libbie took little interest in them. Lynn whined a lot, and Leslie cried when she didn't get her way. It was all too much for Libbie's nerves, so they left early.

Christmas Day at the farm was much more relaxing. Jan was home again that year for winter break, but this time she'd brought home her new boyfriend, Evan Goddard. He was a tall, slender man with blond hair, blue eyes, and a polite personality. He was a junior in college, like Jan was, but he was a business major. Libbie liked him immediately and noticed the way his eyes shined every time he looked at Jan. She remembered when Jack's eyes used to light up when he looked her way, but she hadn't seen them do that in a long time. Jack just looked tired now—whether from overworking or worrying about her, she didn't know.

On New Year's Eve, they watched Dick Clark ring in 1974 with the lighted ball dropping in Time's Square. When they finally went to bed that night, Jack hugged Libbie and curled his body around hers. She tensed—they hadn't made love since she'd come home from the Willow Lake Center, and she thought Jack no longer desired her. Even though he always kissed her goodbye in the morning and hello when he came home, even though he cuddled with her at night, he'd never made a move to touch her in any other way. But tonight, he held her so close that she felt his heart beating against her back.

Jack brushed her hair from her neck and kissed her there, causing delightful shivers to run down her spine. "Don't worry, Libs," he whispered near her ear. "I'd never make you do anything you're not ready to do. I've just missed you so much."

Libbie turned in his arms and looked up into his eyes. Even in the dark room, she saw how much he loved her. She ran her hand through his thick hair and down to his chest. His breathing quickened at her touch. "I'm sorry, Jack. These pills make me feel so dull and empty inside. I don't think about anything else but getting through each day."

Jack kissed her softly on the lips. "It's okay, sweetie. We have time. We have our whole lives to be together. I love you so much. I'm happy just being close to you."

Libbie sighed and snuggled up to Jack. She knew she was lucky to have him, knew that if it wasn't for him, she'd probably be dead by now. She wanted more than anything to feel like she had when they first met—before the pills and the alcohol and all the stress. As she lay in his arms and listened to his steady breathing as he slept, she prayed that she'd always have Jack in her life. He was her lifeline and without him she'd be lost completely.

* * *

The week after New Year's, Libbie was startled by a knock at the front door in the early afternoon. She'd been making a batch of oatmeal cookies. She knew it wasn't Bev because they'd talked on the phone earlier, and Larry never came during the day. When she went to answer it, there stood June and Natalie, carrying a plate of muffins and smiling brightly.

"We just couldn't stand it any longer," Natalie said as they closed the door against the cold behind them. "It's been too long since we've seen you, Libbie. I hope you don't mind us barging in."

"We have blueberry muffins," June said, lifting the plate. "Would you like one?"

Libbie smiled for what felt like the first time in ages. She had missed her friends. "That sounds wonderful," she said. "I was just baking cookies. Why don't you come into the kitchen and we can visit while I finish."

They went inside the cozy kitchen, and the women sat at the table and told Libbie all the neighborhood gossip while she finished getting her cookies in the oven.

"We missed you at the New Year's party," Natalie said, accepting a bottle of Coke from Libbie and picking at a muffin. "You should have been there. The Hendersons both got drunk and had a whale of a fight."

"Why?" Libbie asked, surprised. Kevin and Louise Henderson were a nice older couple with two teenaged children. She'd never seen them even snap at each other, let alone fight.

"Because of Alicia," Natalie said.

"Alicia? She was invited?"

Natalie nodded enthusiastically. "Yes, although no one will admit to having invited her. She came in after the party had started wearing the lowest-cut minidress you've ever seen—it was downright slutty. Of course, all the men stared at her like they'd never seen a woman before. Then Kevin walked right over to her and asked if he could fix her a drink, all the while staring down at her cleavage. It was so obvious."

June jumped in. "Louise went over and tugged at his arm, but he ignored her. Just plain ignored her! She stomped off into the kitchen. Alicia said something to Kevin that none of us could hear, and he hightailed it into the kitchen after Louise. She immediately started yelling at him for ignoring her and told him that if he wanted to spend his time with that little whore, he could have at it. Of course, that didn't go over well with him, so he started yelling back."

"Everyone in the living room tried to politely continue talking, but it was hard to ignore," Natalie said. "And can you believe that Alicia just walked around saying hello to everyone as if nothing had happened? That woman is shameless."

Libbie wasn't one for gossip, but this story did bother her. "Are the Hendersons okay?"

June leaned in closer to Libbie. "We think they might be getting a divorce. Kevin left the next day with a suitcase, and no one has seen him since."

"That's terrible," Libbie said, feeling sorry for the Hendersons. She had really liked them.

Both women nodded their heads. "Every woman in the neighborhood is afraid her husband will be next," Natalie said.

"Alicia is always flirting with the men in this neighborhood. Can you believe she asked my Steve to come over and fix her kitchen faucet? He doesn't know anything about fixing a faucet. Fortunately, he was smart enough to say he couldn't; otherwise there might be another divorce in this neighborhood."

"Well, maybe she does need help once in a while. She doesn't have a man around to do all those things we depend on our husbands to do," Libbie said.

"I don't think she's looking for a handyman," June said. "The way she looks—the tight clothes she always wears—it's obvious to me what she wants."

Libbie shook her head. She remembered how jealous she'd been of Alicia when Jack talked to her. She could understand why the other women would be upset, too.

"I'd be careful of Alicia if I were you, Libbie," Natalie said. "She seems to have her eyes set on Jack, not that I can blame her. He's a good-looking guy."

Libbie had been taking the cookies off the sheet with a spatula when Natalie's warning hit her. She turned and looked at her friends. "What do you mean by that?"

The two women at the table looked at each other and then turned back to Libbie. Natalie spoke. "While you were away, I saw Alicia go inside your house one night after Jack came home from work."

Libbie gasped.

"Oh, but it could have been quite innocent," Natalie rushed to say. "I'm sure Jack would never cheat on you, Libbie. You're a hundred times prettier than she is."

The memory of Alicia touching Jack's arm the night she'd seen them talking out on the lawn a few months before flashed through Libbie's mind. She'd known then that Alicia had eyes for Jack, but why would he let her into their home?

"Libbie? Are you okay?" Natalie asked, concern edging her voice. "I didn't mean to start anything between you and Jack. I'm sure nothing happened."

Libbie stared at the two women. They seemed to be floating in a haze. She blinked. Why were they hazy? "It's okay," she told Natalie. "I'm a little tired. I hope you don't mind, but I think I'll lie down for a while."

June and Natalie stood and said they understood. Libbie thanked them for bringing over the muffins and smiled and nodded at what they said until she could herd them out the door. Once they were gone, she sat down on the sofa and stared out the window. Spence came over from his spot on the window seat and jumped into her lap. Libbie pulled Spence to her and held him tightly. His fur was warm from the sunshine.

"Why would Alicia be in here?" she asked Spence. "Why would Jack let her in?"

The thought weighed heavily on Libbie. Her head began to spin with scenarios of Jack and Alicia kissing in their living room and going into the bedroom. Would Jack cheat on her? Was that why he'd been so eager to take her to the care center and leave her there?

She knew her thoughts were irrational. Jack had never once even looked at another woman. But Alicia wasn't just any woman—she was beautiful and available, and right next door. Libbie's heart pounded and her hands began to shake. She didn't want to think about Jack and Alicia. She had to stop her thoughts. She wanted a drink.

Libbie set Spence down and headed into the kitchen. The cookies forgotten, she rummaged through every cupboard in the kitchen for a hidden bottle of wine. *Where did I put them? I know I hid some around here so Jack wouldn't find them.* But maybe Jack had searched for hidden wine bottles while she was away and disposed of them.

I need a drink. I can't do this without a drink.

Frantically, she started pulling everything out of the cupboards and onto the kitchen floor. As she searched, she smelled something burning and remembered the cookies still in the oven. She pulled out the tray of burnt cookies and just dropped it on top of the stove, then returned to her hunting. *I need a drink now!*

There were no hidden bottles in the kitchen.

She sat on the floor with the mess all around her and closed her eyes. *Jack and Alicia. Jack and Alicia.* She had to get that image out of her head.

Then she remembered another spot where she'd hidden a bottle of wine.

Libbie got up and ran to the laundry room. In the back of the closet, behind a pile of blankets, she found a bottle of red wine. The feel of the long, sleek glass neck felt good in her hand. She pulled the bottle from its hiding place and looked at it longingly. Libbie sighed.

* * *

Jack walked into the house at five fifteen and immediately smelled burnt food.

"Libbie? Is everything okay?" he called out into the silent house. Slipping off his boots, he walked toward the kitchen. "Libbie?" When he walked through the kitchen door, he stopped and stared at what lay before him. Pots and pans, cookbooks, and baking dishes were strewn across the floor. A cookie sheet with burnt cookies stuck to it lay on the top of the stove, and unwashed dishes and bowls sat on the counters. The garbage was tipped over and Spence was eating something out of it.

Jack scooped up Spence and righted the garbage can. Panic spread through Jack. The kitchen looked like someone had been rummaging through it. Why? "Libbie," he said under his breath, before turning to search for her.

"What!"

Jack jumped and dropped Spence. The cat ran out the door, right past Libbie, who was standing unsteadily, staring at Jack.

"Geez, Libs. You scared me to death. What happened in here? I was afraid you were hurt."

Libbie wobbled over to him. He looked at her closely. Her hair was mussed and mascara ran in trails down her cheeks. Her eyes were bloodshot, but not from crying, he realized. She'd definitely been drinking.

"What's going on between you and Alicia?" Libbie said, coming closer to him.

Jack sighed heavily. *Not this again.* "What do you mean? I barely even see Alicia around, let alone have anything going on with her."

Libbie walked right up to him and slapped him across the face. "Don't lie to me, Jack! I know that she was over here while I was at the center. Why would you let that piece of trash in our house? Is that why you sent me away? So you could have her instead?"

Jack stood there, stunned. He raised his hand to his face, shocked that Libbie had hit him. He took a deep breath to steady the anger rising inside him. "You're drunk, Libbie. I'm not going to have this conversation with you." Jack strode past her to the dining room but barely got two steps away when he felt a hand on the back of his shirt.

"Don't you dare walk away from me! The whole neighborhood

knows you're cheating on me with that woman. How could you do that? You said you loved me! Me! Yet you had her here—alone."

Jack pulled away from Libbie's grasp and spun around to face her. She lost her balance and fell toward him, into his arms. Jack held her until she found her balance, but then she pushed him away and started stumbling toward the living room.

"I'm leaving. I can't stand looking at you!" she yelled, heading toward the door.

"Libbie, don't. Just go to bed and sleep it off. We'll talk in the morning."

"No. I hate you! You don't love me anymore." Just as she made it into the entryway, Spence ran across her path, and Libbie tripped trying to miss the cat. Jack ran to her to stop her from falling, but she fell face-first onto the hard floor before he could catch her.

"Libs. Libs! Are you all right?" Jack dropped to the floor and rolled her over. There was blood on her forehead where she'd hit the hardest.

Libbie started sobbing. "Why would you do this to me, Jack? Why would you cheat on me? I love you so much."

"I didn't cheat on you," Jack insisted. "I don't know who is telling you these lies, but I didn't invite Alicia into the house."

"Then why would they say you did?"

Jack gently lifted her into his arms and carried her to the sofa, setting her down carefully. "Stay here. I'm going to get something to put on your forehead." He ran to the bathroom, wet a washcloth, and brought it out, placing it over the spot that was bleeding.

Libbie angrily grabbed it from him and held it to her head herself.

"Libs. The only time Alicia was over here was one night after

I came home from work. I'd just stepped out of my truck, and she caught up with me on the sidewalk. She asked if she could borrow some milk because she was all out and she needed it for her coffee in the morning. So I came inside to get her some, and she followed me in. I swear she wasn't in here for more than a few minutes."

Libbie sat there silently, looking like she was trying to comprehend what Jack had said. Her eyes were glassy, and she was pale.

Jack reached up for the washcloth and pulled it away. The gash was still bleeding heavily.

"Libs, we have to take you to the hospital. You're bleeding pretty badly."

Libbie pulled away, tears still falling down her cheeks. "No. I don't want to go to the hospital. They'll just send me away again. I don't want to go away, or else I'll lose you forever." Her voice was small and pitiful.

"I'm not leaving you, Libs. How can I get that through to you? I love you! No one else. Now, please, let me take you to the hospital."

Jack watched as Libbie's eyelids became heavy and she looked like she was going to fall asleep. He was sure she hadn't heard a word he'd said. He gently laid her down on the sofa and ran to get another washcloth, exchanging it for the bloody one. "Don't move," he whispered in her ear and then kissed her cheek. "I'll be right back." Jack went over to slip on his boots and then back to pick Libbie up. By now, she was sleeping soundly and couldn't fight him. He carried her out to the truck and drove her to emergency.

Chapter Twenty-Eight

Libbie ended up with five stitches in her forehead and stayed the night for observation to rule out a concussion. Jack didn't stay at the hospital that night. He went home and cleaned up the mess in the kitchen before falling into bed.

The night's events kept running through Jack's mind, and he cringed over what had happened. Libbie's eyes had appeared more than just drunk—they'd looked wild, almost manic. And when she'd hit him, he'd been completely stunned. She hadn't been his Libbie that night. She'd been a woman out of control, whether from the alcohol or something else. What if she acted this way again? What if it was directed toward someone other than him? That thought frightened him.

And then there was the drinking. The fact that she had turned to drinking the minute something upset her proved to him that she wasn't well yet. He understood that alcoholism was something that just didn't go away, like the flu or a broken bone. It couldn't be healed entirely and could rear its ugly head at any time. But he'd hoped that Libbie could control it with his love and support—yet he'd been wrong. This was something she would be fighting her entire life. He knew she needed help again, but did he dare suggest she go for treatment? Would she react as violently as she had tonight?

In the end, he was relieved that he didn't have to make that decision alone. The next day, Libbie's regular doctor visited with her and persuaded her to go to another treatment facility where they could work on her sobriety and calm her stress. She agreed, but not without plenty of tears.

When Jack arrived at the hospital that morning, Libbie apologized profusely to him for her behavior and for drinking again. "I don't know what comes over me," she told him in a small voice. "I can't stop my mind from racing when I hear upsetting things. I just can't control it anymore."

"I understand Libs," he told her gently. The doctor had already consulted with him about a different treatment center, and Mr. Wilkens had agreed to pay. "Let's do whatever is necessary to get you well again."

Libbie went for four weeks of treatment, relapsed again, and by the end of the year had been placed in another facility for six weeks. By the time 1975 rolled around, Jack and Libbie were walking on eggshells around each other, trying to figure out how to live a normal life together, because nothing was normal for them any longer.

* * *

That January, Libbie came home from the treatment center feeling lost in her own life. It was a brand new year, and she hardly remembered anything from the year before. It was as if 1974 had never existed for her. She'd spent most of it either in a facility trying to dry out or at home, drunk and trying to hide it. It had been an endless cycle of drinking, arguing, drying out, and drinking again. Now, as she walked through the door of her home with Jack carrying her bags behind her, she didn't even feel like she belonged there. She felt like a stranger in her own home.

"Do you want to rest?" Jack said courteously, as he carried her bags into the bedroom. This time, she'd stayed in a facility just outside of Minneapolis, and they'd had a long drive home. Every mile had been excruciating for Libbie because of the stilted conversation between them. It made her sad that her own husband no longer knew what to say to her.

"I'm not sure," Libbie said, looking around the house. Spence was lying in the window seat, soaking up what little January sun he could get. Libbie walked over and sat down next to him, brushing his soft fur with her hand. "I missed you, boy," she said softly.

"He missed you too, Libs," Jack said, coming up close to them. "He'll be happy to have you home."

Libbie nodded, although she doubted if Spence really missed her anymore. She'd been gone too much the past year—either drunk out of her mind or away from home. If anything, Spence probably only tolerated her now.

Jack drew nearer and ran his hand through her hair. "I missed you too, Libs. So very much." He kissed the top of her head.

Libbie tried not to flinch or back away. She just sat as still as a statue, until Jack stepped back. It wasn't that she was afraid of Jack—she loved him dearly—but every time she came home from a treatment center, she felt as if she were getting to know him all over again. It unnerved her, knowing how close they had been yet feeling so far apart now.

"My mom made some dinners we could freeze and heat up as needed," Jack said. "And there's a fresh pan of her lasagna waiting to be heated up for dinner. Why don't you settle in and relax and I'll heat up dinner." He turned and left the room.

Libbie kicked off her shoes and curled up on the window seat next to Spence. Once again, everyone would treat her like an invalid, now that she'd returned. Bev would make dinners for them and stop by often to "visit," when Libbie knew it was really to check on her. Her father would drop by occasionally, too, and he'd have Sandra come by and clean and do laundry for her for the first few weeks. Libbie loved Bev to pieces, and she appreciated Sandra's help, but it all made her feel so useless. It was like she was a guest in her own home. She should be cooking dinner and cleaning and doing the laundry. But at this point, even she didn't think she could handle the most mundane chores.

This time, at the center, the doctors had given her new prescriptions and more advice on how to maintain her sobriety. "Don't overwork yourself, don't stress about little things, exercise every day to clear your head, and take one day at a time," one doctor had said. Of course, the new antidepressant would make sure to dull her emotions, and the Valium would calm the stress. Between the two, she didn't know how she was going to have the energy to do much of anything, let alone exercise. None of what they said made her feel confident that she could beat this problem.

Nothing had ever helped her mother stop drinking or taking pills. How could Libbie expect her life to be any different? And did she care?

* * *

Jack was tired. He tried to work as few hours as possible while still being able to pay their bills. But after four years of constantly working and almost as long worrying about Libbie, he was exhausted.

Also, his relationship with Libbie was strained. He felt like he was walking a tightrope every time he was home. They were polite to each other and went through the motions of "normal." But as a couple, they were anything but. Whenever he touched Libbie, just to hold her hand or brush a stray hair from her face—something he did as naturally as breathing—she'd tense or pull away. He tried to understand. He knew she was trying her best just to get through each day and stay sober. But he missed kissing her goodbye in the mornings, curling up next to her at night, and making love to her. Despite everything, he still loved her more than anything in the world, so it was hard for him not to be able to show affection to her.

Over the past year, Larry had taken another construction job—this one full-time—and had rented a small apartment. While Libbie was gone, Jack had spent a lot of time with Larry, either at his apartment or at Larry's favorite bar. Jack wasn't much of a drinker, but he and Larry played pool or darts or just watched football on the small television in the corner of the room. Larry never judged Libbie, always asked about her, and never gave Jack advice. He would listen without judgement, and Jack appreciated that very much. Even though he could talk to his mother and father about anything, he felt that Larry understood better. It had helped Jack get through the times Libbie was gone, because without Larry's friendship, he really believed he'd have gone crazy.

By now, all the neighbors suspected that there was something wrong with Libbie. Jack never told any of them where she went, or why, not even June and Natalie who had both asked him outright where Libbie was. But rumors spread, and he was sure they all knew, or at least thought they did. He wanted desperately to protect Libbie from their gossip. She deserved that.

One evening after they'd eaten dinner, Jack and Libbie sat on the sofa with Spence between them, watching a variety show on television. Jack glanced at Libbie, noticing how pale and worn she looked. She slept a lot—he figured it was because of her medications. But now that she'd been home a few weeks, she was doing all the cooking, cleaning, and laundry again. He helped when he could, but he knew it wasn't enough. Libbie was still tired. At that moment, he wished they could go back in time to the day they were married and do everything all over again. He would have watched more closely for signs of her drinking, he wouldn't have accepted the house, and then he could have spent more time with Libbie instead of always working. Jack reached across the cat and gently took Libbie's hand in his. She turned her head and their eyes met, but she didn't say a word.

"Libs. Let's sell this house and start over. We'll buy a place we can actually afford so I can be home every night and we can be together more—like when we were first married. I want us to go back to being that couple again. I know we can do it. I love you. I want us to be happy again."

Libbie stared at him, expressionless. At first, Jack didn't think she'd heard him, but then she finally answered.

"We can't go back to that, Jack," she said, her voice a monotone. "We can't wipe away what's happened. I want to stay in this house. It's familiar. I feel safe here."

Jack sighed. He lifted her hand and kissed it softly. "Whatever you want, Libs. I just want you to be happy."

He hoped they would be—someday.

* * *

That spring, Libbie stopped taking her antidepressant. She was tired of being emotionless. She wanted to feel happy and excited. She wanted to remember what love felt like, but most of all, what being loved felt like. It was worth the risk of feeling depressed again. Even feeling depressed would be better than feeling dull and lifeless. She told herself she could manage without the pills. Libbie hadn't drunk any alcohol since she'd come home from the center in January. She only took her Valium as prescribed. She could do this. She desperately wanted her life back.

That's when the arguing began.

Libbie's emotions returned with a vengeance. She angered easily, felt sad and sometimes even paranoid. She complained to Jack that he was never home. She had trouble focusing on any one project and never seemed to complete anything she started. Laundry would sit damp in the dryer, forgotten. Dirty dishes sat on the counter, not making it into the dishwasher. Dinner would burn. Libbie felt overwhelmed, and it turned into frustration and anger. Jack never complained to her, but she thought she saw resentment in his eyes over work left undone and she'd start yelling. Then the crying would start, the apologies, and she'd do it all over again.

Libbie hated herself for the way she acted. That only fueled her rage more. No matter how hard she tried, she didn't have control over her behavior, and that frustrated her more. Unfortunately, Jack bore the brunt of her frustration.

Jack asked her if she was taking her medication, and she flew off the handle. "I can't take that stuff anymore!" she yelled at him one night. "I might as well be dead than take it because it makes me feel dead inside."

"Libs, please. Take the medicine. You do so much better on it. We can't keep doing this. *I* can't keep doing this. Please. Take your meds," Jack begged, but Libbie wouldn't listen to him. She believed what she'd said. She'd rather be dead than take the meds.

Libbie and Jack spent more and more time apart. Often, he'd sleep on the sofa after a fight. Sometimes, Libbie wouldn't talk to him for several days. Their relationship was shattering into a million pieces, one piece at a time, and yet neither one knew how to stop it. As long as Libbie refused to take her medication, they would continue to fall apart.

Libbie's jealousy over their neighbor returned. She would see Alicia wave to Jack some evenings as he came home or see her start a conversation with him. It didn't matter that Jack barely talked to Alicia or that he came inside quickly—in Libbie's suspicious mind something was going on between them. What had Jack done all those weeks she'd been away? Did he really just sit in the house, pining for her to come home? Seeing how beautiful Alicia was, Libbie doubted that Jack had ignored her the entire time she was at the center.

Libbie kept a watchful eye on Jack and Alicia, and waited.

* * *

Jack came home later than usual one evening in May, hoping, praying, that Libbie was already asleep so there wouldn't be a fight. He'd called her at five to say he had a car to work on at his uncle's garage and then he'd be home. She hadn't seemed upset about it then, but that didn't mean she wasn't brooding about it now. Even though he'd been working late many nights ever since they'd moved into the house, she now complained that he was only doing it to stay away from her. Jack fervently wished Libbie would take her medication. Their lives weren't perfect when she did, but they were better.

And he was too tired to fight with her about it anymore.

He'd talked to Libbie's father about her refusing to take her medication, asking for his help, but Mr. Wilkens only brushed his concerns aside. "If she's not drinking, then leave it be," he'd said. "All you can do is be there for her. That's your job, Jack, to take care of her. If she feels better not taking it, then you shouldn't force her."

Jack felt frustrated and alone. He didn't understand the complexity of Libbie's problems, and no one seemed to have answers on how to care for her. Even the doctors were useless, prescribing pill after pill, none of which helped. All he could do was stick by Libbie and hope for the best.

When Jack stepped through the door that night, his eyes met Libbie's from across the room and he knew immediately that she was angry. *Oh, God. Not again.*

"Where were you?" she asked, her eyes flashing.

"I told you, Libs. I was at the garage, working on a car," he said calmly. He pulled the cash out of his pocket that the man had given him for repairing his steering. "See? Here's the money he paid me."

Libbie's eyes burned into him. "You're lying. I called the garage and you didn't answer."

"Come on, Libs. You know when I'm in the garage I don't always hear the phone in the office. Especially with my head stuck in a car."

Libbie stepped closer. "You're lying."

Jack studied her a moment. Her pupils were dilated and her face looked hard. "Have you been drinking?"

Libbie moved so fast that Jack didn't have time to step aside. She ran at him and shoved him hard. His back hit against the door, and it took him a minute to regain his balance. By then,

Libbie was already across the living room.

"What the hell are you doing?" Jack yelled.

"You were with Alicia, weren't you?" Libbie yelled back.

Jack ran his hand over his face. "For the thousandth time, I do not see Alicia. I'm not interested in her. I'm married to you."

Libbie glared at him. "Then why did Alicia just pull into her driveway minutes before you came home? That's quite a coincidence, isn't it?"

Jack shook his head and started walking toward the hallway. "I'm not doing this anymore. Have your fit. I'm going to have a nice warm shower and go to bed."

A glass ashtray flew across the room and hit the wall in front of Jack. He turned quickly and saw that Libbie had a ceramic figurine in her hand, ready to throw at him.

"Get out! Get out of my house!" she yelled, throwing the figurine. It flew across the living room and crashed into tiny pieces on the floor. "I never want to see you again! I knew you were cheating on me with her. You're going to send me away forever so you can be with her. I won't let you. Get out!" She picked up a glass candy dish and threw it.

Jack ducked as the candy dish sailed by. "Stop it, Libbie," he yelled. "Stop it. I love you. I've always loved you. Why don't you believe me? Everything I've ever done has been for you."

Tears streamed down Libbie's face. "Get out! Get out!" She swayed and almost fell down.

Despite everything, Jack came to Libbie's rescue, grabbing her arm to steady her. He'd been right. She was drinking again. God help them.

Libbie pulled away from him and started screaming again. "Get out! I hate you! I never want to see you again! Get out!" She flailed her arms and hit him over and over, pushing him towards the door. Jack had no choice but to back away from her.

"I'll go, Libs. Just stop yelling. I'll go." He strode outside and climbed up into his truck, then drove off.

Libbie was drinking again. Jack didn't know how much more of this he could take.

Chapter Twenty-Nine

Jack drove into town through the dark streets, not knowing what to do or where to go. Without realizing it, he found himself parked in front of Larry's favorite bar. Jack walked inside and, sure enough, Larry was sitting there, drinking a beer. Jack sat down next to him and ordered a beer.

Larry turned to him. "Something must be terribly wrong if you're here at this time of night. What happened?"

Jack dropped his elbows on the bar and ran his hands through his hair. He turned to his friend. "Libbie's drinking again."

Larry shook his head. "Oh, man. I'm sorry."

"It was terrible. I walked in the door after working all day and all evening, and she just jumped me about Alicia again. I don't even know where it all came from. She has it set in her mind that I'm screwing around with the neighbor, and she won't let it go. I tried to talk to her, but she just erupted and started screaming and throwing stuff at me. She told me to leave, so I finally did." Jack sighed. "I can't take this anymore. It's all too much. Nothing I do makes her happy. She's angry and paranoid all the time. It's so hard."

Larry picked up their beers and nodded for them to go sit in a booth over on the side where they could have privacy. Jack followed and sat heavily on the wooden bench.

"Jack, you're killing yourself over this. I've been silent all these years, but I can't be anymore. Maybe it's time to pull the plug. You know I love Libbie, but she just isn't the girl you married anymore. I don't know if it's the drinking or not taking her meds, but whatever it is, she's out of control and it's killing you."

Jack stared at Larry in disbelief. He'd never said a bad word about Libbie no matter what Jack confided in him, but now he wasn't holding back. "Leave Libbie? How can you say that? She needs me. I promised to take care of her, forever. How can I go back on that?"

Larry leaned over and put his hand on Jack's arm. "You have taken care of her. You've done everything for her. But she needs help, and it's not the type of help you can give her. Do you honestly want to spend the rest of your life doing this? How many more times before you've had enough?"

"But I love her," Jack said, sorrowfully. "I've always loved her."

Larry sat back and said softly, "I know, man. But at what point is love no longer enough?"

Jack sat there a long time, thinking about his friend's words. He and Libbie no longer had the relationship they'd started with. He was right—she needed help—but how could Jack abandon her at a time when she needed him most? But he knew that he couldn't keep doing this. Working all the time, the fighting, and the constant accusations. It was all too hard to live with.

He finished his beer and stood up. "I'll see you around, Lar."

"Tell me if there's anything I can do, okay?"

Jack nodded and left the bar. He got into the truck and headed home. He hoped Libbie had calmed down by now or maybe drunk herself to sleep.

Jack saw the flashing lights the moment he turned into their neighborhood. Panic rose inside him. *What has Libbie done?*

He pulled up to the house and jumped out of the truck. There was a police car in their driveway and several other cars parked haphazardly around. He recognized one as Mr. Wilkens's car. Running now, he stepped into the entryway and his eyes instantly met Gwen's across the room. She glared at him, her mouth set in a hard, thin line.

"What happened? Is Libbie okay?" Jack took a step, and something crunched under his boot. He stopped and looked down. Glass was strewn all over the floor. Photo frames had been torn from the walls and tables and tossed about. Wedding pictures had been pulled from their frames and torn in half. Stunned, Jack bent down and lifted up one of the damaged photos. It was of him and Libbie, standing at the altar, smiling brightly at the camera. Now it was torn and crumpled, just like their life together.

"What the hell are you doing here?" Gwen said, stepping closer. "I thought you were gone for good."

Jack raised his eyes and stared at her. He wasn't going to play games with her. "What happened in here? Where's Libbie?"

"Keep quiet," Gwen said sharply. "She's in the bedroom with Father and the doctor. I don't want her to hear your voice or else she'll freak out again."

"What are you talking about? Why are you even here? Why are the police here and the doctor?"

Gwen drew even closer, her shoes crunching glass as she did. "A neighbor called the police when they heard Libbie in here screaming and breaking things. He said it sounded like you were killing each other. Thank God the officer knew who Libbie was, or else he would have hauled her off to jail. She was uncontrollable, throwing everything in sight and screaming at the top of her lungs. The officer called Father right away and he called me. By the time we got here, she'd destroyed pretty much everything. She screamed over and over that she hated you and never wanted to see you again. So if I were you, I'd leave right now."

Jack's jaw tightened. "This is my house. I want to see Libbie. Now!" He turned to go down the hall but was stopped by Mr. Wilkens, who'd come out of the bedroom.

"No. This is not your house; it belongs to Libbie. Only her name and mine are on the title. So you have no right being here. I want you to leave."

Jack stared at him in disbelief. "But I'm the one who's paid the mortgage all these years. I live here. And I insist on seeing Libbie. I need to know she's okay." He tried pushing through Mr. Wilkens, but the older man stood firm.

"I won't have you upsetting Libbie again. The doctor has given her a sedative, and I won't let you wake her. She made it perfectly clear that she never wanted to see you again. You've failed her, Jack. I trusted you with my daughter, and you broke your promise to take care of her. It's over. Now get out, or I'll ask the police officer to escort you out."

Jack slowly looked around him in disbelief. Everything in sight was crushed, torn, or broken. He took a step back and looked down. He'd been standing on the blue topaz pendant he'd given Libbie one Christmas. The chain was broken, and the setting was bent. She'd destroyed everything he'd ever given her, everything that had anything to do with their lives together. His heart felt as crushed as the glass under his feet.

Defeated, he turned and slowly walked out the door.

* * *

Jack drove to Larry's apartment south of town. He had nowhere else to go. He didn't want to talk to anyone right now, so he didn't want to go to the farm. Larry wouldn't ask questions. So he found himself standing in the small entryway of Larry's building, hitting the buzzer to be let in.

"Hey? Who's there?" Larry's voice came over the speaker.

"It's me." That was all he had to say. Larry buzzed him in.

"Can I stay here tonight?" Jack asked when Larry opened his door and let him in.

"Sure." Larry found an extra pillow and blanket and set them on the tattered sofa. "Do you want to talk about it?" he asked.

Jack shook his head. He was so drained he thought he'd drop on the spot.

"That's fine. Get some sleep." Larry went off to his bedroom.

Jack lay down on the sofa and stared at the ceiling. What had happened? Libbie hadn't meant it when she said she hated him. She'd been drunk. She needed to take her meds. Once she felt better, she'd realize it was all a big mistake.

Somehow, he slept.

Jack woke up at his usual time and heard the shower running. He folded the blanket and put the pillow on top of it, then headed out the door. Last night had been a nightmare. Libbie hadn't meant what she'd said, he was sure of it. They loved each other, despite all that had happened. He'd go home and make up with Libbie, and then make sure she got the help she needed. Everything would be back to normal—well, at least the normal he'd become used to.

When he drove up to the house, it was dark inside and the

door was locked. He tried his key, but it didn't work. Puzzled, he tried unlocking the garage, and that key didn't work either. He tried all the doors, and none of his keys worked. Jack frowned. It was only seven in the morning. How in the world did they get the locks changed so quickly?

He tried looking in the bedroom window to see if Libbie was there, but it was too dark inside. Someone tapped him on the shoulder and he jumped.

"Sorry to scare you," June said. "I saw you trying to get in. Libbie's not here."

"Do you know where she is?"

June shook her head. "An older man, I think it might have been her father, put her in a car this morning and they drove off. It was about an hour ago."

Jack's mind began spinning. *Where has he taken her? To another care facility?*

"Jack? Is there anything I can do?"

Jack refocused on June. "No, thank you. I just have to find Libbie." He got into his truck and drove off, not sure where he was going.

Jack slowly drove by the Wilkens house, wondering if Libbie was there. He parked behind the bushes and sneaked over to the garage. Peering inside, he didn't see Mr. Wilkens's Cadillac. Next, he drove around town, trying to spot his car. Suddenly, it hit him that he might have taken Libbie to the hospital.

Jack drove to the hospital and walked through the front door and over to the receptionist's desk. "Can you tell me what room my wife, Libbie Prentice, is in?"

The receptionist stared at him oddly, and Jack realized that he must look a mess. He was still wearing his greasy uniform from the day before. He stood straighter and ran his hand through his hair, trying to look presentable. "It's been a long night," he said by way of explanation.

The receptionist nodded and told him she was in room 202.

Jack took the stairs up to the second floor. He hoped he could sneak past the nurses' station and go right to Libbie's room. Unfortunately, as he walked onto the floor, he ran head-on into Gwen.

"What are *you* doing here?" Gwen asked, staring daggers at him.

Jack looked her square in the eye. "I'm here to see my wife." He walked right past her and headed down the hall.

"Stop!" Gwen shouted. "You are *not* allowed in there."

Jack ignored her and kept walking, but as soon as he came to Libbie's room, the door opened and Mr. Wilkens barred his way.

"You are not welcome here," Mr. Wilkens said sternly. He looked over Jack's shoulder and raised his hand as if summoning someone.

"Libbie's my wife. I have every right to see her," Jack insisted. He tried pushing past Mr. Wilkens, but the older man shoved him farther away from the door.

"She doesn't want to see you, Jack. Get out of here now, or I'll call the police."

"She's my wife!" Jack yelled frantically. "You can't stop me." He pushed past Mr. Wilkens, almost knocking him down. Before he could reach the door, strong hands grabbed both of his arms from behind.

"Just leave quietly," a man said into his ear.

Jack turned his head. A tall, muscular man wearing surgical greens had hold of him. Jack struggled to get free of his grasp, but the man was too strong. "Let me go! I have to see my wife."

"Not today," the man said, pulling Jack away from the door

and leading him toward the elevator.

Anger flashed through Jack. Just as they arrived at the elevator, he shoved the man backward and rammed him against a wall. The force of his weight caused the man to loosen his grip enough that Jack could run back to Libbie's room. By now, there were several nurses and orderlies heading his way, but Jack pushed past them, desperate to see Libbie.

"Libbie! Libbie!" he called out, just steps from her door. He reached out to push it open. Before he could touch the door, someone tackled him from the side. Jack hit the floor hard, the breath knocked out of him.

The man grabbed him roughly and pinned his arms behind him. Then he pulled him toward the elevator.

"The police are waiting in the lobby," Mr. Wilkens said to the man in green.

Jack tried to struggle but it was no use. He was out of breath and his side hurt from hitting the floor. He was pulled into the elevator as everyone on the floor stared at him. His eyes met Gwen's cold, steely ones just as the elevator doors closed.

Jack spent the next few hours in the city jail until it was determined that neither the hospital nor Mr. Wilkens would press charges. Larry picked him up that evening.

"Well, I never expected to have to do this," Larry said with a smirk.

Jack didn't respond. He'd spent the last several hours rethinking the hand that life had dealt him. He'd spent the past five years building a life with the girl he loved, and it had all shattered to pieces in a few short hours.

"You look like hell, Jack. Why don't you come back to my place and shower, and I'll find some clothes you can wear until you can get your own, okay?"

Jack nodded. The fight had been sapped out of him. He couldn't win against the Wilkenses. They were too powerful in this town. If Libbie never wanted to see him again, her father would make sure of it.

After he showered and changed at Larry's place, he called Gwen's house.

"Now what?" she asked when she recognized his voice.

"I need to get my clothes and personal things out of the house," Jack said. "Can you let me in to do that?"

"Are you going to act like a crazy person again?"

Jack sighed. "I just need my things."

"Fine. But I'm bringing a police officer along just in case you flip out. I'll meet you there in fifteen minutes." She hung up.

"Do you want me to go with you?" Larry asked when Jack told him where he was going.

Jack shook his head. "No. I'm just getting my clothes and stuff. I'm too drained to fight anymore. Then I'm going home to the farm."

"That's probably a good idea. You need family around you right now. But you can crash here anytime you want to, okay?"

"Thanks, Larry."

"Hey. No thanks necessary," Larry said. "I'm sorry, Jack. I wish things had turned out differently."

"Me, too."

Gwen was already at the house when Jack showed up. It was growing dark out, but the nighttime didn't hide the police officer standing on the curb by his patrol car. Jack walked up the sidewalk and through the front door. He glanced around. The entryway and living room were clean now—no broken glass or torn photos on the floor. The house looked perfectly normal, except for the pictures missing from the walls and tables. Twenty-four hours ago, this had been his and Libbie's home. Now he had to ask permission to come inside.

"Get your stuff," Gwen said, standing in the living room with her arms crossed. "But don't you dare take anything else. This all belongs to Libbie."

Jack turned and walked down the hall to the bedroom. This room had been cleaned up, too. Their senior prom photo was missing, as was one of them in the canoe on the lake that Larry had taken. The jewelry armoire that Jack's father had made for her had a broken leg and was lying on the floor. Otherwise, the room looked the same as always.

Jack went through the motions of pulling his clothes out of the closet and drawers and laying them on the freshly made bed. He went to the hall closet and pulled out a suitcase and packed his things inside it. He also went into the bathroom and got his personal items. When he opened the medicine cabinet, Libbie's pill bottles stood at eye level, facing him. *If she'd only continued taking them, maybe this wouldn't be happening.* But he couldn't change that now.

Jack carried his suitcase out into the entryway. He took two coats out of the closet and picked up a pair of winter boots that sat on the closet floor. That's when Spence came running to greet him.

"Spence." Jack bent down to pet him. He wondered if anyone had fed him in the last twenty-four hours.

"You can take that cat with you," Gwen said sharply. "Otherwise, I'm letting it loose."

Jack's mouth dropped open as he stared at Gwen. He knew she was coldhearted, but this topped everything she'd ever done before. He picked Spence up and went back to the hall closet in search of his carrier. He placed Spence inside and carried him to the door.

"Are you almost done?" Gwen asked impatiently.

Jack turned and stared at her. "Where are the pictures that were on the floor?"

A small grin appeared on Gwen's face. "Libbie said she never wanted to see them again. Or you, either."

Jack should have told Gwen right then and there what he thought of her, but he didn't have the strength. He glanced around the house where he'd shared his life with Libbie for the past four years, and his heart grew heavy. Then he walked out into the night, threw his suitcase into the back of his pickup, and placed Spence's carrier on the front seat.

As Jack turned to walk to the driver's side, he noticed a box sitting beside the garbage pails on the curb. He went over and looked down at it. It was closed, but a piece of paper stuck out of it. Kneeling, Jack took a closer look. He slowly pulled the paper out and found that it wasn't paper after all—it was their wedding photo torn in half. Jack's heart constricted. He pulled the flaps of the box open and peered inside. There were the pictures, torn and crumpled, that had been lying on the floor the night before. Photos of their life together. Memories that should have followed them throughout their lives to share with their children and grandchildren. Tossed away in a box on the curb like garbage.

Hot tears stung Jack's eyes. Libbie said she never wanted to see them again. If he'd needed proof that he and Libbie were completely over, he had it right here in front of him.

Reverently, Jack closed the box and picked it up in his arms. He glanced at the police officer, who quickly turned away as if embarrassed by the whole scene. Jack walked with the box to his truck, slid it in on the front seat, then got in and drove away.

Part Two

Emily

Chapter Thirty

Emily stared at her grandmother, stunned by all she had told her. "Poor Dad," she said, tears filling her eyes. "He's lost two women he loved. It's so unfair."

Bev nodded. "Yes, it's very sad. That night, he came home and placed that box on the table, right here," she pointed to the exact spot where it had sat. "He let Spence out of his carrier, and then he carried his bag up to his old bedroom without saying a word. Luckily, Larry had called me to fill me in on what had happened, so I didn't have to ask. Larry"—a small smile appeared on her face—"He was always very protective of Jack, but that night he knew he should tell me so Jack wouldn't have to go through the pain of explaining it. Of course, eventually Jack did tell me what happened, but it was so hard for him. It was all so sad."

"What happened after that?"

"Jack lived here and worked a couple more months at the dealership. I think he was holding on to the idea that he could somehow get Libbie back. But it wasn't to be. After the divorce papers came, he knew it was over. He signed them, and the next day he packed up what little he had and drove away in that old truck. He hadn't even told us he was leaving. He just left."

"Where did he go?" Emily asked.

Bev shrugged. "We never knew. And if Larry knew, he never would say. A little over a year later, Jack just drove up to the farm again and moved back in. He never explained and we never asked. But he did look better—healthier. I think he needed to get out of this town for a while and put his life back together. He worked at a different dealership then and saved up to buy that piece of property on the lake to build a house and start his own garage." Bev looked at Emily. "You do know what property that was, don't you?"

Emily's brow creased. "Dad always said it had been an old resort. Oh"—her eyes widened when the realization hit her—"he bought the Blue Water Resort property. Where he and Libbie were so happy that first year."

Bev nodded. "At first, I thought it wasn't healthy for him to relive the past, but after he tore down those old cottages and began building his house and the garage, I realized he would be fine. He and that orange tabby lived in one of the cottages until he finished part of the house. Then he met your mom in her last year of college, and that was that. Of course, he'd known Kate all his life, her being Larry's little sister, but he'd never paid much attention to her when she was a little thing. They met again when she was twenty, and by then he'd been alone for a few years, so it was time he moved on."

Emily smiled. "Mom always said that she'd had a crush on Dad since she was ten years old, he just never knew it."

Bev grinned. "But their age difference never mattered. Your mother was so good for Jack. She was steady and calm, exactly what he needed after what he'd been through. They both worked hard and built a good life. She was a wonderful woman."

Emily nodded. Her mother had been pretty amazing. She'd raised two children while working full-time as a second-grade teacher. Children adored her, and she was so good with them. Her mother had been gone now for two years, and Emily missed her terribly.

"Do you think she ever resented their living on the same property where he'd once lived with Libbie?"

"No, I don't think so. She never said she did. She loved that property as much as Jack did. She knew all about Libbie and never felt threatened by her memory. Kate created a whole new life with Jack, and he loved her deeply. As far as I knew, Libbie's memory never came between them."

Emily thought about that a moment. She'd never sensed any problems between her parents. They'd been happy, that's why her mother's illness and death had hit her father so hard. They'd been so close that he seemed lost without her.

Emily looked at the box of photos and then up at Bev. "How did the pictures get into this hatbox if dad found them in a cardboard box?"

"I did that," Bev confessed. "I couldn't bear to see these photos stuffed into a plain old box. It was heartbreaking. So I found one of your great-grandmother's hatboxes in the attic and placed them in it. I put it on the shelf in Jack's room, but through the years, it got shoved behind other things. I don't think he ever looked at them again. I'm sure it would have been painful for him."

It was still difficult for Emily to believe that her father had been married to someone else before he'd married her mother. After his heartbreak with Libbie, she was glad he had found happiness again.

"What happened to Libbie? Did you ever see her again?" Emily asked.

Sadness shadowed Bev's usually cheerful face. "No, I didn't. Not many people did. Her family kept her hidden away or in care facilities for years. Through town gossip, I'd hear that she was home at her parents' house, but then she'd be gone again. A few years after she and Jack broke up, her mother died. Some say it was natural causes; others say she overdosed. I'm not sure which is true. Times began to change. Small businesses in town had competition from the chain stores that moved in, and soon the local businesses began closing or selling out. A few years after Abigail died, Randall began selling off his businesses and properties and moved to Florida. I heard he'd left a lot of money to Gwen and Libbie. He remarried but passed away a few years after that. Gwen took charge of Libbie, and for a while, I guess, Libbie lived with her. But then Gwen became sick with cancer, and the last I heard, right before she died she placed Libbie in a care facility for good. That would have been about five years ago. Gwen's husband, Walter, moved away to Arizona and remarried, and that was the last anyone heard from him. Their girls were grown by then and must have moved away, too."

"Poor Libbie. It sounds like she never had much of a life."

Bev nodded. "Yes, it's so sad. She was such a smart, beautiful girl. Even after everything that happened, I always hoped she'd find happiness again."

"Do you think she's still alive?" Emily asked. "Maybe she's living somewhere close by."

Bev shrugged. "She could be. I've never seen an obituary for her in the paper, but that doesn't mean anything. Wherever she is, I hope she's found some happiness."

Shadows grew long through the dining room windows as the sun began to set. Emily looked at the clock on the wall, surprised at how late it was. "I can't believe we spent the whole afternoon sitting here."

Bev chuckled. "I guess we're better at talking than packing."

"I'd better head home," Emily said, standing up and stretching. "I'll be back this weekend to help pack some more. But this time we'll actually do some packing."

Bev laughed and stood also. She glanced at the box. "Do you want to take that with you, dear?"

"Me? Shouldn't they go to Dad?"

"I doubt that your father wants them. You might as well take them. There are still some nice photos of your dad as a young man in there."

Emily stared at the box a moment and then decided she wanted it. The photos were a part of her father's past, so that made them important to her. She hugged her grandmother goodbye before picking up the hatbox and heading out to her car.

* * *

It was dark by the time Emily arrived home at the town house. She walked inside and smelled pizza. Jordan must have given up on her coming home and ordered it. Walking down the hallway to the bedroom, she found him sitting up in bed, his long legs stretched out in front of him and his computer on his lap. He looked up and gave her a small smile when she walked in.

"So, how'd the packing go?" he asked, returning his gaze to the computer screen.

"Good, but we didn't get much done," Emily said, setting the hatbox on the bed and then climbing up to sit beside Jordan. He gave her a brief kiss before turning back to the computer. "What are you working on?"

"My syllabus for the English lit class I'm teaching this summer. The college has made a few changes this year."

Emily glanced at the screen at the list of books the students would be reading. "Nothing like some light summer reading," she said with a grin.

Jordan smiled. He looked so handsome. His sandy blond hair was tousled, and his blue eyes sparkled behind his glasses. "Yes. They can enjoy these tomes on the beach."

"Well, I have a story worthy of one of those literature books you teach about," Emily said, reaching for the hatbox. "Take a look at these." She pulled off the lid and took out a few photos, spreading them on the bed between them.

Jordan set his laptop aside and slipped off his glasses to look at the photos. "Is that your dad? He's so young."

"I know. We found them when we were cleaning out a bedroom closet. Aren't they neat?"

Jordan lifted the photos, one by one, studying them. "Why are they torn and crumpled?"

Emily grinned. "That's the amazing part. My dad was actually married before he married my mom. My grandmother told me the entire story." Emily repeated a condensed version of her grandmother's story. Jordan listened with interest. After she was finished, he whistled softly.

"Wow, that is an incredible story," he said.

Emily began picking up the photos and carefully placing them back in the hatbox. "I wonder if Libbie is still alive. I guess she still was five years ago, when her sister died. It would be so interesting to track her down."

Jordan slipped his glasses back on and picked up his laptop again. "Well, she wouldn't be that old. She might still be alive. But what would you do if you did find her?"

Emily shrugged. "I'm not sure. I'd just like to see if she's still around. Their story never had an ending. Don't you think it would be nice if it did? Maybe even a happy ending. Maybe they could be friends again after all these years."

Jordan laughed. "Well, I guess stranger things have happened."

He turned back to his computer while Emily sat on the bed, thinking about her dad and Libbie. Would they even want to see each other again after all these years? Maybe not. But she decided right then and there that she really wanted to find her. If for no other reason than to just make sure Libbie was okay.

"Hey, I have some news, too," Jordan said, interrupting Emily's thoughts.

She glanced up at him. "What?"

He took his glasses off again as he looked at her. "I've accepted a graduate assistantship down at the University of Minnesota for this fall."

Emily stared at him, stunned. She felt she'd been broadsided. "What? I thought you were teaching here this fall."

"There were no open positions here this fall or next spring. I had to find one somewhere else, and this one opened up. I only have one more year left to finish my PhD, so I had to take it."

"But that means we'd have to move there. I don't want to live in the Cities—I like it here. My family is here and so is my job."

"Yeah, but it's only a retail job," Jordan said dismissively. "You could easily find another one down in Minneapolis. You can probably transfer to another store at the chain you work for. It really won't be a big deal."

Emily frowned. *Won't be a big deal? Leaving my family and friends is a big deal to me.* "I thought you wanted to teach at this college. You've always said that this is where you'd like to stay."

Jordan shrugged. "I have to go where the opportunities are, and right now they're down at the U of M. You know that the graduate assistant position helps pay for my classes. I really have no choice."

Emily didn't answer. She stood up and carried the hatbox out to the dining room and set it on the table. Then she went into the bathroom to get ready for bed. She couldn't believe Jordan would accept a position without discussing it with her first. Weren't they a team? Hadn't she put her life on hold for the past ten years that they'd lived together so he could pursue his degrees? And now he wanted to move, even though he'd told her before that he wanted to teach at the college in Jamison.

What if he were offered a permanent position at the U of M after he finished his PhD? Jordan was from the Minneapolis area, so it wouldn't bother him to move back there. He'd come up to Jamison for college because he'd wanted a quieter lifestyle. Emily had never considered that they might move.

By the time she crawled into bed, Jordan was already under the covers. She turned off the light on the nightstand and laid her head down on the pillow, her mind still spinning. Jordan rolled over and curled up next to her.

"I'm sorry, Ems, but I really didn't have a choice. And we both know that, realistically, as a college teacher, I'd probably have to move to find a job anyway. Maybe someday we may find ourselves in Jamison again."

Emily didn't answer and soon Jordan was sound asleep. Her mind was swirling with a hundred different thoughts. Jordan had accepted a position without even consulting her. He'd assumed she'd go, too, yet not once in the past ten years had he ever even mentioned the idea of them getting married. She'd always thought that eventually, after he was finished with school, they'd marry. But he had earned his B.A., then his master's, and now he was working on his doctorate. There'd also been a couple of years that he hadn't been able to take classes, so he'd worked odd jobs until a graduate assistant position had become available and he could continue his education. Ten long years she had been their main source of support, working in retail, and in one fell swoop tonight, he had dismissed her job as if it was nothing. That had not only hurt her, it had angered her, too. In the beginning, he'd promised that once he was done with school, he'd support her while she went back. Was that ever going to happen, or was she destined to work at an unfulfilling job for the rest of her life? Did Jordan even care?

That was what scared her the most.

Chapter Thirty-One

The rest of that week, Emily spent most of her free time when not at work on searching online for Libbie. She tried not to dwell on her and Jordan moving to Minneapolis. For him, it was a done deal. But for her, she wasn't as sure. Instead, she immersed herself in looking for Libbie.

The first thing she did was search for an obituary, but when none came up for an Elizabeth "Libbie" Wilkens, she set out searching for every care facility in a two-hundred-mile radius. Emily was surprised at how many assisted living facilities, nursing homes, and treatment facilities there were in the northern part of Minnesota. And there was the possibility that Libbie could be as far away as Minneapolis, or even in Fargo or Duluth. The list grew long.

Emily knew she couldn't call every facility looking for Libbie. It was impossible, and due to privacy laws, they probably wouldn't give her any information anyway. She decided she had to find someone who might know where she was.

Saturday she spent the day with Bev at the farm, sorting and packing. They finished the bedroom where they'd found the hatbox and then started working on Bev's closet.

As they worked, Emily asked Bev more questions about Libbie and people she knew. "Do you think anyone around here would know where Libbie is? The library ladies she worked with, or maybe her best friend, Carol?"

Bev thought a moment. "The women she worked at the library with have all passed away. I doubt that they ever saw her again anyway. And I didn't know the neighbor women she was close to, but I doubt if they'd know anything either. Carol may have heard something, though."

"Do you know her last name so I can find her?"

Bev smiled. "Of course I do, dear. You know who she is, too. She was your fourth grade teacher, Mrs. Simmons."

Emily stopped folding the sweater in her hands. "What? Mrs. Simmons was Libbie's Carol? Her best friend?"

Bev nodded.

"That's incredible. No one ever said anything about her and Dad knowing each other."

"I guess they just felt it was better to leave the past behind them. But that's who you should ask."

And that's exactly what Emily did as soon as she returned home. Jordan was out golfing with his friends, so she had the town house to herself. She looked up James and Carol Simmons in the phone book, praying they still had a landline like most people her parents' age did. Sure enough, it was in the book. She dialed the number, hoping she wasn't intruding on their Saturday evening. A kind, soft voice came over the line.

"Hello."

"Hi, Mrs. Simmons?"

"Yes."

"This is Emily Prentice. I was in your fourth grade class years ago."

"Emily? Jack's daughter?"

"Yes."

"Well, isn't this a nice surprise. What can I do for you, dear?"

Emily didn't think this was something she wanted to discuss over the phone. "I was wondering if we could meet this week sometime. My grandmother told me that you and Dad were friends years ago. I wanted to ask you some questions about that time, if you don't mind."

There was a long pause, and Emily worried that she might decline. Finally, Mrs. Simmons spoke. "Yes, that would be nice. Tomorrow afternoon would be good. One o'clock? We can meet at my house. Do you know where I live?"

"I have your address. Thanks, Mrs. Simmons."

"Sweetie, you're all grown-up now. You may call me Carol."

"Okay, Carol. I'll be there."

* * *

Exactly at one, Emily knocked on the door of Carol's lake home. From what she could tell, this was the same house Carol's parents had owned, two houses down from the Wilkenses' old place. It didn't look like a seventies house any longer, though. It had been remodeled outside and looked very nice with a large lawn and paved driveway. Old, tall oak and maple trees lined the perimeter.

Carol answered and smiled at Emily. "Hello, Emily. It's so nice to see you. It's been a long time." They hugged, and then she led Emily through the house into the family room, which had large windows that faced the lake. It was an open floor plan with the kitchen at the other end and the dining room in between. Carol gestured for Emily to sit on the cream-colored sofa and then Carol did also.

Emily noticed how much Carol had aged since she'd been her teacher. She now had silver hair that was cut into a neat bob with fringe bangs. She was still slender, but her skin gave away her age the most, probably from years of suntanning, as everyone had done in the seventies and eighties. But her blue eyes were still bright and her smile genuine.

"How's your father?" Carol asked. "It's been so long since I've run into him."

"He's doing fine. He misses my mother, but he's still working on cars and keeping busy."

"I'm so sorry about your mother, dear. She was such a lovely woman and a wonderful teacher. Students adored her. We didn't teach in the same elementary school, but I always heard good things about her."

"Thank you," Emily said. She cleared her throat. "I guess I should just come out and say why I'm here. My grandmother told me about my dad and Libbie."

A sad look crossed Carol's face, as if Libbie's name caused her pain. For a moment, Emily was afraid she wouldn't want to talk about her childhood friend, but then Carol shook her head slowly.

"Poor, poor Libbie," she said in a soft voice. "You know, Libbie and I were best friends from the time we were old enough to run back and forth between the houses to play together. We were close all through high school, and even for a while after that. But once Libbie's troubles began, she pulled away from me. Then I got married, had my children, finished getting my teaching degree, and began teaching, so I was too busy to try to reconnect with Libbie. I wish I had, though. I feel bad about that. I did try to see her once, when I heard she was back home for a time. But her sister, Gwen, wouldn't let me. Said she was too sick to see anyone." Carol grimaced. "Gwen was a nasty person. It broke my heart knowing that she was in charge of Libbie's welfare."

"I was hoping you might know what happened to Libbie, or where she might be."

Carol looked at her curiously. "Why do you want to know, dear?"

"Honestly, I'm not sure. It's just that dad and Libbie's story is so sad, I feel a need to find out if Libbie is okay, wherever she is."

"You have a kind heart," Carol said, patting her hand. "What does your dad think of your search for Libbie?"

Emily bit her lip. "He doesn't know about it. I haven't even told him yet that I know about Libbie. But I have to find her—or at least try."

"Just a minute, dear." Carol stood and walked over to a bookcase across the room. Emily watched as she studied a row of photo albums before pulling one off the shelf and bringing it over. She laid it on the glass coffee table and opened it up.

"This was Libbie and I at our kindergarten graduation," she said, pointing to two little girls, one blond, one dark haired, wearing graduation gowns and big smiles. Even though the picture was faded, you could tell they were both very cute.

"You're both adorable," Emily said, leaning over for a closer look.

Carol turned several pages. "And here's one of us at our high school graduation." This picture was in color, and both girls were beautiful. Libbie was small and petite; Carol was taller with a mass of auburn hair.

"Wow. That's so amazing, having a friend for so many years. You must have really missed Libbie when your friendship faded."

Carol nodded. "I did. I still do. And I'm sorry I didn't continue my friendship with your father after everything happened, too. He was such a sweet boy and grew into a good man. I was always a little jealous of Libbie for being lucky enough to have someone like Jack. He loved her more than any man could ever love a woman."

"That's what my grandmother said, too," Emily told her.

"Don't get me wrong, I know he loved your mother, too. Deeply. That's the only way Jack loves, with all his heart," Carol said.

"I know he loved my mother. But I appreciate you saying that."

Carol closed the album and turned to Emily. "I wish I could help you, but I'm afraid I don't know where Libbie is, or even if she's still alive. Gwen was so closed-mouthed about where she placed her, and then Gwen died and no one ever said what happened to Libbie. I wish I knew, dear, but I don't."

Emily was disappointed. She had hoped that Carol might know what had happened to her old friend.

"There is someone who might know where Libbie is," Carol said.

Emily's brows rose. "Who?"

Carol grinned. "Your uncle, Larry."

A frown fell across Emily's face. "Uncle Larry? How would he know?"

Carol shrugged. "He just always seemed to know things no one else did. He knew everything shady or good that went on in this town—at least he used to. He and Jack were so close, and Larry was always so protective of Jack and Libbie. He may know something about what happened to her."

Emily doubted it—after all, he'd been living in southern California for the past seven years—but then again, it was worth checking.

She thanked Carol for seeing her and the two women hugged goodbye.

"If you do find Libbie, will you please let me know?" Carol asked as they walked to the front door. "I'd love to see her again."

Emily said she would and then drove away. When she arrived home, she sat in her car, thinking. She had always adored her uncle Larry. He was fun, irreverent, and had often annoyed her dad for teaching her and her brother games like poker or 21, or swearing like a sailor in front of them. It was as if he'd never grown up—which she figured was the reason he'd never settled down and had kids. Seven years ago, he said he'd had enough of living in an icebox and moved to California. He met a woman there soon afterwards and they'd been living together for several years now. Emily wondered if he might know something about Libbie's whereabouts. She didn't wait to get out of her car. She immediately dialed Larry's number.

"Hey, squirt! How're you doing?" Larry said when he answered his phone.

Emily smiled. Larry had called her "squirt" for as long as she could remember. "I'm fine. How's life treating you?"

"I can't complain. Is everything okay there? It's not like you call me every day."

She told him all was fine and then explained why she was calling.

"Hmm. Does your dad know you're searching for Libbie?" he asked, his tone serious.

"No, and I'd appreciate it if you didn't tell him, okay?"

"Sure, sure," Larry said. "Sorry, squirt, but I don't know what happened to Libbie. Cross my heart and hope to die. But I can tell you something I've never shared with anyone else."

"What?"

"Before I moved out here, I was dating a woman who worked

for Libbie's doctor. She'd seen Libbie at the office and said she was healthy looking and just as normal as normal can be. Everyone thought Libs was off her rocker, but if she was, it didn't show. So if she was healthy then, there's no reason why she wouldn't be alive now."

Emily sighed. That was good news, but it still didn't help find Libbie. "Thanks, Uncle Larry. I wish someone knew more."

They talked a little longer, and then she hung up. After all this, she was back to square one.

Jordan was home when she went inside the town house. He'd played tennis that morning with friends, and now he was freshly showered and smelled delicious. She went over to the sofa and gave him a quick kiss before heading to the kitchen for a snack.

"How did your meeting with the school teacher go?" Jordan asked. He was watching a golf tournament on television with the sound off.

Emily came over with an apple and sat down beside him. "We had a nice talk, but she didn't know anything about Libbie's whereabouts. She told me to try asking Uncle Larry."

"Your uncle Larry? Why?"

Emily shrugged as she bit into her apple. "I guess he used to hear about everything in town. But he wasn't living here when Libbie's sister died, so he had no idea."

"Did you talk to him?"

"Yeah, I just did."

"Well, it was a long shot anyway. Finding someone who hasn't been seen in forty years is pretty difficult," Jordan said. He placed his arm around Emily and pulled her closer, grinning down at her. "But I'm easy to find." He tickled her and she squirmed away, laughing, almost chocking on her apple.

"Ha-ha," she said sarcastically.

"Did you think to ask your dad? Maybe he kept track of her all these years."

Emily thought this over a moment. "I doubt he did. He and Mom were really happy together. I think he moved on with his life and left memories of Libbie behind."

"Well, you gave it your best try," Jordan said.

Emily glanced up at him. "What do you mean? I'm not through looking yet."

"Really? What's the point? No one knows where she is, and besides, even if she were alive, she probably wouldn't appreciate being found. After all, you're her ex-husband's daughter—the daughter she couldn't have. She might be really bitter about it all."

Emily hadn't thought about that. "Well, you're a downer, aren't you?"

Jordan chuckled. "Besides, you should be concentrating on getting a job in Minneapolis for this fall, and we should start looking for an apartment instead of wasting time on this wild-goose chase. Libbie is the past—our lives are happening now. That's more important."

Emily didn't reply. It was obvious Jordan didn't understand how important finding Libbie was to her. In fact, the more she thought about it, the more she realized Jordan hardly ever acknowledged what was important to her. He'd often blow off attending family get-togethers with her so he could do something he enjoyed instead. And he rarely asked her what she'd like to do on weekends. He just assumed it was fine that he play golf or fish or meet up with his friends to watch baseball or football. Yet if there was a faculty dinner or a get-together at a department professor's home, she was always expected to attend.

Emily finished her apple in silence. She didn't care what Jordan thought; she was going to keep looking for Libbie.

Chapter Thirty-Two

Another workweek began for Emily. Monday was a rough day because the register system went on the blink for a couple of hours and sales had to be handwritten. This was happening more and more, and Emily wished the store would upgrade its system.

Wednesday, she spent the day at her grandmother's going through boxes and trunks in the attic. There were so many wonderful items up there—an old dressmaker's dummy, more hatboxes, a trunk of clothes from the early 1900s—but most of the clothing had become moth-eaten or rotted from being up there so long. They saved what they could and then disposed of the rest, which Emily thought was a shame.

In the evenings after work, Emily sat at her computer, searching for Libbie. She tried the alumni list at the high school, but there was no new address for Libbie since her parents' lake house. Then she tried finding Gwen's two daughters, Lynn and Leslie, but that was next to impossible. They weren't listed on the high school or college alumni lists, and Emily had no idea if they were married or where they lived now. They'd be in their late forties, so they could be just about anywhere.

On Friday after work, feeling discouraged, Emily drove out to the neighborhood where her dad and Libbie had lived for four years. Back then it had been a brand new development, but now it was old and tired looking with many outdated houses. Some had been remodeled, but most still held traces of the 1970s: old painted brick, wide siding, and doors with gold glass windows on them. Emily pulled up in front of the home her dad had lived in and stopped. It was painted gray with white trim and had a new door with a beveled-glass window. The windows were large and looked newer, and pavers had replaced what Emily assumed had once been a cement sidewalk leading up to the house. It looked like it had been taken care of, and that made Emily smile. She wondered if her dad ever drove by here to look at the house. She supposed not; it would probably bring back unhappy memories.

An SUV pulled into the driveway, and two little kids jumped out and ran to the front door. A tall woman with dark hair followed them inside carrying a bag of groceries.

Emily thought it was nice that children were living in the house where Libbie had so wanted to raise a family.

As Emily drove around the cul-de-sac, she spotted an older woman with short, gray hair placing geraniums in a large planter on her porch. Emily wondered if the woman had lived here a long time. She slowed down, looking for a name on the mailbox in front, but there was only a house address. The woman stood up and stared right at Emily. She must have thought she knew Emily because she waved and then went back to her work.

Emily parked the car and, with all the courage she could muster, walked up the sidewalk toward the older woman. "Excuse me, ma'am. I was wondering if I could ask you a question."

The woman turned and stared at her curiously. She looked to be about Emily's father's age, had a kind-looking face and warm, brown eyes. She picked up a cane that sat against the house and carefully walked a couple of steps toward Emily.

"What can I help you with, dear?"

Emily swallowed hard. She wasn't the type of person to go running around asking strangers questions, but she forced herself to do it. That was how determined Emily was to find Libbie.

"Sorry to bother you, ma'am, but I was wondering if you've lived here a long time."

The woman peered at her though thick glasses and then smiled. "Well, I guess that depends on what you consider a long time." She laughed. "I've lived in this neighborhood since it was first built."

Emily's heart skipped. She took a chance. "Then you must have known my father, Jack Prentice?"

The woman's face softened and her smiled widened. "You're Jack's daughter? Why yes, I can see it now. My, my." She shook her head. "Such a long time since I've run into your father. How is he?"

"He's fine."

The woman nodded. "Oh, where are my manners?" She reached out her free hand. "I'm June. And what is your name, dear?"

Emily shook her hand. "I'm Emily. It's nice to meet you, June."

"Well, aren't you a lovely girl. I'm sorry about your mother's passing, dear. I didn't know her, but I'd read about it in the paper. I'm sure, if she was married to Jack, then she was a wonderful woman."

"Thank you, she was," Emily said. "If you know my father, then you must have known his first wife, Libbie."

The elderly woman nodded slowly. "Oh, yes. I knew Libbie.

She and I were friends back in those days. But then, she backed away from everyone until we rarely saw her. That was before her breakdown, you know. The one that broke her and Jack up. So sad. She was such a beautiful girl and so sweet, until she started changing. I've never quite understood what happened, but I guess it wasn't my business anyway."

Emily's heart sank. It sounded like she hadn't stayed friends with Libbie through the years. She asked anyway. "I've been searching for Libbie. Is there any chance you know where she is?"

June's face turned sad. "No, dear. I have no idea. I never saw her again after that morning I watched her father drive away with her. Never heard about her again, either. It was as if she'd fallen off the face of the earth."

Emily sighed. Another dead end. "I appreciate your time, June," she said. "It was nice meeting you."

"You too, dear."

Emily waved and turned to walk back to her car when June called her name. She spun around. "Yes?"

June walked carefully up to Emily. "If you do find Libbie, will you come back and tell me? I'd love so much to see her again. So many of my friends are sick or dying these days. And with my husband now gone and my children living all over the country, I get very lonely. It would be nice to have someone to visit with every now and again."

Emily's heart swelled. How sad to grow old and have no one around to talk to or go places with. It was why she wanted to find Libbie. She just wanted to make sure she was happy and not alone.

"I'd be happy to let you know if I find her," she said, smiling at June.

June's eyes lit up. "Thank you, dear. And do say hello to Jack for me. We all loved Jack so much. He was a wonderful husband to Libbie and a good friend to everyone in the neighborhood."

"I will. Goodbye."

As she drove away, Emily hoped she would find Libbie. She had to be a good person for everyone who knew her to want to see her again. Emily wondered if Libbie knew how much she was loved and missed. She intended to find her so she could tell her.

* * *

On Sunday, Emily went to her grandmother's for dinner, but Jordan had bowed out—again. He had Twins' tickets, and he and two friends had driven down to the Cities yesterday to spend the night, see the game today, and then come home that night.

"I've flagged a couple of apartment buildings down there that have openings, so I want to drive by them and see what the neighborhoods look like," he'd told her. "At some point, though, you and I have to make a trip down to look at a few."

Emily had no desire to look at apartments or to move at all. She hadn't yet asked about transferring to another store in Minneapolis, either. She knew that eventually she'd have to, but right now her heart wasn't in it.

Her father had come for dinner and so had Ray and his wife, Ellen. Ray was a good-looking man at age forty-seven and was tall and lean, his dark hair showing only a touch of gray. He'd taken over her grandfather's cabinet business after Norman retired and had built it up enough to have a nice shop and show-room in a building just west of town. Through the years, he'd expanded the business to include selling flooring, windows, and several national brands of custom cabinets, but he still made handmade custom cabinets, too. Ellen had come to Jamison to attend college and had met Ray, married, and stayed. She worked in the admissions office at Jamison State College. Their two children were now grown and on their own.

"All we need is Jan and her husband, and everyone would be here," Bev said, as she bustled between the kitchen and dining room. Jan still lived in the Cities and rarely came up to visit. She'd married Evan Goddard, and they'd had three beautiful girls. Evan had worked as a manager for a restaurant for years and then finally opened his own, and now they owned three restaurants around the Minneapolis area. Emily knew that Bev was proud of Jan but wished she could see more of her.

"Once you move into the town house, maybe you can visit Jan more often," Jack said, taking a carrot from the vegetable platter.

Bev nodded but kept on working. Emily glanced at her dad. Like Ray, he was tall and slender, but his dark hair was peppered with gray. His hands were rough and stained from years of working on engines, and his face was lined and weathered. But his smile still came easily, and his eyes twinkled with mischief. He still had that easygoing nature that made people like him immediately. Considering what Emily knew now, how her father had lost not one love in his life but two, it amazed her how he managed to keep his sense of humor and not be bitter.

"Is there something on my face?" he asked, winking at his daughter.

Emily shook herself out of her thoughts. "No, no. I was just thinking."

Jack grinned.

Emily wished she had the courage to tell him she knew about Libbie, but she was afraid he'd ask her not to search for her. And she just had to. She was so drawn to their story; she had to see if it had a happy ending. She knew her father had enjoyed a good life, but she needed to know if Libbie had, too. Every night, she opened the box of pictures and studied them, wondering how such a lovely-looking couple could endure so much pain. It broke her heart to think of Libbie out there somewhere, alone, with no family. She hoped she was wrong and that she was having the time of her life surrounded by people who loved her. At least her dad had his family and children; she hoped Libbie had someone, too.

* * *

The weeks flew by and June came with warm days and cool nights. Emily still hadn't had any luck finding Libbie and had run out of ways to search for her. Short of calling every facility on her list—or visiting them—there was no way for her to track Libbie down. It made Emily sad to think that she might never find Libbie, but what choice did she have?

She and Jordan were having problems, too. He'd begun teaching summer classes at the college, and he was taking a class also, so they were both very busy. But more and more, he was pressing her about moving in the fall. Emily still didn't feel good about the move.

"But it's for our future," he insisted one day when she hadn't reacted to the apartments he showed her online that were possibilities.

"It's for your future," she said, surprising even herself.

"What's that supposed to mean?"

"I don't know," Emily admitted. She didn't understand why she had started to resent his going to school after all these years. She should be happy for him. He'd have his final degree in a year, and then she could move on with her education. Maybe. They'd been focusing on his career for so long, she didn't know how to focus on herself anymore.

She'd ended the conversation there and they hadn't broached the subject again. Yet. But she knew he'd bring it up soon. She had to decide what she wanted to do about it. One choice was to give up the life she'd built here among her family. The other was to give up Jordan. It was a difficult decision.

* * *

Monday morning, Emily walked into work a half hour before it opened to get her department's registers ready for the day. As she was putting her purse away in the employee break room, the store manager, Carson Wheetly, came up to her with a thick manila envelope.

"Hi, Carson. What's up?" Emily said.

"Happy Monday morning," he said, handing her the envelope. "We had problems Saturday with the registers again, and the bookkeeper is in a tizzy. Apparently, none of the registers balanced properly. The cashiers had to write everything down manually, and then they keyed it in later when the registers started working again. We're asking all the department managers to check the credit card and check receipts against the register tape to make sure they are correct. I have a feeling that some cash sales were keyed in as checks or credit cards, so that's why the cash is off."

Emily sighed. "Great. Sounds like this is starting out to be a good day. We really need a new register system. These ones are ancient."

Carson nodded. "I know. We're constantly telling corporate

that, but you know how slow everything goes."

Emily nodded. She went to bookkeeping and retrieved her cash register drawers, then walked out on the sales floor to the women's wear department. She managed both women's wear and outerwear, along with accessories. After locking the cash drawers into the registers at the large square counter that served all three departments, she began working on the long list of credit card and check receipts.

Methodically, she went down the register tape and checked off the amounts against the pile of checks and credit card receipts. She found a couple of instances where a check had been keyed in as cash and one credit card receipt that had also been keyed in as cash. If the register had been working properly, it would never have allowed this to happen.

Allison, a sales associate in her department, came in just as the doors to the store opened for business. She was a short, petite girl with long dark hair, and she had worked with Emily for two years. Allison groaned, telling Emily how crazy Saturday had been—busy, and with register problems. Emily showed her the couple of mistakes she'd found so far, and Allison sighed with relief that it had been another sales associate who'd made those mistakes and not her.

"But you can't blame her. It was so busy."

Emily continued working on her project, while Allison helped customers and rang up sales. Another credit card receipt didn't match any on the register tape, so Emily glanced down the long strip of paper at unmarked checks. There it was, halfway down. She checked it off and made a notation on a pad of paper that it had been keyed in wrong. When she looked at the name on the credit card receipt to write it down for the bookkeeper, she stopped short.

E. Wilkens.

Emily stared at the name. *E. Wilkens.* She looked at the signature on the bottom of the receipt. It was shaky but otherwise a nicely handwritten script. *E. Wilkens.* Elizabeth Wilkens?

"Oh, my God," Emily said under her breath. "It can't be."

Her heart now pounding, she looked at the name of the clerk who'd keyed it in. Allison.

Emily shoved the paperwork under the desk and went in search of Allison. She found her in the dress section, zipping up dresses and straightening a rack.

"Can you believe how messy this is? I swear, the girls on Sunday didn't straighten anything," Allison complained.

"Allison. Look at this. Do you remember who this was?" Emily asked, shoving the receipt under her nose.

Allison glanced at it. "Why? Did I key it in wrong?"

"Well, yes, you did, but that's not why I'm asking. Do you remember who this person was? E. Wilkens. Does the name ring a bell?"

Allison looked at the receipt again and then shrugged. "Not really. We were so busy on Saturday."

"You have to remember," Emily said, exasperated. She looked over the receipt. "It was at 2:35 p.m., and she bought a yellow dress and a cream-colored spring coat. Don't you remember selling a yellow dress to anyone?"

Allison frowned, deep in thought. "Yeah, I do. It was at that time that we had a bus of elderly ladies come in all at once. Oh, yeah, I remember. It was that sweet older lady who comes here about once a month with a group of ladies from some nursing home or something. But her name doesn't start with an E. People call her something else." Allison looked directly at Emily. "You know who she is. You've waited on her before, too. She's short, like me, and tiny, with her long silver hair pulled up. She has a nice smile. I just can't think of what the other ladies call her."

"Libbie?" Emily asked, picturing the elderly woman Allison was talking about.

"Yeah. That's it. Libbie. What's that short for, anyway?"

"Elizabeth," Emily said, hardly able to believe that she'd found Libbie. And here, right under her nose. She'd actually waited on her before and talked to her. She was a quiet, sweet woman who loved blue, emerald, and yellow dresses.

"Are you okay?" Allison asked. "You look dazed."

Emily nodded slowly. "Do you remember where the ladies come from?"

Allison thought a moment. "I think it starts with an S. Spring Valley? No. Wait, it's Spring River, somewhere north of here. That's what one of the ladies said. That they ride almost an hour here from up north."

"Thanks, Allison," Emily said, rushing back to the counter. She pulled out her phone and searched for Spring River, Minnesota, and sure enough, an assisted living facility popped up. Emily stared at it, hardly able to believe it.

She'd found Libbie.

Chapter Thirty-Three

Emily could barely make it through the workday once she'd leaned about Libbie. The moment she arrived home, she sat down at the table where Jordan was working on his laptop and opened her own. She looked over the list of care facilities that she'd composed, and there it was, Spring River Assisted Living.

"Did you have a good day?" Jordan asked.

Emily looked up at him, excitement rising inside her. "I found Libbie."

Jordan's eyes darted up and met Emily's. "Really? I thought you'd given up on all that."

Emily frowned at his condescending tone. "No, I hadn't. But I ended up finding her by sheer coincidence. Her name was on a charge slip at the store for Saturday. She lives in an assisted living facility about forty miles north of here."

"Now what are you going to do?"

"I'm going to go visit her."

Jordan stood and walked over to the fridge, pulling out a bottle of beer. He twisted off the cap and leaned against the counter. "What exactly do you think visiting her will accomplish?"

"I'm not sure. I just know that I have to see her and make sure she's okay."

"I don't understand why you think her happiness is your problem. She was married to your dad long before you were born. You have no connection to her. At the very least, you'll probably annoy her. Or you just might dredge up painful memories that she's tried to forget."

Emily closed her laptop and walked into the kitchen to stand across from Jordan. She hated that he didn't support her on this. Or on much of anything, for that matter. She crossed her arms.

"Or I may make her happy by letting her know there are people who'd love to see her again. My grandmother, Carol, and even June, her old neighbor; they all want to see her. Why can't you see the positive outcomes of my finding her?"

Jordan shook his head. "I think you're trying, unrealistically, to conjure up a happily ever after for Libbie. This isn't a fairy tale or a romantic novel. Not everyone has a happy ending."

Emily looked up into Jordan's eyes. "What about us? Do we get a happily ever after?"

A crease formed between Jordan's brows. "What do you mean by that?"

Emily took a deep breath. "We've been together for ten years, yet in that entire time you've never talked about us some-day getting married or having a family. Our entire life has been about you getting through another semester at school so you could further your career. But what about us? When are we going to move forward in our relationship?"

"I'm with you, aren't I? Why do we have to have a formal commitment to be considered a couple?"

"Maybe I'd like one."

Jordan walked past her to the table and turned around. "This isn't the time to discuss this. I have one more year of school, and then I can teach in a college somewhere. We can discuss our future then."

"So I'm supposed to wait another year? I'm supposed to move away with you and hope that you want a future with me? Why can't we discuss it now?"

"All this nonsense about Libbie and your dad has affected you. I'm with you, Emily. I don't need a piece of paper to tell me to be with you. Besides, there are no guarantees in life with or without a marriage license. If you need an example, look at your dad and Libbie."

Emily's mouth dropped open at the fact that he'd use her dad's and Libbie's relationship against her. She stared at him as he began working again, a sign that the discussion was over. Disgusted, she walked past him and into the bedroom, where she kicked off her heels and lay down on the bed. Jordan was skirting the issue, like he usually did. She'd spent the last ten years putting her life on hold for him, believing that in the end she'd be able to finish college and they'd marry and have a family. But now she didn't believe any of that would ever happen. It saddened her to think that the last ten years may have been for nothing.

* * *

Emily thought of nothing else that week besides seeing Libbie. Even though she now knew who Libbie was and had helped her on occasion at the store, she still didn't know anything about her life other than the fact that she lived at the Spring River Assisted Living facility. She'd looked up the facility online and was pleased to see that they had a detailed website with photos. It looked like a nice place, nestled in a wooded area beside the river just outside the small town of Spring River. The building was painted light gray with white trim, and there were flower boxes at each of the resident's windows. The place boasted lovely apartments with kitchenettes, a shared dining room, entertainment room, and a communal television room with a huge widescreen TV and cushy chairs all around. Outside were a cement patio with beautiful flowers all around and a large lawn with paved walking paths. Emily was pleased Libbie was living in such a nice place.

On Wednesday, Emily took a deep breath and called Spring River to check on visiting hours. She hoped that she didn't have to be a relative to be allowed to visit, and she worried how it might look if a total stranger just appeared to see Libbie. Since Monday, she'd thought about what to say if they asked how she knew Libbie. She knew she should tell the truth, but saying she was the daughter of Libbie's ex-husband would sound strange. Maybe a long-lost relative? But who? Then she thought of Carol. Maybe, if they asked, she could just say she was the daughter of an old friend of Libbie's. It wasn't really a lie—after all, her father did know Libbie.

She dialed the number on the website and waited, her heart hammering in her chest. A pleasant voice answered the phone.

"Spring River Assisted Living. How may I help you?"

"Hello. I was wondering when visiting hours were."

"Oh. Well, relatives and friends can visit anytime they wish between the hours of nine to nine. Are you a relative of one of our residents here?"

"Actually, I'm the daughter of an old friend of one of the residents. My mother wanted me to check up on her." The lie had come out so easily it surprised her.

"Oh, well that would be nice. May I ask who you'd be visiting?"

"Elizabeth Wilkens." Emily's spine tingled just saying her name.

There was a pause on the other end of the line. For a brief moment, Emily feared that Libbie didn't live there after all. But then the woman spoke.

"Elizabeth? Oh, you mean Libbie." Another pause. "You say you're the daughter of an old friend?"

"Yes. Would I be allowed to visit?"

"Oh, of course. Yes. Libbie would love for you to come visit. You can come any time. Or we have a family visiting day every Sunday from noon to five. The residents bake treats, and there's always coffee and punch. It's the day many families come to visit."

"That sounds nice. Thank you."

"You're welcome. Will you be coming that day?"

Emily thought the woman's voice sounded strange, like she was eager, or hopeful, that she'd come visit. "Yes, I think that day will work out fine. Thank you for your help."

"You're welcome. I hope we see you then."

After Emily hung up, she let out a long sigh of relief. It was finally happening. She was going to see Libbie. Suddenly, her excitement turned into panic. *Yikes! I'm going to see Libbie! What am I going to say to her? How will I explain who I am?*

She decided she'd take it one step at a time. She had until Sunday to come up with a plan.

* * *

The week crawled by for Emily. She and Jordan spoke very little to each other all week, and then on Friday night he brought her roses and apologized for being insensitive to her need to see Libbie.

"I should have tried harder to understand you wanting to meet her," he told her as he handed her the flowers. "Sometimes I try to be so logical that I forget that logic doesn't explain everything a person feels. I'm sorry."

Emily accepted his apology and they went out for a romantic dinner that night. Emily couldn't help but feel resentful. This was how Jordan generally operated. They'd fight, he'd apologize with flowers, and then all would be fine again. But he surprised her even further with what he said during dinner.

"I do want us to be married someday, Ems. As soon as I finish my degree and have a full-time teaching position, we can start planning our future."

Emily was taken aback. She'd never heard him utter one word about marriage before. Had her admission that she hoped they'd marry someday jolted him awake? Or was he just trying to placate her so she'd move with him in the fall? She knew she shouldn't feel that way, but that thought sat right below the surface. She pushed it aside for the night and enjoyed the evening.

Sunday morning Emily was nervous as she got ready to see Libbie. Jordan had left early to golf, so he didn't know she was going today. It took her half an hour to figure out what to wear, and then she still changed three more times. Should she dress up? Should she wear jeans? She settled on a pair of black dress pants, a royal-blue silky T-shirt, and a pair of low-heeled pumps. She wanted to look mature and responsible without overdoing it. Emily wasn't sure how Libbie would perceive her, so she thought dressing nicely might make her seem more normal and not like some crazy person butting into her life.

Although, in truth, she felt like a crazy person butting into Libbie's life.

Finally, Emily got into her car and headed north on the highway toward the town of Spring River. The drive was beautiful, with lush pines, oak, and birch trees lining the roadside. In this part of the country, you could drive fifty miles without passing a house or town. Emily drove through only one small town that consisted of two churches, two gas stations, and a bar before she finally saw the sign announcing Spring River.

Emily rode through the sleepy little town before her GPS told her to turn right after crossing a bridge over a narrow river. She followed the winding river for a couple of miles before the assisted living facility came into view.

Emily slowed down and gazed at the place. It was built on a small hill overlooking a wide spot on the river. A sloping lawn stretched from the riverbank up to the front of the facility, and the building curved out slightly on each side of the main entrance. Emily guessed that the curved sections were the resident's apartments, allowing some to have a view of the river. She hoped Libbie's room had a view.

She pulled her car into the crowded parking lot. The woman she'd talked to had been right—many families came to visit on Sundays. As she stepped out of her car, she heard voices coming from the back of the building. She followed a path that led to the back and soon saw all the visitors and residents milling around. There was a big round cement patio off of the main back door that had brick planters filled with colorful flowers separating the sitting areas. Chairs and small tables were set about, and a massive lawn spread out a long distance. The river flowed from the front of the building around to the back, and large, lush trees grew along its edge.

It looked tranquil here, even with so many people milling around. Emily thought it was a wonderful spot to grow old and enjoy your sunset years.

"Hello? May I help you?"

A voice spoke beside Emily, making her jump. She placed a hand over her heart as she turned to see who was there.

"I'm sorry," a woman dressed in a nursing uniform said. "I didn't mean to startle you. You looked a little lost."

"That's okay," Emily said. "I was admiring how beautiful this place is. It's so peaceful."

The woman smiled. She looked to be in her forties and had dark brown hair and friendly brown eyes. "Thank you. That's exactly what we're going for—peaceful and calm. The residents like it that way." She put out her hand. "I'm Angie, the supervising RN here."

"Hi, Angie. I'm Emily."

"Nice to meet you, Emily. Are you here to see a relative?"

Emily paused. *Well, here I go.* "I'm actually here to see an old friend of my mother's. Libbie Wilkens."

Angie's smile faded and a stunned look crossed her face. "Libbie? You're here to see Libbie?"

Emily nodded. "Yes. Libbie Wilkens." Her mind began to race. What if something had happened to Libbie this past week? What if she'd lost her chance to meet her?

Slowly, the smile reappeared on Angie's face and grew even wider. "Oh my goodness. You must be the woman who called earlier this week. You actually came. Libbie has a visitor."

Emily stared at her curiously. "Is it unusual for Libbie to have a visitor?"

The woman wrapped her arm around Emily's shoulders and began leading her across the patio. "Oh, sweetie, you have no idea. Libbie's been with us for five years, and not once has anyone come to visit her." She stopped and pointed toward a woman sitting with her back to them, watching children playing croquet on the lawn.

"There she is. Waiting. Every Sunday she dresses up in a pretty dress and sits out here with the other families and waits. For five long years she's waited, and she's never had even a single visitor. And every Sunday after the other visitors leave, she walks back to her room, alone. She always puts on a smile and says someone will come someday, but we'd all given up hope. And here you are. Someone has finally come to visit Libbie."

Emily stared at the tiny woman in the chair. Her silver hair was pulled up in a twist, and she wore the yellow dress she'd purchased last week at the store with a white cardigan over it. Her hands were in her lap as she watched the children play. Tears formed in Emily's eyes as she thought about how long Libbie had waited. What little family she had left, her nieces, never came to see her. Her friends from the past didn't know where she was. No one knew of the lonely woman waiting here so patiently.

And now, Emily was finally going to meet Libbie.

Chapter Thirty-Four

"She's going to be so happy to see you," Angie said, pulling Emily along toward where Libbie sat. "We're all so happy to see you."

Angie released her hold on Emily as she neared Libbie and gently laid her hand on the older woman's shoulder. "Libbie? I have a surprise for you. You have a visitor."

Emily walked closer to Libbie. The older woman turned and raised her eyes up to Emily's as a smile crossed her lips.

"A visitor? How lovely," Libbie said in a soft, sweet voice.

Emily gazed at Libbie, unable to speak. Bright blue eyes shone in a delicate oval face. Her skin was pale and soft, gently touched by time. Her body was petite, but not too thin, and in her small hands, she held a book of poetry open in her lap.

"This is Emily," Angie continued. "She's the daughter of an old friend of yours."

Libbie set the book on the table beside her and stood, reaching for Emily's hands. "I'm so happy to meet you, Emily. Please, come sit next to me and we can talk."

Emily looked down at Libbie's hands in hers. They were warm and smooth, just as she would have imagined they'd be.

"It's nice to meet you, too, Ms. Wilkens."

"Oh, now, please call me Libbie, dear. Everyone does."

"Okay, Libbie," Emily said, sitting down in a chair beside hers.

"Well, I'll let you two visit," Angie said.

"Thank you, Angie," Libbie said, smiling up at the nurse. She turned to Emily. "She's such a sweet person. All the nurses here are so kind."

"Yes, they seem to be," Emily said. She continued staring at Libbie, unable to take her eyes off of her. She was still pretty, like in the old photos of her father's. Age showed in the lines around her eyes and lips, but her smile was genuine, and her eyes were so clear and alert. The problems that had separated her and Jack had to be in the past. Libbie didn't look like a woman ravaged by drugs and alcohol, she looked like any other woman her age, if not better.

"So, dear. Which old friend of mine is your mother?" Libbie asked, a curious expression on her face.

Emily hesitated. She hated lying to Libbie now that she'd met her. Libbie was no longer just an elusive memory she was chasing; she was real flesh and blood, with feelings and emotions. Lying to her seemed wrong. Yet she'd already started the lie. How on earth could she tell her the truth now?

"Carol." Emily nearly winced when she said it.

Libbie's eyes lit up even brighter. "Carol Raymonds? Oh my goodness. She and I were friends since we were just toddlers. Oh, I should say Carol Simmons, shouldn't I? Did you know I was the matron of honor at her wedding?"

Emily nodded. "Yes, she told me. I actually saw a photo of you then. You were both so beautiful."

"Ah, you're sweet, dear. Well, how is Carol? It's been forever since I've seen her."

Emily told Libbie about Carol's years of teaching and how she now divides her time between the lake house and Arizona.

"She lives in her parents' old house? Well, isn't that nice. I suppose she's changed it to suit her taste."

"Yes, it's very nice now. Of course, I've never seen it any other way."

Libbie nodded and appeared to be studying Emily's face. Feeling nervous at her scrutiny, Emily continued talking.

"Carol . . . I mean, my mother . . . would love to see you. Would you mind if she visited you?"

Libbie raised her hand up and fingered the blue topaz pendant around her neck. "I'm surprised she'd want to see me after all these years. I'm afraid I wasn't much of a friend those last couple of years. But I would love to see her."

"That's wonderful. I'll tell her she can come." Emily wondered how she'd explain to Carol that she'd suddenly become her daughter.

Libbie cocked her head and gazed at Emily. "You have such beautiful blond hair," she said wistfully. "My hair used to be that color, but it was too much trouble trying to keep it blond through the years."

"You have lovely hair," Emily said. "It's a beautiful silver color. I know a lot of women who'd love for their hair to look like yours."

Libbie lifted her hand to her hair, smoothing it down. "I've kept it long all these years," she said. "That's the way everyone always liked it on me. But I love how your hair is cut to frame your face yet is still long. Do you think I'd look good with my hair that way? Even at my age?"

Emily smiled. Libbie sounded so self-conscious about her looks when she didn't need to be. "I think it would look wonderful on you. Just like that yellow dress. It's the perfect color for you."

"Thank you, dear. I've always loved yellow."

Silence fell between them, and Emily searched for something to say. She was so happy to see that Libbie was fine. She lived in a nice place where the people were kind to her. And now maybe her old friends would come visit her and she wouldn't have to sit alone on Sundays anymore. When Emily looked up to meet Libbie's eyes, she thought she saw them twinkle mischievously.

"You're not really Carol's daughter, are you, dear?" Libbie said softly.

Emily's heart sank. She knew she shouldn't have lied. Slowly, she shook her head. "No, I'm not. I'm sorry I lied. I had to meet you, but I didn't think I'd be allowed to visit if I wasn't a friend or a relative. And once I lied, I had to stick to it."

Libbie sat forward, closer to Emily. "It's okay, sweetie. I understand."

"What gave me away?" Emily asked.

"You're much too young to be Carol's daughter. She must be at least ten or fifteen years older than you. I also know that Carol's daughter has the same beautiful auburn hair as her mother."

"I'm sorry," Emily repeated remorsefully. "I really am. But why didn't you tell me you knew right away?"

"I was afraid if I told you I knew, you'd leave. And I so wanted to talk to you."

"Really? Why?"

Once again, Libbie's fingers went to the pendant at her neck. "You're Jack and Kate's daughter, aren't you?"

Emily stared at her, stunned. "How did you know that?"

"I still subscribe to the Jamison newspaper. So much has changed, and I know very few people there anymore, but it is home, after all, and I like to see what goes on there. I recognized you from your high school graduation picture years ago." She gave Emily a small smile. "Besides, you have your mother's lovely eyes and Jack's smile. I'd recognize that smile anywhere."

Goose bumps ran up Emily's arms. Libbie knew who she was, yet she'd wanted her to stay anyway. It all seemed so unreal.

"I'm so sorry about the loss of your mother, dear," Libbie continued. "I didn't know her personally, but I did know her brother, Larry. I'm happy that Jack found a sweet girl like Kate to build a life with. He deserved happiness, especially after all I put him through."

Sadness creased Libbie's face as she looked down at her hands.

"Thank you," Emily said. "My mother was a wonderful person, and I miss her."

Libbie looked up at Emily, her eyes now filled with compassion. "How is he doing? Jack, I mean."

"He's doing okay, keeping busy, working on cars in his shop still. I know he misses my mom terribly, but he's getting through it, like we all are."

Libbie nodded. "That's good. Loss is such a dreadful thing. Did Jack tell you about me?"

"No, he didn't. To be honest, I never knew he was married before, until I came upon a box of photos in a closet at my grandmother's house. She was the one who told me about you and Dad."

"Photos," Libbie said, staring up into the sky as if searching for something. She turned back to Emily. "Jack has pictures from those days?"

"Yes. Well, yes and no. He brought a box of photos to my grandmother's house years ago, and they've been there ever since."

Libbie's face softened. "I'm happy he saved them. I didn't know any still existed."

"I could bring them someday, if you'd like. Some are damaged, but many aren't."

"Yes. I'd like that very much." Libbie's gaze returned to Emily. "Your grandmother. Is that Bev?"

"Yes."

A smile spread across her face. "Bev. How I adored her. And Norman and Ray. And Jan. Tell me everything about them, please. I've missed them all so much."

Emily told her all about the family and also what Larry was up to. She told her about meeting June and how much her old friend would love to see her. The two women talked about people past and present, and Emily told her about Jordan and how he was pursuing a doctorate degree. Time slipped away and before they knew it, they were the only two people left outside. Angie came out to tell Libbie that dinner was being served.

"Oh, I took up your whole afternoon," Emily said.

"I'm so happy you did," Libbie told her. "I haven't enjoyed myself this much in years." She looked at Emily with a hopeful expression. "Is there any chance you might come and visit with me again?"

Emily smiled. "I'd love to come see you again. I work on some Sundays, though. Is it okay to come during the week sometimes?"

Libbie's eyes lit up. "Oh, yes. Please do. Just call ahead to make sure we're here. Sometimes we take little shopping trips to towns."

Emily stood and Libbie did also. Angie had gone inside again, to give them some privacy. Emily walked with Libbie to the doors that led into the building. They both stood there a moment, and Libbie gazed up at Emily, her blue eyes glistening.

"Can I give you a hug goodbye?" she asked tentatively, as if afraid the answer would be no.

Emily's heart swelled. "Of course." The two women hugged and then said their final goodbyes. Libbie went slowly through the doors and disappeared. Emily just stood there a moment, marveling at how quickly Libbie had stolen her heart.

Angie came outside with a wide grin. "You've made Libbie very happy, I just have to hug you, too."

Emily laughed and they hugged. "I think I got as much out of it as she did," Emily told her.

"We adore Libbie here. I know that she's had a rough life, but she's content now."

As they walked together out to the parking lot, Emily admitted to Angie her true identity.

"I'm sorry I lied. I wasn't sure if I'd be able to see her if I wasn't family or a friend."

Angie brushed it off. "After seeing how happy Libbie is, I don't care if you're the Easter Bunny." She laughed, and then turned serious. "I hope you'll come and see her again. This has been so good for her."

"Oh, yes. I plan on coming often. And my grandmother wants to visit, too, as well as a couple of old friends of Libbie's. I hope that's okay. It won't upset her, will it?"

Angie shook her head. "It won't upset her. Libbie's doing so well on her medication. As long as she's okay with it, she'll be fine." They stopped beside Emily's car. "I can't tell you what your visit to Libbie means to all of us here. We've all felt so sad for her, not having visitors. Libbie is such a sweet soul. She deserves to be happy."

Emily nodded. "I could tell that just from the short time we visited. Believe me, I'll be back to see her."

* * *

Emily kept her promise. Over the next month, she visited Libbie every week. Each time, she grew to know her just a little more, and she understood why her father had fallen in love with her all those years ago. Libbie was not only sweet and kind, but she was also smart and had a fun sense of humor. Emily never asked her about her health issues, and they rarely talked about Jack other than when Libbie asked how he was. Instead, they took walks around the property, talked about everything from current events to the latest clothing styles, and once Emily even took Libbie out to lunch at a café in Spring River.

Emily loved visiting with many of the other residents also. Once they recognized her as the manager from the department store they shopped in occasionally, they would ask her questions about styles and mixing and matching their clothes. So many of the ladies took pride in their appearance, especially when they went out with family or as a group on little trips, that they wanted any advice Emily could give them. She enjoyed talking to them about fashion, and on occasion, she and Libbie would go with one of the women to look through her closet and put together outfits. Libbie especially enjoyed this and puffed up like a proud mother at Emily's popularity.

In mid-July, when Emily brought Bev along on a Sunday visit, she and Libbie hugged and cried. Emily stepped away for a time to give them privacy, and her heart filled with joy as she watched them from across the patio, their heads close together, sharing confidences.

"Amazing," Angie said, coming up beside Emily. "So that's Jack's mother."

Emily looked at Angie curiously. "Why is that amazing?"

"Libbie used to talk about Jack often but stopped over the years. I began to think she'd dreamt him up, and the pendant she wore was just jewelry from a relative or something, even though she said that Jack had given it to her. But then you showed up, and now Jack's mother." She turned and looked at Emily. "Will Jack show up next?"

Emily bit her lip. "I haven't told my dad about Libbie yet. I hope to, someday, but I want to get to know Libbie better first. Their ending was so dramatic and heartbreaking. I'm not sure how he'd feel about seeing her again."

Angie shook her head. "Imagine. All those years lost. It's so sad."

Emily thought so, too, and it made her ponder her own relationship. Was she spinning her wheels with someone who may not want the same future she did? She and Jordan hadn't spoken again about the move except for Jordan telling her he'd rented a two-bedroom apartment in a nice area not far from the school. In a month, he'd have to move down there to start the fall semester. He still thought she was coming with him. But Emily hadn't decided yet. And the fact that she didn't want to go told her volumes about where their relationship was headed.

She looked up and saw Bev wave her over to join them. Leaving her thoughts behind, she hurried over with a smile.

Chapter Thirty-Five

At the end of July, Libbie asked Emily if she'd like to go with the group on an overnight shopping trip to Fargo. "We do this once a year and the other women invite their daughters or grand-daughters along. I usually don't go since I've never had anyone to invite. I'd love it if you'd come along with me. I'll pay for everything, of course."

"I'd love to go," Emily said, elated that Libbie would ask her along. "And you don't have to pay for everything. We'll have fun."

Libbie's eyes sparkled. "I'm so happy you agreed to go. I was afraid I was being too forward, asking you like this. I can't wait."

But when Emily mentioned to Jordan that night that she'd be going on a shopping trip with Libbie the second week in August, he flipped out.

"You can't go then. That's the week before we move to the Cities. We have packing to do."

"I'm sorry, Jordan, but I'm going on the trip. Besides, I've never said I was moving to Minneapolis. That's your plan. I haven't decided yet."

"What do you mean you haven't decided? Of course you're going. We're a couple. If I move, you move, too."

A crease formed between Emily's brows. "You made the decision to take the grad assistant job without discussing it with me first. If we were a couple, you would have considered my feelings in this. Now I have to do what's right for me. I'm not sure I want to move there. I like my life here, and besides, I still want to go back to school someday. Here. Not in Minneapolis."

Jordan stared at her, crossing his arms. Emily could tell he was composing himself so he could play the logical one. He did that when he felt he was losing a fight. He always turned it around on her. She hadn't noticed it until recently, and when she realized he'd been doing it all along, it made her angry.

"Let's discuss this like adults," Jordan said, his tone condescending. "I had no choice but to take the position, so discussing it with you wouldn't have made a difference. This is for our future together, Emily. Why don't you see that?"

Emily sighed. "I know you see it that way, but I'm afraid I don't. This is my home. My family is here. I like living here. I can't picture myself living in a busy, crowded city. If you'd discussed it with me before taking the position, I would have told you that. I'm not going, Jordan. I'm sorry."

Jordan stared at her, looking as surprised as she felt. Up until that moment, she hadn't realized that she absolutely wasn't going with him. But now she knew she couldn't go. She was willing to give up on their relationship to stay here. They hadn't moved forward as a couple for ten years. She couldn't see a future with Jordan any longer. It tore at her heart, but she knew it was true. It was over.

"You're not thinking straight," Jordan said calmly. "I'll give you time to think about it. You've been so wrapped up in this nonsense about Libbie and the past that you've lost sight of your own reality."

Emily shook her head. "No, Jordan. It doesn't matter what you think about Libbie or me or my life here. I'm not leaving."

No matter what Emily said, though, Jordan wouldn't believe her. He was holding out hope that she'd move with him. Sadly, Emily realized it had more to do with his financial need for her than with their relationship. He didn't say it, but she knew that was why he was so desperate for her to come along. She'd supported them all these years so he could follow his dream. Without her support now, he'd never be able to afford basic living expenses. It made her sad to think that that was all their relationship had come down to—money.

* * *

Two weeks later, on a Friday afternoon, Emily boarded the charter bus with Libbie and twelve other residents and their relatives for the two-and-a-half-hour drive to Fargo. Angie and two other nurses were along as well to supervise the trip. Some of the residents, Libbie included, depended upon them to help them take their medicine regularly, so it was important that they come along.

All the women talked, laughed, and had a wonderful time during the ride. The atmosphere felt like being on a field trip with a bunch of sixth graders. Emily enjoyed meeting the other family members, and it looked like they were having a good time, too. Before they knew it they arrived at their hotel, situated close to the shopping mall, and soon had their bags stowed in their rooms. Emily and Libbie were sharing a room with two queen beds. Once they were settled, the group got into the hotel's shuttle bus, which drove them to the shopping mall.

"Okay, ladies," Angie said when they all entered the mall. "Let's meet back here at six o'clock so we can go out for dinner."

Everyone went off in their own direction, but they ran into each other at the various shops. Libbie wanted to look for some new clothes and asked Emily if she'd help her pick out some nice things.

"That's what I do best," Emily said, laughing.

They went into a store that catered to mature women, and soon Emily was bringing items back and forth to the dressing rooms for not only Libbie, but also two of the other women from the home. She suggested colors to them and found scarves and necklaces to accent the outfits they were trying. Their daughters helped, too, and they all had a great time trying on clothes.

Angie came in and joined the fun. Soon, they were having a mini fashion show in the dressing rooms, and even the store's sales associates were enjoying watching the ladies.

Emily came into the dressing rooms after one of her searches and knocked on Libbie's door. "I have the perfect dress for you, Libbie."

Libbie opened her door, and her eyes lit up when she saw what Emily was holding. It was a soft-pink dress with a crisscross pleated bodice and a fitted waist that flared out into a full skirt.

"Oh, I love pink," Libbie said, taking the dress.

Emily had known this. She remembered the pink dress in the prom photo with her father.

Once Libbie had the dress on, Emily helped her zip up the back, and she came out to look in the three-way mirror. The other ladies exclaimed at how lovely it was when they saw Libbie.

"It's so beautiful on you, dear," one lady said.

Emily agreed. "It's perfect. The color makes your skin glow."

Libbie turned first one way and then the other, making the skirt swish around her legs. She seemed entranced by the dress, her gaze far, far away.

"I love it," she whispered, looking over at Emily. "But where on earth would I wear it?"

"I'm not sure," Emily said. "But it looks like it was made for you."

Libbie agreed, and she purchased it along with several other items that Emily had helped her find.

As the women waited in line to pay for their purchases, Emily and Angie stood aside.

"You sure are good with Libbie," Angie said. "Look at how happy she is. And the other women, too. You must be very good at your job in the department store."

Emily shrugged. "I've been doing it a long time. But some-day I hope to go back to school."

Angie glanced at her. "What would you major in?"

"I'm not sure. That's the problem. I don't know what I want to do with my life. I've been so focused on my boyfriend's career, I put my own future on hold."

"That's a shame," Angie said. "Have you ever considered becoming a nurse? You're good with people, and you have so much compassion for them."

Emily shook her head. "Oh, I could never do what you do. I hate needles and the sight of blood."

Angie laughed. "But you have a good heart, dear. What about social work? You could be an advocate for the elderly. There are many programs that could use a good person like you."

Libbie came over with her bags then, and Emily never had a chance to answer Angie. But as the evening continued and they ate dinner as a group at a nice restaurant, Emily thought about

Angie's suggestion. Social work. It was an interesting idea. She loved working with people, and she would enjoy being able to help people in need. The more she thought of it, the more the idea grew on her.

Later that night, as Emily and Libbie crawled into their beds, Emily asked Libbie what she thought of her going to school to become a social worker.

"I think that's a wonderful idea," Libbie said. "You have such a kind heart. You'd be perfect for that kind of work."

Emily decided it was something she'd look into when she got home.

They turned out the lights, but both women lay in their beds, wide-awake. Soon, Libbie spoke.

"Thank you for coming along, Emily. This has been such a special day. I know I have no right to say this, but I like thinking of you as my own daughter. Ever since you've come into my life, it's been so much fuller. You've made me very happy, dear. I hope you don't mind my saying that."

Emily swallowed the lump that had formed in her throat. "I don't mind at all," she said quietly. "I'd love to be thought of as your daughter."

"I've always wanted a daughter," Libbie said wistfully. "But of course, it never happened. I was happy that Jack found Kate and was able to experience being a father. He's such a kind soul, and he deserved a happy life. I knew he'd make an amazing father."

"He was," Emily said, holding back tears. Poor Libbie, who'd wanted a child so badly and had never been able to have one. Emily's heart broke for her. She was only too happy to be like a daughter to her.

"You've never asked me what happened all those years ago," Libbie said.

"I didn't think it was my business," Emily replied.

"Yet you took the time to find me. Why?"

Emily thought about it a moment. She wasn't really sure why she'd sought out Libbie. She'd just felt so badly for the beautiful young woman whose life hadn't turned out as she'd hoped. "I just wanted to make sure you were okay, after everything."

"It took a long time," Libbie said. "So many doctors and so many different diagnoses. Everyone thought I was an alcoholic and drug abuser, but those were just symptoms of the real problem. For years I was in and out of hospitals, recovery centers, and even mental institutions while doctors tried to figure out what was wrong with me. And every time, they failed, only giving me drugs that didn't work, and I'd slip back into drinking and abusing pills to feel better. Back then, women were considered nervous and overly sensitive anyway, so doctors didn't think twice about handing out drugs to calm me down."

"That's terrible," Emily said.

"Yes, it was." Libbie paused, then spoke softly. "I don't remember anything about the night that Jack left. I just remember waking up early the next day with my father sitting beside my bed and my sister cleaning up the house. They told me that Jack and I had fought, and he'd left."

Emily stared at Libbie, stunned. "They didn't tell you the truth?"

Libbie shook her head. "I begged and begged my father and sister to let me see him, or at least talk to him one last time. But they told me that he never wanted to see me again. I was angry at first, but then, when I realized he was gone for good, I felt so useless and depressed. I'd lost Jack and my entire future, and I just didn't care about anything anymore. No sooner would I dry out in one facility than I'd sink back into abusing drugs and alcohol and end up being sent to another one."

"They lied to you," Emily said. "Dad tried to see you several times and even ended up in jail for storming the hospital. Your father and Gwen wouldn't let him see you. He had no choice but to give up."

Libbie sighed. "I always wanted to believe that Jack didn't leave me on his own. I know my behavior was intolerable, but he would have given me another chance. I'm very glad to hear you say that. I spent years believing that Jack had stopped loving me, and it made living almost unbearable."

"Oh, Libbie, that's so sad."

"After a few years, I stopped obsessing about the past. I wanted to get better. I knew I'd just slip away, like my mother did, if I didn't try harder to get well. Time and advances in medicine finally caught up to my condition, and they were able to diagnose me properly. They found that I'm bipolar, which caused my mood swings and deep depression. It took a while to get the medication right, but now I'm feeling so much better. I'm calmer, and more in control of my emotions. I haven't abused alcohol or drugs in over eight years, and I feel good about myself again."

"I'm so glad they were finally able to help you," Emily said, her heart aching for Libbie. "It's terrible that it took them so long to figure out what was wrong, though."

"Yes, I know, but I'm happy that I feel better now. It didn't help that my father and sister didn't want to face reality and get me the proper treatment. They thought I was overly sensitive, like my mother. Of course, I figured out that my mother had mental health issues, too, but no one would admit it. I know my dad meant well—he didn't want the stigma of a mental disorder to be attached to me or my mother. In those days, you hid people with mental health issues away. I guess my family thought it was better for me to be considered an alcoholic rather than mentally impaired. Strange, isn't it? The way people used to think."

"It's a terrible shame. If you could have gotten help sooner, maybe you and my dad could have had your happily ever after," Emily said. Libbie couldn't help her behavior all those years ago, and there had been no way for her father to know that.

Libbie sighed. "I try not to think of that. Poor Jack. He tried so hard. He had no way of knowing why I acted the way I did. It was better that he started his life over. A life with me would have been too painful for him. He deserved happiness."

Tears filled Emily's eyes. "You deserved happiness, too."

"Oh, sweetie. I'm happy now, and that's what counts. You're here. I'm grateful for that."

Long after Libbie had fallen asleep, Emily thought about all that she'd learned. It was sad that Libbie and her father had been torn apart by something neither one could control. It made her feel even happier that she'd found Libbie. At least now Libbie had people in her life again who loved her and cared about her. If only Jack could see Libbie now. She wondered what he'd think.

Chapter Thirty-Six

Two weeks later, Jordan was gone. He finally left after holding out as long as he could for Emily to change her mind and go with him. After she'd registered for fall semester at Jamison State College, he realized at last that she was serious about staying.

He packed up his things and gave her a kiss on the cheek. "I wish you were coming along," he told her. "But I guess you have your mind set on staying."

"I want to build a life, Jordan. We've just been playing house, but now I want more. I hope you understand."

"No, I don't. But I wish you all the best anyway," he said. Then he gave her one of his cute grins and left.

For a brief moment, Emily felt like she'd made a huge mistake. But then she remembered her dad, and her grandmother, and Libbie, and she knew her place was here.

Since the night Libbie had confided in her about her medical condition, she talked more openly about her and Jack's life together and how much she'd loved him. Emily began to wonder if her father and Libbie should meet. If nothing else came of it, they could at least be friends. Her father was so lonely now without her mother, and Emily thought it would be nice if he had someone to spend time with. Libbie had told Emily that she didn't have to live in the assisted living facility; she chose to stay there because she didn't want to live alone. Maybe, if her father finally understood what had happened to Libbie all those years ago, just maybe they could come together again. Emily knew it was a stretch of the imagination to believe they could have their happily ever after all these years later, but it wasn't completely out of the question.

Was it?

So Emily gathered up all her courage, put the hatbox of photos in her car, and headed out to her dad's house.

She parked in front of her childhood home. The lake was smooth as glass on the warm August day, and the old oak and birch trees shaded the yard to a nice temperature. Emily gazed around the yard, trying to picture where Jack and Libbie's cottage had once stood. It amazed her that her father had bought the land where he'd once loved Libbie and had been able to live there with the memories surrounding him all these years.

Maybe her idea wasn't so ridiculous after all.

Emily found her father in his large garage, under the hood of a car.

"Hey, stranger," Jack said, smiling widely as he wiped his hands on a rag. "What a great surprise."

Emily set the hatbox on his workbench and walked over to give him a kiss on the cheek. His hair was longer than usual and mussed, and his coveralls needed washing, but the grin on his face was all that mattered to Emily.

"I see you're hard at work again," she said. "I thought you were going to start taking it easy."

Jack shrugged. "It fills the day," he said. "Hey, your grandmother told me about you and Jordan. I'm sorry to hear that it ended. Are you okay?"

"I'm fine. Jordan's life plan didn't fit with mine anymore. I'm going back to school and moving on with my life. And I'm excited about it."

"Your grandmother told me that. I think it's wonderful that you're going back to school. You know that if you need extra money you can count on me to help, right?"

Emily smiled. "Thanks, Dad. I'm sure I'll take you up on that."

"This weekend is the big move. Your grandmother is getting excited about moving into the town house and not having to take care of that big place anymore," Jack said.

Emily nodded. "Yeah. It'll be good for her. It will be a fresh start."

Jack glanced over her shoulder. "So, what's in the box?"

Emily walked over to the bench where the hatbox sat and looked up at her dad. "It's old photos Grandma and I found when we were packing up the house."

"Really? Why'd you bring them here?"

Emily took a deep breath and then looked up into her father's eyes. "They're photos of you, Dad. When you were young. Of you and Libbie."

Jack stood silent a moment, his expression unreadable. "So, your grandmother told you about Libbie, huh? Well, I guess it's no secret." He gazed at the box. "I'm surprised she kept those after all these years."

"They're amazing, Dad. You and Libbie were so adorable together. Do you want to look at them?" Emily stared at him, hopeful.

Jack slowly shook his head. "No, sweetheart. The past is best left in the past." He turned and walked back toward the car.

Emily's excitement faded. She followed her father across the garage. "Dad. Haven't you ever wondered what happened to Libbie? Where she is? How her life turned out?"

Jack turned, a crease forming between his eyes. He didn't look angry. He looked pained.

"I loved your mother, dear. We had a good life together and had you and your brother to fill our lives with happiness. I left the past behind me and built a new life."

"Yet you chose to build that life on the same property where you and Libbie were once so happy," Emily said gently.

"Leave it be, okay, honey?" Jack bent over the open engine.

"She's alive, Dad," Emily blurted out. "Libbie is still alive and doing well. She's the prettiest, sweetest woman you could ever meet. She's had a hard time through the years, but now she's better. She's content."

Jack's head rose up sharply as he stared at Emily. "How do you know this?"

Emily took a step closer, feeling braver now. "Because I found her and I've been visiting her for the past few weeks. She's amazing, Dad. She lives in an assisted living facility about forty miles north of here. Everyone there just loves her. I've grown to care about her, too."

"Why would you do that? What on earth made you want to find her, to talk to her?"

"After Grandma told me your story, I had to find her. I needed to know if she was okay. You had your happily ever after with Mom. I needed to know if Libbie got hers."

Silence swelled between them. For a moment, Emily thought her father wasn't going to say another word. But then he turned to her.

"Did she?" Jack asked softly, his face suddenly looking tired and worn.

Emily slowly shook her head. "Libbie never had the chance to love again or have a family of her own. But she isn't sad or bitter about it. She says she feels lucky to finally feel well and to have so many good people around her. And she's happy that I found her. For the first time in years, she has visitors, like Carol, and your old neighbor, June, and even Grandma."

"You've all been visiting her? Even your grandmother?"

Emily nodded. "Yes. And it would be wonderful if you'd go see her, too, Dad."

Jack raised his hand as if to ward off the idea. "No. I can't do that. I'm happy that Libbie is fine and her friends have found her again. But I can't go. Libbie can't possibly want to see me."

"But she does want to see you, Dad. She's talked often about your years together and how much she loved you."

Jack shook his head. "No. I can't see her. You don't understand everything that happened."

Emily crossed her arms. "Then tell me. Tell me why you can't go see the woman you once loved?"

Jack's shoulders sagged. He looked over at Emily and spoke quietly. "I failed her, Ems. That's what happened. I promised to love and take care of her until the day I died, and I didn't keep my promise. Believe me, Libbie doesn't want to see me again."

Tears welled in Emily's eyes at her father's sad words. She pictured him as a young man, heartbroken, being thrown out of his own home by Libbie's father and sister. He hadn't failed Libbie, her family had. "You were so young then, Dad. You can't blame yourself for everything that happened. You didn't know how sick Libbie was. No one knew. But that's changed. She's better now. Please, come with me on Sunday to see her."

Jack shook his head. "No. I'm sorry, dear, but no." He turned and walked a few steps away.

The tears Emily had tried so hard to hold back trailed down her cheeks. "Dad. Listen to me."

Jack stopped but didn't turn around.

"For five years, Libbie dressed up every Sunday on family visiting day and waited for someone to come visit her. And for five long years, no one did. Yet every Sunday, she waited. She waited for someone, anyone, to remember her. Now she has me, and her other friends, but still, I see it in her eyes. She's still waiting. She's waiting for you, Dad. I know she is. Only you can give her the peace she's been waiting for. Please, Dad. Please come to see Libbie."

Through her tears, she watched her father, his shoulders sagged, his head bowed.

"I can't," Jack said hoarsely. Then he walked out of the garage.

* * *

That Saturday, Jack, Edward, and Emily moved Bev into her new home. As the men lifted the heavy furniture into the trailer attached to Jack's truck, Emily and Bev carried the smaller boxes, stacking them into the trailer and Emily's car. Emily and Edward had both chosen a few pieces of furniture they wanted, and the rest was being stored at Jack's place. It was a bittersweet day, emptying the farmhouse they'd all known as a home in one way or another, knowing that by this time next year it would be torn down and new houses would be sprouting up on the property. Yet Bev was excited to begin a new phase in her life of less work and more fun.

All day as they worked, Jack didn't say much to Emily.

She'd hoped that he would have had time to think about visiting Libbie and change his mind, but it was obvious he hadn't. It made Emily sad to think that her father blamed himself for Libbie's unhappiness all those years ago. She wished he'd visit, if not for Libbie, then to heal his own past demons.

On Sunday, she visited Libbie, and they walked along the winding path near the river. They talked about the Prentice farm and how sad it was to see it disappear. Libbie told her stories of a white horse named Sprite that she and Jack had ridden several times and of the small lake that sat on the back forty. Emily shared stories from her childhood about visiting the farm and all the fun she and Edward had there.

"Everything changes eventually," Libbie said. "But this sounds like a good change for Bev. She can enjoy her life with friends and family close by."

Emily nodded. Life was changing for her, too. She was living alone for the first time in ten years, and she was starting college classes next week. After Jordan left, she'd found that she didn't miss him, which was sad, yet also a relief. She realized that they had both been living their own separate lives, just sharing the same space. That wasn't what she wanted in a relationship. She wanted one like her father and mother had, where they lived, loved, and worked as a unit, always considering the other's needs, too. She wouldn't have had that with Jordan. Emily hoped that someday she'd find the right person to share her life with, but for now, she was fine living alone.

* * *

The weeks sped by once classes began for Emily. She'd chosen to take two night classes and one morning class so she could still work full-time at the store. Eventually, she'd have to take a heavier class load to finish her degree, and then she'd need to ask her father for help. But for now, she could do this on her own.

Emily found that she enjoyed the challenge of school. She didn't even mind her retail job anymore. She had a new future to look forward to, and that made her feel more energetic and excited about life.

Emily continued to visit with Libbie on Sundays. She enjoyed spending time with her, and they had forged a strong relationship. She also saw her grandmother more, having dinner or lunch with her a couple of times a week since they lived so close to each other. She enjoyed her grandmother's company, and they always had a good time. And, to her surprise, her grandmother did go on weekly senior bus trips to the various casinos in the area, and she was also planning an Alaskan Cruise for next year with two of her friends. Bev was "living it up," just like Emily's grandfather had wanted her to, and Emily was very happy for her.

Her father, however, was a different matter. Since the day she'd told him about Libbie, she hadn't seen much of him. Emily knew her father wasn't angry with her—he was never angry with anyone—but it made her sad that he was keeping his distance. She'd hoped he'd changed his mind about visiting Libbie, but as August slipped into September, he hadn't come. Emily worried that maybe she shouldn't have ever told her father about Libbie. It obviously only brought him pain to remember the past. She'd been naïve to think that he would want to see Libbie after all these years. Maybe he was right— the past belonged in the past.

* * *

September settled in, with warm temperatures making the trees erupt into rich colors of orange, red, and gold. In a place that was used to cooler temperatures beginning early, a warm, dry September was a lovely gift. Emily didn't have much time to enjoy the autumn colors or warm days, though. Her hours were filled with school, work, and homework. Sundays were the only days that she allowed herself a few hours off, and that was to visit Libbie and the other residents at the home.

You never know what the day will bring. Her grandmother's words filled her thoughts as Emily visited with Libbie the last Sunday in September. Emily was sitting in a chair on the patio beside Libbie, enjoying the autumn sunshine. They were looking at a winter clothes catalog Emily had brought along to show Libbie a dress she thought she might like. Angie stood behind them, bent over to see, too.

"Emerald green," Libbie said excitedly. "I love that color. It changes my eyes to green."

Emily smiled over at her. Today Libbie wore a sapphire-blue dress with long sleeves. Her eyes shone brightly, their color brought out by the blue in the dress. The blue topaz pendant hung around her neck, as it always did. "I think all colors look good on you," Emily said.

Emily noticed Libbie had raised her head and was staring straight ahead. Her fingers had gone to the pendant around her neck. Glancing up, Emily stared in the direction Libbie was gazing. Across the yard, a tall, slender man was walking toward them. He wore jeans with a casual brown blazer over a light-blue dress shirt. In his hand was a bouquet of colorful flowers. Emily recognized him immediately. She turned to Libbie, who was staring at him, her face serene and her eyes bright.

"Jack," Libbie said softly.

Emily's heart swelled as her father drew nearer. He looked so handsome with his suntanned face and freshly cut hair. His steps slowed as he approached the group of women, and then he stopped, gazing down at Libbie as if she were the only one there.

"Hello, Libbie," he said, smiling at her.

"Hello, Jack." Her words came out in barely a whisper. A smile slowly appeared on her face, and her skin nearly glowed. Emily could have sworn she looked twenty years younger in that moment.

"These are for you," Jack said, handing Libbie the flowers.

Libbie accepted them and lifted the bouquet up to her nose, inhaling deeply. "They're beautiful," she said, locking eyes with Jack.

"You look beautiful," Jack said, his eyes sparkling.

Their gaze didn't waver. To Emily, it was as if in that very moment the years and all that the two of them had endured melted away. All they saw was each other.

"Will you walk with me a while?" Jack asked, holding out his hand to Libbie.

Libbie accepted his hand and stood, her eyes twinkling mischievously. "I'd love to. But you'd better behave like a gentleman, Jack Prentice."

Jack grinned. "I always do."

Libbie turned to Emily and handed her the flowers, then she slipped her hand around Jack's proffered arm. As the two walked away, Jack placed his other hand over the one Libbie had on his arm.

Emily rose and watched as her father and Libbie made their way to the path by the river. His head was bent toward Libbie, giving her his full attention. Tears filled Emily's eyes as she thought of what they must be saying after all these years.

A loud sob from behind her shook Emily from her thoughts. She turned, finding Angie there, crying uncontrollably.

"That's just about the most beautiful thing I've ever seen," Angie said through her sobs.

Emily smiled through her own tears and put her arm around Angie. She pulled a tissue from her jacket pocket and handed it to her. "It is, isn't it?" Emily said softly. "After all these years, he's finally found Libbie."

Epilogue

On a warm spring day beside the blue waters of Lake Ogimaa, Libbie and Jack were married in a small ceremony. Guests included immediate family; Libbie's old friend, Carol; Larry, who'd flown in especially for the ceremony; and Angie. Libbie wore the beautiful pink dress she'd bought on her trip to Fargo with Emily, and Jack loved it, saying it reminded him of the pink dress she'd worn to their senior prom, the night he'd proposed to her the very first time.

Since his first visit, Jack and Libbie had spent countless hours together throughout the fall and winter. At first, he'd visited her several times a week, and then it turned into nights out, going to dinner, seeing a movie, taking a drive on a crisp winter day. There was no denying that the deep connection that had brought them together years before was still there, and Emily was thankful that they didn't resist it. She hadn't seen her father this happy since before her mother died, and Libbie practically glowed with happiness.

After they were married, the couple moved into Jack's home on the lake and slowly made it their own. Jack helped Libbie keep track of her medicine—which she took religiously—and Libbie took care of Jack and their home. They traveled all over the country together, took Caribbean cruises, and even went to Hawaii one winter for two weeks. Jack worked less and less, preferring to spend his time with Libbie. They were both happy and content, finally enjoying a life together as it was always meant to be.

Emily finished college and began working, first as a social worker in the hospital, and then for the county as an advocate for the elderly in nursing homes and assisted living facilities. While she was working at the hospital, she began dating, and eventually married, a doctor, Aaron Bennington, a handsome, easygoing man who put family first, even with his busy schedule. By the time Jack and Libbie celebrated five years together, Emily and Aaron had a two-year-old daughter, whom they'd named Katherine Elizabeth. Emily thought it was only fitting to name their daughter after two special women—her mother and Libbie, who felt like a mother to her.

At last, Libbie had a little girl to love and spoil, and she thought of little Katie as her own granddaughter. It wasn't unusual at a holiday or family gathering to find the two off playing dolls or coloring together. Emily was happy to have been able to bring so much joy into Libbie's life. She truly deserved it.

Everyone mourned when Bev died at the age of ninety, simply passing away in her sleep one night. But they were thankful to have had her in their lives, and that she'd been able to live her life fully to the end and enjoy every minute.

For ten years, Jack and Libbie enjoyed a life filled with love and happiness, until one summer day when Jack passed away unexpectedly. Libbie moved back to the assisted living home where she'd lived before because she didn't want to be a burden on Emily and her growing family. By then, Emily and Aaron had another young child—a boy, whom they'd named Lars after Emily's uncle Larry. Libbie was content to live out her days in the home, happy to have been able to share a portion of her life with her beloved Jack. Because of Jack, she was no longer lonely, having gained a new family who loved and cared about her. Emily brought the children to visit her often, and that brought joy to Libbie's last years.

Emily once asked her father what had made him change his mind about visiting Libbie that first time.

"It was the pictures you left at the house," Jack had said. "I finally opened the box, and all the memories of the past came flooding back to me. But instead of being sad memories, they were happy ones. After that, I had to see her again. And I was so glad that I did."

Because of Jack, Libbie finally had the loving family she'd always wanted and a caring husband to make her feel loved. She lived her happily ever after. Emily knew that finding Libbie again had given her father a second chance to prove his love for her. Jack had finally been able to keep the promise he'd made to Libbie so long ago when he'd first proposed to her on that warm spring evening. He'd loved and cared for her until the day he died. And he died a happy, fulfilled man.

-End-

About the Author

Deanna Lynn Sletten is the author of THE WOMEN OF GREAT HERON LAKE, MISS ETTA, MAGGIE'S TURN, NIGHT MUSIC, THE LAKE HARRIET SERIES, and several other titles. She writes heartwarming women's fiction, historical fiction, and romance novels with unforgettable characters. She has also written one middle-grade novel that takes you on the adventure of a lifetime.

Deanna is married and has two grown children. When not writing, she enjoys walking the wooded trails around her home with her beautiful Australian Shepherd, traveling, and relaxing on the lake.

Deanna loves hearing from her readers. Connect with her at:
Her website: http://www.deannalsletten.com
Blog: http://www.deannalynnsletten.com
Facebook: http://www.facebook.com/deannalynnsletten
Twitter: http://www.twitter.com/deannalsletten

Made in the USA
Middletown, DE
03 August 2021

45287885R00219